MURDER ON THE BAHAMA PRINCESS

The Casserole Ladies Mix Homicide and Humor

Billy and Linda Johnson

Other Books in the Casserole Ladies Series
By Billly and Linda Johnson

THE CASSEROLE LADIES
Zany Misadventures in the Quest for Postmortem Romance

AREA 53
The Casserole Ladies Go Where No Woman Has Gone Before

Other Books by Billy Johnson

ATTACK OF THE iFONES
And Other Vertically Challenged Stories

A collection of eight short stories

LION IN MY BACKYARD

A Children's Picture Book

The characters and events portrayed in this book are fictitious. Any similarity to real persons, living or dead, is coincidental and not intended by the authors. The Bahama Princess is a fictional cruise ship.

Cover design:
Kindle Cover Creator was used to create the cover and incorporated a man overboard picture of Danny Tucker as taken by Rannie Tucker.

ISBN: 978-1-7374282-4-4

Acknowledgements

Danny and Rannie Tucker who have been Casserole Ladies boosters from the first book in the series.

Dr. Tammy Winner, Professor in the English Department at the University of North Alabama who has generously allowed her professional editing classes to edit all three Casserole Ladies books as class projects, including MURDER ON THE BAHAMA PRINCESS

Tony Gorody for beta reading the book and providing valuable feedback.

MURDER ON THE BAHAMA PRINCESS

The Casserole Ladies Mix Homicide and Humor

Casserole Ladies: Older unmarried women in towns throughout the South who appear on doorsteps of recently widowed or divorced males. These women bring casseroles and other homemade dishes, such beneficence occurring when these men are most vulnerable to feminine sympathy. Potential companionship and/or matrimony often are motivating factors.

Chapter 1

12° 6' 13.6116" North, 62° 41' 26.808" West
November 15th

Light from an orange-red sunrise glinted off of eight long rows of tinted glass on the starboard side of the ship. The emerging sun provided enough light for a few early risers to appreciate stunning emerald-blue water. The Bahama Princess had sailed from Grenada several hours earlier, and in this area of the Caribbean, gentle morning waves made the ocean seem tranquil, unlike its true nature. Gidget took note of the gorgeous new dawn only in relation to the ugliness of yesterday's tragedy.

"I was just thinking about how much we've enjoyed walking… and the beauty of these sunrises… until today," Gidget said, struggling to catch her breath. The brunette's short legs churned to keep up with her taller companion. This was lap two of their daily powerwalk, and she huffed and puffed in between words. "I was thinking how much this cruise has mostly been good for me… I've been in a funk way too long… I was getting out of it on this cruise…"

Daffy, her long-legged seventy-year-old companion slowed her pace to let Gidget catch up.

Gidget continued her thoughts among numerous pauses to catch her breath. "Remember how nervous I was about going on this cruise? I was becoming more confident about my decision to go… even after those strange things in the Bahamas, Gibbs Cay, Antigua, and Saint Lucia… But after what happened yesterday… Now, it's hard for me to enjoy things this morning. I worry about what's gonna happen next."

"He was so young. Too young," said Daffy. There was a time when she would have called a sixty-seven-year-old man 'old.' That was two decades ago.

Gidget was sixty-two. Her age and the extra pounds gained since leaving the Port of Jacksonville on October 15th made these powerwalks necessary. She knew growing older had contributed to her long-standing melancholy.

"Everything is relative… Compared to us, Brad Pitt is young, but my oldest grandchild thinks he's ancient…"

Daffy smacked her lips. "Brad Pitt. Yum-yum! I wouldn't mind robbing that cradle."

Gidget and Daffy's mouths motored overtime as they powerwalked the ship's promenade deck—an enormous oval almost a third of a mile in circumference. They were casserole ladies, and as with all of their kind, talking was more than a way of life. It was life itself. Both women simultaneously engaged in a flurry of texting with their offspring, mingling the gist of those exchanges into their conversation. Walking, talking, and texting—multitasking at its finest.

Gidget said, "I still feel… I don't know… guilty about going on our regular powerwalk this morning… as if nothing had happened yesterday. Maybe, we should have stayed in and tried to comfort his brothers." One of the five brothers who were the two ladies' traveling companions had bizarrely died the day before. He'd choked on an order of Sonoran empanadas at breakfast.

Daffy took a different view. "I understand where you're coming from, but I look at it this way. We laid our grief on them all day yesterday, but I didn't see them grieve much in return."

Gidget nodded. Daffy continued. "Maybe I'm exaggerating a little—"

"I've never known you to exaggerate." Gidget rolled her eyes.

"They did seem upset at first. But then, last night, the VERY day their brother dies, they had to watch the 'Citizen's Arrest' episode on *The Andy Griffith Show*! I don't get it. I mean… I don't expect them to flagellate each other with a… What's that whip thing called? The thing that monks use to flagellate themselves with?"

"A scourge…"

Powerwalking while talking began to take a toll on Daffy as well as she now paused between sentences to catch her breath. "Yeah. I don't expect them to flagellate each other with a scourge, but… I bet these guys wouldn't even use a wet noodle… Mmmm… Now, that's an interesting image…"

"The brothers scourging each other with a wet noodle?"

Daffy shook her head. "Nope. A much better image than that. Brad Pitt is scourging me. He's shirtless like he was in *Thelma and Louise*, and he's smiling at me like he smiled at them."

The Bahama Princess was a massive vessel. It weighed over a hundred and fifty tons, had twelve levels above its waterline, and half that number below. A crew of twelve-hundred and fifty served twenty-eight hundred passengers. Everything about the ship was impressive, but none of it impressed Gidget at the moment. Her mind could not rid itself of questions regarding yesterday's tragedy.

"Back to what we were talking about before Brad Pitt. I know I'm a pharmacist, not a doctor… but I've had enough clinical experience to have my doubts about Doctor Mokulus." Gidget, aka Gloria Smurfitt, earned a doctorate in pharmacy from the University of Georgia while married to Sam Smurfitt. She buried him three years earlier after thirty-eight years of marriage. Sam owned Thomasville, Georgia's only remaining independent pharmacy, which Gidget inherited and now managed.

"I got the impression from you yesterday that Chef Dreyfus was your prime suspect. He made the Sonoran empanadas. And his chicken liver pâté and how we were weirdly attacked by those… What were they?" asked Daffy.

"Triggerfish."

"Yeah, triggerfish. And I know you think Dreyfus' Sonoran empanadas could be a likely cause of Larry's death. You even imitated Chef Dreyfus' French accent when you said, 'He iz about az French az ze French booldog.' But now you think it's Doctor Mokulus instead of Dreyfus? You're usually not this wishy-washy. What's changed?"

Daphne Belvedere graduated in 1969 from Thomasville High, which took its name from the small South Georgia town where and Gidget now lived. Like many other casserole ladies on the Bahama Princess, she was a widow, having planted her deceased husband Royce Belvedere five years ago. Royce did all right by Daffy. He owned Sawgrass Bank and passed ownership to her. He also left her a mansion in Thomasville's Tockwotton Historic District, two Mercedes, several pecan orchards outside of town, and so on.

"I don't know what's changed… The more I think about Mokulus, things just don't seem right. If Mokulus had started CPR on Larry right there in the restaurant like I was about to do, maybe there'd be five brothers now instead of four? I don't know. I've been going back and forth between Mokulus and Dreyfus all night. I guess my mind's kind of acting squirrely right now."

"I bet it's the seasickness you've been having every morning lately. Your seasickness seems to be getting worse."

"Yeah, and walking this far ain't doing it any good."

"I believe the deck on this boat is almost as long as any of its all-you-can-eat buffet lines. My gut is testimony to how long they are." Daffy had put on eight pounds herself, which did less damage visually on her tall and lanky frame, than six pounds did on Gidget's short, compact frame.

Gidget said, "I think they could use this promenade deck for the Daytona 500."

The Ladies continued to chatter as the sun continued to rise. It now cast a much brighter light on the upper levels of the ship where their traveling companions' two staterooms were located. Daffy and Gidget's suite was sandwiched between those two on the eighth level of the ship. All three suites had balconies with beautiful views.

Although Daffy and Gidget each had a special relationship with two of their five, now four, traveling companions, they playfully referred to all of them as their boyfriends. Every morning for the last thirty days, a boyfriend or two would be on his balcony as they powerwalked beneath. Whoever it was would wave, and Daffy and Gidget would look up and wave back. Daffy always made the same comment. "Ain't it just like being back in high school? Down on the football field, cheerleading and waving at your boyfriend up in the stands. Gettin' all hot and bothered when he waved back."

Daffy wisely withheld that comment this morning, and instead asked, "Wonder if any of our boyfriends will be on a balcony this morning?"

"I doubt it after yesterday," said Gidget. "But with the Marx Brothers, who knows?"

Marx Brothers was the nickname Gidget and Daffy used for their five boyfriends. The nickname seemed appropriate. All were brothers, and all wore the same outfits every day—oversized brightly colored Hawaiian flower shirts, Bermuda shorts, white crew socks, and sandals. They were all short, bald-headed, and retired old rich guys.

As Gidget spoke, she noticed a familiar powerwalking couple further up the deck abruptly stop. It was the same elderly man and his wife who usually approached them from the opposite direction. The old guy always said, “You two girls slept so long last night that you grew hair on your heads.” His wife always rolled her eyes as Daffy and Gidget laughed politely, then all exchanged pleasantries before continuing their walk. The elderly couple now stood stone cold in their tracks, looking skyward in horror.

Gidget and Daffy looked up to see what was commanding their fellow passengers’ attention. It was something more astonishing than yesterday’s choking death. One of the four remaining Marx Brothers plummeted through the air, having apparently fallen off his balcony eight levels above the promenade deck—well over a hundred feet above the ship’s waterline. He did not drop straight down like a hundred-pound gunny sack of potatoes, which would be an apt description of his physique. Instead, he tumbled head-over-heels, his multi-colored Hawaiian flower shirt mimicking the image one sees when one looks into a child’s kaleidoscope while twisting its lens. Red, green, yellow, orange, blue, and black continually tumbled over and over and mixed and sparkled in the bright sunrise light. Had it been something other than a human body, it could have been described as flashy or even psychedelic, depending on one’s predispositions.

“OH, MY GOD!” Both women screamed simultaneously in horror and panic. To their credit, they both remembered what to shout next. “MAN OVERBOARD! MAN OVERBOARD!”

Other passengers on the promenade deck also began shouting. Daffy and Gidget ran to the railing and watched the tumble of colors pass by about twenty feet in front of them. It cleared the railing by only yards. The body violently plunged into the water, making a tremendous splash and leaving a hole that quickly disappeared as water rushed back in.

Daffy, Gidget, and a dozen other passengers ran around like chickens with their heads cut off, sporadically leaning over the railing, frantically looking for a body to surface. Cries of 'MAN OVERBOARD' constantly rang out in frustration. Several passengers grabbed life preserver rings in anticipation of throwing one to the drowning man once he surfaced. That was not to be. One minute passed, and no body surfaced. Two minutes, three minutes. By this time, members of the ship's crew had converged on the area. The ship's captain had ordered the ship to initiate man overboard protocols, but this was a major effort taking too much time.

Daffy and Gidget stood paralyzed, too stunned to move. They looked at the other passengers, everyone in a state of shock. Gidget glanced up in the direction of their staterooms and spotted someone. A person stood inside one of the Marx Brothers' rooms—too far inside from the balcony to be identified—and quickly stepped back and disappeared.

Gidget pointed up in the direction of their staterooms. "Someone was standing in the jumper's stateroom. Did you see who it was?"

Daffy said, "Nope. It was probably one of the Marx Brothers."

"That didn't look like any of the other Marx Brothers. Way too tall to be one of them."

"Wonder who it could have been?"

"I've got my suspicions, but it didn't look anything like one of the Marx Brothers. Wonder where they are?"

Daffy said, "Doing what men always do—either sleeping on the couch, reading on the toilet, or watching cable news on the TV."

Gidget shook her head. "Sometimes your sense of humor escapes me, and this is one of them."

"I can't help it. Four decades of living with someone like Royce does that to a person. I don't know whether to stay here and look for a body or go up and see which of the Marx Brothers are still alive. We've grown pretty close to all of them. I'd hate to think it was…" Daffy had become especially close to one of the five brothers and could not bring herself to say his name.

"No need to go up there right now," Gidget counselled. "I know which one fell overboard."

"Which one? I couldn't see his face, and it was hard for me to tell who it was with all that psychedelic mix of colors tumbling over and over through the air. They all wear Hawaiian flower shirts. It definitely wasn't Larry."

"Yep. Definitely not Larry."

"Gary?"
"Nope."
"Barry?"
"Nope."
"Harry?"
"Nope."
"That only leaves Jerry."
"Yep."
"I couldn't make out his face. Could you?"
"Nope."
"Then how do you know it was Jerry?"
"He was wearing huarache sandals."

Chapter 2

Thomasville, Georgia
October 13th

Someone looking to purchase huarache sandals might have had a tough time finding a pair in Thomasville in October. Like November, when Jerry plunged overboard, it was a month in the Autumn/Winter fashion season when retailers tend to stock fewer sandals. Perhaps that's why the closest thing to huaraches at Al Dixon Men's Wear that month was an expensive pair of Johnston & Murphy Woven Italian Calfskins. The upper part of the shoe had the woven leather look of a huarache, but its overall look said shoe. Al Dixon's website labeled the Calfskins as 'shoes.' Lilly believed it was a worthy debate as to whether huaraches were sandals or shoes.

Lilly White's surname resulted from three decades of marriage to Wendell, who died the year before. It also appropriately described the fifty-five-year-old platinum blonde's skin complexion. She was always happy to discuss whether huaraches are shoes or sandals. Lilly had a shoe fetish and sometimes unintentionally reminded her close friends about it, as she did once again on a pleasant autumn morning at breakfast with Gidget and Daffy.

The three of them met with best friends Babs Neauxgeaux (pronounced NoGo) and Lizzie Sherbert. The five older women are prime examples of casserole ladies, and locals in Thomasville recognize this by openly referring to them as 'The Casserole Ladies.' All five are among Thomasville's most wealthy and most eccentric residents. They typically get together several times a week to catch up on Thomasville gossip, the latest news on each other's children, and updates on their various ailments. It was a busy Monday morning at the local IHOP, and after a fifteen-minute wait, they sat down for breakfast.

Before the subject of huaraches came up, they first updated each other on their ailments. They had not yet progressed to the latest Thomasville gossip when the Director of Tourism for Thomasville stopped by their table.

"Hey, Casserole Ladies. I knew y'all would be here."

Daffy replied, "Have a seat and sit a spell. We haven't ordered yet."

"Babs can't make up her mind between the Rooty Tooty Fresh 'N Fruity Pancake Combo or a Grand Slam." Sarcasm oozed from Lizzie's observation.

"They don't have Grand Slams at IHOP. Those are at Denny's," the Director said.

"That's what we been trying to tell her for the last ten minutes."

Babs stuck her tongue out at Lizzie but said nothing, which surprised the Director. Babs was known for being ditzy and chatty.

The Director bit her tongue before replying. "Wish I could stay and jaw with you ladies, but I can't. I just *had* to come by and alert y'all to expect some visitors. Five older, odd-looking gentlemen came into the Visitors Center earlier this morning. They wanted to find the five women in the 'Widows of Thomasville' calendar."

The Casserole Ladies posed for a risqué (some say scandalous) calendar in September, thinking it would be a way to attract some eligible bachelors. Their calendar ripped off the famous calendar which pictured artfully posed, semi-nude older women from Rylstone, England. The photographer of the 'Widows of Thomasville' calendar truly earned his fee from the extensive airbrushing it required.

"Your calendar sales have gone through the roof, Casserole Ladies. Y'all are famous throughout the Deep South. Those old boys came up here from The Villages in Florida and are tracking y'all down because they saw your calendar. I tried to put them off your scent, but they seemed determined to meet y'all. We couldn't stop laughing after they left. One of the girls at the Visitors Center nicknamed them the Marx Brothers. If you see them, you'll know why."

"I can hardly wait," Daffy said.

Gidget was doubtful. "Ain't it strange that they would want to meet five women they've only seen on a calendar?"

"It must be something like when fans fall in love with movie stars," said Lilly, the romantic of the group. "I did that when I was a young girl with Robert Redford when I saw him in *Butch Cassidy*."

Lizzie, generally considered the most lustful member of the group, nodded enthusiastically. She said, "Same for me and Clint Eastwood. I loved his cute little butt in *Play Misty for Me*."

"I don't remember him showing his butt in that movie."

"Your memory's better than mine. Lord knows, I can't even remember what I ate for breakfast in the morning, and I eat the same thing every morning. Maybe his cute, naked little butt was just wishful thinking on my part. Give a sixty-five-year-old a break and let me keep my delusions." Lizzie had recently gone through her fourth divorce and needed all the delusions life offered.

The Tourism Director said, "Anyway, I just stopped by to warn y'all. Hate to leave, but I gotta go."

"What's up?"

"The Thomasville Accordioneers are performing at lunchtime. I've got to haul five chairs they're borrowing from the Visitors Center over to Big Oak Park for their concert."

"Only five chairs? Which one of them died?" asked Babs anxiously. One of her many paranormal interests included the afterlife. The youngest of the six Accordioneers was fifty-nine, and Gidget suspected Babs' excitement may have been prompted by the prospect of a séance with a recently deceased Accordioneer.

The Director said, "No. None of them died that I know of."

"Then why only five chairs?" Lilly asked.

"They're not for the Accordioneers. It's seating for the number of expected attendees. Not a big audience for accordion music. Bye."

Five older gentlemen shuffled into the restaurant foyer while Babs and Lizzie argued over whether or not the Rooty Tooty Fresh 'N Fruity Pancake Combo was better than the Italian Cannoli Pancakes. The old boys appeared to be looking intently for someone as their five bald heads simultaneously swiveled back and forth 180 degrees. One of them spied the Casserole Ladies, nudged his companions, and pointed. Four other bald heads rotated until all five were fixed on the girls' table. The old boys grinned as they stared.

Mouths open, the Casserole Ladies stared back. Lizzie was the first to break the silence. "Those old boys look like they bought their clothes at a Jackson Pollock estate sale."

"Yeah, except Pollock's paintings are less chaotic," said Gidget.

Daffy said, "I see why the girls at the Visitors Center nicknamed them the Marx Brothers."

Noting the gentlemen's protruding tummies, Lilly said, "Looks like the Marx Brothers have been enjoying the Endless Buffet at the Golden Corral."

"I'm not gonna talk," said Babs, whose short frame exaggerated any extra pounds. "Those shirts kind of remind me of the Tiki Room at Disney World. Would you look at those Hawaiian flower shirts! Where are my sunglasses?"

Daffy shook her head. "Looks like some of them have more tummy than available shirt. I think I see a couple of exposed hairy belly buttons."

"Men should never wear Bermuda shorts unless they have some hair on their legs," said Lilly. "And those pastel-colored shorts definitely do not go with the primary colors in those shirts. It just reinforces what I've always said about the horrors of mixing pastels with primary colors."

Lizzie had forgotten her glasses again. She squinted as she said, "I never realized until now that there are five different shades of pastel. I thought there were only three."

Daffy said, "I haven't seen that many bald heads since the last time I looked through the picture window at the newborn nursery in the hospital."

"On the bright side, I don't see any walkers or Hurrycanes." Gidget referred to the elaborate walking stick for old people often advertised on cable television.

Babs said, "The second one on the right does have a pretty nice comb-over."

"I bet the tallest one is only five and a half feet tall."

"I'd say that's also the height of the shortest one," said Lizzie.

"Bald and short. What a sexy combination." Daffy rolled her eyes. "They must all be retired."

"How so?"

"Old retired men always wear sandals unless someone's died. Death is the only reason they ever wear shoes. These guys are all wearing sandals."

Lilly was doubtful. "Maybe, maybe not."

"You think they're not retired?" asked Babs.

"Not that. I was talking about what Daffy said about them *all* wearing sandals. That one guy in the middle, the guy with the Hawaiian shirt with the Woodie station wagons and surfboards on it. He's wearing Nisolo huaraches, which ain't cheap. The cheapest I've ever been able to find them at Nordstrom is $130 a pair. And that's for the Nisolo women's huaraches. The men's huaraches are probably thirty or forty bucks more. But you pay for what you get. You can buy a pair for $19.99 on eBay, but—"

"Lilly sweetie, your shaggy dog story is losing us again." Daffy used a term referring a long-winded, meaningless anecdote. "I thought you were talking about them *all* wearing sandals, not the price of huaraches."

"I'm getting there. I'm talking about whether or not huaraches are sandals or shoes."

Gidget said, "That probably depends on one's footwear belief system."

"No, silly," Lilly said. "I was gonna say whether huaraches are sandals or shoes depends on who's selling them. Nike calls them shoes, while Zappos calls them sandals. Most shoe retailers call them sandals. *Footwear News* is the bible on shoes, and I've seen that magazine call them shoes sometimes, but most of the time they call them sandals—"

Daffy looked around the table. "Will someone please call Shoe-a-holics Anonymous? We need an emergency intervention here."

"Anyway, the guy with woodie station wagons and surfboards is wearing huaraches, which may or may not be a sandal… or a shoe." Lilly had a satisfied look on her face when she finished.

"What about the guy wearing the crew socks?" asked Lizzie.

"They're all wearing crew socks," said Gidget.

"The guy on the end… on the left side. Whatever he's wearing on his feet looks kind of weird, if you ask me." Lizzie looked at Lilly. "Would you call them sandals or shoes?"

Lilly said, "They're not sandals… or shoes. They look like McGuffey slip-ons to me. They're more of a slipper than a shoe or a sandal. They ain't cheap either. Johnston & Murphy don't make cheap slip-ons."

"At least the blue denim color of his slip-ons doesn't clash too badly with his orange socks," mused Daffy.

Always in search of another meal ticket, Lizzie said, "I don't care about any of that. Get a load of that bling. I see two solid gold Rolex watches, one gold Patek Phillippe, and two gold Vacheron Constatin watches. There's some serious money ogling us right now."

Expensive watches were only the tip of the iceberg, emphasis on *ice*. Diamonds adorned multiple strands of 18-carat solid gold link chains around each man's neck. A variety of gemstones encrusted numerous rings on each man's hand.

"Looks like they all got the same diamond-studded pinky ring," said Lilly.

"Maybe they all belong to the same men's club," said Gidget.

Daffy nodded. "At their age, they must belong to something like the Elks Club or a Moose Lodge."

"Lions Club?" asked Babs.

Gidget shook her head. "Nope. With the colorful outfits these guys are wearing, they've got to be Shriners. It's probably some sort of ring Shriners wear. Like a Masonic ring, but more expensive."

The IHOP hostess seemed as stunned at the Marx Brothers' fashion statements as the Casserole Ladies. The young woman stared speechless at the new guests as they ogled the objects of their search. Her limited life experience in her small hometown never prepared her for a Rio de Janeiro Carnival in the foyer of the IHOP. She finally asked, "Would y'all like a table?"

One of the old boys pointed to the Casserole Ladies' table and said, "Tanks, but ah tink we ah gonnah go ovah dere an meet doz lovely brahds."

Chapter 3

Thomasville, Georgia
October 13th

The hostess stood dumbfounded. She understood seven of fifteen words spoken by the old man. He might as well have been speaking Mandarin Chinese. The best she could manage was, "Huh?"

Another of the old men stepped forward.

"What my bruddah..." he stopped himself. "What my bro-ther meant to say is that we are go-ing to go ov-er there and meet those love-ly la-dies."

She pointed and asked, "Oh, y'all want to be seated with the ladies at that table?"

"Yeah, dat's right."

"Let's go see if they're okay with that."

She led them to the table. One of the gentlemen bowed slightly to the Casserole Ladies, and in a heavy Brooklyn accent, said, "Hello. Ain't youse duh goils in duh 'Widows of Thomasville' calendah?"

The Casserole Ladies experienced the same language barrier as the hostess. Before any of them could respond, one of the other older gentlemen looked at the previous speaker.

"Larry, remember we ain't in Brooklyn no more. These people down here speak English."

Lilly said, "Correction. We speak the Southern version of English, thank you."

"I beg your pardon, Miss. What my brother meant to say was aren't youse the girls in the 'Widows of Thomasville' calendar?"

With the translation completed and understood, Lilly said, "Yes, that was us in the calendar. And who are y'all?"

"My name is Harry. Harry Vanderhoff. And these are my brothers Jerry, Larry, Barry, and Gary. Would youse mind if we join youse? We are big admirers of your calendar. Especially Miss May."

Harry lasciviously eyed Daffy. She had posed for the month of May *au naturel* in a profile shot, sitting in a swing and leaning back. But for an extended arm holding onto a chain, Harry would have seen Daffy's lovely breasts.

Lizzie said, “We ain’t ordered yet, so why don’t ya’ll pull up some chairs? We’d love to sit a spell with y’all.”

“We can do better than that.” Larry turned to the hostess. “Miss, we’d like a table big enough for all of us.”

“But, Sir. We don’t have a table big enough to accommodate all of y’all right now—” she said.

Larry cut her off when he reached into his shirt pocket—the one with a red, green, and yellow parrot on it—and pulled out a thick wad of hundred-dollar bills.

Gidget looked at Daffy. Daffy looked at Gidget. Gidget mouthed, “That’s a lot of dough.”

Lizzie was not as tactful. “I ain’t seen that much money in one place since Ken Jennings won on *Jeopardy*.”

“What? This? This ain’t nothing.” Larry peeled off two of the hundred-dollar bills and handed them to the hostess. “Keep one for yourself and give one to the manager. Get us another table and five chairs over here.”

Jerry looked at Larry and frowned. “Tsk, tsk, tsk. Ain’t you even gonna say please?”

Lizzie said, “If he don’t, I will.”

Ten minutes later, everyone began getting acquainted around two tables joined together.

“So, y’all are all brothers?” Gidget asked.

Gary said, “Yep. Harry’s the oldest, Barry’s the ugliest, Larry’s the laziest, Jerry’s the shyest, and I’m the smartest.”

Jerry said, “Only in your mind.”

“Where are you gentlemen from?” asked Daffy.

“We currently live in The Villages. Been there about five years,” Larry said. “Ever hoid of it?”

Lilly said, “Oh yeah. We almost went there in September. We would have made it if Lizzie here hadn’t gotten into an argument with my Mercedes’ GPS, and the thing decided to shut down—"

Five quizzical looks prompted Daffy to say, “It’s a long story.” Lilly’s GPS was enabled with Artificial Intelligence, and it did not appreciate Lizzie calling it a stupid bitch during the September trip.

"Say no more," said Jerry. "I got so pissed at the GPS in one of our Mercedes, I took it back to the dealer and made them turn it off. Who can understand how to work all this new technology nowadays? We just use the map on our iPhones now. Problem is iPhones don't have a voice with a Brooklyn accent, so it's hard to understand her directions."

Everyone gave a short laugh, followed by a question from Daffy. "Y'all aren't originally from The Villages, are y'all? The lovely fifty-five plus community in Central Florida?"

Barry said, "Correct. Only been there about five years now. We're originally from New York. Brooklyn actually."

Gary nodded. "Yeah. The Vanderhoff family goes way back in New York history. Our ancestors come over to Manhattan in the Mayflower with the rest of the Dutch settlers."

Gidget made a skeptical face and asked, "What prompted y'all to move to The Villages?"

Larry shook his head sadly. "High taxes and crime in New York. It was gettin' so bad a guy couldn't go out for a bottle of pop for the weekend up there without dodging bullets."

"Yeah, so we turned over our businesses to our associates, retired, and come down to The Villages to take it easy," Gary said.

"What kind of businesses were y'all in?" Babs asked.

"Oh, various things…" Harry paused, refreshing his memory. "We been in things like restaurants, convenience stores, some entertainment investments in Vegas, a few things in Hollywood."

Jerry said, "Don't forget our waste management business."

"And the credit business in Chicago," Barry added. "That's still a significant portion of the portfolio. Anything else we forgot?"

"There's probably a lot of other things we forgot," said Larry, "but memory is the first thing that goes when you get old."

Jerry shook his head. "I wish. The prostate is the first thing that goes."

"Jerry… that ain't the kind of thing to talk about around these nice ladies." Harry eyed Daffy as he spoke. "I apologize for my brother's lack of couth."

Daffy returned Harry's look. "No need to apologize. I was married for over forty years, so I know all about men's prostates."

The conversation meandered for a while as they got to know each other. The Marx Brothers talked about life back in Brooklyn and their family, especially their father Sal and their mother Angie. Sal was a strict disciplinarian, and Angie was a wonderful cook.

"Mamma made the best gnocchi," said Larry.

"No-kee? What's that?" asked Lizzie. "It sounds like a dirty word I know."

Jerry laughed. "You roll out some flour dough, cut it into small squares, put a mixture of mashed potatoes and egg in the middle of each square, roll 'em into little balls, and boil 'em. I can still taste 'em. Mamma made gnocchi every Sunday for dinner."

"My momma made chicken and dumplins' every Sunday for supper. It was so good, but lordy did it put on the pounds," said Babs.

One unmentioned topic continued to bother Daffy. When she sensed an appropriate opening, she asked, "What about your wives? Do they like life in The Villages?"

"No, we ain't got no wives. Three of us been married a couple of times." Barry looked at three of his brothers. "These three was so consumed by our business ventures that, unfortunately, their marriages suffered. That's a problem when your work is high-stress. They all got divorced. Several times."

Lizzie looked at Larry, Jerry, and Gary. "You boys and I are simpatico."

"Me and Harry… we took a different approach. We decided long ago to keep our options open, so to speak. We were lucky that we had very understanding lady friends."

Harry nodded. "They was all very understanding."

"We made it worth their while," said Barry. His comment failed to endear him to any of the women except Lizzie. She appreciated men, especially husbands, who took care of women financially after the relationship ended. Lizzie had engineered generous alimony settlements in all of her four divorces. She considered herself an expert in family law.

A different issue disturbed Lilly. She knew it might be an etiquette blunder of enormous proportions to address it, but she could no longer restrain herself. "Mister Jerry, I just got to ask you about your sandals. Those are some of the most beautiful huaraches I ever seen. What brand are they?"

"Yuketen Alejandro," Jerry said.

"Oh my God!"

Jerry's brow wrinkled, more so than its normal state. "Yeah. It took some doing to get myself a pair. The smallest size Yuketen sells to Saks is an eight. I had them custom order them direct from Yuketen."

"It must have cost you a fortune."

"Nah, chump change."

"I was looking online at Saks the other day and saw a pair of Yuketens for two-seventy-five."

"That's what I said… chump change."

Gidget winced. Talking about the cost of someone's shoes was clearly a breach of etiquette. "How'd y'all wind up coming up here to Thomasville just to see us? I'm surprised *our* calendar would have tempted y'all to drive all that way."

"It's like this," Larry said. "We're sitting by the pool playing canasta recently, and one of the older gentlemen at another table is looking at this calendar what has these good-looking babes in it, and we borrows his calendar, and Jerry says, 'Who the heck is these good-looking broads?' I mean women. And I says, 'We gotta meet these good-looking fillies. There's five of them and five of us, so it's a match made in Heaven.' And, here we are."

Barry nodded. "That's the way we are. We sees something we like, we go for it. So, we hopped in one of the Mercedes and drove on up here."

Babs said, "That reminds me of the time when my momma's two sisters came to visit my momma here in Thomasville. I drove the three of them to the new Walmart in Tallahassee because her sisters forgot to pack their bedroom slippers. This was when one of my oldest girls was only six months old, and so I had to drive all the way to Tallahassee with them three old women and a six-month old baby in a tiny Toyota Corolla. Those three old women wouldn't stop talking about stuff that had no business being discussed in front of a six-month-old—"

"Babsie," Daffy said, "let's make sure this story is going somewhere."

"Oh, it is. Anyway, they start talking about the Pope, and tampons in the ear, and how urine is sterile, and sex with a husband after prostate surgery, and…" Babs put her hands over her ears. "It got so bad I had to put my hands over my ears—"

"I thought you were driving?"

"I was. Anyway, it was so risqué I had to put my hands over my ears and keep saying 'Happy Place' 'Happy Place.' You know the drill—"

"Have you gentlemen had breakfast yet?" Gidget asked.

"That sounds great, but I want to hear the rest of this lovely lady's story first," said Larry.

Three minutes more into Babs' story, Harry said, "I like your story, Babsie, but I gotta take my pills. Let's get the waitress over here and order some breakfast, then you can finish."

Gary looked at Harry and said, "Harry, you took your pills with the bagel you ate on the way up here. Remember?"

"Now, that's a stupid question. If I'd remembered I'd already taken my pills, I wouldn't have said 'I gotta take my pills,' would I? I'm seventy-five, after all. Give me a break." Harry looked at Daffy for sympathy.

Daffy nodded. "Old age bad memory is why God invented the medicine pill organizer."

"Mine has an alarm," said Gary.

As the laughter died down, Larry signaled for a waitress. The restaurant's four waitresses had all heard about his wad of hundred-dollar bills, and three rushed to the table.

The first waitress to arrive asked, "What can I get y'all?"

Jerry looked at the Casserole Ladies. "What would youse like?"

Babs had forgotten her reading glasses and had to telescope the menu back and forth to get it in focus. She said, "I'll have the Rooty Tooty Fresh 'N Fruity Pancake Combo. But could I have a side order of grits with it?"

Harry said, "Grits. God, how I love 'em."

Larry said, "God's gift to the South. You know, until I come down to The Villages, I always thought you ate a grit, then asked for another grit if you wanted more."

In a moment of sibling rivalry, Jerry tried to one up his brother. “First time I ordered grits, I thought they’d made a mistake and served me mashed potatoes with my poached egg.”

Rambling, a tendency displayed in many older men, accounted for the next five-minute discussion about grits. The subject only changed when Daffy said, “Maybe we should finish our orders so our waitress here can go on about her business.”

Orders taken, the discussion continued for two and a half hours and included a variety of topics of interest to almost no one under the age of fifty-five.

Chapter 4

Thomasville, Georgia
October 13th

Time flew for all the oldsters. They discussed everything from favorite foods—Gidget noticed a lot of soft foods in the Marx Brothers' diet—to the good old days. Harry showed the Casserole Ladies the scar on his calf.

"I accidentally shot myself while showing my oldest son how to load a Colt semi-auto pistol," Harry said, forgetting Barry had told the ladies he and Harry were never married. Gidget and Daffy glanced at each other, and the latter winked.

Gary told a story about getting mugged on the subway in high school. "A buddy dared me to wear a dress and ride from the 34th Street station to the 59th Street station. The problem was that part of the subway goes through the Hell's Kitchen neighborhood."

"What's the problem with that?" asked Babs.

"The toughest thugs in New York City roam there."

"Why'd you do that?" asked a horrified Lilly.

"We did that kind of stuff all the time in high school. We was batshit crazy back then. We pulled all sorts of pranks—"

"Yeah. All five of us even streaked the Macy's Thanksgiving Day Parade when we was in high school—" Jerry abruptly stopped his narrative when he noticed a look from his older brother Harry.

Babs said, "Oh my gosh! Ain't that a coincidence?! The five of us just streaked the Georgia-Florida game in Jacksonville this last Saturday."

Larry asked, "You mean those five streakers we saw on TV was youse? All of us thought it was the Kardashians."

"Nope. It was us." Babs did not exaggerate. They had disguised themselves—Babs went as Kylie Jenner—and ran across the field naked at TIAA Bank Stadium during halftime of the nationally televised college football game. All of Thomasville currently debated whether the streakers were the Casserole Ladies or the Kardashians. Daffy shot Babs a look, but she continued talking anyway. "We had to do it when we lost a bet with some other women after one of them insulted Daffy's granddaughter's plié—"

Daffy said, "You'd have have had to have been there."

"Good disguises." Larry glanced at his watch. It was a Patek Phillippe, and Lizzie had shamelessly ogled it. "We been enjoying yakking with youse so much that we forgot the time. Unfortunately, we must depart. It's three hours back to The Villages. None of us drives very well in the dark."

The five women's heads empathetically nodded. Old age is hell.

"Can't y'all stay overnight?" asked Daffy. "We could spend some more time together and get to know each other better."

"I wish we could, but my brothers and I can't stay. We're leaving on a month-long Caribbean cruise Wednesday, and we gotta get back to The Villages today so we can pack tomorrow."

"I hope we'll see y'all again soon," Lizzie said. As she spoke, she did something all Southern women learn how to do at an early age. She batted her eyelashes.

"I am sure my brothers will agree with me when I say I hope that is *real* soon," Jerry said.

Barry's eyes lit up. "Hey! I just got an idea. Why don't youse go with us on the cruise? We'll spring for all the costs. It'll be our treat."

As if on cue, all his brothers nodded.

Gidget grimaced. "Uh, I don't know. I've got a pharmacy to run. I can't just take off out of the blue."

Barry looked at Babs. She said, "I wish I could go with y'all, but three of my grandchildren have birthdays later this month, and I can't miss any of them. They kick you out of the grandmothers' union for missing your grandchild's birthday."

Harry looked at Daffy.

She said, "I don't know. I need to check my calendar. It's back at the house."

"What about you?" Larry asked as he looked at Lizzie. He was the one who pulled the roll of hundred-dollar bills out of his Hawaiian flower shirt.

"I'd love to, but I got a doctor's appointment this month." Lizzie purposefully did not mention the appointment was with her plastic surgeon for a tummy tuck.

Jerry looked at Lilly. "That leaves you."

Lilly said, "Oh, my goodness. I'd love to go on a cruise. I haven't been on a cruise in ages—"

"You went on a cruise last spring," said Daffy.

"Oh, I forgot that one. Anyway, I'd love to go with you boys. A cruise sounds like a great idea. Get away from this cold weather—"

"It's seventy-nine degrees outside."

"Anyway, I'd love to go with you boys," Lilly said, "but I'm having my shoe closet remodeled this month."

Barry asked, "Shoe closet? I never heard of a shoe closet. A closet for just shoes?"

Lilly sheepishly nodded.

Gidget said, "Lilly's a shoe-a-holic. Tried several times to kick the habit, but…"

"So, reschedule the remodel," Larry said.

Lilly vigorously shook her head. "No way. Getting a contractor this close to the SEC Championship is tough enough. I'll have to wait months if I cancel. My shoe closet is in real bad shape."

"Besides," asked Gidget, "how will we be able to get rooms on board your boat this late in the game?"

"Youse let us worry about that. We're gonna make 'em an offer they can't refuse." Barry's grin reached ear-to-ear.

Larry furrowed his brow, then relaxed and smiled. "Barry was just trying to be funny. Ladies, we'll take care of everything—the rooms, food, booze, you name it. We'll get youse great staterooms, or my name ain't uh… Vanderhoff. The cruise is on us."

"That's very tempting, but—" Daffy said.

"Look. Youse don't have to make a decision right now. We're gonna head on out." Larry passed out his card to each woman. "Call me on my cell phone this afternoon if any of youse changes your mind and wants to go. We'd love to have youse join us. Otherwise, we'll text you pictures of the cruise. And this breakfast is on us."

As the Marx Brothers stood, Larry pulled several gold coins out of his pocket to pay and asked, "Do they take Bitcoin in this here joint?"

"I… I don't think so," said Gidget.

Larry put the coins back in his pocket, then pulled out his wad of cash. "That's okay, we still got plenty of dough."

The women stared as he motioned for their waitress. He plopped down five one-hundred-dollar bills on the table and told the young lady, "We're covering these nice ladies' bill as well as ours. Divide what's left over between yourself and the rest of the crew."

"Meeting youse has been wonderful," said Gary. The Marx Brothers bowed slightly and hobbled off, leaving their waitress speechlessly staring at more money than she had ever seen in one place in the IHOP.

After their waitress scooped up the money and left, Gidget said, "The English language sure could use a plural form of the word 'you' besides just 'you.'"

"We already got y'all," said Babs.

"It ain't the official plural of you."

"You sure about that? I always assumed y'all was a real word."

"I'll take anything but 'youse,'" said Lizzie.

"I wonder if youse is a real word, and we just ain't heard about it down here," said Babs.

"It's as real a word as y'all," said Gidget.

"I vote for 'y'all' myself," said Lilly.

"The other language difference between those New Yorkers and us Southerners is their term for their mothers."

"How so?" asked Daffy.

"Y'all notice how Jerry talked about his 'mamma' instead of his 'momma?' He pronounced it with a definite M-A instead of M-O like we do."

They discussed the pros and cons of accompanying the Marx Brothers on the cruise. The main objection centered on the propriety of such an action. As Lilly said, "We just met them. Think of what Thomasville would say about us going on a cruise with five strange men."

Lizzie said, "Emphasis on the word *strange*."

"I think they're kind of cute," said Babs.

"You gotta be kidding." As Gidget spoke, she nodded in the direction of the foyer. "Look who's here."

Sonny Biskit, a minor celebrity in Thomasville, stood in the foyer. He glanced in their direction, then headed their way. His red Def Leppard t-shirt strained to contain his belly, as did his snug, well-worn jeans. Both emphasized a paunch ravaged by McDonald's Big Macs and middle age. His chubby cheeks sported three days growth of whiskers. As he approached, his hand attempted to tame a flyaway combover to no avail. He said, "Hey, y'all. No need to avert your eyes. Unlike the sun, ya'll can look directly at me as long as y'all want to."

"Sonny gazing is usually measured in nanoseconds, isn't it?" After Lizzie spoke, a puzzled expression came over Sonny's face.

Locals sometimes debated whether Sonny's personality more closely mimicked Barney Fife on *The Andy Griffith Show* or Ted Baxter on *The Mary Tyler Moore Show*. As with both of those characters, Sonny displayed a pretentious swagger, belying mediocre abilities. In testimony to the severity of the shortage of eligible bachelors in Thomasville, two of the Casserole Ladies had dated him on the sly. Most recently, he had squired Babs to a tractor pull in nearby Waycross, where they experienced an embarrassing incident involving a Viagra-induced visit to the local hospital's ER.

"What's up, Sonny?" asked Gidget.

"I'm meeting Bob in here for lunch," Sonny said. Bob Biskit was his older brother. He owned Biskit Buick in Buckee, Georgia. "He's bringing me a '09 LaCrosse. My Electra is on its last legs. He just got the LaCrosse on a trade-in and thought of me. Say, was them five old boys that I passed coming in here the Marx Brothers?"

"Yeah. How'd you know their nickname?"

"Olive at Flash Foods told me. She said they drove up here from that old folks' place in Florida just to see y'all. She said they'd seen your calendar." Sonny chuckled. "She said they was barely understandable when they talked. Said they kept saying 'youse' instead of y'all."

Daffy rolled her eyes. "Word sure travels fast in Thomasville, especially when Olive gets involved. They must've stopped at Flash Foods to gas up before they came to the IHOP."

Sonny shook his head. "She didn't meet 'em. She got word about them from Jasmine at Harvey's. Her sister Connie at the Visitors Center called her to tell her about the five strange men who stopped by. Hey, I see Bob just walked in. Gotta go. Bye, y'all..." Sonny turned to leave, then looked over his shoulder as he walked away.

"Oh, 'fore I go, there's a tractor pull at the fairgrounds in Valdosta this Saturday if any of y'all wants to go."

"We'll let you know. Bye," Lilly said.

As they watched the hostess seat Sonny and Bob, Daffy said, "Sonny seems to shrink every year. Why are all older men so short nowadays?"

"It's because you're so tall," said Lizzie.

Babs said, "Sonny should wear things that make him look taller."

"Why? So, he could take you to the tractor pull in Valdosta?"

"I wonder what Sonny could wear that would make him look taller?"

"Stilts."

Chapter 5

Thomasville, Georgia
October 13th

The Ladies quickly returned to the main topic of discussion. Daffy channeled Shakespeare when she asked, "To cruise, or not to cruise? That is the question."

Babs voiced the thought running through everyone's brain. "Is it safe to go on a cruise with five strange men?"

Gidget said, "Running off with five old bachelors like the Marx Brothers will be grist for the Thomasville gossip mill."

Lizzie agreed. "It'll make the gossip mill's analysis of my third divorce look tame by comparison."

Lilly looked puzzled. "Wasn't it your third husband who tried to sell Sunrise Senior Care on the idea of building a second nursing home across the street from Sunset Memorial Cemetery?"

"It was either him or my second husband. What hustlers those guy were. He told the manager at Sunrise it would be real convenient for their residents when they passed away—just a short ride across the street to their final resting place."

"Which husband was it—the second or third?" Gidget asked.

"I can't remember. After two, they all run together." Lizzie scrunched her eyes and nose. "What were we talking about?"

"Going with the Marx Brothers on their Caribbean cruise."

"The Marx Brothers do look kind of strange, although I wish I could tan like them," said Lilly whose fair skin freckled at the mere thought of going into sunshine.

"I bet they get those tans from playing pickleball in The Villages, which pisses me off," said Lizzie. "They get some sun and they get good tans. I get some sun, and all I get is wrinkles and age spots."

Gidget said, "They are dark complexioned. They look like they have some Mediterranean mixed in with their Dutch blood."

Babs had a warm fuzzy about the Marx Brothers. "They look like five harmless old men to me. Heck, they're almost as short as me. The more I think about it, it would probably be safe to go on a cruise with them. I can't imagine a bunch of short, old retirees hurting someone. I wonder how old they are?"

"I wonder how old their money is?" asked Lizzie.

"I'd say the youngest is in his mid-sixties," said Lilly.

"Oh God. We're robbing the cradle again."

Other than a lot of money—which the Casserole Ladies already had—and a free cruise, the Marx Brothers appeared to offer little else. For years, four of the Casserole Ladies had been engaged in a quest for postmortem romance, i.e., marriage and/or sex after their spouses' deaths. Lizzie's quest focused on acquiring another meal ticket. The Marx Brothers certainly seemed to be good meal tickets, but ill-equipped to meet the sex requirement.

Daffy said, "None of them Marx Brothers is the kind of man I envisioned waking up next to on a Sunday morning after a little fun Saturday night."

Lizzie made a face. "At our ages, we gotta take what comes along. It looks like those old boys got money. What more could you ask for? The staterooms they've reserved for the cruise sound great—guest suites, Jacuzzis in each stateroom. But great sex with a Marx Brother? Hard to imagine. I just wish I didn't have my tummy tuck scheduled with Doctor Beauvisage."

"Reschedule it," Lilly said.

"I'd love to, but my tummy tuck can't wait."

"You should go on the cruise and get the tummy tuck after you get back. That way, you could visit the buffets on the cruise as much as you want and have the surgeon remove all of the fat you put on after you get back," Babs said, for once sounding sensible.

Daffy was surprised. "Out of the mouths of babes occasionally come pearls of wisdom."

"You can always reschedule your tummy tuck," Lilly said.

Lizzie shook her head. "You know how hard it is to get on his surgery schedule. He's the only plastic surgeon in Thomasville."

"But I thought that's why you had him on retainer. For priority."

"I do, but I'm not the only ugly, old broad in Thomasville."

Analysis of the pros and cons of going continued. Babs said, "I thought we had a great time talking with them."

"Some of their stories, like the ones about those guys swimming in the Hudson with the fishes and opening the fire hydrants on cop cars, were outrageous," said Lilly, "but that's Yankees for you."

"I loved the one about Jerry and Larry lighting firecrackers during Mass when they were ten."

"It's hard for me to imagine the Marx Brothers as ten-year-olds."

"Why?" asked Lizzie. "They were probably the same height then as they are now."

Babs said, "Now that I think about it, the Jacuzzis in their rooms are probably for their bad backs. I put in more than thirty years listening to a man whine about his bad back." She made a face.

Lilly frowned. "It'd be hard for me to love a short, bald-headed old man that dresses the way they do."

"Why is it with an old man that if his head isn't bald, it's grey, and if it's not grey, it's dyed?" asked Daffy.

Lizzie said, "I did notice some dye jobs when they sat down with us, and I can always spot a dye job. Even a good one like mine."

A wistful look came over Babs' face. "It would be kind of nice to have a man to spoil again."

"Babsie, get yourself a male dachshund," Daffy said. "So long as you do whatever a dachshund wants, they're a piece of cake."

Lilly shrugged. "Remember that old song about marrying an ugly woman if you want to be happy for the rest of your life. Maybe it's the same way with men."

Lizzie shook her head. "It didn't work that way with any of my four husbands, and they were all pretty ugly."

Babs asked, "We know very little about the Marx Brothers. They might be sex perverts—"

"They might even tie us up and do who knows what to us," said Lilly.

"Say no more. I'll cancel my tummy tuck and go," Lizzie joked.

Babs' thinking continued to harden. "Them paying for our way is like we're from some sort of escort service. Like we're prostitutes."

Lizzie smiled. "You and Lilly are definitely trying to convince me to go."

True to form, Gidget had said little during much of the discussion. She was known as the quiet intellectual of the group. Despite a few negative comments initially, the Marx Brothers' offer began to intrigue her. Other than a few Casserole Ladies misadventures, family and work had dominated her life for many years.

Daffy noticed her silence and asked, "Whatcha thinking about, Gidge?"

"Nothing…" Gidget lied. Her brain never ceased thinking and Daffy knew it was a lie. She, Lilly, Lizzie, and Babs had often discussed their friend's increasing melancholia since Sam Smurfitt's death. Each had her own ideas as to its cause. Daffy thought it resulted from being a widow and had told them as much one day:

> "Royce's death never bothered me, but I was odd in that respect. Gidget is normal, and normal people need to go through the grieving process after a spouse's death. It's much needed mental therapy. Poor Gidge has been so busy running the pharmacy by herself, she's never had time to grieve."

It now occurred to Daffy that a cruise might be an opportunity for her friend to grieve. "I think you should go, girl."

Lilly felt Gidget's moodiness was a sign of a mid-life crisis and had told the others as much. After all, Gidget was sixty-two. She said, "I agree with Daff. You need a break in your routine. Go."

For Lizzie, money and sex motivated all human behavior. To her, Gidget's melancholy stemmed from her being a sex-starved widow for the last three years. A lecherous smile spread over Lizzie's face. "I think a little romantic getaway with a couple of old men might put a little bloom back in your cheeks."

Babs thought Gidget's moods resulted from all her children being grown and gone—no one to look after. "A cruise would do you good. Instead of children, you could fuss over five old men. Afterall, there's no difference mentally."

Widowhood, mid-life crisis, lack of sex, no kids running around the house—all these things *had* contributed to Gidget's increasing melancholy. But there was something else. She had been in her husband's shadow for over three decades. Mother to *his* children. Working in *his* pharmacy. Even after running it by herself for the last three years, locals still called it *Sam's* Smurfitt Phamily Pharmacy. It would be nice to do something independent of him. Something that would show Thomasville that she was her own person. Nevertheless, she felt compelled to push back.

"I can't leave the pharmacy for a month. Sam always said, 'There's money in them there pills,' but he never talked about how much work it takes to make that money."

"Those women that work for you can run the pharmacy," Daffy said.

"What about the Thomasville gossip? Running off with a bunch of men I never met before. And like Babsie said, the Marx Brothers might be a bunch of perverts… or even criminals."

"Who gives a rat's ass what the Thomasville rumor mill says? And, as far as the Marx Brothers being dangerous, you're gonna be on a ship with thousands of passengers and crew. It'd be tough to get murdered on a cruise with all those people—"

Lizzie cut in, "I'd be more likely to die on a cruise from overeating at the buffets than from being murdered."

The idea of an adventure increasingly appealed to Gidget. This cruise would show Thomasville that she was an independent woman. "Now that I think about it, I don't see anything wrong in accepting a gentleman's offer so long as there's no strings attached. We'll have our own stateroom. I'm going to check with Cheryl about running things in the pharmacy for a while. Anyone else going?"

Lilly shook her head. "I can't abandon my shoe closet remodel."

"You just had it remodeled last spring."

"Yeah, but I've added more shoes to my collection since then."

"How many you got now?" asked Babs.

"Last count a month ago was four hundred and thirty-six. I forget how many I've bought since then. I've reached a point where I'm gonna have to start getting rid of shoes if I don't remodel."

Lizzie nodded. "Getting rid of old shoes would be more traumatic for you than me skipping my monthly hair coloring appointment."

Gidget looked at Babs. "What about you?"

Babs said, "I can't go. I'd miss too many grandkids' birthdays."

"I understand, and Lizzie, you've got your tummy tuck, so Daff, that leaves you."

Daffy hated denying her close friend but felt it best to decline. None of the Marx Brothers appealed to her in the least. Besides, it would be cruel to give them hope that one of them might have a chance for romance with her, which would be an impossibility. She envisioned going on a cruise with someone sexier, someone much more Italian-y than any of the Marx Brothers. Tall, dark, handsome. Someone whose chest circumference exceeded the circumference of his abdomen. She tried to visualize a young sexy male Italian movie star, but realized no such person currently existed. She fell back on one of her go-to erotic images. A shirtless Chris Hemsworth sashayed into her brain.

Lost in this image, Daffy was startled when Gidget asked, "Are you going?"

Daffy turned to decline Gidget's request and saw Sonny Biskit and his brother sitting in a corner booth. The reality of her situation hit her like a blow from Apollo Creed to Sylvester Stallone's head in *Rocky*. Sonny Biskit, not Chris Hemsworth, typified the eligible bachelor available to a casserole lady in Thomasville. She thought about a quote attributed to Einstein, 'Everything is relative.' When she thought like Einstein about Sonny Biskit, the Marx Brothers began to look a little better. *And* a cruise might be a good venue to meet some really sexy eligible bachelors.

"Now that I think about it, I can't let my good friend go with five strange men by herself. The Marx Brothers seemed friendly and looked harmless enough, but still, I better go along. Two women together are more formidable than one. And I am twice their size. I could probably beat the hell out of any three of them at the same time."

Lilly said, "Maybe you could talk them into wearing Polo shirts occasionally."

Babs looked at Daffy. "It's like Lizzie told Gidge. A cruise with the Marx Brothers might put a little bloom back in your cheeks."

"Especially if you get a chance to sleep with Larry's wallet," Lizzie said.

"Sounds like you're going with me," said Gidget.

Daffy nodded. "Just you and me, kid. Count me in."

Chapter 6

Thomasville, Georgia
October 14th

Daffy whistled in awe as a black stretch Cadillac limousine pulled into her driveway at ten o'clock in the morning. She and Gidget watched from her front porch.

Gidget said, "That's one of the longest limos I've ever seen. It must have a bowling alley in it."

When Daffy had called Gary, he told her that he and his brothers would drive from The Villages directly to Jacksonville and meet them at the ship. They would have a separate limo pick her and Gidget up in Thomasville.

Daffy said, "Gary told me they'd have a limo pick us up, but he never said he was borrowing the President's limousine. You and I have ridden in many limos but never one this glitzy."

They watched as a man wearing a black suit, white shirt, black tie, and chauffeur's hat exited the limo. He said, "Ms. Belvedere?"

"Yep, that's me."

"I'm Edmund, and I'm here to drive you and Ms. Smurfitt to the Port of Jacksonville to embark on the Bahama Princess. If you are ready, I'll load your bags, and we'll leave."

The number of suitcases impressed Edmund, who was a professional driver and had transported a lot of women and their luggage. He filled the limo's large trunk and put the overflow in the passenger compartment.

Daffy made light of their overpacking. "You're lucky we ran out of suitcases before we ran out of clothes."

Daffy whistled again as they settled into the limo's luxurious leather seating. Gidget said, "Looks like you finally found a vehicle large enough to accommodate those long legs."

"I do have a lot of leg," agreed Daffy. She took inventory. "It looks like the Marx Brothers made sure that the limo is well stocked. Check out the bar—Glenmorangie, Blanton's, Patron Anejo, Grey Goose, and Bombay Sapphire."

Gidget opened the limo's built-in refrigerator. "Here's two bottles of Dom Perignon champagne, and it looks like one more in this ice bucket. The Marx Brothers must think we like to drink."

"Our reputations have preceded us."

The glass partition separating the chauffeur's section slid open and Edmund said, "Ladies, we'll be leaving in a minute. Enjoy yourselves. It's a two-and-a-half-hour ride to Jacksonville. Please help yourselves to anything in the bar. There is a nice selection of hors d'oeuvres in the refrigerator. If you need anything, just push the talk button on the intercom system to speak to me. Have a pleasant trip." With that, the partition window closed again.

They began shifting some of the luggage around to get more comfortable. Gidget struggled to shift Daffy's tote bag and asked, "What the heck you got in this thing? I believe the boat already has an anchor."

"That's my reading material," Daffy said.

"What you reading now?"

"My usual stuff—*Fifty Shades of Grey* series, *The Thorn Birds,* the *Story of O*. And some of the newer stuff."

"Nothing like a little soft porn to make five short guys look better," said Gidget.

"What did you bring with you?"

"A few Jane Austen novels. Several John Sanford and Jonathan Kellerman murder mysteries. Also brought a couple of Agatha Christie's books. They showed Kenneth Branagh's *Murder on the Orient Express* on HBO recently, and it motivated me to re-read some of her books."

Daffy wasted no time popping a champagne cork. "Let's get the party started. THREE BOTTLES! How in the heck could the Marx Brothers imagine we could consume three bottles of champagne during a three-hour drive?"

Gidget smiled. "I guess they're hoping we'll lose our inhibitions."

"They obviously don't know that when it comes to sex, I have no inhibitions."

Daffy did the honors, and soon she and Gidget relaxed with champagne while viewing the scenery along Interstate 10.

"Nothing but pine trees and palmetto bushes," Daffy said. "That's all you see along I-10."

"Not all you see. You forgot one other prominent feature of the I-10 landscape."

"What's that? Live oaks with Spanish moss?"

"Nope. Rest Areas."

Daffy nodded as they passed a 'Rest Area 2 Miles' sign. She said, "You're right. I-10 does have a lot of Rest Areas, all built by the State of Florida. There's a Rest Area every thirty minutes along I-10. Royce timed them when we drove to Jacksonville one time. He had an enlarged prostate so it was an important issue for him."

"What man over fifty-five doesn't have an enlarged prostate? I bet all of the Marx Brothers have 'em. They're all overweight. I wonder if anyone's ever done a study on the correlation of weight, age, and prostate size?"

Daffy quipped, "Royce's prostate alone probably weighed five pounds. But I'm surprised you don't know the answer, Little Miss Factoid. You're like my grandson. You always know something about everything."

Forty-five minutes out of Thomasville, Daffy popped the cork on their second bottle of Dom Perignon. Gidget was feeling its effects. "Little Miss Factoid. An intellectual. That's all people in Thomasville ever say about me. The short one with the brain—"

Daffy also felt the alcohol's effects. "That's better than calling you a gold digger like they do Lizzie."

"One of my older sisters always used to tease me about being an intellectual. She always said, 'You and Sam are so smart. So brainy. How do two intellectuals like you two ever do something as physical as have sex? Sex between you and Sam must be something like a Vulcan mind meld.'"

"I wish you hadn't said that. I'm trying to get that image out of my brain. I always thought you and Sam were such a good match—both of you good at math. And as everyone knows, math is the basis of good marriage, especially the multiplication aspect of it."

"Keep trying. You'll say something funny eventually."

"Your moodiness is showing," said Daffy.

Gidget nodded. "I've been moody for a long time now. Work, marriage. Work and marriage were all I had for over thirty years. It was all about Sam. I was just his companion. It was always Sam Smurfitt this, and Sam Smurfitt that. *He* ran Smurfitt Phamily Pharmacy. The *last* of the independent pharmacies. I just did what he told me to do, and *his* pharmacy made a lot of money. It'd be nice to be known for something *I* did... without Sam. I don't want to seem like I didn't love him and enjoy my life with him. I did, but I want to do something just as Gidget, not as Sam's wife. I'd like to achieve something on my own for a change."

"Like what?"

"Anything."

Daffy listened for the next two minutes to Gidget's Dom Perignon-fueled bitching before she changed the subject. "Let's talk about the Marx Brothers."

"There's something strange about them," Gidget said.

"You must be thinking about Larry wearing socks with his Crocs? He *was* taking 'dad fashion' to a new level."

Gidget laughed. "Not that. They seemed harmless enough, but the more I've thought about it, there's something about them."

"What? Make it juicy."

Gidget was a pharmacist by trade and possessed a pharmacist's mindset. She examined things carefully, looked for incompatibilities and inconsistencies, and paid attention to detail. She possessed three things helpful to a pharmacist: good analytical skills, problem-solving abilities, and a photographic memory.

"The way they all dress alike. I mean those oversized Hawaiian flower shirts. I know all old retired men wear them, but these guys take it to an extreme. It's almost like some sort of secret society."

Daffy said, "Maybe those shirts are their camouflage uniforms in case they ever have to invade the rain forests of Brazil."

"Okay, what about all that bling? All the Marx Brothers had gold chains dripping from their necks and wrists, gold watches, and those diamond studded pinky rings. Each of those rocks must've been at least three carats. Seems like an excessive display of wealth. What kind of people do that?"

Daffy refilled their champagne glasses. "People with money."

"And that wad of hundred-dollar bills. And what a weird collection of businesses they've been in—convenience stores, Vegas entertainment, credit business in Chicago. Seems like a strange conglomeration."

"And all my Royce ever owned was one measly ole bank."

"And all that BS about them having Dutch ancestry. Their ancestors coming over on the Mayflower. The boat must've dropped the Pilgrims off in Massachusetts, then gone on down to Manhattan with the Dutch."

"It was called boat-pooling, the forerunner of carpooling. All good points, but so what?" Daffy asked. "They're weird Yankees, but aren't most Yankees weird?"

"True, but these guys seem weird in a weird sort of way," said Gidget. "But let's face it. Anyone not from Thomasville will seem weird to us. We're going with them because there's not much to choose from in Thomasville, and we're not exactly *Playboy* centerfolds."

"We'd be lucky to be centerfolds for a Tractor Supply catalog."

This kind of conversation went on for another hour and on into their third bottle of champagne. A small green light on the intercom lit up, and Edmund's voice announced, "Ladies, if you look to your right, you can see the Port of Jacksonville."

Daffy focused on the bottle of Dom Perignon she held upside down over Gidget's empty champagne flute. Sadness in her voice, she slurred, "All gone," as a large ship loomed in the distance.

Chapter 7

Jacksonville, Florida
October 14th

Standing on the pier, Daffy and Gidget gazed at eleven hundred feet of ship moored beside the dock. A cobalt blue hull extended sixty feet from the waterline up to the main deck. Two levels above that, eight rows of tinted windows reached from stem to stern. Three smaller decks were scattered around the ship along with another larger deck, the promenade deck. The weather deck, the highest one on the ship, contained a hodgepodge of things on it, including more passenger accommodations, pools, and a variety of entertainment venues. The Bahama Princess was impressive.

Gidget said, “That’s what I call a big boat.”

“That’s what I call a long gangplank.” Daffy pointed at the offending obstacle in front of them. “Its designer must have hated seventy-year-old women.”

“There’s the Marx Brothers.” Gidget waved at five men in Hawaiian flower shirts standing on the main deck near the end of the gangplank leading into the ship’s entrance. All smiles, they waved back.

“They look much shorter up there, don’t they? And the closer we get to them, the taller they’ll look. Maybe by the time we’re standing next to them, they’ll be taller than me.”

“Talk about wishful thinking.” Gidget looked at the gangplank. “Let’s get started up this abomination. Where’s a wheelchair when you need it.”

The Casserole Ladies’ ages caught up with them about a fourth of the way up. Both were groaning and huffing, but between breaths, Gidget managed, “You know, I just thought of something. Without Lilly, Lizzie, and Babs, there’s five of the Marx Brothers and only two of us.”

“And the problem is?” asked Daffy.

“Seems kind of unfair to the other girls. We get first dibs on the booty.”

“True, but so what? All’s fair in love and war and chasing male booty.”

"Miss Daffy, you are so bad. You should at least try to limit your amorous attentions to *one* of the five Brothers."

As they plodded further up the gangplank, Gidget noticed a large man on a deck further up ship who seemed to be looking down at their five boyfriends. He noticed Gidget looking at him and quickly walked away. She said, "Look at the guy on the deck just above the Marx Brothers. The one walking away."

Daffy looked, then whistled. "All I see is a large back, but it looks like it belongs to one big dude. He looks like he could kick Arnold Schwarzenegger's ass."

"Front the front, he looked vicious... like some sort of special operations kind of guy. Not exactly someone you'd expect to see on a vacation cruise."

A little further up the gangplank, Daffy said, "It just occurred to me that I'm probably going to embarrass myself."

"How so?" asked Gidget.

"I'm not going to be able to remember which Marx Brother's name is associated with each face when we meet them."

"Just follow my lead." Gidget's photographic memory could sometimes be useful outside of her pharmacy.

At the top of the gangplank, the ship's photographer took a picture of the two women. She said, "Bahama Princess takes a photo of each group of passengers as they board. We post them on the bulkhead outside of the cruise director's office if you want to see them. You'll get a copy of yours after the cruise is over as a souvenir of a wonderful vacation."

A flurry of hugs followed as the Marx Brothers crowded around the Casserole Ladies. It sounded like a movie scene from a 1930s comedy as Gidget, then Daffy was groped and smooched sequentially by each Marx Brother. "Gary." "Gidget." "Gary." "Daffy." "Larry." "Gidget." "Larry." "Daffy." "Barry." "Gidget." "Barry." "Daffy." "Harry." "Gidget." "Harry." "Daffy." "Jerry." "Gidget." "Jerry." "Daffy."

After they finished, Daffy said, "Y'all should have your names embroidered on your shirts. Those Hawaiian flower shirts make y'all all look alike."

Larry had a lecherous look on his face. “You look good enough to eat.”

“You almost did when you kissed me… but I’m not objecting.”

“I guess you Dutch-Americans must be huggers,” Gidget said.

“Dutch-Americans!?” Larry looked around at his brothers.

Harry nodded. “That’s us all right. Dutch-Americans through and through. Huggers, not fighters.”

Jerry said, “Too bad the other girls couldn’t make it.”

“*C'est la vie*. How long have y’all been on board?” asked Gidget.

“About three hours. Would’ve been here longer if one of us hadn’t had to stop at every gas station on 301.”

“Can I help it if there were no rest stops on 301?” asked Larry.

“You just *had* drink all them Budweisers this morning.”

Harry looked at the women. “Ignore those two morons. Let’s get youse up to your rooms. Just follow me.”

A fall festival corn maze could not have been more confusing than the winding route to their suites. Barry apologized, “Sorry about the long walk. Our rooms are on the eighth floor.”

Daffy said, “Y’all might as well have blindfolded me. I’ll never remember the route we’re taking.”

“And no bread crumbs to mark our trail,” added Gidget.

The ladies’ suite, which was sandwiched between the Marx Brothers’ two suites, contained a large sitting area with a sixty-five-inch TV, leather seating, matching mahogany cocktail table and end tables, and original works of art on the walls. Most impressive were sprays of red roses throughout the suite.

Daffy said, “Looks like this boat has a florist shop.”

“This is a Premier Suite, just like ours. Everything is included—top-shelf booze, the finest dining, health spa with massages, you name it,” said Gary. As he spoke, two crew members, a man and a woman, suddenly appeared in the doorway. “These two will give youse the tour of your suite, while me and my brothers adjourn to the Barbados Lounge. Please join us there after you finish your tour.”

After the Marx Brothers exited, the man stepped forward. He wore a white long-sleeve shirt, black bow tie, black vest, and light grey pants. His thinning black hair, thick black eyebrows, and sallow complexion gave Gidget the willies. In a clipped British accent, he said, "Hello, my name is Stokes, and I am your butler. This is Yvette, your maid."

Yvette wore a classic French maid's uniform. Low-cut, black bodice with a short skirt hemline, and white apron. Her dark hair was tied up in a bun. She curtsied and spoke with a French accent. "I am so ha-py to be of ser-veece to you *mesdames*."

Stokes said, "We come with the Premier Suite—"

Daffy quipped. "I didn't know indentured servitude still existed."

"I do not believe I have heard that one before. If you will follow me, each of you has your own master bedroom suite. A thirty-five-day cruise demands the privacy afforded by one's own suite. One suite is off of this sitting area, while the other is accessed via that stairway." Stokes pointed to a set of steps. "It goes up to a second level. Please walk this way, and I'll show you the downstairs bedroom first. I trust the suite's decor will meet with your approval."

The downstairs bedroom included its own *en suite* bathroom. The bedroom and bathroom's interiors could have graced the glossy pages of the high-end decorating magazine *Veranda*. Stokes next showed them a small combination kitchen and bar, also off of the sitting area.

"This bar is even better stocked than the limousine," Gidget said.

Stokes nodded. "I am quite sure. However, Yvette and I will be at your beck and call should you need any food or drink any time of day. Also, you may have noticed the advertisement touting Premier passengers' exclusive dining privileges in Azul, an amenity not available to other passengers. After you dine in Azul, eating food prepared in this kitchen will seem absurd. Please follow me up the stairs."

The bedroom upstairs mirrored the one downstairs in terms of amenities. Both bedrooms as well as the sitting area downstairs opened onto balconies. Daffy and Gidget walked outside onto the upstairs balcony. Gidget stepped up to the railing and looked over the railing.

"Thank God none of my grandchildren are here. They would be climbing all over this railing. It looks like a long way down to the water."

"At least they'd have a beautiful view on the way down," said Daffy.

Stokes seemed disgusted. "If you ladies will pardon me, I need to go downstairs and coordinate some details of your stay with Yvette."

After Stokes left, Gidget moved close to Daffy. "There's something about that butler that bothers me."

"What?" asked Daffy.

"His name for one thing. Sounds like a villain character in a movie. There's something about him."

"It's probably his British accent."

Gidget nodded. "That accent sounds contrived. Did you hear the way he pronounced PRIVa-see and ad-VERTIS-ment? His heavy British accent sounded faked to me. I'm not too sure about Yvette either. Wasn't the maid in that old movie *Clue* named Yvette? If I remember the movie correctly, she had been a call girl before becoming a maid. This Yvette certainly has a body for that kind of work. And that fake French accent."

"I think you're going a little overboard with your suspicions. Take a Xanax and chill."

Back downstairs, Stokes said, "I took the liberty of scheduling a tour of the ship tomorrow for you and your five traveling companions. It begins at nine-thirty, if that is acceptable to you."

Daffy still felt remnants of the champagne. "You may go now, my good man."

Not to be outdone, Stokes replied, "Very good, milady."

After the Stokes and Yvette closed the door behind them, Daffy asked, "How you like our digs?"

"Two balconies and balcony suites are at a premium on cruise ships. Unbelievable interior decorating. They must have hired Bunny Williams. And these flowers are over the top. Is this how rich old men treat their whores? We did do some risqué poses for our *Widows of Thomasville* calendar."

"Sounds like you're beginning to regret our decision to tag along. It's not too late. The ship doesn't set sail until tomorrow morning."

Gidget decided to let that idea percolate overnight.

Chapter 8

Jacksonville, Florida
October 15th

While the ship was being towed out of the Port of Jacksonville's harbor the next morning, Stokes knocked on the door of the Casserole Ladies' suite. He opened it, looked into an empty room, and announced, "Breakfast is served, Ladies. Remember, I signed you up for a 9:30 tour of the Bahama Princess. Your male companions are finishing breakfast in their suites. It is a three-hour tour with lunch at the end. Your guide will be Rachel, the Assistant Cruise Director."

A voice from the bedroom above shouted, "Go away!"

A voice from the bedroom below shouted, "And don't come back!"

Both women nursed hangovers from late-night cocktails with the Marx Brothers in the Barbados Lounge. Accordingly, Stokes made a pot of Ethiopian Sidamo Guji French Roast coffee. As they sipped it on their balcony and watched the Bahama Princess being towed, Gidget said, "I guess it's too late to change my mind about going on the cruise."

At 9:30, the Casserole Ladies and the Marx Brothers met Rachel on the main deck along with a dozen other passengers. She said, "On behalf of Captain Omen, the ship's skipper, I want to welcome you aboard the Bahama Princess, the crown jewel of the Caribbean. This is one of the newest and largest cruise ships in this part of the world. By the way, the Princess is ship, not a boat. That small craft you see off the starboard side," she pointed to a small catamaran sailing several hundred yards away, "is a boat. Calling the Bahama Princess a boat is a no no—"

Larry said, "Boat, boat, boat—" until Gary punched his chest.

Rachel said, "This will be a three-hour tour—"

Harry interrupted, "Just so long as I don't miss my afternoon nap."

"A man after my own heart. I love afternoon naps," said Daffy.

"They're much better when you cuddle next to someone."

"Would you two take it to a motel?" Barry joked.

"I think a cruise ship is kind of like a motel."

Rachel smiled and said, "As you may know, this will be a thirty-five-day cruise. We'll be stopping at ports in the Bahamas and Turks and Caicos before touring the islands in the Lesser Antilles. These islands include the Virgin Islands, Martinique, Antigua, Saint Kitts, Barbados, Grenada, and Aruba to name a few. We'll finish with a stopover in the Cayman Islands before returning here. Any questions so far?"

Harry said to no one in particular, "I bet they're making that many stops because of my prostate."

As Rachel guided them, she pointed out various features of the ship. "We are on the main deck, one of five. The weather deck is the uppermost deck on this as with all ships. As we enter the ship's interior, we'll pass by Unlimited, one of the Bahama Princess's fourteen restaurants."

Gidget said, "I can feel my shorts getting tighter already."

Barry looked at her. "You fill those shorts out pretty nicely."

"Flattery will get you nowhere, but don't stop trying."

Pointing to several serving stations, Rachel said, "Unlimited is a complementary buffet, meaning that any passenger can eat here as often and as much as they desire. There are nine complementary restaurants on the Princess, including four that are set up buffet style like Unlimited—"

"I don't like buffets," said Daffy to Harry.

"Why not?" asked Harry.

"I don't like to work for my food."

"A woman after my own heart."

"In addition to the complementary restaurants, the Princess has five specialty restaurants such as Buongiorno which specializes in Italian cuisine," said Rachel. "The Bahama Princess has some of the most talented chefs onboard any ship in the Caribbean. Azul, one of the five specialty restaurants, is available only to our Premier passengers and is world renowned. Chef Dreyfus, is a graduate of *Le Cordon Bleu*, the famous culinary school in Paris."

Larry asked, "Can he cook Sonoran empanadas?"

"I'm not familiar with Sonoran empanadas. What are they?"

"Sausage, potatoes, and cheese. Mexican food southwestern style. I couldn't get enough of 'em last time I was in Arizona."

"I'm sure Chef Dreyfus can cook anything you want."

Four levels higher, Rachel pointed to a large clear plexiglass tube on the port side of the ship running diagonally from ceiling to floor. Water gushed through it. She said, "This is a segment of the MegaSlide, the longest water slide on any cruise ship. The entrance to it begins on the Weather Deck, next to one of the ship's five pools. We'll eventually go there. MegaSlide terminates into a pool on the stern of the main deck. It's four hundred and thirty feet long."

Barry said, "It's almost as long as my *mufff—*"

Harry punched him in the stomach. "There's ladies present."

Daffy leaned over and whispered to Gidget, "I'm beginning to rethink my desire to be a kept woman."

On the fifth level, Rachel guided them into a large room with a stage, tables, and chairs. She said, "This is Neptune's Spectacle, one of five clubs on the ship. It hosts bands, singers, dancing, and a variety of shows. There is something happening here every night."

"What kind of shows?" asked one of the passengers.

"You name it. Musicals like *The Phantom of the Opera*. Bands—we have jazz, rock, and so forth. Singers like David Yates from the 1960s band Bread is on this cruise. Entertainers like Harold the Hypnotist, Manfred the Mind Reader, and Moriarty the Magician."

"I've seen Moriarty before," Gary said, then pointed to Daffy. "I want to see him saw this gorgeous lady in half. You're so tall, you won't miss the other half."

Daffy asked Rachel, "Can Moriarty make this guy disappear?"

Rachel laughed. "Absolutely. Making members of the audience disappear is the highlight of his act. See that black cube at the back of the stage?" She pointed to a six-foot high, solid back cube. "That's Moriarty's Magic Cube. That's what he uses to make people disappear... Okay, next we'll head go to the ship's sports complex."

As they filed out, Gidget again saw the large, ominous man she had seen when they boarded. This time, she was closer and able to see the distinguishing features of his face. His hair was cut short, and its light brown color complemented his fair complexion. Wide-set, almond-shaped grey eyes sat astride a broad nose, which appeared to have been broken. A scar ran along the base of his broad chin. He loitered in the hallway but immediately turned and walked in the opposite direction after his eyes met Gidget's.

She nudged Daffy. "It's that guy again. The Arnold Schwarzenegger guy we saw yesterday. He looks even more menacing today than he did yesterday."

"Stop it. You're badmouthing the man I'm planning on including in a pleasurable dream tonight," Daffy said. "He reminds me of Arnold Schwarzenegger when he was in that movie… What was it? True Guys or something like that—"

"*True Lies*."

"Yeah, *True Lies*. Just the kind of hunk you want to take home for a night of fun."

"He's sure dressed kind of funny for a Caribbean cruise. Black t-shirt, black cargo pants, black suede Chukka boots."

"I'm all in on that tight t-shirt. Look at those pecs."

Rachel led them out onto a large outdoor area. She said, "This is the sports complex. Volleyball, Bocce ball, shuffleboard, pickleball are just a few of the outdoor games you can participate in."

Larry said, "Bocce ball, the national sport of Italian-Americans."

"Shuffleboard, the national sport of older Americans," Gidget said.

"Pickleball, the national sport of tennis-impaired Americans," added Daffy.

Jerry bragged, "I won The Villages' pickleball tournament last year."

Gidget craned her head in Barry's direction. "I do believe you're blushing."

Two older passengers and Larry dropped off of the tour, one citing issues with COPD and the other with bronchitis. At the weather deck, Rachel pointed to a pool. "This is one of the largest pools on board. It has a high diving board in addition to the two standard boards. Next to it is the entrance to the MegaSlide. The young man standing by the slide is the attendant, Freddy. Wave to Freddy."

Rachel showed them the bars, restaurants, shopping facilities, gyms, and spas on the way back down to the main deck. At the ship's stern, she said, "Look over the railing and you'll see a small platform that juts out below this deck. It's on the waterline for a reason. The Princess has a number of smaller crafts—speedboats, jet skis, sailboats, and so forth, and you can board them from that platform. We offer a lot of water activities for you. There's Tyler. Hey, Tyler!"

A shirtless, tanned hunk turned and waved, then climbed up to the main deck. He said, "Hey folks. I run the water activities program. We have five speedboats. We can take you water skiing, snorkeling, whale and dolphin watching, parasailing, anything else you can think of doing in the water."

Daffy whispered into Gidget's ear, "I can think of one thing I'd like to do in the water with Tyler."

Harry said, "Parasailing! That's what I want to do."

"Not exactly what I had in mind."

Rachel smiled. "Folks, it's twelve o'clock and the end of this part of the tour. We'll take a lunch break here at Chips Lounge. After lunch, we'll tour the rest of the ship if you want to join."

"What's on the rest of the tour?" asked a passenger.

"It's about an hour and is a short tour below deck."

"Below deck?"

"There are six levels below the main deck, and we'll tour some of them. They house a number of support functions."

"Such as?"

"Engine room, crew's quarters, medical clinics, food and non-food storage rooms, water tanks, sewage processing system, and morgues."

"Morgues?"

"Yes. All cruise ships have to have morgues. Deaths do occur on cruises at sea, statistically about two hundred a year, mostly from natural causes. Smaller ships typically have three morgues, while the larger ships have more."

"How many does this ship have?'

"Bahama Princess has five morgues."

Chapter 9

Nassau, Bahamas
October 16th

The Bahama Princess docked in Nassau shortly before sunrise. Gidget and Daffy rose early to powerwalk in penance for visiting three different buffets the night before. The Marx Brothers slept late, so Daffy and Gidget breakfasted in Azul by themselves after their powerwalk. As they were eating, three women entered.

Daffy nodded in their direction. "Check those three out."

Gidget casually craned her neck to observe the new diners. "That one in the middle looks okay, but the other two look a little rough around the edges."

"All look to be in their late thirties or early forties, no kids, no husbands. I see three girls gone wild."

"I see divorce city, otherwise their hubbies would be with them. If they had kids, they'd be eating in one of the buffets, not Azul."

"I bet the one in the middle is a divorcee and the other two are air traffic controllers," Daffy said.

Gidget asked, "Why air traffic controllers?"

"They look rode hard and put up wet. That's probably the result of high stress jobs."

The hostess seated the trio at a table close by, passed out menus, and took drink orders. The new diners seemed to be having trouble deciding what to order from the breakfast menu. One of them turned to Gidget and Daffy.

"Would y'all mind if we asked y'all what's good on the menu? We just boarded this morning and have never eaten in this here restaurant."

Gidget and Daffy looked at each other. Daffy said, "This is our first time in here as well, so I don't know if we can be of any help."

"If you can translate the French titles of the dishes, that would be helpful. Like this here." She turned her menu around and pointed to *Chaussons aux Pommes*. "What the hell is this anyway?"

"Probably something titled more fancy than it really is. I can tell by your accent that you're from the South. Maybe we can get someone to scrunch these here tables together and get acquainted?"

Azul staff were able to comply with Daffy's request, and everyone got acquainted. The two 'rough around the edges' women turned out to be Veronica from Dallas and Naomi from Kentucky. The divorcee turned out to be Louella, an old maid from Nebraska. Naomi said the three of them were long-term friends from college who sometimes vacationed together, this time on a cruise. Veronica and Naomi proudly announced they were divorcees. None of the three had ever been air traffic controllers.

"You two and our friend Lizzie would hit it off very well. She could probably give you some points on negotiating your alimony," Daffy said.

Louella explained she owned one of the largest farms in Nebraska. "My daddy left me with a big fifty-thousand-acre, thirty-million-dollar headache, and this cruise is my annual escape."

The three had decided to spend a week shopping in the Bahamas before boarding the ship and had become experts on where to shop and dine.

"Why don't we all go shopping this morning and have lunch together?" asked Veronica.

"We'd love to," said Daffy, "if y'all don't mind having lunch with our boyfriends. They're five older men that are our traveling companions on the cruise. We told them last night we'd do lunch with them today in Nassau."

Gidget interpreted the looks on Veronica and Naomi's faces as expressions of mild disdain and Louella's as envy.

"Sure. Bring them along," Louella said.

Back in their stateroom, Gidget was upbeat. "This is good."

"How so?" asked Daffy.

"Five men, and now five women. We can pawn three of the Marx Brothers off on these other women. That way, you and I don't have to juggle more than one Brother apiece."

"Let's keep the two best and pawn the other three off on them."

All five women spent the morning in Nassau shopping for hand woven beach bags in the Straw Market before meeting the Marx Brothers for lunch on the wharf. They rendezvoused at Sharkeez Bar and Grill.

Veronica said, "Sharkeez has the best conch chowder in Nassau."

"What are youse doing taking a cruise? Relaxation or rehabilitation?" asked Larry.

"Both. I just divorced my husband after his picture appeared in the *National Enquirer* with another woman."

"That can be pretty bad. My last wife two-timed me for a stockbroker. Can you believe it? Screwing a stockbroker. Thinking of it makes me want to vomit." Jerry's face testified to his disgust.

"Two-timed for a stockbroker." Daffy made a face herself. "That's worse than being jilted for a telemarketer."

"Needless to say, the stockbroker's clients dried up within a year." Jerry looked at Veronica. "It sounds like you got pretty insulted yourself."

"It was very insulting. He was wrapped around a woman half my age." Veronica held up her hand, displaying a large diamond ring on it. "This is what you get after five years of marrying a man twice your age."

"I didn't realize the Smithsonian had sold the Hope Diamond." Daffy's quip brought a round of chuckles.

"I propose a toast to Veronica's successful divorce." Harry stood and raised his glass.

His brothers stood to join in the toast. As they were about to drink, an odd-looking person approached. He was of medium height, bald, and wore a black guayabera shirt, white linen pants, and leather sandals. He strode up to their table, and they could see beads of sweat dripping down his forehead and cheeks.

The Guayabera Guy circled their table. As he did, everyone turned to follow his progress until he stood in front of Larry and grabbed him. His two big hands gripped the smaller man's shoulders.

Larry stood frozen as Guayabera Guy said, "Little Titty! It's been a long time. Surprised?"

Larry said nothing and was obviously uncomfortable. The man's hands moved up from Larry's shoulders to encircle his neck. Everyone looked on stunned, anticipating something ugly. Guayabera Guy's hands looked powerful. Their roughness bespoke previous use for brutal purposes. What happened next dumbfounded everyone.

The Guayabera Guy tightened his grip on Larry's neck, leaned in, and kissed him directly on the lips. The mouth-to-mouth contact generated a smacking sound so loud that diners at nearby tables turned their heads. He released his grip on Larry's neck, then took a step back.

"I gotta go now, Little Titty." Guayabera Guy's head swiveled as he looked at the other standing Marx Brothers. "Wish I could spend more time with you and your bruddahs. Just dropped by to let you know I'm thinking about youse. Maybe we'll see each other again soon, huh?"

"What the hell was that all about? And why did he call you Little Titty?" asked Gidget after the strange man was out of sight.

The five Marx Brothers nervously sat down and said nothing. Larry was visibly shaken. Their silence prompted Daffy's attempt at humor. "Must've been one of your kissing cousins, right?"

Gidget repeated her question. "Who the *hell* was that?"

"Never saw the guy before in my life." Larry looked around at his brothers. "Any of youse recognize him?"

Head shakes and a chorus of "Nah's" replied.

Jerry nodded. "It's like Daffy said, that man must've thought Larry was a long-lost cousin. Some of these older guys gets a little confused, you know. We deal with 'em all the time in The Villages."

"Yeah, looked to me like an old geezer with a touch of dementia," Larry said.

Gidget was puzzled. "I don't know. He didn't look that old to me."

"Fuhgeddaboudit and him. Let's order some of that conch chowder."

Daffy and Gidget somehow managed *not* to discuss the kissing incident in front of the Marx Brothers and their three new lady friends the rest of the day. But it was tough. In their stateroom that night, they first critiqued Veronica, Naomi, and Louella.

"What's the verdict on our new friends?" asked Daffy.

Gidget said, "We got enough players for Mexican Train or Five-person rummy but not enough for Bunko."

"Besides that."

"They're all friendly enough, although not as talkative as most women I know."

Daffy recycled a stale old joke. "I resemble that remark. You're just used to Babsie. What else?"

"A little on the rough side, both looks-wise and personality-wise."

Daffy nodded. "I thought so too."

"I guess it's where they're from. Texans are kind of wild, and Nebraskans are a little less sophisticated than Easterners. And you've been to the Kentucky Derby with me. Kentuckians think the other forty-nine states are irrelevant, although Naomi seemed focused on the Marx Brothers."

"Let's make sure she only gets *one* of them. What do you make of a total stranger mistaking Larry for someone he knows?"

"I'm still processing it," said Gidget. "Our new lady friends must be processing it as well. Did you see the looks of shock on their faces? I bet they're having second thoughts about hanging with us."

"They didn't back out of swimming with the pigs with us tomorrow."

"True."

"That Guayabera Guy must've really liked whoever he thought he was kissing. That was a helluva smack."

Gidget scrunched her face. "I didn't get those kinds of vibes from the guy."

"What kind of vibes did you get?"

"Good question… Ill will? 'Youse bettah watch out' vibes?"

Daffy shook her head. "I wouldn't try to go on *America's Got Talent* with that Brooklyn accent imitation. You don't think the guy mistook Larry for someone else he knew?"

Gidget said, "I doubt it."

"Why you say that?"

"He knew the four other men at our table were Larry's brothers. How would he know they were his brothers unless he knew them all beforehand?"

"Guayabera Guy did call them his brothers, didn't he? But all five of the Marx Brothers look alike, so that would be an easy call."

Gidget nodded. "True."

"Why wouldn't the Marx Brothers acknowledge him if they knew him? I know you got ill will vibes, but he seemed friendly enough."

"Why they wouldn't acknowledge who Guayabera Guy is, my dear Daffy, the sixty-four-thousand-dollar question."

"Wasn't that the name of a TV gameshow in the fifties?"

"Yes, it was. Contestants were asked questions and won money if they got the right answers. It got canceled when they found out there was cheating going on. Things were rigged."

Daffy exchanged exciting texts with Babs that night.

Babs
One of my old boyfriends from FSU, Cordell Isler, came to Thomasville yesterday. He met with me, Lilly, and Lizzie but had wanted to also meet with you and Daffy to talk about all of us doing a pilot for a reality TV show called The Real Widows of Thomasville. He saw us streak the Georgia-Florida football game last Saturday and recognized me, even though I looked like Kylie Jenner, at least in the face.
Daffy
How did he recognize you if you looked like Kylie? Sounds like your disguise wasn't that good. Wink, wink.
Babs
We did <u>streak</u> the game, you know. He told me there were some things about an old girlfriend that a man never forgets, especially when she's naked. Laugh, laugh. Anyway, he went to work in Hollywood right after graduation from FSU and is now a big Hollywood producer. When he recognized me, he did some research on the Internet and saw our calendar. The idea came to him to do a reality TV show. It's an emergency replacement for another reality show that just got cancelled. We start filming this week for the premiere on October 30. Will keep y'all posted.

Chapter 10

Nassau, Bahamas
October 17th

Gidget, Daffy, their three new women friends, and the Marx Brothers boarded a Kodiak seaplane early in the morning. Their destination was Pig Beach on Big Major Cay in the southern end of the Bahama Islands chain. Barry was still puzzled over their anticipated undertaking.

"People actually swim with a bunch of pigs at this beach we're going to?"

Daffy said, "That's what Rachel says."

Gary made a face. "Swimming with a bunch of pigs don't sound too sanitary to me. Sounds kind of gross."

"Couldn't be any grosser than swimming in the Hudson River." Jerry spoke from experience.

"Swimming with pigs ain't *that* bad," Veronica said.

"Why you say that?" asked Gidget.

"I slept with three different pigs during twelve years of marriage. Swimming with 'em for a few hours should be a piece of cake."

When the laughter died down, Daffy said, "You don't sound too enthusiastic about marriage."

"I'll never make that mistake again. Three times is enough."

"No marriage is ideal, just ask me. But look on the positive side. You always got a date for movies, concerts, and dinner."

Veronica was unconvinced. "You always got a date except during football, basketball, baseball, and golf seasons. My last husband ran around on me. The one before that was a dud in bed. And my first marriage taught me that a good male body don't necessarily come with a brain."

Jerry asked, "Was you one of my wives?"

After takeoff, their pilot/guide enlightened them over the plane's intercom. "Over six million tourists annually visit Big Major Cay to swim with the pigs. No one knows how a group of wild pigs got introduced to this island, but they are there. They wander along the white sand on the shore and swim in the clear aquamarine water.

Tourists have fed them for so many years that they're very friendly. They'll follow you into the water and swim alongside you."

"Do they give you mouth-to-mouth if you drown?" asked Gary.

"Tell 'em I got a pacemaker before they start CPR," Larry said.

"You have a pacemaker?" asked Gidget.

"Don't every man over fifty?"

"Larry is the only one of us that does," said Barry. "The rest of us are behind him on the pacemaker curve."

The Kodiak slowly circled the beach three times, giving its passengers excellent views of crystal-clear aquamarine water in harmony with pristine white sand. A dozen oblong shapes with stubby appendages meandered on the beach, one or two occasionally ambling off to into the water or scrub brush. They came in a variety of colors—some solid light brown, others light brown but speckled with black spots, and a few resembling Holstein cows, white with black splotches.

Jerry's smile stretched ear-to-ear. "How about that? Them little porkers look like a bunch of the boys from Brooklyn."

"Yeah. But a dozen of the Brooklyn boys in one place usually spelt trouble," Harry said.

"Ladies and gentlemen, please make sure your seat belts are secure. We're starting our landing approach," the guide/pilot announced.

He slowly nosed the plane down until its pontoons began splashing in the water, then leveled out. He taxied the plane to a point about fifty yards from shore, cut the engines, and let the plane drift closer to the beach. Once it was in waist-high water, he threw an anchor overboard. "Y'all can hop out now. The water is shallow enough to wade ashore. I'll follow y'all. I'll be pulling a raft with all of our supplies in it." He hopped out and stood in the water next to the plane, assisting each passenger in deplaning.

The trip to the beach was short, uneventful, and met with greetings from other tourists mingling with the pigs. Their guide/pilot provided them with treats for the pigs who eagerly crowded around. He pointed to the largest of them. "That one is Big

Daddy. He's one of the oldest of the swimming pigs and quite a lusty old boy."

"He kind of reminds me of Burl Ives," said Daffy, referring to the actor who played Big Daddy in *Cat on a Hot Tin Roof*. "Although he's not as tubby as Burl Ives."

"Go ahead. Take a swim and see what happens."

Daffy, Gidget, Harry, Veronica, and Barry slowly backed away from the pigs and entered the water. The water was crystal clear, and they could see the pigs' little feet vigorously paddling. They felt very safe thinking there was no way a pig struggling to stay afloat could harm them. It was delightful.

Several pigs, including Big Daddy followed. They paddled around the swimmers, entertaining them in the process—until Big Daddy got amorous.

"Daffy," said Harry, "I think Big Daddy is giving you the eye. I'm getting jealous."

"Looks like a match made in Heaven," Veronica said.

Daffy immediately turned to see Big Daddy paddling toward her, loudly snorting.

Daffy screamed and began furiously walk-swimming toward the shore. Her actions prompted Big Daddy to paddle faster.

The women tourists on shore began chanting, "Go, girl, go! Go, girl, go!"

The men, apparently favoring Big Daddy, took up a different chant. "Go, Big Daddy, go! Go, Big Daddy, go!"

Daffy made it to shore just ahead of Big Daddy and in time to be rescued by their guide/pilot. He shooed Big Daddy back into the water with a switch, then looked at Daffy. "I ain't seen Big Daddy get amorous like that in a long time. You must have something he can't resist."

"He must've got his vet to write him a prescription for Viagra," Jerry said.

Daffy had her standards. "That's his mistake. I never have sex this soon in a relationship."

"Big Daddy doesn't look like your type anyway," Gidget said.

"I don't know. He's got possibilities, especially considering his competition." Daffy pointedly looked at Harry.

After they finished swimming with the pigs, Gidget and the others found a spot up the beach to picnic by themselves. While relaxing on their blankets, movement in clump of nearby trees caught Gidget's eye—a familiar figure seemed to be lurking in the dark foliage. She nudged Daffy. "Look over there."

Daffy turned. "What? I don't see anything."

"I think I saw the Arnold Schwarzenegger guy in those scrub bushes."

"Him? Out here? On this island?"

"Yeah. He was over there but moved further back into the woods when he saw me looking."

"What would he be doing here? And how did he get here?"

Gidget shrugged. Loud, frightened squealing from the opposite direction interrupted her response. Everyone looked in the direction of the squealing. A small pig floundered about twenty yards offshore. Daffy panicked. "That poor little pig is drowning!"

Jerry jumped up and shouted at his brothers, "One of youse come with me!"

Barry followed suit, and the two old men ran as fast as their arthritic legs could manage. They splashed into the water and waded out to the little pig with great difficulty. It was a young pig and new to swimming. He squealed loudly and splashed violently.

"You grab his hind legs, and I'll grab his front," said Jerry as they closed in. They had a devil of a time, as the piglet was in no mood to cooperate. The water came up to their chest, hampering their ability to gain purchase in the sandy ocean floor. Between that and the pig's resistance, it took a massive effort to subdue the animal. By the time they waded ashore, both brothers were exhausted. The piglet squealed as it ran off to its mother.

Harry patted both brothers on the back. "Youse was very brave, little brothers."

"You boys are lucky," Louella said. "A young pig like that can take a chunk out of you. I know."

Barry had an empathetic side to his personality. "Yeah but, downing's no fun. I felt sorry for the little fella. I almost drowned once swimming in the Hudson."

Jerry had a good side as well. "I hate to see any animal suffer, especially a cute little porker like that one."

Daffy sighed. "Our heroes."

After they finished their day of swimming with the pigs and drinking beer, they packed up to return to the Kodiak. Gidget looked at the Marx Brothers. "Did any of y'all see that big man in the woods earlier today? I think he was spying on us."

"What guy?" asked Barry.

"A big guy. He kind of looks like Arnold Schwarzenegger. Dresses like some sort of soldier or Navy SEAL. Wears a tight black t-shirt and black cargo pants."

"And you think he's spying on us?" asked Larry. "What makes you say that?"

"I've seen him before, several times on the ship. He seems to be looking at us—all of us, but especially y'all. He always walks away really quickly when he sees I'm looking at him."

"A guy from the ship. And you saw him on this here island?" A touch of skepticism tinged Barry's question.

Gidget was irritated. "Yes, I did. A couple of hours ago. Not long after Big Daddy tried to have his way with Daffy."

"You think it might've been the guy what smooched Larry yesterday?" asked Jerry.

"Nope. Definitely not him."

"I didn't see him." Larry looked at his brothers. "Any of youse see him?"

A chorus of "Nah's" replied.

Gidget knew further discussion was useless.

Chapter 11

Grand Turk Island, Turks and Caicos
October 21st

The suggestion that a group of senior citizens scuba dive caught Gidget and Daffy off guard. Louella had brought it up at dinner one night several days before. She had seen a video on the ship's info channel and thought it would be fun. Perhaps she thought that way because she was in her early forties instead of her sixties. Naomi and Veronica both declined, citing mild cases of aquaphobia—fear of water. Larry and Gary did not think scuba diving at their ages was a good idea, evidence at least two of the Marx Brothers possessed good judgment.

Despite their misgivings, Daffy and Gidget relented after badgering from Harry, Jerry, Barry, and Louella. Now, all six sat within a Sea Ray power boat doing twenty-five knots over beautiful calm, blue-green water. Tyler navigated the boat toward Gibbs Cay, a small island off of Grand Turk Island. All of them had spent four hours over the last two days in one of the Bahama Princess' eight pools learning how to scuba dive. Tyler taught the class, which was a requirement in order to be able to scuba dive in the Cay's shallow waters.

It was getting close to lunch time, and Harry kept eyeing the large picnic basket next to Louella. "What's for lunch? Smells like roast beef."

"No roast beef. I asked Chef Dreyfus to prepare a special picnic lunch for us," Louella said. She opened the top of the basket. "Let's see, we got a bunch of French picnic dishes starting with French lentil salad—"

Harry made a face. "I ain't ate a salad in fifteen years."

"Roasted red pepper tapenade, salad Niçoise, zucchini and olive breakfast cake..." Louella noticed frowns on the other brothers' faces. "Don't look so disgusted. Okay, who likes chicken livers?"

Everyone, including Daffy and Gidget, perked up. Louella smiled. "I knew it. No one doesn't like chicken livers. That's why I asked Chef Dreyfus to prepare some. He made a French Chicken

Liver Pâté and included homemade toasted French baguette slices to spread it on. He told me the pâté is based on a Jacques Pépin recipe, but he puts his own spin on it."

Harry grimaced. "Ehh, I don't know. I love chicken livers, but in a pâté… I don't know."

"Oh hell, Harry," said Daffy. "Grow a set. Be daring. It all sounds yummy to me. Especially the chicken liver pâté."

While Tyler piloted the powerboat, his passengers chowed down. Everyone loved the pâté, even Harry, and devoured every bit of it. By the time they reached Gibbs Cay, they had consumed most of the contents of the basket, along with three bottles of Louis Dumont Brut.

After Tyler threw the anchor overboard, he reminded them of the rules. "The water here is shallow. Nevertheless, we all stay together. Remember who your dive buddy is and stay with that person. You all did well in the lessons, so don't forget the scuba techniques and rules I taught you. Don't hold your breath while breathing through the regulator. The water here is shallow, but you still want to ascend slowly when coming up. Don't touch anything down there—fish or the coral. Touching the fish can be dangerous, and touching the coral starts a process of decay for it—"

By this point, all the Marx Brothers had tuned out. They looked forward to the feeling of weightlessness they experienced underwater. It offset the feeling of obesity they experienced on land.

Tyler finished. "And that's about it. Let's all get suited up and get in the water."

The Marx Brothers removed their Hawaiian flower shirts and Bermuda shorts to reveal an unusual collection of bathing suits. Barry wore baggies—the loose-fitting swim trunks in style during the Beach Boys era. They were light aquamarine with tiny pink flamingoes on them. A large yellow banana adorned the crotch of Harry's lime-green boxer-style suit. In a fashion statement most rational people would abhor, seventy-year-old Jerry wore a mint green Speedo.

The three women dressed more fashionably. Daffy and Gidget wore multi-colored one-piece suits. Louella also wore a one-piece, solid red suit. She lamented having to wear a bathing suit. "Too bad the warm temperature of these shallow waters makes wetsuits unnecessary. A wetsuit would hide my flab better than this thing."

Harry said, "I'm up for skinny-dipping myself."

Daffy scowled. "That image scars me for life."

Tyler led the group, followed by swim buddies Harry and Jerry, then Barry and Louella, and finally Daffy and Gidget. The water was a crystal-clear light aquamarine color, affording spectacular underwater views. They glided over a variety of beautiful coral formations, including peach-tinted Bubble Coral and multi-spiked orange-yellow Elkhorn Coral. Best of all was the Open Brain Coral, so named for its shape. Its neon pink and blue colors appeared luminescent in the water. As Tyler had ordered, they were careful not to touch the coral as they floated over it.

They also observed a variety of marine life. Schools of fish would casually swim up to them, circling as they inspected the colorful intruders. While circling, the fish often lightly touched the intruders with their mouths, a not uncommon exploratory behavior displayed by many of their species. Unlike the fish, hawksbill turtles, dolphins, and stingrays glided along on their own paths, paying the intruders little attention. They saw an occasional barracuda and small shark, but Tyler had told them they did not typically attack humans in Gibbs Cay.

Twenty minutes into the dive, Louella made a circular motion with her hand at Tyler. It was a pre-arranged signal indicating something was wrong. He swam over to her, and she pointed to the regulator on her scuba tank. This is the device attached to the top of the tank. It attaches to the rubber hose through which the diver breathes the oxygen-nitrogen gas mixture in the tank. Tyler understood she meant that her regulator seemed to be malfunctioning. He turned so the others could see him and pointed to Louella and himself, then upward, then downward. This meant he would accompany her topside, then return. With that, Tyler and Louella ascended.

Tyler climbed onboard the powerboat and helped Louella up. After she had shed her scuba gear, he asked, "What was wrong?"

"I don't know. It just seemed that I was having trouble breathing."

He looked over her equipment and then took a few breaths from its rubber hose. Satisfied with his inspection, he said, "The equipment seems okay. Were you breathing slowly and regularly like I showed you?"

"Well… I was trying to."

"That was probably it. You might've not been breathing slowly and steadily. You may have unconsciously held your breath. When that occurs, its easy to think the regulator is acting funky. Nothing wrong with it. It sometimes happens—"

Splashing next to the boat interrupted Tyler's explanation. A head surfaced—Jerry's. It was followed by Harry's, then Barry's. Daffy and Gidget surfaced last. They were supposed to remain in the place where he left them underwater until he returned. As Tyler helped each one aboard, he saw the reason why they failed to obey his orders. The three men were covered with small bites, except Harry. A large gash leaked blood on his right forearm.

"What the hell happened to you?" asked Tyler.

"Some damn fish decided I looked pretty tasty," Harry said. He pressed his hand over the cut.

"What did it look like?"

"Oval-shaped, thin body, large face. Grey on top, white on bottom. Beautiful yellow streak running from the tip of its mouth to about midway on its body."

"Four white diagonal stripes on each side of its body?"

"Yeah."

"It was a triggerfish. They have a small mouth that houses eight sharp teeth—four uppers and four lowers. Pretty powerful jaws."

"I know that… now." Harry rolled his eyes.

"Let me get the medicine kit and temporarily fix you up. We'll have Doctor Mokulus put a few stitches in this gash when we get back."

Gidget asked, "I wonder what made them come after y'all? We were where you left us just minding our own business, looking at the fish swimming around us—"

Daffy said, "And the number of fish swimming around us kept growing and growing, and then those triggerfish swam over, then came at the boys, and—"

"We were lucky to get out of there alive." The expression on Jerry's face said it all.

Harry tried to calm his brother. "Cool down. We're okay. Those damn triggerfish weren't very big, and they looked harmless."

Tyler nodded. "Around here they get about a foot long, and they do look harmless."

"All I did was try to pet one."

Tyler shook his head. "Next time, try petting a butterfly fish instead. Their bite's not nearly as bad."

"There ain't gonna be no next time," said Jerry.

"And y'all say the schools of fish around you seemed to grow and grow?"

Five heads nodded.

Tyler's face scrunched in an expression of puzzlement. "Odd. Okay, let's pack up, and get Mister Harry to Doc Mokulus."

Gidget's analytical mind kicked in once she and Daffy were back in their stateroom that night. She looked at her laptop. "Daff, look here. I got curious about how the fish started swarming around us today. So, I did a couple of Internet searches and found this info on what attracts fish."

"What did you find out? Our boyfriends smell like fish perfume?" quipped Daffy.

"Don't laugh. Here's an article on what attracts fish. Get this. Two of the things that attract fish are certain smells and certain colors—"

"Our boyfriends were dressed colorfully. Especially Barry. I mean those pink flamingoes on his aquamarine bathing suit."

"You joke, but it says here that green is the color that most attracts fish. The article talks about how fishermen buy these green lights to attract fish. Barry wore aquamarine, Harry wore lime-green, and Jerry's bathing suit was mint green."

"No wonder they made a beeline for us. And I thought it was Jerry's Speedo turning on the female fish."

Gidget shook her head. "I wish you hadn't reminded me of Jerry's junk. I'll have nightmares tonight. But it wasn't just the color of their bathing suits that attracted all those fish."

"No. What else?"

"It was Chef Dreyfus' chicken liver pâté."

Daffy licked her lips. "Oh, man. I salivate thinking of that stuff. His pâté leaves fried chicken livers in its dust."

"Check this out." Gidget pulled up and read from an Internet article titled 'What Attracts Fish the Most?'

"On their bodies, there are a lot of sensors that pick up chemical traces and hence react to them. Fish remarkably use their sense of smell to find food, find their way to home, as well as to hide from active predators too."

"You think it was the chicken liver pâté that attracted the fish?"

"Absolutely. That and the onion and garlic he put in it. Those spices probably enhanced the chicken liver smell. Another article ranks the smells that attract fish, and chicken liver is the best. They're very popular as bait among fishermen."

"But we didn't put the pâté on our skin."

"We did eat it. When the fish touched us with their mouths, they must've detected the chicken liver via our skin's pores."

"I guess Christian Dior couldn't have made a fish perfume any more irresistible than Dreyfus' chicken liver pâté."

"Correct, my dear Daffy. And fish can communicate with each other. They probably communicated to other fish in the area that we smelled very good. That's why more and more kept coming up to us."

At that moment, Yvette entered their stateroom. "*Excusez-moi, Mesdames*. Would you like me to turn down your beds now?"

Gidget looked up and asked, "Yvette, did Stokes lay out Harry, Barry, and Jerry's swimming attire this morning, or did they pick their swimsuits themselves?"

"*Oui, Madam*e. *Monsieur* Stokes laid out all the gentlemen's attires this morning as he does every morning, just as I laid out yours and *Madame* Daffy's."

Chapter 12

Various Maritime Locations
October 15th - October 22nd

Aside from the same-sex smooch in Nassau, the run-in with Triggerfish in Grand Turk, and occasionally spotting the ominous-looking Arnold Schwarzenegger guy, monotony ruled life aboard the Bahama Princess. Monotony and romance.

Two close relationships developed during the first two weeks. Daffy gave in to Harry's persistent whining and had sex with him three days after sailing from Jacksonville. Two days later, he discovered he was out of Viagra and sponged from his brothers. He boasted. "It's a problem those of us with a golden dick often have."

Daffy had a different take on it. As she told Gidget, "He's a three out of a ten who thinks he's a fifteen out of a ten. But it's partially my fault for being such a good actress in bed. I had to learn how to act, or Royce was moody all the next day."

Gidget tsk-tsked as she shook her head. "Three out of a ten."

"I'll be generous. Maybe a three and a half. But what do you expect from a man who wears boxer shorts under his pajamas?"

Gidget said, "Sam always wore boxer shorts under his pajamas."

"I'm sure it works on some men."

Gidget needed a little more time. She gave into Barry's whining after five days at sea. Daffy asked the morning after, "What did you lovebirds do last night? Back rubs after shuffleboard? You turned in a little late last night, didn't you?"

Gidget turned crimson. "We didn't do much of anything."

"Don't be coy with ole Aunt Daffy. You've got a glow on your face this morning that I haven't seen in years. Out with it."

"Okay. Barry invited me into his stateroom for drinks after our swim. The other brothers were conveniently watching *MASH* reruns in the other stateroom, and one thing led to another, and…" she shrugged.

"I knew it, I knew it, I knew it! Give me all the details."

"Barry may not be Frank Furillo, but he still managed to deliver the pizza." Gigdet referred to a character in the TV series *Hill Street Blues*. A thoughtful look came over her face. "You know. It was my first sex since Sam died. God, I'd forgotten how much I had been missing some good, hard sex.

"I always knew you were a postmortem virgin."

"How did you *always* know?"

"For one thing, you've gotten moodier every year since Sam passed. And you've never been on a date with Sonny Biskit."

"I have to admit that part of my moodiness has been a lack of… shall we say male attention. Barry was so polite about sex. He kept asking, 'Is it okay if I do this? Is it okay if I do that?' I finally had to tell him to go ahead and do what he wanted to. He was too much of a perfect gentleman in bed."

Daffy joked. "Sounds like you need to borrow one of my leather whips and a set of my hand cuffs."

Gidget laughed. "What did you do last night?

"Drank and gossiped with the other three broads. I made sure they knew Harry and Barry were ours and that they could have the dregs, although dregs *is* a relative term. I think I must've had a little too much to drink."

"Why?"

"I told them Harry's nickname when he lived in Brooklyn. He had made me promise to keep it a secret. Shows you how naïve men are. For some reason, he wants it kept a secret."

"What was his nickname?"

"Big Banana."

"I can guess the reason behind the nickname." Gidget smiled again. "Like older brother, like younger brother. Barry told me what his nickname was—Medallions."

"As in Swinging Medallions? Did you make his swing?"

"Like a pendulum on a grandfather clock."

Typical days onboard the Bahama Princess for the Marx Brothers consisted of games favored by older people such as Bocce ball, pickleball, pinochle, and canasta. Watching *Andy Griffith* and *MASH* reruns was a must. The women spent time on powerwalks, pickleball, rummy, card games, spa treatments, and chitchat.

Louella told her life story one day during rummy. "I inherited a pretty big farm in Nebraska. One of the largest producers of corn in the state. I take these annual ocean cruises for mental therapy."

Daffy said, "That's a smart idea, to get away from the headaches of running a big business like a farm. Being chairman of Sawgrass Bank is a pain in the butt. I have to deal with twenty old men."

"It's different with me. My life is boring. A cruise is my time away from having to look at nothing but a flat field of corn."

"I would think looking at nothing but a flat ocean would be as boring as looking at a flat field of corn," said Gidget.

"A flat sea of corn is bad karma. A flat sea is good karma."

Naomi pinched an inch of tummy. "Speaking of corn, I think I've already put on five pounds from all these all-you-can-eat buffets."

Daffy couldn't resist. "All-you-can-eat buffets and paddle ball. That's what I call senior living on steroids."

One evening four of the Marx Brothers picked up Daffy and Gidget to eat dinner. They decided to dine in Buongiorno for a change. After they were seated, Jerry asked, "Where's your three girl friends?"

Gidget shrugged. "Louella didn't answer her phone."

Daffy said, "She always turns it off when she watches *The Talk* and forgets to turn it back on."

"Veronica said she was getting a pedicure and would join us later, and Naomi is having a personal moment. Where's Gary?"

Harry shot Larry a look. Larry lowered his head as Harry said, "Him and jerk-wad here got into an argument, and Gary took a poke at Larry, so Larry coldcocked him."

Daffy and Gidget were horrified. The latter said, "Is he okay?"

"Oh yeah. He's okay. We left him lying there, sleeping like a baby. They're brothers. They fight. This happens all the time."

"Why? What was the argument about?" asked Gidget.

"Circumcision. Gary's the only one of us who's circumcised, and he gets upset when we tease him about it. It was Larry's turn this time. Circumcision is a very touchy subject among us."

"A touchy subject about a touchy thing," Daffy said.

Chapter 13

Saint Thomas, U.S. Virgin Islands
October 23rd

Daffy, Gidget, Naomi, Veronica, Larry, Barry, and Harry descended the gangplank into a hoard of local guides waiting on the dock in Charlotte Amalie. Many competed for tourist business in the capital city of Saint Thomas, but fewer drove trams able to accommodate seven passengers. One of the trams caught Larry's eye. "Over there."

After all were seated in the vehicle, Daffy frantically searched her pocketbook.

"What's up? What are you looking for?" asked Veronica.

"My reading glasses," said Daffy. "I can't find them. I had them on a minute ago. I wanted to read this brochure."

Gidget rolled her eyes. "They're on top of your head."

Daffy looked up and rolled her eyes as well. "Talk about going senile."

The brochure Daffy wanted to read described the capital city's attractions. Larry had given it to her and pushed visiting one in particular. He asked the driver, "99 Steps? Can you take us to 99 Steps?"

"Excellent choice, *Monsieur*." Callix, the driver, spoke English with a slight French Creole accent. "It has beautiful views of the city, and its ninety-nine steps are good exercise. Please, step this way into my trolley, and I will take you there."

Gidget patted her tummy. "Ninety-nine steps—just what I need."

Barry said, "I ain't walked that many stairs since we moved out of the tenement in the Bronx."

Daffy nodded. "I ain't walked that many stairs since I quit going to the gym."

"I ain't walked that many steps since last time the power went out in my condo. That happens a lot in Chicago," Veronica said.

"You got a condo in Chicago?" asked Gidget. "I thought you lived in Dallas."

"Oh, it's just one of my ex's investments."

"I can definitely use the exercise," said Barry, looking down. "Look at this gut."

Gidget reached over and patted his stomach. "But it's such a cute little gut."

As they rode up, down, and around curvy hilly streets, Gidget kept thinking about her new romantic relationship. If nothing else, it kept her mind off of what the bouncy ride was doing to her stomach. Barry was a funny-looking little guy, but there was something about him that tugged at her heartstrings. And the sex… So absorbed in reliving their last encounter, she almost missed a motor scooter speeding by their trolley. She nudged Daffy.

"Isn't that the Arnold Schwarzenegger guy?"

Daffy leaned her head out the window. "Ehhh… I don't know. Maybe. He went by too fast for me to get a good look. Whoever it is, it looks like he's heading the same way we're going. And whoever it is, he's wearing the same outfit. How the heck does he stand it in those black clothes in this tropical weather?"

Veronica overheard their conversation. "Who is the Arnold Schwarzenegger guy? You mean the guy wearing the black t-shirt that just went by on the scooter? What a hunk."

"Yep. He's someone you wouldn't want to meet in a dark alley."

Gidget saw no more of the mysterious man for the rest of the fifteen-minute journey to 99 Steps. The tourist attraction was located in the middle of the city and surrounded by residential houses, all painted in different pastel colors. Callix delivered them to the bottom of the attraction's stairs. His passengers exited the tram and looked up.

Harry said, "I can't see the top of these stairs, but I forgot to bring my glasses."

"I can see a heart attack waiting for me at the top," Larry said.

Gidget winced. "I can see my bunions waiting for me at the top."

"You got bunions?" asked Barry. "I never noticed."

Gidget imagined the others were thinking, 'Barry was too busy enjoying the other parts of Gidget's body to notice her bunions.' She indignantly replied, "What do you think you get after thirty years of standing at a pharmacy workstation filling prescriptions."

Harry started to climb. "Come on, youse lazy bums."

After thirty steps, Daffy became concerned. "You gonna make it, Larry? Maybe you should turn back."

Larry could not catch his breath sufficiently to respond.

After forty steps, Gidget said, "Either Larry's panting for breath, or a train is coming at us."

"It's Larry," said Barry. "He's struggling."

After seventy-six steps, everyone heard the theme from *The Godfather* being played. Larry extracted his phone and put it to his ear. "Yeah, this is Larry."

Pause.

"Hell no, I ain't okay! I'm struggling with ninety-nine friggin' steps."

Pause.

"I'll tell you what's wrong. I'm over halfway up a stairway that don't have no end in sight. I'll be lucky if I'm alive *IF* there is an end."

Pause.

"It's a little too late for that."

Pause.

"Because it's shorter to keep going up than to turn back. Besides, I don't do too well going down stairs… I wear bifocals."

Pause.

"Tell the doctor that I'll call you back when we get to the top, if I'm alive. If not, one of my brothers will call you."

Pause.

"*Ciao.*"

After Larry rang off, Gidget asked, "What was that all about?"

"My heart… it had some sort of arrhythmia that caused my pacemaker to set off an alarm that my phone transmitted to my cardiologist."

Gidget pointed down. "Sit. Let me check your pulse."

Larry resisted. "There's no need for that. It's just this stupid technology screwing up or something. I'm fine."

Gidget said, "I didn't spend six years at the University of Georgia getting my Pharm D degree for nothing. Give me your wrist."

She took Larry's wrist and remained quiet for fifteen seconds before pronouncing, "Your heartbeat is racing faster than a Porsche's engine… about one-twenty a minute. Let's rest for a few minutes. Who's your cardiologist?"

"Doctor Corazon," Larry said.

"You dear boy," said Naomi, "you're lucky we have enough cell reception here to transmit to Florida."

"Corazon ain't in Florida."

"Where is he?" asked Gidget.

"In Arizona."

"You have a cardiologist in Arizona? I'd have thought your cardiologist would be in The Villages."

Larry looked as if it was common knowledge. "Banner Health has one of the best heart institutes in the States."

"They do," said Veronica. "One of my friends in Dallas goes there for care. You'll have to stop over and see me next time you go there for a checkup."

Daffy looked at Gidget and mouthed "flirt."

Gidget nodded.

A few minutes later, Gidget stood and glanced up at the top of the stairs. Someone stood at the top but immediately turned and walked away. She climbed several stairs to where Daffy stood.

"Daff, did you see the person at the top of the stairs? I bet it was the Arnold Schwarzenegger guy again."

Daffy looked, then shook her head. "I didn't get a good look."

"My vibes about him are getting worse. Seems like every time he's around, something strange or bad happens. Like just now with Larry's pacemaker problem."

"You think there's a connection?"

"That is a good question, my dear Daffy."

Harry huffed and puffed his way up the steps to Daffy and Gidget. "What youse doing up here by yourselves?"

"Did you see that man at the top of the steps?" asked Gidget.

He looked up. "What man? I don't see no man."

"Yeah. He walked away just a few seconds ago. He was standing up there looking down at us."

"You see another man again? Like when we swam with the pigs?"

"I think it was the same man."

"The same man what you seen on the ship?"

"Yep."

Harry had joined them and shrugged. "If you say so. Let's finish these steps before Larry goes tits up."

Larry shook his head. "Let's finish these steps so I can have a beer."

"You make it up the rest of these stairs, and we'll find some place around here where you can get a cannoli."

Larry salivated. "Ooh, that brings back memories. I'd give my eye tooth for a cannoli from Monte's Trattoria. That restaurant knows how to make cannoli."

Harry eyed Daffy. "Larry never could resist a good cannoli, and neither can I."

"You old lecher," said Daffy.

Chapter 14

Saint Johns, Antigua
October 26th

Rough seas before the Bahama Princess docked in Antigua portended a perilous event, which would happen on the island later that day. The Casserole Ladies and their companions descended the gangplank as if something horrible awaited them. All, that is except Veronica, who picked on the Marx Brothers.

"Where's your testosterone? Grow a set, guys."

Gidget had misgivings. "I'm with the guys. This ain't something sixty- and seventy-year-old senior citizens should even be considering, much less actually doing. You and Naomi and Louella are a little younger than us."

Naomi smiled. "That just means we got more to lose."

Daffy also had trepidations. "I've seen this stuff on Discovery TV and Travel Channel, and it don't look too safe to me."

Larry said, "Look. Why don't we do the tourist thing in Saint John's instead? We can hire a tram, take a nice comfortable ride, enjoy the sights, and have lunch."

Four other bald heads nodded. Louella and Naomi forced smiles.

Veronica chided, "No, no, no. Y'all ain't getting out of it that easy. Y'all were all really courageous last night after four rounds of Bahama Mammas. I seem to remember a lot of bragging. We're going through with this even if I have to hogtie y'all up."

"Why are you so intent on doing this?" asked Gidget.

"Because *Condé Nast* says ziplining is a must do in Antigua. The tropical rain forest on this island is perfect for it. Now, let's find transportation and get on with it."

"It would help if we could stop along the way and have four more Bahama Mammas," said Harry.

They walked up the street to Hemingway's for rum cocktails and sat at the bar. Shortly after their drinks arrived, a woman entered the restaurant.

Gidget leaned into Daffy and said, “Look at what just stepped through the door.”

Daffy turned and appraised the newcomer. “I’d hate to meet her in a dark alley. She looks like a refugee from WWE’s women’s division.”

“You sure she’s a woman?”

The woman scanned the room, then headed straight for Jerry’s barstool.

“Heyyyyy Tushie,” she said loudly as she walked up to him. She grabbed his head and planted a big, wet kiss on each of his cheeks. “You look at little peaked. Feeling okay? Hope you get better. Gotta run. Bye-eee.”

“What was that all about?” asked Daffy after WWE Woman left.

“Reminds me of that guy in Nassau,” said Gidget.

Jerry shrugged and turned to his brothers. “Any of youse recognize her?”

A chorus of ‘nahs’ followed.

“Tushie?” Gidget’s tone implied a question.

“He does have a cute little butt.” Gary’s quip brought a swift hand slap to his head from Jerry.

Jerry said, “Let’s get outta here before any more of these kinds of nutcases come in.”

Outside, Veronica spotted a Toyota van taxi and waved it over.

“We got some very windy, curvy roads to go over through the mountains, and we don’t want anyone to slide out of the open side of a tram. We’ll have to squeeze ourselves into this van. Gidget and Daffy, y’all might find it tight after the buffet last night, but y’all will have to make do.”

Daffy said, “I think we should take a tram and let Veronica sit next to the open side.”

The route through Antigua’s mountains afforded the van’s passengers some beautiful scenery but was fraught with curves and stomach-churning hills. An hour-and-a-half later, the van pulled into a small gravel parking lot at the top of a mountain, thirteen-hundred feet above sea level. A thick forest of mahogany, acacia, and tamarind trees surrounded a rustic one-story wooden building. The sign atop its green-painted tin roof announced their destination as ANTIQUA RAINFOREST ZIPLINE RIDES.

"Here we are!" Veronica shouted as she jumped out, all smiles.

Jerry and Gary followed but did not smile. Instead, they threw up as soon as they stepped out of the vehicle.

After he finished, Jerry said, "This road makes riding the Thunderbolt at Coney Island look like a merry-go-round."

"What a bunch of wussies. Let's go."

Two light-skinned, mixed-race men greeted them once they were inside. One of them spoke with a slight accent, undeterminable as to its the ethnicity. "Welcome, my friends, welcome to Antigua Rainforest Zipline Rides. I am Terrence, and this is Horace, my zipline technician. I will assist your takeoffs, and he will assist your touchdowns. You have come at a most propitious time. Our tourism business seems to be at a lull, so you pretty much have the run of the ziplines today."

"I read where you have six ziplines," said Veronica.

"Yes, indeed. They vary in terms of distance and slope. Our longest is a little over ninety yards long, while the shortest is fifty-yards long. The gentlest slope is twenty degrees, while the steepest is forty-five degrees. Take your pick based on your appetite for thrill."

"I know what I want. Number Six."

Gidget guessed Number Six was the worst. "I'll take Number One."

Veronica had her mind made up. "We can all start at Number One, but we're *all* going to do Number Six."

Daffy said, "I'll probably do a number two on my way down no matter which ziplines you choose."

Harry paid for three rides a piece. Interestingly enough, Zipline Rides was able to process his transaction in Bitcoin. They started with Number One, which began on a platform attached to the back of the building. Terrance gave each rider a protective helmet similar to those worn by bicyclists as well as a pair of thick leather gloves. They donned the equipment and then followed him onto the attached wooden platform. It was fifteen feet above steeply sloped ground below.

"Here. Wrap this around your waist and buttocks," Terrence said as he helped Veronica slip into a zipline harness. Using a mountain-climber's carabiner, he next attached her harness to a nylon strap two inches wide. In turn, the strap was connected to the uppermost of two parallel, thick metal cables attached to the roof of the building. The other ends of the two cables sloped downward at a twenty-degree angle and disappeared into even thicker rainforest forty feet below the platform.

"Grip the top of the harness with one hand and the bottom cable with your other hand." Terrence showed her. "When you are ready, simply step off and let your weight carry you down—"

"It should be a fast trip for Ronnie," said Daffy.

Veronica's dry mouth prevented a comeback.

Terrence said, "If you want to slow your rate of descent down, simply tighten your grip on the bottom cable."

He stood next to Veronica, expecting her to step off. Instead, she remained on the platform, summoning her nerve. After several shouts of "Do it, Girl!" from the crowd, she stepped off. Veronica's trip from the platform to the rainforest trees passed so quickly that those standing on the platform were surprised when she disappeared.

A look of horror on her face, Gidget said, "She's still alive. I can hear her screaming."

"Who's next?" asked Terrence.

Chapter 15

Antigua
October 26th

Everyone completed Number One successfully, even Larry whose erratic heart palpitations generated another pacemaker alert in Arizona. Harry said, "You need an on-off switch on that thing."

"You need an off switch on your mouth," said Larry.

Number Three was much more terrifying and generated much louder screams.

Daffy leaned into Gidget and whispered, "Do I see some dark wet spots on a couple of the boys' Bermuda shorts?"

Gidget nodded. "I'm so glad I wore navy blue shorts myself."

"I'm glad I wore my depends."

By the time everyone reached the platform for Number Six, even Veronica was reluctant. "Who wants to go first?"

Terrence pointed at the long cables. "This is a three-hundred-yard line with a fifty-five-degree slope. Not for the faint of heart."

Gidget said, "But you said forty-five degrees was the steepest zipline y'all got."

"My bad."

Daffy smiled vindictively at Veronica's hesitation. She had noticed the Texan rubbing thighs with Harry during the entire trip up the mountains and silently vowed to get revenge even if she killed herself in the process. She said, "I'll go first."

Terrence helped Daffy hook up to the cable. Looking over the edge of the platform, her bravery rapidly evaporated, and she froze. Veronica gave her a push, which generated a loud scream that continued all the way down. As they listened to her, Louella said, "If there's any graves around here, I bet their occupants are awake by now."

It seemed as if each rider tried to outdo the previous one in terms of how loud he or she could scream. After forty-five minutes, eight riders—four women and four men—stood in a clearing three-hundred-yards below and out-of-sight of the platform far above them in thick rainforest. They awaited Jerry and Veronica's arrival.

"Where are they?" asked Gidget. "Seems like they're taking a long time. One of them should've been here five minutes ago."

"Jerry always was the slowpoke among us," said Gary.

"He probably had to stop along the way to go to the bathroom," said Harry. "His prostate's even larger than mine."

Daffy shook her head. "No one's prostate is larger than yours."

Ten minutes later, a faint scream announced someone was on the way down. It increasingly grew louder until Jerry suddenly emerged from the rainforest on the other side of the small stream opposite them. The stream separated the rainforest from the clearing in which they had all landed safely, with Horace's help.

As Jerry flew over the stream, the wide nylon strap attaching his harness to the top metal cable suddenly snapped. His scream immediately doubled in loudness. But for his grip on the bottom cable with his right hand, he would have immediately dropped twenty feet straight down into the stream below.

"Hold on! Hold on!" shouted Larry. Others joined in the chorus.

Jerry flailed with his left hand, trying to grab the cable so as to hold on with two hands. All could see his right hand slowly losing its grip.

"He shouldn't have eaten so much at the buffet last night. His weight is too much," said Larry.

Gary also had a morbid sense of humor. "Remind me to avoid all buffets on the Bahama Princess."

"Would you two please get serious." Gidget glared at them. "That's your brother up there."

Unable to bolster his grip with his left hand, his right hand finally slipped, and he fell straight down. He landed on his back in the water with a huge splash. Horace and the Marx Brothers rushed to the bank of the stream and waded in. Jerry floated on his back about fifteen feet away, so they dog-paddled the last few feet to reach him. He seemed unconscious at first but quickly revived. His brothers pulled him ashore and helped walk him back to the clearing. Horace said, "It's a good thing he was able to hold on for a while. If he'd fallen as soon as the strap broke, the fall would have killed him, coming down the zipline as fast as he was."

Veronica's scream could be heard almost immediately. She soon zoomed out of the trees opposite the stream bank and smoothly landed in the clearing. She saw the others standing around Jerry, who sat on the ground, looking very battered. She asked, "What the hell happened?"

"The strap to Jerry's harness broke, and he fell into the water," said Harry.

"He almost bought it," said Barry. "If he'd a fell in the woods, he'd be a goner."

On the ride back to Saint John's, Gidget quizzed Jerry and Veronica. "What happened?"

Jerry was so shaken by the trauma he said nothing, leaned back in his seat, and tuned out.

Veronica said, "I… I teased Jerry. I said, 'Gentlemen before ladies,' and I think he sensed I was a little nervous about Number Six, so he went before me."

"Did you help him hookup to the zipline?"

"Yeah. Me and Terrence."

"Did you notice anything about the strap?"

"No, but I didn't pay much attention to it."

Louella asked, "Why are you grilling Ronnie so? It wasn't her fault. It was probably an old worn strap. Terrence should have inspected them better. I know I didn't pay too much attention to mine."

Back in their stateroom that evening, Daffy asked, "You think it was an accident that Jerry's strap snapped?"

Gidget shook her head. "It didn't look like an accident to me."

"Why you say that?"

"Why did it take Jerry so long to follow us down Number Six? What was Terrence doing after I left Number Six? Jerry and Ronnie were the last ones after me. Didn't Terrence check the strap before he attached it to the cable? If he didn't, he should have."

Daffy's face showed skepticism. "You think Terrence purposefully sabotaged Jerry's strap?"

"Maybe him... or the Arnold Schwarzenegger guy."

"Why you say that?"

"I thought I spotted him or someone in the forest on the way down Number Three. I didn't say anything because I didn't want to give that damn Veronica another opportunity to make fun of me. It was either him or *someone* in camouflage sneaking around in the rainforest."

Daffy shrugged. "Who else could it be?"

"Maybe the woman in Hemingway's?"

"Why her? The boys thought she was just another nutcase like in Nassau."

"People have been murdered by nutcases before."

Two days later, they visited Anse Trabaude at the suggestion of Yvette who described it as "The most beautiful beach. Blue waters, gentle white surf, and lots of white sand. Marvelous for sunbathing." She neglected to tell them bathing suits were optional, thinking it was an unimportant detail. Yvette was French, after all.

They lay sunbathing at Anse Trabaud—Harry, Gary, and Veronica *sans* swimsuits—on beautiful white sand. The beach was sprinkled with dozens of sunbathers, a fair number of whom also were nude.

A young male lifeguard approached. "Folks, I hate to say this, but I've had several complaints from some of the other sunbathers about a couple of you."

Jerry sat up. "What kind of complaints? We haven't been noisy or playing our music too loudly, have we?"

"No sir. Not those kind of complaints."

"Then, what's the problem?" asked Barry.

The lifeguard nodded at Harry and Gary. "Other sunbathers have asked me to ask these two gentlemen to put their bathing suits back on."

Chapter 16

14° 14' 39.9048" North, 60° 18' 39.5172" West
October 30th

All five women and the Marx Brothers scrunched together on the massive sectional in the Casserole Ladies' stateroom. The Antigua zipline incident was history, and on this night, something else grabbed everyone's attention. Tonight's premiere episode of *The Real Widows of Thomasville* overshadowed everything else.

Daffy held up a hand. "Quiet! It's about to begin."

Babs had been texting Daffy and Gidget for days, relaying enticing tidbits about filming their new reality show. As Daffy shushed everyone, Jerry said, "This better be good. You know we're missing the *Andy Griffith Show*."

Gidget said, "We know, we know… as you've told us many times."

The Marx Brothers managed to stay awake during the introductory scene where the show's narrator, a shapely but slightly-past-her-prime actress, introduced Babs, Lilly, and Lizzie to the TV viewing audience. She described the beautiful town of Thomasville and revealed several juicy tidbits of gossip about local personalities and rivalries.

The Marx Brothers could not stop laughing during an early scene in Babs' house, in which she educated Lilly on the latest paranormal phenomena updates available on the Internet. All watched as Babs raved about a web site devoted to the Loch Ness Monster. This was followed by a closeup shot of her computer screen showing a live video feed from a volcano in Mexico famous for UFO sightings.

Next, Babs narrated a closeup shot of her computer screen showing live video from a 24x7 webcam set up to record appearances of leprechauns and Irish fairies.

"Where's the leprechauns and fairies?" Gary asked as they viewed a pleasant video of a forest in Ireland. No living beings were to be seen.

"Probably in a bar," said Harry. "You know how the Irish are."

Babs navigated to a live webcam set up to record ghost appearances in a Greenville, South Carolina auditorium. Viewers saw only an auditorium empty except for a whiteboard and podium on its stage. When Lilly pointed out that the auditorium was, in fact, empty, Babs became incensed. She said, "Just because it's not showing a ghost on the screen don't mean that one might not be in that auditorium right now."

A subsequent live webcam set up to record any appearance of Bigfoot only displayed a pastorale forest in Washington State. The scene showed no live human or animal, including Bigfoot.

"Babs takes her paranormal stuff seriously," explained Daffy. "She's obsessed with it."

"Has she ever been evaluated by a psychiatrist for it?" asked Jerry.

Gidget shook her head. "Nope. So far, we've managed to keep it sufficiently contained."

"But we don't know how long we'll be able to keep it contained," said Daffy. "That girl is really into the occult."

"Such as?" asked Louella.

"Voodoo, fortune telling, séances with the dead. Stuff like that."

All five Marx Brothers were fast asleep by the time the shapely narrator mentioned the Widows had recently met five new potential boyfriends. She explained the Widows had nicknamed them the Marx Brothers and that they lived in a seniors' development in Florida called The Villages. Barry and Gary subsequently woke up in time to watch Babs' voodoo scene.

<u>EXTERIOR SCENE: THE BIG OAK, THOMASVILLE, WEDNESDAY NIGHT 8:00 PM</u>

The three women sit in a circle on a large light blue blanket beneath a huge live oak known locally as The Big Oak. It is pitch-black at nighttime. The women are the only people in the area. A black cat runs across the screen behind them, chasing a possum. Their blanket has a variety of voodoo symbols on it: a skull-and-crossbones wearing a top hat, a crudely drawn voodoo doll with pins in it, an elaborate drawing of Baron LaCroix, and another of a large python snake.

NARRATOR: [Speaks off camera] Babs is a voodoo aficionado. She visited Port-au-Prince on a cruise two months ago and stocked up on voodoo supplies. Tonight's ritual is a follow up on Lizzie's warning that the Mahjong Mammas might attempt to steal the Marx Brothers away from them. Babs selected The Big Oak as the location for the ritual due to its status as a historic landmark and the site of many outdoor weddings. Also, Lilly and Lizzie refused to go back to any cemetery at midnight for any more of Babs' voodoo rituals.

BABS: Okay. Lilly, hold the book open to the page I showed you, and Lizzie, you pass me the things I gave you as I call for them. [Lilly nods. Lizzie smirks, then nods.]

BABS: Hold the book still. Hand me the doll. [Lizzie passes Babs a small, crude burlap doll. Babs looks down at the book Lilly holds for her.] All y'all repeat after me. *o gwo lespri.*

ALL OTHER LADIES IN UNISON: *o gwo lespri.*

BABS: Hand me the powder. [Lizzie passes Babs a small jar.] All y'all repeat after me. *kite mwen jwenn yon etranje tou pre isit la.*

ALL OTHER LADIES IN UNISON: *kite mwen jwenn yon etranje tou pre isit la.*

BABS: *se konsa, mwen ka fe yon nouvo zanmi.*

ALL OTHER LADIES IN UNISON: *se konsa, mwen ka fe yon nouvo zanmi.*

[Babs tilts the jar in her hand and sprinkles a small amount of the powder from inside it onto the doll.]

BABS: Okay, that's it. That's all. It's over.

LIZZIE: I hope you didn't screw this one up like you usually do in all your other voodoo rituals. You really should take lessons in how to speak Haitian Creole.

LILLY: What'd we all say?

BABS: We said, "Let our boyfriends tell them Mammas to kiss their asses and think only about the Widows of Thomasville." [Looks at camera.] Is it okay to say asses on the air? Gee, I wish I knew what Mitzi's name is in Creole so I could've included a special hex on her.

LIZZIE: Her name in Creole would be the same as it is in English.

After the voodoo scene finished, Barry asked, "Who are the Marx Brothers?"

"Just some guys back in Thomasville," said Daffy.

Gary asked, "You really think Babs actually believes that voodoo crap?"

Gidget nodded. "You better believe she believes in it. She believes in almost anything paranormal. Especially voodoo. I think next to palm reading, that's her favorite paranormal phenomenon. She enjoys it and thinks she's an expert. Y'all won't believe how many of those voodoo rituals Daff and I have had to go through with her. One of the last ones was recently in Sunset Memorial Cemetery at midnight. We almost got arrested by Thomasville police that night."

"Gidg and I have participated in several of Babs' voodoo rituals," said Daffy. "A Good Luck Floor Wash, several love rituals, a fertility ceremony—"

"What the hell is a Good Luck Floor Wash?" asked Gary.

"It's a voodoo ritual that supposedly brings good fortune… at least according to Babs."

"I wanna know why youse participated in a voodoo fertility ritual?" asked Barry. He shot Gidget a worried look. "Aren't youse a little too old for that?"

Gidget shot Barry an 'if looks could kill' look in return. "You're as young as you feel, thank you very much. Babs performed the fertility ritual for Daffy's female dachshund, Sophie. Daffy wanted to breed her."

Daffy frowned. "And poor little Sophie never got pregnant."

Louella managed to fake sympathetic look. "Is Sophie your emotional support dog, or are you her emotional support human?"

Harry shook his head then looked at Daffy and Gidget. "Youse gets into the craziest stuff."

"Y'all ain't seen nothing yet." Daffy's prediction unfortunately proved to be accurate.

Chapter 17

Castries, Saint Lucia
November 5th

The Bahama Princess docked in the capital city for a two-day layover before the next leg of the cruise. The first priority on day one for the group was a visit to Sulphur Springs on the southwestern part of the island. An inactive volcano provided visitors with heated mud baths—a good therapy for old-age musculoskeletal ailments. By mid-morning, everyone sat waist-deep in a ten-by-twenty-foot pool of warm, black mud.

Veronica made a face. "This stuff smells like rotten eggs."

"It's the sulfur in it from the volcano," said Gidget.

Daffy also made a face. "I could've skipped the Chanel No. 5 this morning."

Naomi agreed, "Ditto on my Dior Poison."

"This mud smells worse than my dachshund's poop."

"Ain't no dog poop smells nearly as bad as my Yorkie's," said Veronica. "After that little bitch takes a dump, you wanna bring in a hazardous waste cleanup team."

"Bitch, bitch, bitch. This mud is just what the doctor ordered for my arthritis." Harry smeared mud all over his shoulders. "Someone do my back for me."

"It does so much for your appearance," Daffy said.

"Baby, we could have some real fun in this stuff if the rest of them wasn't here."

All of them had participated in a three-day mixed-doubles pickleball tournament on board the ship. Resulting ailments in addition to Harry's aggravated arthritis included Larry's exacerbated peripheral neuropathy, Jerry's irritated sciatica, Gidget's pulled calf muscle, Barry's mildly sprained ankle, Daffy's inflamed tennis elbow, and Gary's shin splints. Louella, Veronica, and Naomi managed to survive the tournament injury-free—they were relatively younger—but decided to go along anyway.

The mud baths and hot springs alleviated some but not all of their misery, so they decided to do something that did not involve walking. The next morning, they chose to ride Segways. These are two-wheeled, self-balancing electric scooters on which a rider stands. They travel at speeds up to twelve miles an hour over a distance of up to thirty miles.

Harry had spotted a brochure at breakfast about Segway tours in Saint Lucia and signed them up, explaining, “All we gotta do is stand on ‘em.”

Naomi opted to enjoy a massage in one of the Bahama Princess’ six spas instead.

At nine o’clock, a tour bus pulled up to the dock, and thirty passengers from the Bahama Princess boarded. After a short, pleasant ride along the northwest coast of the island, the bus dropped them off at Rodney Bay. The Segway brochure explained that the area had been an anchorage for pirates at one time. Now, it was covered in condos, houses, and greenery.

A Saint Lucia Segway Tours guide greeted them. With a French Creole accent, he said, “Welcome folks. I am Julien, and I will be your guide. It is my job to ensure you enjoy the next two-and-a-half hours. First, we will spend about twenty minutes on a practice track, and then you will take a beautiful tour through lush forests and along beautiful vistas. Even though Segways are easy to learn how to maneuver, a little practice helps. Don’t worry. It is impossible to fall off of them, as they are self-balancing.

“After the practice session, you will ride your Segways over a two-mile nature trail up Mount Pimard. Mount Pimard is 662 feet in elevation or a little over two of your American football fields high. It covers seventy-eight acres of nature preserve. You will see a variety of plants, old historic ruins, and beautiful vistas. Any questions?”

Julien fielded several questions, then pointed. “Follow me to the building over there, and we will get you outfitted.”

Inside the building, they received bicycle safety helmets, knee and elbow pads, and Segways. On the practice track behind the building, their guide explained the operation of the Segway and demonstrated it. Afterward, the adventure began.

“Where’s the gas pedal?” asked Barry.

"If you'd been listening," said Gidget, "you'd have heard that there is no gas pedal. You lean forward to go forward, and lean backward to go backward. Left to go left. Right to go right. Lean backward a little bit to stop."

"No gas pedal just ain't right."

Not trusting the vehicle's self-balancing capability, Jerry kept stepping on-and-off the machine and made no forward progress as a result. Contrary to Julien's assertion, Gary fell off twice. Daffy screamed "Ohhhhhhh sh—" before she hit the ground. For the next five minutes, Daffy only moved backward until she felt confident leaning forward.

Larry said, "Learning to ride a unicycle has gotta be easier than this."

"Let's rethink these Segways," said Harry. "Do they have a go-kart track on this here island?"

Jerry, Veronica, and Louella finally managed to maneuver their Segways. The others turned the practice session into a mini version of a NASCAR pile-up. Julien steered his Segway over to the group.

"Folks, it appears a little more difficult for some of you. I must leave you so I can start the rest of the Bahama Princess passengers on the tour." Julien pointed at Jerry, Veronica, and Louella. "You three can come with me and the others while they continue practicing. I will come back for you three after the rest of the class reaches the first stop."

Fifteen minutes later, Julien returned. By then, everyone had managed to maneuver their Segways successfully enough to proceed. He led them out of the practice track and onto the nature trail. They traveled on a smooth, packed-clay pathway through thick tropical forest.

At one point, Julien said, "You all seem to be doing very well. I will go ahead and check on the others. We will wait for you at one of the overlooks." With that, he sped up and soon vanished.

The pathway inclined up Mount Pimard through lush tropical forest woodland and along cliffs providing scenic overlooks. These afforded beautiful views of Rodney Bay down below. As they traveled, a man riding a bicycle approached from behind. At first, it appeared he would pass them, but instead, he pulled up alongside Gary.

The stranger wore a black, tight cycling jersey and matching cycling pants. Three parallel white stripes along the side of his black mountain bike shoes branded them as Adidas. He wore a bicyclist's helmet that covered his head and somewhat obscured his face.

Daffy steered close to Gidget. "That guy looks rough around the edges. A real tough guy. Look at those pecs. His jersey looks cramped."

"If you don't look at him above his chest, he'd be perfect for a Saturday night in the sack," said Gidget.

"Definitely a double-bagger."

They approached a narrow point in the pathway overlooking the bay a hundred feet below, and Gary slowed down to let Bikeman pass. This was a prudent move on his part as all that separated him from the bay below was a two-foot-high wooden guardrail. Instead of passing, the other man also slowed his speed. Clearly annoyed, Gary sped up but was matched by the other rider. Again, Gary slowed, and again, his speed was matched. This duel continued until Bikeman sharply swerved into Gary, pulled away, and sped off. Gary tumbled off the vehicle just as it crashed through the wooden guardrail and plunged hundreds of feet down the side of Mount Pimard.

The others steered their Segways up to Gary who lay on the ground. Daffy asked, "Are you okay? You're lucky to be alive."

"What was that all about? Do you know who he was?" Gidget asked.

Gary was stunned and merely shook his head.

Gidget looked at his brothers. "Any of y'all know that guy?"

Her question was answered with negative head shakes.

"Let's go find Julien and report this. That guy is a dangerous menace. Maybe the local police can find him and arrest him."

Back in their stateroom that night, Daffy asked, "Any ideas on the guy on the bike?"

Gidget shrugged. "I think the Marx Brothers acted strange. They didn't react as negatively as I would have if it had been one of my brothers. Gary would have died if he'd fallen over the guardrail."

"It was a pretty long drop to the water."

Travel with the Marx Brothers seemed to have gotten weirder with every island they visited. Gidget's misgivings had multiplied ever since the WWE woman kissed Jerry on Antigua.

"All of 'em, even Gary, acted like they just wanted the incident to go away."

Daffy nodded. "Veronica looked pretty shook up. She was pretty close to Gary when that jerk ran him down. I bet she's thinking but for the grace of God go I."

"For sure."

"We've had the Triggerfish, the zipline, and now the Segway accident. I'm beginning to think the Marx Brothers are bad luck magnets."

Gidget's face revealed a measure of unease. "I'm beginning to wonder if what's happening to the Marx Brothers *is really* just bad luck."

Chapter 18

12° 25′ 52.3632″ North, 60° 5′ 58.9524″ West
November 13th

After Saint Lucia, the Bahama Princess leisurely toured the Windward Islands, most notably Saint Vincent and the Grenadines and Barbados. The Casserole Ladies and friends visited rum distilleries on several of the islands in the chain, much to their regret the following mornings. Veronica, Naomi, and Louella seemed better able to hold their liquor. After every visit, they all swore off rum only to violate their oaths on the next island. Mount Gay Distillery on the island of Barbados resulted in the worst of the hangovers.

The Bahama Princess weighed anchor two days after the Mount Gay visit and sailed for Grenada at a leisurely pace. Most passengers were glad to enjoy a few restful days at sea, but Larry complained about a nagging upset stomach. At a table in the Tiki Tiki Lounge, he renewed his pledge for the eighth time.

"No more rum for me ever again. I wish I'd never heard of Mount Gay rum."

"Maybe you should drink rum by the ounce and not the gallon," said Daffy.

Jerry shot his brother a look of scorn. "Larry never could hold his liquor. He's a wuss."

Gidget was doubtful. "It might not be the liquor. I hope it's not food poisoning. I'd hate to think we got salmonella or some other bacteria in the ship's food supply. Or maybe he's just seasick. I threw up myself this morning."

Larry's stomach complaints continued into the evening when the third episode of the *Real Widows of Thomasville* was scheduled to air. Daffy and Gidget had watched the second episode by themselves. The Marx Brothers missed that one because it aired in the same time slot as a must-see episode of *The Andy Griffith Show*. Harry had explained, "We missed a classic *Andy Griffith* episode during the premier of Babs' show. 'Barney's First Car' is one of my favorites. We ain't missing 'The Pickle Story' tonight."

The bloom of the romance had definitely worn off by November 6th when that episode of *Real Widows* aired.

Texts received from Babs said the third episode of *Real Widows* airing on November 13th would be the one *not* to miss. Talking with Barry, Gidget said, "I promise y'all will wanna watch this one. Babs says it will vindicate what she's been saying about UFOs in Area 53."

But Barry was the holdout on November 13th. He said, "Hon, I'd love to, but tonight's *Andy Griffith* episode is a classic. 'Opie the Birdman.' Youse might wanna skip your *Real Wid*ows and watch it with me. It'd be worth your time."

Harry nodded. "'Opie the Birdman' is probably the best *Andy Griffith* episode ever made."

Daffy asked, "What's so great about it?"

"Opie kills a momma bird with his slingshot and has to raise her baby bird by himself. I cry every time I watch it."

Barry agreed, and Gidget thought she saw a tear in his eye. She said, "Let's let Barry watch *Andy Griffith*. It means so much to him. The rest of you with him?"

Gary said, "Not me. 'Opie the Birdman' is too sad for me. I'm gonna watch the *Widows* show with youse."

Jerry nodded his concurrence. Harry thought about how sad 'Opie the Birdman' was, changed his mind, and nodded his concurrence as well. Larry said, "I'll watch the *Real Widows* with youse, but with this throwing up, I might not make it all the way through."

Gidget and Daffy looked around as *Real Widows* began. Larry was in the bathroom, and the other three Marx Brothers had nodded off.

Daffy said, "Tsk, tsk, tsk. The little dears. It is past their bedtime. Royce used to do this to me all the time."

"Same with Sam," Gidget said. That's why I always got to choose what to watch on TV because he'd sleep through whatever was on. Let's wake these boys up. The show's about to start, and they'll be pissed if they miss it."

Real Widows' premiere episode had introduced the public to Lilly, Lizzie, and Babs by delighting its viewers with the women's quirks. Lilly's shoe closet reorganization, Lizzie's alimony strategy, and Bab's obsession with the paranormal generated huge ratings for that episode. The highlight of the second episode was a food fight among Thomasville elites in Halloween costumes at one of the city's historic plantations.

Daffy explained, "Tonight's episode is titled 'Area 53.' Babs says it is actually going to show the real aliens they met in Area 53 in Northwest Florida."

"Yeah, right," said Harry. "And next week they're gonna go to Oz and meet the Wizard."

Gidget said, "Y'all met Babs before we sailed. Y'all know what she's like."

"Shhh, I can't hear what this broad's saying," said Jerry who was enjoying the narrator's sexy voice and cleavage.

Gary asked, "Why? You can't hear anything anyway."

Harry put on his glasses as he spoke. "None of us can, but we *can* look at that broad."

The 'Area 53' episode began with Lilly, Lizzie, and Babs sitting in her Escalade, which was parked next to an electrified fence on an desolate road in Northwest Florida. The narrator detailed speculation on the Internet concerning a top-secret government facility called Area 53 located somewhere behind the fence. It was supposed to be a repository for an overflow of UFOs from Area 51 in Nevada.

The episode then showcased the three women's grueling trek through a snake- and alligator-infested swamp. Finally, they found Area 53, a spaceship within, and three aliens on a diplomatic mission to Earth. One of the aliens invited Babs, Lilly, and Lizzie to tour the inside of the spaceship, all recorded by *Real Widows* cameramen.

Jerry said, "Those are some wild alien costumes. The show's makeup artists are pretty good."

"Would you wake Gary up? I can't hear what they're saying for his loud snoring," Harry said.

Jerry nudged his brother. "Gary! Gary! Wake up! And wipe the drool off your chin."

"Those costumes are good, but the inside of the spaceship is even more impressive," said Harry. "Hollywood knows how to build a realistic movie set."

Jerry shook his head. "It ain't makeup, and it ain't a movie set. It's CGI. Them aliens and that spaceship are computer generated. Like the scene in the outer space bar in *Star Wars*."

"Whatever it is, it's pretty good," said Gidget.

Scenes showing the interaction between Lilly, Lizzie, Babs, and three Aliens were hilarious. One example involved a discussion about grandchildren.

INTERIOR SCENE: ALIEN SPACESHIP PARKED IN THE AREA 53 HOLDING FACILITY, MONDAY MORNING 3:15 AM

Babs, Lilly, and Lizzie sit at a kidney-shaped table opposite an alien, whose name is pronounced in English as Monroe.

MONROE: It has been very informative, being able to talk with you about life on Earth. We are here to study Earth people in order to gain a better understanding of your species. I have asked the three of you a lot of questions. Now, you may ask me anything you would like to know about life on our planet.
BABS: Mister Monroe, how long have y'all been on the road, so to speak?
MONROE: It has been approximately one-hundred and three of your Earth-years since Ramone, Salome, and I left our home planet, KOI 5715.01.
BABS: [Look of shock on her face.] My goodness. You must miss your family… especially your children and grandchildren.
MONROE: Yes. I miss all eighty-seven of them.
LIZZIE: Sounds like you got quite a bit of testosterone inside you. My kind of guy.
BABS: But, eighty-seven children and grandchildren! That's more than every woman in my garden club has all put together.

MONROE: Eighty-seven only includes my children. I have one-thousand nine-hundred and fourteen grandchildren.
BABS: My goodness! That *is* a lot!
MONROE: The Supreme Authority on KOI 5715.01 only allows each citizen no more than four spouses and twenty-two offspring per spouse.
LILLY: I bet you have a devil of a time shopping for Christmas presents for all of them grandkids.

The group laughed throughout 'Area 53,' or at least those who were awake. Larry missed out on much of the fun as he had to excuse himself several times to visit the toilet. Sounds of vomiting echoed from the bathroom each time.

Daffy texted her and Gidget's congratulations on another brilliant episode to Babs, Lilly, and Lizzie. She also texted that she and Gidget would be back in Thomasville on November 19th.

Harry said, "It's amazing that Hollywood could pull something like that off on such short notice."

"What do you mean?" asked Gidget.

"I mean, spaceships, aliens, and that massive hangar with the spaceship in it. Getting all that built in a couple of weeks."

"It's like I said. It's all CGI. None of that was real," said Jerry.

"How do you know it wasn't all real?" asked Gidget. "Babs says Area 53 is for real. Maybe it really does exist."

Harry shook his head. "No way. Those girls would never have gotten into an Air Force base like your friends did. They'd have been arrested the minute they got over that electric fence."

"I don't know," said Daffy. "Y'all don't know Babs. Every time we pooh-pooh her weird ideas, she proves us wrong."

Barry said, "Trust me. All that stuff was made up. None of it was real. Those Hollywood people are experts in making you think you're seeing one thing when something else is really going on. Don't believe everything you see."

Chapter 19

12° 22' 29.568" North, 60° 21' 42.354" West
November 14th

Except for Larry and Gidget, everyone slept in late the morning after watching *Real Widows of Thomasville*. The program had started at 8:00 PM and kept them up an hour past their usual bedtime. Gidget opened the door to her stateroom at 7:00 AM and stepped out into the hallway. She saw Stokes emerging from the stateroom Larry shared with Harry and Jerry.

"Morning Stokes. How are you?" Gidget asked.

"Very well, thank you, Mum," Stokes said.

"Are the boys stirring yet?"

"Only Mister Larry. He complained of throwing up all night and rang for me earlier. He needed my help preparing something to calm his stomach."

"Poor dear. I was throwing up myself this morning. That's why I'm up. The seas must've been a little rougher last night. Is Larry in the room?"

"No, Mum. He already left to go to Azul to put some food in his stomach. He told me he would get a large table for everyone to join him for breakfast after everyone gets up."

Louella joined them on the way to the restaurant. Harry shook his head. "Poor guy. I heard him throwing up all night. He needed breakfast in order to have something to throw up."

"God, how I hate the dry heaves," said Daffy. "Little Miss Gidg was throwing up this morning herself. Her seasickness seems to be getting worse."

They entered Azul and saw Larry drinking a Bloody Mary.

"You look like hell," Barry said.

"Like something the dog dragged in that the cat wouldn't have," added Jerry.

"You got that wrong Bro," said Gary. "It's something the cat dragged in that the dog wouldn't have."

Larry looked terrible. “Whatever. I already ordered Sonoran breakfast empanadas. Gotta get something in my belly.”

“You finally found someone who knows how to cook those things?” asked Gidget.

“Yeah. Chef Dreyfus told me he has a recipe for them that has his own twist to it.”

Their waiter took their orders shortly before Larry’s empanadas arrived.

Gidget said, “Please. Eat. Don’t wait for us. You need something on your tummy.”

“Listen to her,” said Daffy. “She *is* a registered pharmacist.”

Larry extracted large chunk of empanada with his fork. “Here goes nothing. Geronimo!”

After eating five large chunks of the empanada, he suddenly raised both hands and covered his mouth. His eyes rolled up, and he started shaking. He slumped forward, and his head smashed into the plate of empanadas. The shaking became more violent and was accompanied by vomiting and foaming at the mouth. Daffy and Gidget screamed and were joined by Louella. A waiter ran to their table and helped manhandle Larry’s shaking body down to the floor.

“Let’s turn him on his side to keep his airway open,” said Gidget. “Don’t hold him down, and get the doctor here, *quick*!”

The waiter hollered at the hostess who picked up the phone. He looked at Gidget. “Should we put something in his mouth? To keep him from biting his tongue.”

“No. That’s a popular misconception. Best thing for us to do is let the seizure take its course until the doctor gets here. Looks like a grand mal to me.”

“She’s dead,” said Barry.

Harry shook his head. “Grand mal—a seizure—you idiot. Not our grandma. You need a new hearing aid.”

After a minute, Larry stopped shaking. Gidget took his wrist in her hands and felt his pulse. After fifteen seconds, she said, “He’s got no pulse. Let’s flip him on his back and start CPR.”

Gidget took a cloth napkin off of the table and cleaned the foam, vomit, and saliva from around Larry’s mouth. She said, “I’ll administer mouth-to-mouth resuscitation. Does anyone know how to do chest compressions?”

Five blank stares answered.

"Harry, you put your hands like this on his chest and push down about an inch or two, while I do the mouth-to-mouth to Larry." Gidget put her hands on Larry's chest to show him.

Gidget was about to start CPR when Doctor Mokulus arrived. He was followed by two crew members carrying a lightweight collapsible stretcher. The doctor kneeled and felt Larry's pulse.

"He's got no pulse."

"He hasn't had one for about three minutes now," Gidget said.

"Let's get him on the stretcher and to the clinic. Quick!"

They laid Larry on the stretcher, raised it, and hustled off. As the medical crew passed through the entrance to the restaurant Gidget noticed the Arnold Schwarzenegger guy standing just outside, talking on a mobile phone. She nudged Daffy and whispered, "It's him again."

"Yeah, and he's talking on the phone."

"Looks like he's having a real serious conversation."

"Ladies," Gary said, "we're gonna head on down to the medical clinic. I'm sure the Doc will get Larry to come around, so why don't youse stay here and eat your breakfast? They ain't brought it out yet, so it'll still be warm. And Gidget, you probably need to get something on your stomach after throwing up this morning."

"Oh no, we'll go with—" Daffy began.

Gidget shook her head. "Let's stay here for a while, Daff. They may need some time with their brother by themselves."

Louella pooh-poohed Gary's suggestion she remain and instead, accompanied the Marx Brothers. After they departed, Daffy asked, "What's up? Why didn't you want to go with them?"

"It's like I said. They may want to be with their brother by themselves. You know, all the excitement has robbed me of my appetite. I'm going to go check on Larry."

Gidget still held the napkin she had used to clean his mouth. She walked back to the table, picked up an unused napkin, wrapped the other one in it, and placed the bundle in her pocketbook.

"You going to stay and eat?" Gidget asked.

"Nah. My appetite's gone too."

As they left Azul, Daffy asked, "What's up?"

Gidget said, “Something’s not right here. I want some time to think.”

“Larry’s been feeling sick ever since Mount Gay. His seizure was probably a result of that. What’s the problem?”

“I don’t know.” Gidget touched her pocketbook. “What’s on the napkin in here may provide an answer.”

Chapter 20

12° 22' 29.568" North, 60° 21' 42.354" West
November 14th

Twenty minutes later outside the ship's medical clinic, Doctor Mokulus huddled with the Marx Brothers. Louella stood nearby. Everyone looked serious as Daffy and Gidget approached.

"How is Larry?" asked Gidget. "Why are y'all standing out here?"

Harry wiped a tear away. "Larry's dead."

"Oh, my God!" Daffy shrieked.

Doctor Mokulus nodded. "I just informed his brothers that Mister Vanderhoff is dead. My assistants are prepping the body and will take it down to the morgue shortly."

"What did he die from?" asked Gidget.

Mokulus looked at the brothers. "Do I have your permission to discuss your brother's death with these ladies?"

Harry nodded. "Yes. Please. They're close friends."

"My preliminary cause of death is choking while having a seizure. The seizure was brought on by acute alcohol poisoning. What did he have for breakfast?"

"Bloody Mary's and Sonoran empanadas, but we don't know how many bloodies he had before we got there."

Jerry said, "And he'd drank a lot of rum in Barbados. What was that? About two days ago? He'd been throwing up ever since."

"And then he was eating them empanadas when he had the seizure," Gary said.

Mokulus nodded. "It all fits. All the alcohol he consumed this morning must have triggered the seizure. The empanadas were what choked him. Seizures are one of the symptoms of alcohol poisoning. Your brother is a small person. Small people don't have a lot of body weight to be able to absorb a lot of alcohol. The seizure caused him to choke on the empanadas. Are all of you next of kin?"

"We're all his brothers." Harry sighed. "There's no one else."

"Very well."

At that point, the doors to the clinic opened wide, and two medical assistants rolled a stretcher past them. A white sheet covered the small body on it from head to toe. One of the assistants turned to look back at the doctor and said, "Which morgue do you want him to go into, Doc?"

"Put him in Number One," Doctor Mokulus said, then turned to the Marx Brothers. "I'll need to get some information from you for some of the forms I'll have to complete. Please step inside."

Gidget stepped up and placed her hand on Harry's shoulder. "Guys, we're so sorry. If there's anything we can do, let us know. Daffy and I will head back to our room. We'll see y'all later."

Louella said, "I'll head back to my room as well."

On the way back to their rooms, Louella said, "This is just terrible. Larry dead. I feel so bad for the four remaining brothers."

"I can imagine how they must feel right now. One of their brothers gone. They looked like they were holding up well enough," Daffy said.

"Doctor Mokulus had just informed them that Larry was dead when you came up. I think they were in a state of shock. Well, here's where I gotta leave you. Are you girls okay?"

Gidget nodded. "I'm good."

"Me too," said Daffy.

"I'll let Naomi and Ronnie know," said Louella. "Maybe we'll see y'all in Azul later on."

After Daffy and Gidget had separated from Louella, Daffy said, "You haven't said much."

Gidget's brain raced. "Something's odd about this."

"What?"

"First off, he spent a lot of time throwing up all day yesterday and last night. He should have gotten rid of a lot of alcohol that way."

"Maybe he didn't get rid of enough. Plus, who knows how many Bloody Mary's he had before we got to Azul this morning? He was putting the rum away in Barbados and more bloodies this morning."

"Mmm… I wonder about Larry's seizure. Foaming at the mouth. To me, his seizure looked more like symptoms of some sort of poisoning."

"Food poisoning?"

Gidget shrugged. "I wish it was something as innocent as food poisoning."

"You don't think someone *meant* to kill Larry, do you?" asked Daffy.

"I don't know. I'm not Sherlock Holmes, but I am suspicious. That's why I kept the napkin I used to wipe Larry's mouth with. I'd like to have it checked out. Some of his symptoms—the nausea for instance—are symptoms of poisoning. And he was rubbing his forehead like he had a headache when we walked up to the table. His seizure and losing consciousness and then going into cardiac arrest—all those things are symptoms of poisoning by cyanide."

Daffy whistled. "*Phwee*! Girl, that's a serious accusation."

"But some of those symptoms are also classic symptoms of arsenic poisoning. Did you notice how flushed his skin looked? The abdominal pain, nausea and vomiting. His abnormal heart rhythm—I guess I should say no heart rhythm. All those are classic arsenic poisoning symptoms."

"Which is it? Arsenic or cyanide?"

"Can't say without more info. And it may be some other kind of poison I don't know much about. I do know one thing that is strange about this poisoning, if it is poisoning."

"What's that?"

"Foaming of the mouth is not a symptom of either arsenic or cyanide poisoning," Gidget said.

"Wow! I'm amazed that you know all that off the top of your head. But after all, you are a pharmacist."

"When you're a pharmacist, you have to know this stuff. People may call you day or night about someone they're with who's showing poisoning symptoms, and you have to be able to diagnose it and tell them what to do."

"So, who could have or would have poisoned Larry?"

"Good question, my dear Daffy. I've read enough murder mysteries to know that you start with the obvious and then work your way through the less obvious. Occam's Razor."

"Occam's Razor? I always use a Gillette Venus. Handles both fine and coarse hair. Great for your bikini area."

Gidget rolled her eyes. "Sometimes your sense of humor escapes me. The guiding principle behind Occam's razor is that for any problem, first look at the simplest explanation."

"So, what is the simplest explanation? What is most obvious?" asked Daffy.

"The simplest, most obvious explanation is that if Larry was poisoned, Chef Dreyfus or one of his staff must have poisoned him. Someone in Azul prepared Larry's breakfast. Either Dreyfus or someone under his supervision. Dreyfus is obsessive compulsive, from what I gather, so whether he or someone under his supervision prepared Larry's Sonoran empanadas, Dreyfus would be complicit in Larry's death. Another thing—Dreyfus made the chicken liver pâté that attracted all those fish. I've wondered about that ever since Gibbs Cay."

Daffy nodded. "He always gives me the willies."

"How so?"

"He just looks shifty. Those dark brown, almond-shaped, narrow-set eyes—very shifty looking. And his teeth. His upper canines are so long they look like vampire fangs. He always seems nervous every time he visits our table when we're dining. You know… he acts kind of jumpy."

Gidget frowned. "Brown eyes, long canines, always nervous and jumpy at the dinner table. Sounds like your dachshund, Sophie."

"What are you going to do now?"

"Eat breakfast, then visit the dead."

Chapter 21

12° 20' 33.666" North, 60° 33' 34.7328" West
November 14th

The Bahama Princess' size warranted a morgue large enough to accommodate five bodies. The morgue's location, below deck in a dark deserted area within the bowels of the ship, befitted its occupants. To get there, one passed by the sewage processing facility and the brig, spaces unlikely to be visited often. Gidget felt confident they could prowl around without being seen. They walked cautiously, with Gidget leading and ready with an answer for anyone who might question them.

We're just looking for the Purser's Office. Need to get some spending cash for shopping in Grenada this afternoon.

"I hope you remember where the morgue is," said Daffy. "I had too many loco mojitos at lunch before we took the second part of Rachel's tour of the ship."

"As best I remember, it's just up the hallway from sewage processing."

"Convenient location if someone needed to get rid of a body real fast. Why do you want to look at Larry's body anyway?"

"I want to see what it looks like postmortem. I didn't get much of a chance to check it out while we were in Azul. I remember his face seemed kind of flushed, but I don't remember much else. There may be things… indications of cause of death in the way his skin and fingernails look."

"Really?"

"Yeah. Poisoning can cause skin rashes and redness. Liver and kidney failure or certain kinds of respiratory problems can cause your fingernails to change color."

"Tough way to get out of having your nails painted."

Gidget shook her head, then held up her iPhone. "I'm going to take pictures with my phone and check against some online medical databases."

"Won't the morgue be locked?"

Gidget held up two bobby pins. "When we stopped by our room, I looked up info on the Internet on how to pick a lock. I remembered from the tour that the morgue doors have standard door locks on them. According to the video I watched, it's pretty simple to pick a door lock. All you need is two bobby pins."

Past the empty brig, the words 'Ship's Morgue' were printed above a series of five stainless-steel doors. The doors appeared similar to those found on commercial refrigerators in grocery stores. They were numbered one through five. Each had a shiny pull handle with a key lock on it.

"Doctor Mokulus told his tech to put Larry in Number One," Gidget said as she pulled on the handle to the door labeled with the number '1'. The door easily opened toward them. "I'm surprised they don't have it locked with a dead body inside. Anyway, no need to pick this lock."

Daffy said, "Maybe they want to make it easy for potential morgue customers onboard to check out their future accommodations. The average age of people onboard must be at least sixty-five."

They looked at a stainless-steel pullout drawer tray into which a body would be lain.

"This is it," said Gidget. She had visited a few morgues during her education and thirty-plus year pharmaceutical career.

"I figured it wasn't a fancy filing cabinet," said Daffy.

"In a way, it is." Gidget grasped the handle of the pullout drawer tray and slowly pulled it toward her.

They looked down. Daffy shrieked, "Oh my God! Where is Larry?"

"Not where he should be. No wonder the door wasn't locked. I guess they leave the morgues unlocked unless a body is inside."

"Mokulus' assistants must be bad at math. Check Number Two."

Gidget opened the second morgue door and pulled out the drawer tray. "Nothing."

Daffy quipped. "Puts real meaning to 'The Walking Dead,' don't it?"

"Something's wrong. Let's check the others."

"This is just like *Let's Make a Deal*. Gidget Smurfitt! Which door is Larry behind? Door Number Three, Door Number Four, or

Door Number Five?!" Daffy parodied Monty Hall, host of *Let's Make a Deal*, a TV gameshow of the 1960s.

Gidget frowned, opened the third door, and pulled out its stainless-steel drawer. "Damn! He's not here either."

Morgue doors four and five also failed to produce Larry's body.

Daffy asked, "We saw them taking his body to the morgue, didn't we?"

"We saw them taking Larry's body somewhere. Apparently, it wasn't here."

"We've got to tell someone about his body being missing."

Gidget shook her head. "We can't do that. We'd get into trouble. We're not supposed to be down here snooping around for a dead body. The ship's Security Officer might not appreciate it. And if Larry was murdered and his murderer gets wind that we're snooping, whoever it is might come after us."

"Okay. Now what? Why would they not bring his body down here and put it in the morgue?"

"Someone is trying to hide something suspicious about the body," said Gidget. "I bet it's because it wasn't just a simple case of choking."

"Makes sense, but what does that tell us?"

"I don't know at this point." Gidget pulled the napkin out of her shorts pocket. "This napkin may contain clues about Larry's death."

"What next?"

"We get the residue on this napkin analyzed, and I know someone in Grenada who can do it for us."

Later, Gidget and Daffy met Louella, Naomi, and Veronica for an early lunch. The Bahama Princess was scheduled to dock in Grenada early in the afternoon.

"Louella told us about Larry," said Veronica. "How are the boys taking it?"

"We haven't seen them since it happened, so we don't know how they're doing right now. They were kind of in a state of shock when we left them, and we thought it best to leave them alone," Daffy said.

Naomi frowned. "Larry was such a cutie. A real treasure. Louella gave us her version of his death. What's yours? Tell us all about it."

"Not much to tell," said Gidget. "Doctor Mokulus said he choked to death…"

"Sonoran empanadas'll do it to you every time," Daffy said.

"Louella says he didn't say anything before he choked," said Veronica.

Gidget nodded. "Only that he wanted to get something in his belly and that Chef Dreyfus cooked them special for him."

"Don't forget," said Daffy. "He shouted 'Geronimo' before he started eating. I guess he expected the empanadas to be pretty hot."

Veronica said, "I was visiting an old boyfriend of mine at Fort Campbell in Kentucky one time. He's a retired Army colonel. Fort Campbell is the home of the 101st Airborne. When we toured their museum, they told us paratroopers shout Geronimo when they jump out of airplanes."

"Why?"

"To show their bravery when they're about to risk dying."

As they finished eating, Naomi asked, "Y'all want to go with us this afternoon? I suspect the guys will want to be by themselves, so we're going to leave them alone and do a little shopping."

"I'm itching to spend some more of my divorce settlement," said Veronica. "Saint George's is nirvana for a shop-a-holic like me."

"Lizzie should be here," Daffy said.

"Wasn't she one of them on *The Real Widows*?"

"Yep. She's been diagnosed with Compulsive Buying Disorder by one of her psychiatrists."

"She's got more than one?"

Daffy nodded. "Oh yeah. Lizzie has two psychiatrists and one psychologist. CBD is one of the worst kind of addictions for a woman."

Gidget worried about the direction this discussion might take. She had plans for their time in Saint George's. "Ladies, we wish we could go with y'all, but Daff and I promised a close friend of ours in Thomasville that we would go check on her son. He's going to med school at the University in Saint George's."

"Robbing the cradle," said Veronica. "Don't let Barry find out, or he may go game hunting elsewhere."

"You should send that one into one of those late-night TV comedy shows. I hear they use that kind of lame humor all the time."

Daffy was surprised at Gidget's harsh reply to Veronica's snide remark. After they had left the restaurant, Daffy said, "Your reply to Veronica surprised me. What gives?"

"She's been flirting with Barry too much lately," said Gidget.

"It's not as if you two have gold bands on your ring fingers."

"No… but we might as well."

They stopped by the stateroom Larry used to share with Harry and Jerry. No one answered, so they knocked on Barry and Gary's door. Barry answered. "Come on in."

The other three brothers sat on the room's sectional sofa watching *The Young and the Restless*. A cloud of gloom hung over the room's occupants. Daffy asked, "How y'all doing?"

Harry said, "About as well as could be expected. Needed something to take our minds off what happened to our brother, and this soap was one of Larry's favorites."

"Yeah. He loves… loved the woman who played Phyllis Summers. Called her the Cleavage Lady," Jerry said.

Gary choked back tears. "We're gonna miss our brother. He could be an old coot at times, but he would do anything for any of his brothers."

Barry looked at Gary. "Even coldcock them once in a while."

"Ah, he didn't mean nothing by that. I deserved it anyway."

"We're going ashore this afternoon to do some shopping," Gidget said. "Don't wait on us to join you for supper. We'll eat in St. George's. Did the doctor tell y'all what they're gonna do with Larry's body?"

"Yeah. After we dock in Grenada, they're going to take it to the medical school there for autopsy, then ship it back to the States."

After they left Barry and Gary's stateroom, Daffy said, "They didn't look that shook up."

"It hasn't hit them yet. They're probably still in a state of shock," Gidget replied.

"Losing a 'bruddah' does that to you."

Chapter 22

Saint George's, Grenada
November 14th

Saint George's is not only the capital of Grenada, but also the location of a famous educational institution. Concerns for safety of Americans studying at Saint George's School of Medicine was one of the motivating factors behind Operation Urgent Fury in 1983. President Reagan authorized the invasion of Grenada in part to rescue students at the medical school. That was where Gidget and Daffy were headed.

As they stood on the dock waiting for a taxi, two Bahama Princess crew members rolled a stretcher down the gangplank. A black polyethylene body bag lay on top.

Daffy nudged Gidget. "Look. That's Larry."

Gidget turned her head to look. "Yeah. It is."

"You can tell Larry's inside it—outline of a short body and a huge bulge where his stomach is."

"Talk about kicking a guy when he's down."

"I wonder if getting him ready for the autopsy was why he wasn't in the morgue? You think they'll fly him back to The Villages after the autopsy?" asked Daffy.

"We should have asked the Marx Brothers. I guess that's where they'll want to bury him. Either there or back in New York City. Maybe they have a family plot up there."

"Why would anyone want to be buried in New York City?"

"New York City or The Villages? Neither possibility appeals to me."

"I know what you mean... Which is worse? Resting eternally in the city that inspired the movie *Escape From New York* or in a community populated by the living dead."

They watched as an ambulance pulled up, and the crew members loaded the body bag inside. As it pulled away, Daffy asked, "What do you plan on doing at the medical school besides checking on Louie? Take an afternoon seminar on the latest in poisonous substances?"

"No, nothing that entertaining. I'm hoping to get Louie's help understanding the cause of Larry's death." She opened her pocketbook. It still had the napkin she had taken from Azul in it.

At the medical school, Gidget and Daffy tracked Louie down after checking with the school's administration. A young clerk had suggested he was probably in the library studying for mid-terms. They recognized the tall, lanky twenty-year-old's curly dark hair as he sat looking down at several books spread out on a table in in front of him.

They approached him, and Daffy said, "Louie, my, how you've grown. You look as skinny as ever. Don't they feed you at this place?"

"I ain't got time to eat," said Louie, imitating Jesse Ventura's voice in the movie *Predator*.

"Sounds like the fifteen pounds in the 'freshman fifteen' is a negative number at Saint George's," said Gidget.

"That's for sure. What brings my mom's two favorite sources of Thomasville gossip to Saint George's?" he asked.

"It's a big blue and white thing called a ship," said Daffy.

"I left myself open for that, didn't I?"

Gidget nodded. "Yes, you did. Seriously, Saint George's is one of the regular stops on our cruise's itinerary, so we thought we'd stop by and see how you're doing. Your mom wants a report when we get back. We do also have an ulterior motive."

Gidget looked around to make sure no one else was watching and extracted the napkin. "One of our traveling companions… you wouldn't know him, just died this morning. Kind of suspiciously. I think he might have been poisoned, and some of the poison may be on this napkin. Can you run a chemical analysis on the substances on it?"

Louie was eager to help. "Sounds exciting. CSI at Saint George's. The medical school lab has several excellent gas chromatographs—an Agilent, a Thermo Fisher, a PerkinElmer."

"When can I get the results?"

"The test itself shouldn't take too long. Let's say about two hours to be safe."

Daffy and Gidget went shopping in the city of Saint George's while they waited. They visited many shops and dragged bags loaded with souvenirs back with them. At four-thirty in the afternoon, they picked Louie up in a taxi and took him to eat at a local restaurant favored by med students. After they ordered, Gidget asked, "So what you got?"

Louie handed her several sheets of computer printout. "A lot. The napkin revealed a variety of compounds. These are in no particular order: $C_{10}H_{20}O$, NaC1 and carbohydrates, mostly glucose and sucrose; H2O; several proteins and fatty acids; a couple of minerals; bioactive compounds include conjugated linoleic acid, L-carnitin, and carnosine; cholesterol—"

Gidget said, "They sound like compounds contained in sausage—the chorizo sausage in the empanadas he ate. Let's keep going."

"Carotenoids including lutein and zeaxanthin; some proteins including ovalbumin and conalbumin; fatty acids including oleic acid, palmitic acid, and linoleic acid. Something on the napkin had a real high level of cholesterol."

"That's the eggs in the empanadas. They account for the high cholesterol."

Daffy frowned. "Poor Larry. The cholesterol will kill you every time."

Louie plowed on. "Fatty acids—triglyceride, stearidonic acid, gamma-linolenic acid, oleic acids, erucic acid—"

"Vegetable oil for cooking. Everything checks out so far as legitimate ingredients for empanadas," Gidget said.

She continued looking at the computer printout as Louie rattled off a long list of organic and inorganic chemical compounds revealed in the chromatograph analysis. It took ten minutes to go through the list on the printout. By the end, Daffy said, "Looks like you've successfully identified all the ingredients in Chef Dreyfus's secret recipe for Sonoran breakfast empanadas. He'll be pissed if he finds out we broke his code."

Louie said, "The napkin had a lot of vomit, foam, and saliva on it. Excellent samples and why the chromatograph was able to reveal so many different chemical compounds on it."

"It sounded like there were a ton of green chili pepper compounds in the sample. No wonder Larry croaked. That much green chili peppers will do it to you every time."

Gidget shook her head. "You already said that about the cholesterol."

Louie continued, "There were *a lot* of those compounds. The other thing I noticed was the high levels of anhydrous citric acid, sodium bicarbonate, and aspirin in the sample. They were through the roof."

"That doesn't surprise me."

"Why is that?" asked Daffy.

"Because they're the main ingredients in Alka-Seltzer. He was probably guzzling the stuff all night for his nausea." Gidget's lips turned down in a noticeable frown.

"What's wrong?" asked Daffy.

"I didn't see any traces of any compounds typically found in poisonous substances." Gidget looked at Louie. "Did you?"

Louie shook his head. "Nope. None at all. About the most noxious substance in the sample was the hydrochloric acid."

"Hydrochloric acid. What's that?" asked Daffy.

"Stomach acid in his gastric juices. In his vomit."

"It's too bad. I was hoping we'd find some sort of poison that might give us a clue as to the identity of the murderer. You didn't see anything suspicious?" asked Gidget.

"I wouldn't call it suspicious, but I did see something weird." Louie held up one of the printouts.

"What did you see?"

"Look near the bottom of the list. See the traces of several plant alkaloids—cephaeline, methyl-cephaeline. You don't often see those."

Looking at the relevant section of the printout, Gidet shook her head. "Not enough info here to determine exactly what kind of alkaloid compound this might be."

"What's an alkaloid?" asked Daffy.

Gidget said, "Alkaloids are chemicals composed of carbon, hydrogen, nitrogen, oxygen, sulfur…"

"That's more info than I need to know. What do alkaloids do anyway?"

Louie was eager to show off his medical knowledge. "They're a wide variety of organic nitrogen-based compounds that have a diverse array of physiological effects on humans."

"Such as?"

"Quinine, ephedrine, morphine to name a few."

Gidget asked, "Can you do me a favor, Louie?"

"What's that?"

"Can you run the sample again and get me a more detailed breakdown on this alkaloid compound? I'd like to find out exactly what it is."

"I should be able to. There's enough sample on the napkin to run another test. I'll run it on the Aglient analyzer. It gives more detailed analysis. I would've used it before, but it was in use."

"Excellent. Also, I understand one of the pathologists at the Med School is going to do the autopsy on his body. Can you find out what the results are and let me know?"

"Sure. That should be easy. The instructors at the school are very open to sharing clinical autopsy info with their med students. What are you going to do next?" asked Louie.

"We've got to head on back to the ship. It'll be sailing in a couple of hours. Daffy and I have some more shopping to do. You can text or email me the results. Don't include his name of course," Gidget said.

Chapter 23

Saint George's, Grenada
November 14th

The ship's public address system sounded its last 'All Aboard' as Daffy and Gidget struggled up the gangplank, loaded down with shopping bags. The Bahama Princess was scheduled to cast off at seven o'clock on the dot—in ten minutes. The gangplank would have already been raised but for the kind heart of a bosun's mate. He saw two elderly women overloaded with shopping bags, chugging toward the ship, and decided to keep the gangplank lowered for them.

Daffy and Gidget had spent too much time dining with Louie, leaving little time for shopping afterward. True to form, they went shopping anyway. Both needed more souvenirs for their large assemblage of grandchildren. Daffy spotted a taxidermized iguana which she thought would be perfect for her ten-year-old grandson. No sooner had she purchased it than she remembered she had two ten-year-old grandsons, each by a different child. An iguana for one and not the other would engender angry charges of favoritism, both from her grandsons and their mothers.

Daffy reasoned that the same gift for each grandchild would be equally disastrous, so she continued shopping until her eye spotted something just as hideous as a dead iguana. The hideous item sat on a shelf filled with one-and-a-half foot young, taxidermized alligators. She looked at the store clerk while paying and said, "You watch. This is a no-win situation for me. They'll still fight over who gets which of these." Both dead animals lay in the bottom of one of Daffy's bags as she toiled up the gangplank.

As Daffy and Gidget entered the passageway to their room, they spotted the back of the Arnold Schwarzenegger guy at the other end, walking away.

"I wonder if he just came out of Harry and Jerry's suite?" asked Gidget. "The one they used to share with Larry."

Daffy said, "I don't know. What would he be doing in there?"

"Let's find out."

After depositing their shopping bags in their room, they knocked on Harry and Jerry's room and were invited inside.

The four remaining brothers sat on the room's large sectional sofa, intently watching an episode of *The Andy Griffith Show*.

"Y'all already ate?" asked Daffy.

Harry kept his eyes glued to the TV. "Yeah. We did a pretty thorough number on the Paradise Buffet. What about youse?"

"We ate at a restaurant in Saint George's, then went shopping for presents for the grandkids. By the way, we saw the crew rolling Larry's body off the ship as we were leaving—" Gidget stopped, regretted reminding them of their brother's tragic death. Not wanting to further their grief she added, "They off-loaded it in a very tasteful, dignified manner."

"Super."

"By the way, who was that guy that just came out of your suite?"

"What guy?"

Daffy said, "The big guy. Black, tight t-shirt. Lots of muscles. Looks like a smaller version of Trump Tower."

"Wasn't no one else in here but us," said Jerry.

Gidget shrugged. "Okay. He must've just been walking past your door.

Barry looked up from the TV. "Youse wanna stay and watch *Andy Griffith* with us? It's one of the show's best episodes. The one where Gomer makes a citizen's arrest when he catches Barney making an illegal U-turn."

Gidget looked at Daffy who shook her head. Gidget said, "Nah, I think we'll pass. All that shopping tired us out. We're gonna take it easy for a while. See y'all at breakfast."

"See youse."

Daffy and Gidget returned to their stateroom. Daffy was puzzled. "They certainly didn't seem too depressed about Larry's death. We've only known him for about a month, but I kind of developed a liking for the little guy. I think I was sadder to see him go than they were."

Gidget nodded. "I agree, but it's probably because they're still in a state of shock. When you lose a close friend or relative, a lot of times, you kind of go numb. Know what I mean? I was like that for a year after Sam died. Also, New Yorkers like them see so much death up there, they probably get kind of get even more numbed to it."

"Agreed, but you still look perplexed."

"I am. That guy we saw in the passageway worries me. I've seen him sneaking around this ship at odd times wearing that black, secret ops-like outfit. My gut feeling is that he's up to no good."

"You sure your gut isn't feeling the chicken pelau we ate in the restaurant this evening," Daffy said, referring to a spicy popular dish on the island.

Gidget rolled her eyes in disgust at her friend's poor taste in light of Larry's recent death.

Daffy hung her head in shame. "I know, I know. Bad taste, but I couldn't resist it. Anyway, you should always trust your gut. Should we alert the Marx Brothers about your gut feeling? That guy might be up to no good."

"Nope. I need more than a gut feeling. They'd probably think it's some sort of silly women's intuition thing. Besides, I don't think they would appreciate us interrupting *Andy Griffith* again. It *is* the citizen's arrest episode after all. Nevertheless, I'd like to find out exactly who that guy is. If I could just find out his name."

"What if you find out his name? What good does that do you?" asked Daffy.

"If I knew his name, I could try to find out more info about him on the Internet."

"Good luck with that."

"I could get my daughter who worked for that company that did security background checks for the Federal government to help. She knows how to find out everything about everyone."

"Yeah. She did do that for what…about five years?"

Gidget nodded. "She found out some good stuff on Sam."

"Such as."

"Eef I toll you, I'd haf to keel you."

"So, how do we find out the Arnold Schwarzenegger guy's name?" Daffy asked.

"Good question, my dear Daffy. Follow me."

Shortly afterward, Gidget and Daffy stood outside the Cruise Director's Office looking at the Bahama Princess Organization Chart. It showed all the ship's departments and names of the heads of each of those departments. As they studied it, the Assistant Cruise Director walked up.

"May I help you ladies," he said.

"Yes. We're wondering what department to check with to locate another passenger," said Gidget. "We saw him from a distance. Good looking guy. A real hunk. We'd like to meet him."

He smiled. "I understand. A little shipboard romance. Maybe I can help. What's his name?"

"We don't know. We've seen him once or twice from far away, but we were never able to get to him. It's a big ship, and he's a big guy."

"Several big guys on this ship, but mostly around the middle… if you get my drift." He patted his own stomach. "If you don't know his name, it's going to be kind of hard to find him. You may be able to identify him from one of the group photos we take when passengers board the first time. I could give you his name from that."

"Oh, yeah! I'd forgotten about the souvenir photographs."

"We also take them for security reasons. That way, we have pictures of *all* of our passengers in case something happens."

"Where do you keep the photos?" asked Daffy.

"Right around the corner here in another passageway. We always line the bulkhead with copies of the photographs so passengers can see whose on board if they want to."

Gidget and Daffy followed him to the other passageway. Three long rows of pictures lined it.

"There must be over a thousand pictures here," said Daffy.

The assistant director said, "We have twenty-one-hundred and thirty-three passengers, but we don't take individual photographs of each of them unless a passenger boards alone. We photograph each group of passengers as they board."

Gidget said, "There's still going to be a lot of pictures for us to look at."

"Let me know when you finish, and I'll help you find his name."

An hour later, Gidget and Daffy found the assistant director. He asked, "Did you find the person you were looking for?"

Gidget frowned. "We looked at every damn picture on the wall, and he wasn't in any of them. Two hours of squinting."

"The number of wrinkles around my eyes doubled," said Daffy.

"You ladies must have *thought* you saw someone you knew. *Every* passenger absolutely gets his or her picture taken. Like I said, it's for security as well as souvenir reasons."

"So, you're saying the huge guy we saw is not on board this ship?"

"All I can say is that we photograph everyone who comes on board this ship."

Daffy and Gidget dragged themselves to the nearest lounge afterward. Gidget said, "My brain is fried."

"I've gone cross-eyed, just like that guy in Miami that was looking at all those hanging chads," said Daffy. "Did you notice who was in one of the photos?"

"No. Who?"

"That senator from… Lord, I am going senile. I can't remember his name or even what state he's from. I just know I recognized his face. He's on the cable news shows all the time."

"I never picked up on it."

"Maybe it'll come to me. Anyway, back to the Arnold Schwarzenegger guy. What now?"

Gidget said, "This is strange. The Assistant Cruise Director said *everyone* who boards the ship gets his photograph taken as a memento and for security reasons. We did see our guy on board, but he's not in a cruise photograph."

"Correct, but what does that mean?"

"That means we saw someone on board who's *not* on board."

Chapter 24

12° 6' 13.6116" North, 62° 41' 26.808" West
November 15th

The gentle motion of the ship acted like a dose of Ambien, and Daffy was sound asleep when her alarm went off at five o'clock in the morning. She got out of bed, put on a Lululemon tank top with matching running shorts, and hollered for Gidget to wake up.

Gidget hollered back from the kitchen. "I'm already up. Been throwing up again. What are you doing up so early?"

"I gotta powerwalk off that dinner in Grenada yesterday if I'm ever gonna see my feet again," Daffy said.

Gidget winced. "Do you think it might seem disrespectful to powerwalk the morning after Larry's death? Like nothing ever happened? Maybe we should take a day off and be more solemn."

"You said yourself last evening the other brothers might be in a state of shock. Kind of numb. I doubt they'll care what we do so long as it doesn't interfere with them watching *Andy Griffith* or *MASH*. Besides, it might be good for us. Clear our brains."

Gidget gave up. "Alright. Let me get my workout clothes on."

"You sure you're up for walking after throwing up?

"Yeah. It's passed. I'm fine now."

Fifteen minutes later, they huffed and puffed around the promenade deck. Their conversation mixed yesterday's tragic event in between texts from their offspring. Gidget's iPhone buzzed, and she began reading.

"What's up?" asked Daffy.

"Latest granddaughter calamity," said Gidget. "A week before we sailed… I gave Susan her first bottle of perfume for her eighth birthday… a bottle of Poison. Now, Cheryl says Susan drowns herself in it every morning when she dresses for school. Here, look at her text."

> "The cloud of Poison around Susan is so thick, you can barely see her when she walks out of her bedroom every morning. Her

teacher has complained. Can you text her and tell her to tone it down? She won't listen to me, but she'll listen to Mimi."

"Another grandmotherly intervention. Happens more and more the older my grandchildren get," said Gidget.

Daffy nodded. "It does. Sounds like your daughter still needs her mother."

"Yeah, they all do. Susan's at that age… Whatever mom says, she wants to do the opposite."

"My granddaughter Amelia listens to me better than her mother. And I don't blame her." Daffy looked down at her iPhone as an incoming text arrived.

The conversation had returned to the Marx Brothers and Larry's strange death yesterday by the time the body tumbled head-over-heels into the emerald blue waters of the Caribbean. After Gidget and Daffy screamed "MAN OVERBOARD," the ship's alert sounded, and Captain Omen initiated standard man overboard protocols.

The quartermaster made the ship come full stop. Omen ordered lifebuoys emitting smoke and signals be deployed over the starboard side. Lookouts assumed their assigned positions. The communications officer broadcast man overboard notices to all ships at sea as well as to the required nautical authorities.

The quartermaster began hand steering the ship, allowing her to execute a Williamson turn. This complicated maneuver, when executed correctly, would eventually result in the Bahama Princess returning to the body's point of entry into the water.

Meanwhile, Daffy, Gidget, the other passengers, and the members of the crew continued to lean on the deck's handrail, desperately looking for a body to surface, which did not happen. The body had most certainly fallen from one of the Marx Brothers' staterooms, and the kaleidoscope of colors suggested it was one of them wearing a Hawaiian flower shirt. Daffy knew it could not be Larry, who had choked yesterday morning.

"It definitely wasn't Larry."

"Yep. Definitely not Larry."

"Gary?"

"Nope."

"Barry?"

"Nope."

"Harry?"

"Nope."

"That only leaves Jerry."

"Yep."

"I couldn't make out his face. Could you?"

"Nope."

"Then how do you know it was Jerry?"

"He was wearing huarache sandals."

"Huarache sandals? How could you see his shoes when we couldn't even see his face?" asked Daffy.

Despite the solemnity of the moment, Gidget couldn't resist. "Watch what you say. Don't let Lilly hear you refer to the footwear Jerry was wearing as *shoes*. You know she believes huaraches are sandals, not shoes."

"And you gig me about my morbid humor!" Daffy unsuccessfully tried to stifle a snicker.

Gidget looked up at the balcony again. "I still don't see any Marx Brothers. I wonder if something is wrong up there. Let's go check and see who's left. I'd like to find out who that was looking out from the room. I'm sure it wasn't one of the brothers."

"Whoever goes in their room first will have to tell them they've lost another brother."

Ten minutes later, they hurried up the stairs to their floor. As they entered the passageway to their rooms, Gidget spotted someone heading in the other direction, away from them.

Gidget tried to holler at him to stop but was out of breath from the climb and could only manage to cough. She looked at Daffy and breathed heavily. "Was that Stokes coming out of Jerry's stateroom? Tell him to stop."

Daffy was also out of breath. "It's too late. He disappeared."

They knocked on the stateroom formerly occupied by Harry and Larry and Jerry, now occupied by only Harry. No answer.

"Keep knocking," said Gidget. "Maybe Harry's still asleep."

"Either that, or he forgot to put in his hearing aid this morning."

Repeated knocking again resulted in no response. They tried Gary and Barry's stateroom with similar results.

"No one here and it's not even seven o'clock. I'm worried. Let's get Stokes or Yvette to open the doors for us," Gidget said. At that point, a door three doors down opened, and Yvette stepped out. She saw Gidget and Daffy and froze, a look of shock and horror on her face.

"Yvette," Gidget said. "Can you come here?"

Yvette tugged at the hemline of her uniform's short skirt. It was a classic French maid uniform—short black dress, low-cut bodice, and white apron. The dress had ridden up, exposing too much thigh, resulting in her attempts to lower it.

"*Oui, mesdames*. How may I help you?"

Gidget asked, "Can you let us into our traveling companions' staterooms? We don't seem to be able to rouse them."

"*Oui*, *madame*."

Yvette opened the door and led them into the stateroom Harry had shared with Larry and Jerry. Gidget and Daffy were shocked. Half of a dozen empty bottles of vodka and three empty bottles of gin lay strewn on the sitting room floor and out onto the balcony. They had to watch their step as the bottles were surrounded by pools of clear liquid. Gidget walked over to the bar.

"It looks like they cleaned out the bar last night."

Yvette nodded. "*Oui madame*. *Monsieur* Stokes told me zey rang for him about eleven o'clock last night and ordered more vodka and gin."

"Let's check the other stateroom."

"*Oui madame*."

Barry and Gary's stateroom was empty.

Gidget asked, "Where is Stokes? Usually both of you are busy in our suite this time of the morning. What have you been doing?"

"I… I have been engaged elsewhere."

"You were not in Mister Vanderhoff's stateroom when he fell?"

"No *madame*! He has fallen?"

"Yes. What have you been doing?"

I… I cannot say. Eet was a private matter."

Chapter 25

12° 6' 13.6116" North, 62° 41' 26.808" West
November 15th

Just as Gidget was about to press Yvette for more information, her phone rang. She answered. "Hey sweetie. I'm kinda busy right now. Make it quick."

There was a long pause as Gidget listened.

"I told you to buy at least five or as many as they have on the shelf. Tootie is only three, you know. You always want a backup that you can sneak in while they're asleep, then tell them the little critter found his way back while they slept."

Pause.

"I know, I know, but trust me. She'll take her favorite stuffie to college with her just like you did. All girls take their favorite stuffie to college with them."

Long pause.

"Look, I gotta go now. Got something important going on. We'll talk later. Toodeloo."

Daffy smiled. "I bet Tootie lost a stuffie and won't stop crying."

Gidget nodded and turned back to Yvette. "You realize you will not be able to keep it a private matter when you are questioned by the Chief Security Officer, don't you?"

Yvette pouted. "*Oui, madame*."

"So, you might as well tell us anyway."

"*No madame*. That will be between myself and the Chief Security Officer."

Gidget saw she was not going to get any further with Yvette. "All right, Yvette. You may go now."

"*Oui, madame*." Yvette turned and exited.

After Yvette was gone, Daffy asked, "Wonder what Yvette was so nervous and flustered about?"

Gidget said, "Good question. She acted as if she had been up to no good. I wonder if her nervousness is in any way connected with Jerry's plunge?"

"She is French. Don't they just naturally act strange?"

"Sounds like you have a case of Francophobia to me. I think later on we need to pursue an answer to your first question. Why was she so nervous and flustered? First, let's go see if the remaining Marx Brothers are in Azul."

Gidget proved correct. Harry, Barry, and Gary sat gorging themselves on eggs Benedict. Harry looked up as they approached.

"What youse been doing?"

"Looking for y'all," said Gidget. "Eating kind of early aren't y'all?"

"Had to. Drank *waaaaay* too much last night and had to get something in our bellies."

"Why didn't Jerry come with you?"

"He drank more than all of us combined. We hollered at him before we left but got no response. He must've been dead to the world."

"Moreso than you know," said Daffy.

"Whatcha mean?"

Gidget sat next to Barry and placed her hand on Barry's shoulder. "I hate to have to tell you this, but it looks like Jerry fell overboard from your balcony. He fell right in front of us as we were walking underneath our staterooms. We watched him tumble over and over before he hit the water. He hit it so fast that his body never surfaced. Didn't y'all hear the man overboard announcement?"

"We did but didn't know it was about Jerry." Gary wiped Hollandaise sauce off his mouth.

Daffy said, "It's like Gidg said—we were powerwalking almost underneath when he fell. He just missed us by a few feet. He was revolving like a top, but Gidg was able to make out his huaraches."

Barry shook his head. "Jerry loved his huaraches."

"It figures," Gary said.

Gidget was surprised. "What do you mean it figures—revolving like a top or wearing huaraches?"

"Neither one. Jerry was real depressed last night after Larry's death. We all were, but he seemed a lot more depressed than the rest of us. That's why we drank so much, but he drank even more."

Harry nodded. "He must've been so depressed that he decided to sleep with the fishes."

Harry signaled the waiter so Gidget and Daffy could order something to eat. After he left to place their orders, Harry became thoughtful.

"Larry and Jerry was good little brothers. They was crazy at times, but they had good hearts."

Gary nodded. "That's two of our brothers in two days. This boat must be jinxed."

"Two back-to-back like that is weird, but Jerry was so depressed last night about Larry's death," Barry said.

Harry observed, "Jerry always was the moodiest of us. I remember him pitching fits all the time when he was growing up."

Gary managed a small smile. "He was a pistol when his hormones kicked in when he turned thirteen. The stories I could tell."

"He couldn't keep his mind off the girls. Mamma used to find dirty mags under his bed all the time."

"Remember… what was that girl's name?" asked Barry. "When he was fifteen."

"Gianna. He moped over her day and night for months, then that… What's that ass—" Harry blushed. "Ladies, please excuse my language. What's the name of that jerk that gives her a ring, and they goes steady? Crap, my memory gets worse every year. Anyway, Jerry got back at the guy. He takes a dump in the jerk's school locker."

The brothers reminisced about Jerry for thirty minutes before Harry returned to the main topic.

"What can youse tell us about his fall?"

Daffy shrugged. "Not much other than what we already said. We were walking almost under our staterooms when he fell. It must've been a hundred feet down. He just missed hitting the deck of the ship. He was so close that we could've shook hands with him on the way down."

"Tell us about last night. Sounds like he was very upset last night," Gidget said.

Harry said, "Not much to tell. He was depressed. We all was, which is why we was watching *Andy Griffith* when youse came by.

To take our minds off of Larry's death. When did youse come by? Must've been a little after seven o'clock because that's always when the first of the *Andy Griffith* shows starts."

Harry looked at Barry and Gary, and they nodded.

Gidget put on her best Perry Mason face. "Okay. What next? Give me all the details."

"Well… uh. It was the 'Citizen's Arrest' episode. The one where Gomer makes a citizen's arrest when he catches Barney making an illegal U-turn—"

Excitement in his voice, Barry interrupted, "Can youse believe it? The guy directing that episode was the guy what played Luke McCoy on the *Real McCoys* TV show back in the fifties. We noticed it when the credits came on after the show was over dat Richard Crenna directed dat very episode—"

Daffy got excited. "I never knew dat… uh… that. Citizen's Arrest was one of my favorite *Andy Griffith*'s. And you say Richard Crenna directed it. I loved him in *Rambo*."

"I talked to a guy once—one of them special ops kind of guys—and he said the Richard Crenna character in that *Rambo* movie was unrealistic—"

Gidget said, "Let's get back on track here. So, the four of you continued to watch TV after Daffy and I left… right?"

The three remaining Marx Brother's all nodded. Harry said, "That's correct."

"And Jerry was with y'all?"

"Yep."

"What happened next?"

Chapter 26

12° 6' 13.6116" North, 62° 41' 26.808" West
November 15th

Before the Marx Brothers could answer Gidget's question, Harry and Gary had to use the bathroom, making their usual prostate jokes before leaving. When they returned, Harry set the tone for his brother's untimely death.

"It's like I said before we had to go pee. We was all feeling kind of low due to Larry's death that morning, so we decides to do a toast to him—"

"To honor his memory," said Gary.

"Yeah. To honor his memory. So's, we pull out the hooch—"

"Was it vodka?" asked Gidget. "We saw clear liquid on the floor."

Harry nodded. "Yeah. I believe we did start with vodka, and after I pours us a round, Barry says 'Here's to our brother. May his next destination be a warm one.' And—"

Barry interrupted. "Let me clarify that. By warm one, I did *not* mean that his next destination should be in hell. I meant someplace warm… like a desert. He would have loved it if he was going to a desert somewhere."

"Yeah. Larry was the main reason we moved to Florida in the first place… its warm climate. Anyway, I added my thoughts to Barry's toast. I says 'He is… was a loyal goombah,' uh, I mean brother—"

Gidget was getting impatient. "But what happened after the toast? That's what I'm interested in."

"We had another toast."

"What about after that?"

"Another toast."

Gidget feared Harry's response if she asked another "What happened after that," so she tried another tact.

"I'm sorry to be so inquisitive. It's just that I loved your brother so. He was dear, sweet man. Anyway, it sounds like you kept drinking—"

Barry nodded vigorously. "You can say that again."

Gidget had to resist the urge to repeat her last sentence. Instead, she said, "And was Jerry with you the whole time?"

"Yeah. The whole time."

"How long did you drink? What time did you go to bed?"

Harry took his time answering. "That's a good question. Let me see. I think we turned in sometime shortly after midnight."

He looked at his brothers for confirmation, and both nodded.

Gidget looked at Barry and Gary. "And you two went straight back to your room?"

The brothers looked at Harry. He seemed okay with the way the broad was questioning them. Both brothers said, "Yep."

Gidget looked at Harry. "Jerry was with you when you went to sleep?"

"Hell no!" Harry exclaimed.

Gidget felt slightly satisfied. Now, she was getting somewhere. "He wasn't?"

"Of course not. I ain't had a brother sleep in the same bed with me since I was five-years-old."

"I didn't mean that. What I meant was when you went into your bedroom to go to sleep, was Jerry by himself in the living room… drinking?"

"Yeah."

Gidget sighed. Progress with the Marx Brothers was measured in inches not feet. "And when you woke up this morning, where was Jerry?"

Harry shrugged. "I guess he was in his room. I didn't see him."

"What happened next?"

"I turned on the TV and watched the morning news shows for a while till Gary and Barry pops their heads in and says, 'Let's go to breakfast.' We needed something on our guts after all that booze."

"Where was Jerry when Gary and Barry came into your room?"

"Still in bed, I guess."

Gidget looked at Barry and Gary. "Did you boys see Jerry?"

Gary and Barry shook their heads. "Nah."

Gidget weighed asking the next question. It might make Harry defensive. "I guess you didn't you peek in on Jerry before you left?"

"You know the old saying 'Let sleeping dogs lie.' Thats what I did."

Gidget said, "Then the three of you came here to Azul, leaving Jerry alone in his and Harry's room… as far as y'all know?"

Harry looked at his brothers for confirmation. They nodded and he said, "Yeah. As far as we know."

"No one, neither Stokes nor Yvette for example, came into your room before you left, and you didn't see anyone hanging around your stateroom when you left?"

"Nope. No one at all."

"Why're you asking all these questions?" asked Gary. "You ain't no cop."

Barry came to Gidget's defense. If he wanted more nookie, he had better cooperate with her investigation.

"She can ask any and all the questions she wants to. It's like she said, she loved Jerry like a brother."

Gidget figured she had pressed them for enough information for the time being and decided to let the conversation drift back to other topics. An incoming text on Daffy's phone provided the perfect excuse to do just that. She extracted it and began reading.

"It's Olivia, my daughter."

"What does she want?" asked Gidget.

"It's Amelia again. Another crisis. She wants to get her ears pierced. Oh, to be eight-years-old again."

"Don't tell me. All the other little girls have pierced ears. My daughters always used that one on me."

"Yep."

"And Olivia wants you to text Amelia and talk her out of it."

"Yep."

"What you gonna say?" asked Gidget.

"I'm going to scare the crap out of her. Tell her she could lose her earlobes from an infection."

After Daffy finished keying her frightening message to Amelia, Gidget resumed questioning. "I can believe it when you say y'all put away the booze last night. We saw a lot of empty liquor bottles and spilled vodka all over the floor of your room."

"Youse went into our room?" asked Harry.

"After Jerry went overboard, we were concerned and went back upstairs. We got Yvette to let us into your room to check on you and saw the bottles and spills. Then we came up here to Azul to see if y'all were here. What about the bottles and spills? How'd they get there?"

"I noticed them myself while I was watching TV this morning. We drank a whole lot last night. That's for sure. I'm not sure how it got spilt. We all might've done spilt the booze, or maybe Jerry might've done it by himself."

Barry nodded. "Like we said, we was all very bummed out about Larry's death."

Gidget said, "I guess that explains the bottles and alcohol on the floor, but it doesn't explain the person I saw in your stateroom right after Jerry fell this morning. Like I said, a real big guy… looking down at the crowd on the deck."

"And you don't know who it was?" asked Harry.

"Yeah. I don't know who it was. Couldn't see who it was. He or she was standing back… inside the stateroom. They backed away from the door real quick when they saw me look up."

Harry looked at Daffy. "You see him too? In our room?"

Daffy shook her head. "Not really. By the time I looked up, he or she was gone."

Harry grimaced. "Ehhhh… You know, maybe you saw someone who was in a different room. Maybe a floor or two above or below ours. Maybe a room or two down the hall."

Barry nodded. "Yeah. They wasn't no one in our room when we left to go to breakfast, and we locked it when we left."

Gary said, "Jerry was probably still asleep when Barry and I came to Harry's stateroom *and* when we left."

"Wasn't nobody else in the room when we left."

"And I locked it when we left," Harry said.

"And you are sure you didn't see Stokes or Yvette anywhere around when you left?" asked Gidget.

"Well, we did see Yvette going into one of the rooms down the hallway. A couple of doors down."

Gidget composed her next words carefully. "I wonder if the stuff on the floor… the empty bottles, the alcohol, might have been put there on purpose."

"You mean to *make* him slip?" asked Harry. "No way!"

"No way," echoed Gary. "Who would've done that anyway?"

"Look. What probably happened was all of us did mess up the place with all our boozing last night, and Jerry got up to pee this morning after we left and was on his way to get something to drink in the kitchen and he slipped along the way. He was probably still groggy from all the booze, staggered onto the balcony, and slipped in whatever was spilled on the floor."

"Yeah. Yeah. I bet that's it," said Barry.

"That's good," said Gary.

"What are y'all gonna do now?" asked Daffy.

"We're gonna go check in with Captain Omen to see if they've found Jerry yet. What about youse?" asked Harry.

"We'll be in our room," said Gidget. "I don't feel much like doing anything today after Jerry's death."

Chapter 27

12° 6' 13.6116" North, 62° 41' 26.808" West
November 15th

Back in their stateroom, Gidget expressed her frustration. "I don't think I ever heard that many duh's and dat's at one time. After a while, it can be tough translating from Brooklyn English into Southern English. And getting answers out of them was like pulling teeth."

"But you were impressive!" said Daffy. "I've never seen you like that before. The way you questioned Harry… You were Hercule Poirot on steroids."

"I feel more like Inspector Clouseau on steroids. I was merely questioning like any investigator would do."

"Questioning? Girl, you even made me nervous. This cruise has brought out the real Gidget Smurfitt. What next?"

"Let's check out Jerry's stateroom again. I didn't have enough time to do a thorough job this morning."

They summoned Yvette, and she let them into Jerry's room again. After she left, they stood still for a while in the living room.

Daffy asked, "Whatcha looking for?"

"I'm trying to get a better feel what could have caused Jerry to go over the balcony," said Gidget. "Notice how Harry acted at breakfast?"

Daffy shrugged.

Gidget explained, "His Noo Yark accent. The more I questioned him, the more nervous he got, and the thicker his accent got."

"You're right. All three of 'em—their accents regressed."

"That was symptomatic of some sort of defensiveness. When someone gets defensive, they forget and let their façade drop. Their true persona comes out. I got the same vibes from Harry I usually get from doctor shoppers when I start to question them."

"What's a doctor shopper?"

"A patient who goes from doctor to doctor until he finds one willing to write a prescription for a controlled substance he wants."

"You must be the Agatha Christie of controlled substances."

Gidget said, "Look around and see if there is anything unusual in this room. I'm gonna check out Jerry's bedroom."

Daffy walked around the living room carefully so as not to disturb the empty bottles laying on the floor. She gingerly stepped over the puddles of clear liquid. She noticed no new clues.

"Daff!" Gidget shouted. "Come here into Jerry's bedroom."

Daffy hurried into the room. "What's up?"

"Look at this." Gidget held up a three-inch thick black binder.

"What is it?"

Gidget opened it and read, "U.S. Navy Diving Manual. Revision 7. Dated December 1st 2016."

Daffy took it and turned to the Table of Contents. "Someone's highlighted a couple of chapters—one on Open-Circuit SCUBA, Closed-Circuit SCUBA, Rebreathers. Why would Jerry do that?"

"Look at this." Gidget held up another binder.

Daffy opened it and read, "FINA High Diving Manual. This is all about how to dive off of high diving boards."

"Yeah. I found this box with this stuff in it under Jerry's bed."

They sat on the bed and rummaged through the box, finding more materials on underwater and high diving. Gidget asked, "Did you see anything odd in Harry's room the nights you spent there?"

"Nope. It was too dark to see anything. We always kept the lights off so we didn't have to look at each other's wrinkles and age spots."

"Let's go back into the living room."

Gidget and Daffy stood motionless in the living room, looking at empty bottles and spills. Gidget asked, "Harry told us he didn't know who made this mess, didn't he?"

Daffy nodded. "It might've been all of them, or just Jerry."

"Either way, the mess would have been made accidentally?"

"That's what he implied."

"Then why does this mess not look accidental?"

"Whatcha mean?"

"Look at the way these bottles are laying. It's like someone carefully placed them. Almost equally spaced."

"You're right."

"And look at the spills."

"Okay. What about them?"

"What happens when you spill a liquid?"

"It splatters all over the floor. You have a big mess to wipe up. After five kids and a dozen grandkids, I should know."

"Correct, my dear Daffy. When a liquid hits the floor, it splashes everywhere. Lots of drops, small puddles, big puddles and all scattered randomly everywhere. Look at these spills. Each is about the same size and a perfect circle. Each looks carefully poured."

Daffy looked at the spills, remained silent, and slowly nodded.

Gidget asked, "What's odd about all them empty bottles?"

"There's no messages in them? It's spin-the-bottle on steroids? That many empty bottles is a recycler's wet dream? I give up."

Gidget rolled her eyes. "No broken bottles. Four old men get drunk, and no bottles are broken? At least a few should be broken."

"Yeahhh! You're right. Great point. Anything else?"

"It's as if the bottles make a pattern leading you to the balcony as if someone wanted you to go there. And one empty bottle on the balcony. Did someone place the bottles so as to lead an investigator to the balcony with a trail of spilled alcohol along the way? To make it look like Jerry was drunk and accidentally fell from the balcony. I've seen enough in here for now. Let's go."

Daffy walked to the door, opened it, and screamed!

The Arnold Schwarzenegger guy stood there, his hand reaching out to turn the doorknob. He looked at the room number on the door, then at Daffy.

"Sorry, wrong floor." He abruptly turned and briskly walked away.

Daffy turned around and looked at Gidget. "What the hell was he doing here?"

Gidget said, "That was just your imagination. He doesn't exist. Remember?"

At twelve thirty, Daffy and Gidget headed to Glutton's Paradise for lunch. The remaining three Marx Brothers were already there along with Veronica and Naomi.

"What's the latest on Jerry?" asked Gidget.

"Nothing so far," said Harry. "He's disappeared. No body at all. A bunch of ships and aircraft are circling the area. The Bahama Princess has resumed course."

"We feel so sorry for y'all," said Daffy. "It must be terrible to lose two brothers, one after another like that."

"Yeah, it is."

"What are y'all gonna do now?" asked Gidget.

Gary said, "I'm gonna go play some Bocce ball for a while. Kind of take my mind off of Jerry… and Larry."

"I'm gonna go take a snooze. Too much for me this morning," Barry said.

"I'm gonna take a nap like Barry. Wanna join me?" Harry looked at Daffy. "Big day tomorrow."

"Big Day? How so?" asked Daffy.

"I'm going parasailing." There was a noticeable lack of enthusiasm in Harry's voice as he spoke.

"Parasailing at your age! I had hoped you were joking about that. Surely, you're not gonna still go parasailing after Jerry's death?"

Veronica said, "We were discussing it before y'all got here. Naomi thinks like you do, Daffy. That he shouldn't go. I say he should. Jerry and Larry aren't here, so they won't mind. And life goes on. After all, Harry is only seventy-five. He's been talking about parasailing ever since I boarded. It's like when George Bush senior skydived. He was ninety when he made his last jump."

Naomi shook her head. "I say skydiving *and* parasailing is lunacy at any age."

"Have you talked to Tyler about this?" asked Gidget.

Harry shrugged. "Yeah. He's okay with it if Doc Mokulus says it's okay, and the Doc's already said it's okay. We'll be anchoring offshore in Aruba tomorrow."

Veronica said, "Just think. Harry will get to sightsee the whole island of Aruba from five hundred feet up."

Back in their stateroom, Daffy looked at Gidget. "He's talked about it ever since we went on the tour of the ship, but I never thought he'd go through with it. I thought he was trying to impress me—like the teenage boys did in high school."

Gidget was exasperated. "Parasailing after two brothers have died. What's going on in his head? I can understand Jerry committing suicide after his brother dies. But parasailing after Jerry drowns?"

"These brothers are strange."

"I wonder if it's some sort of suicidal death wish after his two brothers' deaths? That damn Veronica seemed awful anxious for him to go parasailing, didn't she?"

"I got the feeling that Harry would've canceled if she hadn't been pushing him."

"Daff, why don't you go take a little nap with him and pick Harry's brain?"

"Might as well. Might be the last nookie I get for a while if he breaks his neck parasailing. What're you gonna do?"

"I'm gonna find Barry and engage in a little afternoon delight myself."

Afternoon delights were followed by dinner where they discussed what everyone was doing that night. Daffy already knew the answer.

"Don't tell me. You boys are gonna watch *Andy Griffith* and *MASH*."

"Why don't youse join us? Tonight is the Captain Tuttle episode," Harry said.

Gary agreed, "Captain Tuttle was the best *MASH* episode ever."

"I don't remember Captain Tuttle. Who was he?" asked Gidget.

Barry got excited. "How could *anyone* forget Captain Tuttle? He was a non-existent Army officer Hawkeye and Trapper invented in order to steal supplies for a Korean orphanage. They have to keep making up more stuff about him in order to keep fooling everyone."

"They even make up a personnel record for this Captain Tuttle, like he's a real person. And the stupid Army people send his back pay to the MASH unit, and Hawkeye gets it donated to the orphanage—" Gary was laughing so hard he could not continue.

Barry took over. "And they had made Tuttle look like such a great hero that the Army was gonna award him a medal, so Hawkeye and Trapper had to kill Tuttle off before the general could present him the medal—"

Harry picked up. "The best part of the show is when Hawkeye gives Tuttle's eulogy after he supposedly dies. Hawkeye says Tuttle jumped into combat without a parachute. He forgot his parachute! It's a classic case of fooling people with something that ain't real."

Daffy and Gidget looked on in bewilderment. Could these guys be for real?! Gidget said, "I think we're gonna have to pass on *MASH*. Too much sun today. See y'all in the morning."

Back in their stateroom, Gidget said, "I guess we needn't have worried about the Marx Brothers taking Jerry's death too badly. Watching *MASH*! Unbelievable!"

"Find out anything during your afternoon delight?" asked Daffy.

"Nothing. We talked about his dead brothers, and he was real broken up about it. I knew he was grieving over them when he declined my offer of sex. You?"

"Harry enjoyed having his way with me as if nothing had happened, so I enjoyed having my way with him as well. Harry has got a strange way of dealing with losing two brothers… although I can't say it's not a pretty good way. I think he overdosed on the Viagra this afternoon. Other than that, I didn't find out anything more than we already know."

"Barry acted depressed, while Harry takes it in stride. New Yorkers deal with personal tragedy in different ways, I guess. I can't believe Doctor Mokulus okayed a seventy-five-year-old man to parasail. I'd feel better about his clinical skills if he'd been able to revive Larry while he was choking. That's one reason why I don't feel too confident about him okaying Harry to parasail."

"Too bad the Bahama Princess doesn't have a minimum height requirement on their parasail ride like some of them rides at Disney do—the ones where you have to stand next to a ruler. None of the Marx Brothers would be tall enough to parasail."

Chapter 28

13° 4' 53.8284" North, 68° 55' 6.582" West
November 16th

Gidget and Daffy slept in the next morning. Both woke up groggy after a night of restless sleep. Two deaths in two days had taken its toll. They met several times in the dark of the living room, either pacing the floor or medicating themselves. At seven-forty-five, they sat on their balcony guzzling coffee.

Daffy said, “My alarm went off at five-fifteen, but I couldn’t get up for another sunrise powerwalk. Especially after yesterday’s sunrise surprise. My get-up and go done rolled over and hit the snooze button.”

Gidget suggested, “Let’s powerwalk later this morning, about ten thirty—”

“Powerwalk after two deaths?”

“Hey, if Harry can parasail today, then we can powerwalk and grab a bite to eat afterward for an early lunch. The ship should be anchored off Aruba by then. We can shower and change clothes after lunch before Harry parasails.”

“Yeah. That way, any calories we lose powerwalking will be offset by the calories we consume at lunch. I hate losing weight.”

Gidget made a face. “Wasn’t that an example of sarcasm? You forgot I flunked my sarcasm classes in college.”

“Not me. I made an A in Sarcasm 101.”

“When is Harry going parasailing?” asked Gidget.

“One o’clock.”

“He’ll have a lot of witnesses.”

“A lot of witnesses? Why would anyone want to watch a seventy-five-year-old man parasail?”

“I see why you made A’s in sarcasm.”

Gidget and Daffy tried to get their brains around the perplexing investigation as they walked around the promenade deck later that morning. Gidget expressed their frustration.

“Even after all our efforts, about all we can say is that two of the Marx Brothers are dead. No trace of poison in the sample I took from Larry. I wish Louie would get back to us with the autopsy results.

And I'm still suspicious about whoever it was in Jerry's stateroom when he went overboard."

"And who is this Arnold Schwarzenegger guy?" asked Daffy.

"And why is he not on the passenger rolls? Things seem to get more and more confusing the further along this goes."

"And don't forget the empty bottles and spills in Jerry's room. Who made them?"

Gidget nodded. "Good point."

"It's a mystery, but I know Gidget the Gumshoe is going to get to the bottom of it."

Gidget's phone buzzed. She pulled it out and looked at it. "I just got a text from Lizzie."

"What's she say?"

"They appreciated the text congratulating them on the success of the *Real Widows*. She says the show's a megahit. They can't wait for us to get home. She says with you and me on the show with them, Cordell thinks it will get even better ratings."

"True. What else?" asked Daffy.

"She's been so busy with the show that she had to cancel her tummy tuck."

"That's too bad. She was looking forward to buffing up her belly. Rescheduling a tummy tuck with Beauvisage will be tough. I hear it's a popular procedure, and from what else I hear, he's booked up for months."

"Get this. She says she's not going to have him do a tummy tuck after all. She's going to get Beauvisage to do a vampire breast lift instead—" Gidget interrupted her narrative. "Look, it's Veronica and Naomi coming toward us."

Daffy lowered her voice. "Doesn't look like their powerwalks are doing them any good."

"Don't let them hear you say that, or our Mexican Train games will probably get pretty hostile."

"I'd say they're pretty hostile already. Afterall, five women are playing the game."

Gidget said, "Well, I'm not gonna talk about others being overweight. I live in a glass house in that respect. Although, you are correct about their lack of success in weight loss from powerwalking."

"Part of the reason they're not losing any weight is they're walking in the wrong direction," Daffy said.

"What do you mean?"

"They're walking clockwise around the ship."

"So?"

"They should be walking counter-clockwise like us."

"What's the direction you walk got to do with losing weight?" asked Gidget. "Veronica! Naomi! How good to see you!"

The other women said, "Daffy! Gidget! It's wonderful to see both of you too."

Thus began fifteen minutes of gossiping and lying.

"We heard about poor Jerry," said Naomi. "We heard y'all were real close when he dove—er, fell off his balcony."

"He whizzed by us through the air… must've been spinning through the air at a hundred miles an hour… ten yards away from us," said Daffy.

"That must've been terrible seeing all that money go down the drain."

"Naomi!" said Veronica.

Gidget restrained herself. "We never thought of Jerry in that way."

"Ignore her. Tell me… Are y'all sure it was Jerry? How could y'all tell it was him and not somebody else? Was it his Hawaiian flower shirt?"

Naomi said, "All of those brothers wear Hawaiian flower shirts. Most of the old men on this boat wear Hawaiian flower shirts."

"The shirt was part of it," said Daffy. "I think I saw an old woodie station wagon and some Dos Equis beer bottles spinning through the air—like the ones on one of Jerry's shirts. But it was the huarache sandals he was wearing. Gidget spotted them. Y'all know how much Jerry liked huarache sandals."

"I always though huaraches were shoes, not sandals," Veronica said.

"It depends on your footwear belief system."

The discussion continued to deteriorate for several minutes until Gidget received a text from one of her daughters.

"What's up?" asked Daffy.

"Gloria needs my help," said Gidget. "She's dreading taking Bobbie for her flu shot and wants my advice."

"Oh God. She has my sympathy."

Veronica said, "Bobbie must be Gloria's child."

Gidget nodded. "Eight-years-old. Screams and cries every year when Gloria takes her for the shot."

Naomi said, "Don't tell her they're going for the shot. Tell Bobbie they're going to Chuck E. Cheese or some place."

Veronica advised a more aggressive technique. "Tell her to tie her hands and feet and gag and blindfold her."

Gidget did not look up from texting. "Actually, Gloria *has* contemplated binding and gagging the child—"

"Doesn't every mother?" asked Daffy.

"But she's worried Bobbie might call one of those child abuse hotlines. Bobbie's got all the numbers memorized and threatens her mom all the time."

"My kids used to threaten me about calling one of those hotlines all the time," said Daffy. "What are you telling Gloria to do?"

Gidget looked up. "I told her to use Xanax."

"I know you make your living off of pills, but giving a child Xanax?" asked Naomi.

"Not for Bobbie. For Gloria."

Veronica said, "Good advice. That's what mothers are for."

After Naomi and Veronica resumed powerwalking in the wrong direction, Daffy said, "I haven't lied that much since I completed that Medicare questionnaire at my spring checkup."

Gidget smiled. "That Medicare questionnaire is a joke."

Daffy began critiquing the questions on the questionnaire. "How many alcohol drinks do you consume a week? The Feds would make me enroll in Alcoholics Anonymous if I answered that question truthfully. Do you ever feel overwhelmed? Only when I think about all the things the Federal government is trying to do for me. How many servings of fruit and vegetables do you eat in a typical day? I wanted to write 'What's a vegetable?' I thought that's what they made Metamucil for. I mean, who's going to answer those kinds of questions honestly? Get real."

"Big Brother *is* watching."

"Getting back to the important stuff, what is a vampire breast lift? I'm dying to know."

Gidget said, "According to Lizzie's text, it's the latest rage in Thomasville. Everyone wants one."

"Why? What's so great about it?"

"Hold on. Lizzie's text is long, she had to split it into several messages. Here it is. A vampire breast lift is some sort of non-invasive procedure. The surgeon draws blood from your breasts. Yuck! Then extracts plasma from it, combines it with some stuff. She doesn't say what. Then injects it back into your boobs."

Daffy made a face. "What's that do for your boobs?"

"Wait a second. It's a long text. Oh, here it is. It 'smooths wrinkles, reduces stretch marks, and lifts saggy skin.' Hmmm, I may look into this myself."

As they powerwalked, Daffy and Gidget discussed techniques for dealing with eight-year-old females until a text came over Gidget's phone.

"What is it?" asked Daffy.

Gidget said, "I just got a text from Louie about the autopsy of Larry's body."

"What'd it say?"

"It says the Med School didn't do an autopsy. They never received Larry's body, so there was no body to autopsy—"

"No body to autopsy?! What does that mean?"

"That means someone doesn't want Larry's body autopsied," said Gidget.

"But why? And who?"

"Excellent questions, my dear Daffy. We know from Louie's chromatograph analysis there was no poison, so that eliminates Chef Dreyfus as a possible suspect. Someone doesn't want the body autopsied probably because it shows what really killed Larry."

"But who could the killer be?"

"We don't know because there was no autopsy."

Chapter 29

12° 29' 53.7288" North, 69° 52' 56.5464" West
November 16th

At one o'clock, hundreds of passengers crowded every deck on the Bahama Princess, with prize locations found on the stern of the ship. Two of the Marx Brothers and the five women squeezed in on the crowded helicopter deck. It overlooked a platform dock, from which the parasailing speedboat would be launched. Daffy and Gidget listened to the crowd's speculation.

Time: "They should've gone in the morning. I was always told the best time of day to parasail is in the morning before the winds get too strong."

Weather: "Look at all those clouds in the sky. Feel that wind picking up. He's going to get bounced around up there."

Water: "Look at the water, how choppy it is. Water always gets a lot choppier in the afternoon. It's tougher to maneuver a boat on choppy water. It's even tougher for someone five-hundred feet up in the air."

Age: "Tyler says the guy is seventy-five and will be the oldest passenger to have ever parasailed on the Bahama Princess."

Death: "Isn't he the guy whose brothers died mysteriously over the last two days? And now he's going parasailing? He must want to join them."

Gidget looked around. "Look at the size of this crowd. Talk about morbid curiosity."

Daffy said, "The reason there's so many people here is that Harry's been bragging to all his canasta and Bocce ball buddies about parasailing."

Gary appeared detached. "Nothing wrong with that."

"A seventy-five-year-old man parasailing reminds me of going to NASCAR to watch a massive car pileup—"

Gidget leaned in and sharply nudged her friend. Two of the Marx Brothers had died in the past two days. No need to remind Barry and Gary of the dangers in parasailing.

"I'm sure Harry will be just fine."

Barry said, "I tried to talk him out of it. With Jerry and Larry gone, I told him that we don't wanna lose another brother."

Barry's two last words came out as 'anudder brudder.'

"Harry's always been the daredevil among us," Gary said.

"Y'all amaze me," said Daffy. "You New Yorkers seem to accept your brothers' deaths much better than I would've."

"Us New Yorkers is… what do they call it? Stoic," said Barry. "Southerners is… un-Stoic. Our two deceased brothers was in their late sixties, early seventies, and they led good lives, so we ain't gonna sit around and mope over them. When I die, I don't want people moping over my death. I want them to remember me, of course, but I want them to go on living. I know Larry and Gary would want us to act that way over their deaths. It'd be disrespectful to them to act any other way."

Barry's comments showed he had taken offense at Daffy's comment. Gidget feared her friend had committed one of a Southerner's worst sins—accidental rudeness. Besides, maybe the Marx Brothers' attitudes were the best way to approach death. Gidget promptly changed the subject. "Oh, look, here they come."

Tyler and Harry emerged from a nearby door. As if in a biblical scene, the crowd parted in order to allow them to pass. A small, dark, brutish-looking man followed. Rachel, the ship's Entertainment Director, made up the fourth and final person in the entourage. All females in the crowd of spectators began chanting, "Tyler! Tyler! Tyler!" He waved at them.

"That guy with Tyler and Harry looks like the hunchback guy in *Young Frankenstein*," said Gidget.

Daffy asked, "Didn't Marty Feldman play the hunchback? What was the character's name? Uh… uh, Igor." She pronounced it the way Feldman pronounced it in the movie: I-gor, not E-gor.

"Now that we got that out of the way, take a look at Harry."

Harry wore his best Hawaiian flower shirt, the one with large pink flamingoes surrounded by green tropical plants, all on a black background. He chose more subtle swim trunks. A bunch of small, hot pink sharks floated on the swimsuit's aqua canvas background. He also wore a pair of Merrell Hydro Moc Water Shoes. Many small oval cut-outs in their EVA foam uppers enhanced an olive green, black, and grey camouflage pattern found on many swamp reptiles and extraterrestrial aliens.

Gidget leaned into Daffy and whispered, "All in all, Harry is a picture of excessive style gone wild."

"I hope he doesn't get hurt. I'd hate to think of him showing up in the emergency room in that outfit."

"Yeah. How would an ER doc treat a being not from this world?"

Tyler led Harry, Igor, and Rachel through the crowd, passing by the Casserole Ladies and the Marx Brothers. As they neared, Gidget leaned into Daffy and said, "That guy following Harry looks awful."

"Yeah," Daffy said. "Look at the scar on the side of his jaw. I bet he didn't get it cutting himself shaving."

As Harry passed by, Daffy wrapped her arms around him and planted a big wet kiss on his lips. "Love your outfit! Are you sure you want to go through with this?"

Though he tried to hide it, Harry's face advertised his fear. The best he could manage was a slight nod. Gidget pulled him over and gave him a great big hug. Barry pulled him away and said, "Good luck, brother. Bring us back a seagull."

"Keep it up, brother," said Gary. "No pun intended."

Harry and Rachel followed Tyler and Igor to a set of stairs leading down to platform dock where a wicked-looking speedboat was moored. Tyler and Igor helped Harry get onboard.

The word '***Raptor***' emblazoned on the side of the boat identified the model built especially for parasailing. Thirty-six feet long and four-hundred fifty horsepower, its sleek design and bright yellow color made it look like a banana on steroids.

While Tyler checked the controls, Igor helped Harry put on a life vest, get seated, and then connected the parasail and harness system to a mechanical winch. Everything shipshape, Tyler looked up at the crowd and waved.

Standing on the platform dock, Rachel spoke into a megaphone and said, "Everyone give big hand to Mister Harry Vanderhoff, the oldest Bahama Princess passenger to ever parasail!"

Chants of "Ha-reee! Ha-reee! Ha-reee!" spontaneously arose. Cheers accompanied the crowd's clapping. Barry raised his voice in order to be heard over the crowd's noise.

"It makes me proud that he's my brother!"

"Larry and Jerry would both be proud if they could be here," said Gary.

Gidget noticed a single tear dripped down Gary's left cheek. She felt a tingle run down her spine and joined in the chanting. Daffy soon followed.

Tyler started the Raptor's engine. The noise was deafening.

"God that thing is loud," said Gidget. "Sounds like it could be used to launch spaceships into orbit."

"Or replace dirt-track racing in Waycross," said Daffy. Waycross was well-known throughout South Georgia for the horrendous noises echoing throughout the small town on Saturday afternoons during racing season.

Igor cast off, and Tyler shifted into a low gear. He slowly pulled away from the platform and steered them on an elliptical course close to the ship's stern. The crowd got a good view of Harry sitting in the bow of the boat, head lowered.

"Is Harry reading something?" asked Gidget.

"Probably praying," said Daffy.

"That's as pale as I've ever seen Harry. I hope he doesn't get too sick."

"Hope he doesn't throw up while he's floating over us."

Barry heard her comment. "Or pee. He's got an enlarged prostate, you know.

"And I thought his frequent bathroom visits were in connection with some sort of handwashing fetish."

"You must be practicing your sarcasm again," said Gidget.

"*Moi*?"

"Moe? What's he got to do with this?" asked Barry.

As Tyler slowly cruised circles and figure eights near the ship's stern, Rachel narrated.

"Folks, Tyler will make a series of maneuvers for about fifteen minutes near the Bahama Princess. He does that to make sure the Raptor's engines are running smoothly. It would be disastrous to have the engines fail while Mr. Vanderhoff is five hundred feet in the air. Dropping from that far up too fast would probably result in serious injury. Also, Tyler's checking out the wind speed and the water currents. He wants to make sure he knows what's going on aero- and hydrodynamically, so he can compensate for any anomalies."

During this time, Igor stood on the Raptor's launch platform. He appeared nervous and fidgety, almost as if he had never done this before. Gidget and Daffy took little note of his behavior as they were more interested in ogling Tyler. He wore a sleeveless pale blue Adidas tank top revealing the swollen veins in his shoulder and arm muscles.

Daffy leaned into Gidget. "I tried to count the veins in Tyler's biceps when he walked by me, but I gave up. My eyesight ain't what it used to be."

Tyler finally gave a thumbs up, turned the boat away from the Bahama Princess, and headed out to sea.

Chapter 30

12° 29' 53.7288" North, 69° 52' 56.5464" West
November 16th

The Raptor gathered speed until it reached a point a hundred yards from the Bahama Princess and three hundred yards offshore. At that point, Igor assisted Harry into the parasail harness and attached the harness to a towline held tight by the winch. The process went surprisingly well given the seventy-five-year old's bum knees and tendinitis in his left rotator cuff.

Tyler kept the Raptor slowly cruising at five miles per hour during this process. After Igor finished, he double-checked his work, then gave Tyler a thumbs up. Tyler shouted, "You good to go, Harry?"

Harry gave a tentative thumbs-up signal. Tyler increased the boat's speed to ten miles an hour which allowed Igor to unfurl the parasail into the oncoming wind. It inflated and gracefully lifted upward. The winched towline kept Harry steady on the platform.

Tyler looked back and shouted again, "Ready for liftoff?"

Harry again gave a thumbs-up signal, and Tyler increased the Raptor's speed to twenty miles an hour. Igor began turning the winch's handle, letting the towline play out.

Back on the Bahama Princess, Gidget pulled out her iPhone. "I'm so glad I bought this new phone last month. It's got a helluva zoom lens so I can get good closeup video of our boy's adventure." She aimed it at the Raptor and began videoing as Harry slowly lifted upward. She said, "There goes Harry—rising up in the air."

Daffy said, "Some short guys will do anything to increase their height, although three-inch shoe lifts would be easier."

"That's got to be the lamest joke you've made so far on this cruise."

"That bad, eh? How would you rate it on a scale of one to ten?"

"I'd give it an F."

"I hope youse learned your lesson to never doubt it when a Vanderhoff says he's going to do something," said Barry.

"When are you going skydiving?" asked Daffy.

They watched Harry continue to rise as the Raptor picked up speed. Gidget asked, "I wonder how fast it's going?"

A passenger close by had a set of binoculars with a built-in rangefinder. He looked through them. "Looks like about thirty miles an hour."

A man standing next to him said, "Thirty's the max a boat's supposed to go when towing a parasail."

The Raptor followed a course away from the ship and parallel to the beach as Harry kept rising.

"Wonder how high he is now?" asked Gidget.

Binoculars looked again. "About three hundred feet up, so far."

"Harry told me he was going to go up to the full five hundred feet," said Gary.

"Five hundred's the max for parasailing… at least in Florida. He just passed the three-fifty mark."

"I bet he *is* peeing in his swimsuit right now."

"At least he's not over our ship," said Daffy. "How high is he now?"

"About four-ten," said Binoculars.

Daffy leaned in close to Gidget. "Four-ten… isn't that Harry's original height?"

Gidget frowned and looked at Binoculars. "Let us know when he reaches five hundred, would you?"

"He just hit it. Now, he's five-twenty-five."

"Five-hundred and twenty-five feet?"

"Yep."

Gidget had her iPhone's zoom set to it maximum power and could just make out Harry's face. Even with the phone's poor resolution at his distance from the Bahama Princess, she thought she saw fear on his face "Is that safe?"

Binoculars kept looking upward. "Nope. Not safe in the least bit. FAA regulations limit parasailing to five hundred feet… but that's only enforceable in the States."

"You sure know a lot about parasailing."

"I should. I've done enough of it. That's why I *had* to see a seventy-five-year-old do it."

By the time the Raptor was half a mile away, Tyler began turning it around to head back toward the ship. Turning became a chore as the chop was now over two feet high and beating against the sides of the boat. Making matters worse, offshore winds had picked up. The towline strained. Half a mile away, the crowd on the Bahama Princess could see Harry's parasail continue to rise.

"How high is he now?" asked Daffy.

"Seven hundred feet," said Binoculars. "Uh oh. Looks like his parasail is pegged."

"Pegged? What's that?"

"It's when the wind gets rough and the parasail begins to oscillate violently. That sometimes happens when the parasailer's tow angle is too steep. Tyler should slow down to decrease the tow angle."

"Tow angle?"

"Angle made by the towline and the surface of the water."

"What is Tyler doing?" Panic screamed in Gidget's question.

Binoculars lowered his binoculars. "Looks like Tyler's gonna give him a thousand-foot ride come hell or high water. That's why Tyler's making the tow angle so steep. A thousand-foot ride is against FAA regs."

"Against FAA regulations!" Gidget could not mute her panic.

The man next to Binoculars said, "Yeah. So unsafe, the FAA outlawed parasailing a thousand feet up. Out here off Aruba, who knows?"

Barry seemed complacent. "Harry told me he was gonna get Tyler to take him up a thousand feet. I just thought it was something standard."

"He only told me five hundred," said Gary.

Binoculars said, "He's at nine-seventy-five."

Gidget continued to video Harry's ride and caught a crucial moment when the Raptor was halfway through its turn. The towline suddenly separated about thirty feet below Harry. A collective scream arose from spectators onboard the Bahama Princess. Harry continued to float in the air, now untethered to the Raptor.

Binoculars again lowered his binoculars. "The stress of turning that high up in high wind must've been too much for the towline."

The passenger next to him asked, "I wonder what the rating on the Raptor's towline is?"

"With those winds and choppy seas, I have to wonder who approved that area as his flight zone."

"Flight zone?" asked Gidget.

"Area where you're going to parasail. It's supposed to be predetermined and approved before you parasail."

The other passenger said, "This is bad. I hear that hitting the water that high up, even with a parachute, is like hitting a slab of concrete."

Thinking Daffy would probably be upset at this bit of information about her boyfriend, Gidget quit videoing and turned to her. In doing so, she noticed the Arnold Schwarzenegger guy standing at the railing on the main deck along with other spectators who had witnessed the horrific event. She quickly pointed her phone at him and snapped a photo. He immediately turned and hurried away. Gidget looked back to see what was happening with Harry.

Harry floated in a direction taking him further away from both the Bahama Princess and the shore. Tyler turned the Raptor back in the direction of Harry's parasail. It continued to rise and headed out to sea.

"He must be caught in some sort of an offshore updraft that's taking him higher and further out. This is really bad," Binoculars said.

Gidget looked over at Barry and Gary, who remained stone-cold frozen. She leaned into to Daffy. "What are we going to do? Gary and Barry look like corpses."

"I don't know. Poor Barry and Gary. I hope Harry makes it back somehow," Daffy said.

Harry floated higher with the Raptor following him as he headed away from shore. It became harder to see both Harry and the boat. They became mere specs, then disappeared. Binoculars gave up and lowered his binoculars for good. "I can't see them anymore."

Captain Omen and several of his senior officers arrived. He looked around. "Are the other Vanderhoffs here?"

Gary and Barry nodded and walked over to him.

The captain said, "Tyler called us on his ship-to-ship radio. He's following your brother as best he can. He indicates the wind is pretty strong at the elevation your brother is gliding at, and it's propelling him out to sea. I told Tyler to stay with him."

Gary said, "Thanks. Please keep us informed."

Thirty minutes passed while the crowd waited for the Raptor to return. Gradually, other passengers began to wander off. After fifteen more minutes, another crewman showed up and spoke with the captain. He moved close to Barry and Gary.

"I'm sorry to say that Tyler tells us that he is going to have to turn back. The seas have gotten too rough for a boat the size of his."

Another thirty minutes passed, and a small yellow dot appeared on the horizon. The Raptor made a beeline for the Bahama Princess. By then, the captain and his other officers had returned to the bridge to await Tyler's report. Before he left, the captain told Barry and Gary that the ship had put out a distress call to the Aruban Coast Guard. He had requested they conduct a search and rescue effort.

The helicopter deck was deserted except for Gidget, Daffy, Barry, Gary, and a few deckhands by the time Tyler docked the Raptor. They watched as Igor tied the boat up and Tyler shut down its engine. He climbed out of the Raptor and headed for the ship's bridge. As he passed, Barry asked, "Tyler, what about Harry?"

"I… I… got nothing to say. The captain told me to report to the bridge the minute we docked," Tyler said as he briskly walked away.

Barry said, "Gary and I are gonna go find out what happened."

Both brothers left Daffy and Gidget standing there. Gidget said, "Let's snoop around."

Daffy pointed to Igor, stowing gear away on the Raptor. "He might be a problem."

"Let me handle him."

"You know, I can't make up my mind."

"About what?" asked Gidget.

"Whether Igor's an escaped animatronic character from the DINOSAUR ride or the Monsters Inc. ride in Disney World."

Chapter 31

12° 29' 53.7288" North, 69° 52' 56.5464" West
November 16th

Gidget intently studied Igor as she and Daffy descended the stairs. She thought about Daffy's animatronic character comment and shook her head.

"Nope. He's that long-snooted snitch that turned Luke and Obi-Wan in to the Empire in the first *Star Wars*… or was it actually the fourth one? Whichever, I bet Igor's nose has been broken at least twice."

Daffy said, "It looks like a parrot's bill. That reminds me. What did the duck say to the drugstore clerk when he bought a tube of ChapStick?"

"Put it on my bill. That's an old one. I've lost count of the number of times I've heard that joke. I did work in a drugstore for over thirty years."

"Anyway, Igor's nose does have a helluva curve. It probably sounds like a French horn when he snores."

"Look at those arms. They're pretty big for such a small guy."

"They are pretty gnarly. He looks like he could play King Kong in the movies."

"More like Cheeta in the Tarzan movies."

Gidget and Daffy stepped onto the platform dock and watched Igor. He paid no attention as he made things fast and stowed equipment away. After he finished, he walked around the Raptor, taking his time, perhaps in an effort to avoid dealing with the two women watching. After no more tasks remained, he climbed onto the dock and headed for the stairs.

Gidget rushed up to him. "Can you tell us what happened? We're Mr. Vanderhoff's friends."

Igor did not stop nor look at them as he said, "No."

Gidget moved to block his progress. "Come on. Tell us what happened."

Daffy also moved in front of Igor. She towered over him. He nervously looked around, realized he was trapped.

"Look, he got caught in a big wind that comes along while we's turning, an' whoosh, the towline snaps. We follows him a long ways out. That's about it."

"What caused the towline to snap?" asked Gidget.

"Don't ask me. I don't know."

"Didn't you check the towline before you left?"

"Sure we did. We always checks the towline before hitchin' someone to it."

"Why did y'all take Harry out in the afternoon? I thought mornings were the best time for parasailing. The wind's calmer."

Igor shrugged. "I don't know nothing 'bout that. Youse gotta talk to Tyler about that. He's the captain of this here boat. He makes those kind of decisions. Not me."

"Why did he pick that flight zone?"

"What's that?"

"Who approved the flight zone?"

"I don't know nothing 'bout that."

"One of the other passengers said that y'all were giving Harry a thousand-foot ride," Daffy said.

"I don't know what that is."

"He had binoculars with a range-finder on it, and he measured Harry's height at nine-hundred and seventy-five feet," Gidget said.

Igor shrugged again and said nothing.

"Thousand-foot rides are against FAA regulations. Did you know that?"

"I don't know nothing 'bout that," Igor said.

"Why didn't Tyler slow down and decrease the tow angle when the winds got too rough?"

"I don't know nothing 'bout that."

"Couldn't you see the parasail was pegging?"

"What's that? You sure does ask a lot of questions."

"Enquiring minds want to know," said Daffy.

"Curiosity killed the cat."

"But satisfaction brought him back."

"I gotta go now." Igor said nothing more and climbed the stairs back up to the helicopter deck.

Gidget and Daffy did not follow Igor and instead remained on the dock. Daffy was impressed.

"Wow! You really grilled that guy. He was a scary guy, yet you handled him like a pro. Sherlock Holmes would be proud of you. Only one thing."

"What's that?" asked Gidget.

"All your interrogation got us nowhere."

"*Au contraire*, my dear Daffy. We learned a lot."

"Such as?"

"I heard a lot of duhs and dats and a few youses. Sounded like the same Brooklyn accent as the Marx Brothers?"

"I'll never get used to the word youse."

"It is kind of puzzling—the same accent. And he didn't seem to know much about parasailing, yet he crews on a parasailing boat. He didn't know what the best time for parasailing was. He didn't know what pegging was. He didn't know what tow angle was. He didn't know what a flight zone was or who approved it. Or what a thousand-foot ride was."

"I doan know nuttin 'bout dat stuff myself," Daffy quipped. "What now?"

"Why was someone that ignorant of parasailing crewing the Raptor anyway? I don't see any of the deck crew around. Let's do a little snooping to see if we can find out why."

With no one else around, Gidget and Daffy climbed from the dock onto the Raptor and slowly made their way from stern to bow. Daffy asked, "Whatcha looking for?"

"Nothing in particular," Gidget said. "I just want to get a feel for the boat and see if anything jumps out at me. I think it's good to get the overall picture before diving into details."

In the bow, Daffy reached down and picked up a small pamphlet. "I wonder if this fell out of Harry's pocket. He seemed to be looking at something while Tyler was warming up, remember?"

Gidget took the pamphlet. "Let me see. GL300 GPS Tracker Instruction Manual. These are the instructions for a GPS device that allows someone to track whomever has the it with him via an iPhone. Why would Harry need to have someone tracking him via a GPS tracker on a twenty-minute parasail ride?"

"Yeah. Why?"

"Isn't it obvious? Harry didn't think it would be a twenty-minute ride."

They edged their way back to the mechanical winch system. Gidget opened the compartment in which Igor had stowed the towline.

"Help me get this out. It's heavy. Must be hundreds of feet of towline. I guess when it breaks like it did, they have to get rid of it, but why'd he stow it away?"

"Good question."

"Maybe he didn't want anyone to examine it before they could get rid of it?"

"Looks like it's made of some sort of nylon stuff," said Daffy.

"Yeah. Some sort of woven fibers. Definitely nylon or some other man-made material."

In fact, it was made of polyester double-layered fiber, was fifteen millimeters thick, and specifically manufactured to withstand the stresses of parasailing up to five hundred feet above sea level.

Gidget handed part of the large loop of towline to Daffy. "Hold this up. I want to look at the end of it that broke."

Gidget knelt and began maneuvering through the towline, trying to find the end that had snapped. Much of it remained, and it took a lot of time and effort to reach the end. Finally, she stood and held it up. "Would y'all lookee here at this."

"What? What?" asked Daffy.

"If this towline snapped in two, why does this end look like it was melted?"

"Melted?"

"Yeah. See how smooth and rounded the tip looks."

"What does it remind you of?"

"Keep your mind on snooping, not sex," Gidget scolded. "If it had been snapped into by all that force, you would think it would have a frazzled end… jagged… with individual strands all different lengths. The end of this towline reminds me of when you want to prevent a nylon cord from unraveling, you hold a lighted match under it and melt it together."

"By golly, you're right. What could have done that?" asked Daffy.

Gidget pulled out her iPhone. "I got the part where the towline snapped on video."

She played back the video until she got to the part where it snapped, then handed the phone to Daffy and said, "Look."

Daffy played the video of the towline snapping several times. "It's hard to tell even with your phone's zoom, but it looks like a small puff of smoke right when it snapped."

"I'm gonna take a picture of this end of the towline."

Chapter 32

12° 29' 53.7288" North, 69° 52' 56.5464" West
November 16th

Daffy and Gidget headed for the ship's bridge to check on Harry's status. They were torn over what to do with the findings from their investigation. Igor had behaved suspiciously when questioned, but so what? They found suspicious physical and video evidence that the towline break was not accidental. Again, so what? Who is going to listen to two old women? Gidget adopted a cautious strategy.

"Let's play it by ear."

They found Gary and Barry huddled outside the bridge. They stopped talking as Daffy and Gidget approached.

"What's the latest?" asked Daffy.

Gary said, "They got the Aruban Coast Guard out looking for Harry. The Aruban Coast Guard did find the parasail, but Harry wasn't in it. U. S. Navy planes will be over the area soon to join in the search."

"Where was the parasail?" asked Gidget.

"About three miles offshore."

"Three miles!?"

"Yeah. The captain said the Coast Guard said the offshore winds were pretty strong. His parasail must have drifted that far out."

"No body?" asked Daffy.

"Nope. They sighted sharks in the area. They're still searching."

Gidget subtly introduced her reservations about Harry's accident. "Does anyone have any idea as to how this could have happened? How did his towline get broken?"

Gary shook his head. Barry took over.

"It's tough to say. Captain Omen said he might have drowned although that's not certain. There were sharks, and well… you know. No way he could've swum three miles to shore. The United States Navy was in the area and has joined in the search. They're searching all the area between the shore and where they found the parasail. We've got several more hours of daylight, and they'll continue searching—even after sunset."

"Let's pray they find him. By the way, I got the entire ride on video," Gidget said.

Barry shook his head. "I don't think I want to look at that right now."

"I've got the part where the towline broke."

"So what? A thousand passengers on the ship saw it."

"I had it zoomed in and saw something fishy about the towline breaking. It looked like a puff of smoke happened at the point it broke. Let me show y'all." Gidget replayed the video of the towline snapping. "What do y'all think?"

Barry was skeptical. "It was too fuzzy to say that was smoke. It might've been a small cloud somewhere between the towline and your phone."

"I think we're gonna talk to a lawyer when we get back," said Gary.

"About what?" asked Daffy.

"We heard what those guys with the binoculars were saying. About going higher than Federal regulations allow, parasailing in bad weather, and so forth. We're gonna talk to a lawyer about suing this here cruise line for some sort of malpractice or incompetence."

Gary and Barry decided to stay on the bridge in case the Aruban Coast Guard found Harry.

"Youse don't have to stay. Probably a waste of your time," said Barry.

When they were out of earshot, Daffy said, "I can't believe another Marx Brother disaster has happened. Harry's the third in three days. What in the hell is happening? Something's not right here."

"Let's pray they find him floating in the water alive," said Gidget. "But you're right. Something's not right here. It's as if someone is trying to get rid of them."

"Who could that be?"

"That's another sixty-four-thousand-dollar question, my dear Daffy."

They headed back to the stern of the ship where they saw Tyler on the Raptor coiling up the towline.

"Damn! We forgot to put the towline back in the compartment," said Gidget. "Maybe Tyler will think Igor forgot to stow it away."

"Dementia strikes every thirty minutes at my age," said Daffy.

"Let's get down there and see if we can get anything from Tyler."

Tyler was so busy with the towline he did not notice them until they stood on the dock next to the boat.

"Miss Gidget and Miss Daffy. "I uh can't tell you how sorry I am. He was such a great guy."

"We know. He was a precious man," said Daffy. "What are you doing?"

"My crewman forgot to stow the towline away. There's going to be a preliminary inquiry tomorrow morning, and they'll want to inspect it."

"Oh?" asked Gidget.

"Yes, ma'am. Harry's accident is the uh… third mishap reported to authorities in three days. Bahama Princess is an American-registered vessel, so the United States Coast Guard is sending in a team tomorrow to conduct an inquiry."

"Wow!" Daffy's phone buzzed—an incoming text. "Hold on a minute. Uh oh. More grandkids excitement. Beth Anne just had one of them new Dr Pepper milkshakes at the Whataburger in Tallahassee and couldn't wait to tell me about it."

Tyler's eyes lit up. "Dr Pepper milkshakes? And I thought no one would ever top fried Oreos. Leave it to Whataburger."

Gidget rolled her eyes. "Tyler, you said the Coast Guard is sending a team in tomorrow to conduct an inquiry?"

"Yes ma'am. The Seventh District has a base in San Juan, Puerto Rico. They're sending in a team. They've ordered the Bahama Princess to remain here off of Aruba and wait for them."

"What can you tell us about the accident?" asked Gidget.

"I'm sorry, ma'am, but I can't tell you anything about it. Captain's orders because of the upcoming inquiry."

"Can you answer one question?"

"Depends on the question, and I just answered one."

"Everybody's a comedian. Your crew member who forgot to stow the towline. Has he been with you a long time?"

"No. He just hired on in Grenada. The guy he replaced had to take emergency leave and fly back to Florida."

On the way to their stateroom, Gidget said, "I'd say interrogating Tyler was mostly a waste of our time."

Daffy put on her most lecherous expression. "*Au contraire*. Talking to eye candy like Tyler is never a waste of time."

"I noticed you never took your eyes off of him."

"I may be seventy, but I still got a few hormones left. You said 'mostly.' What part was not worthless in your mind?"

"Igor just came on board in Grenada after the regular crewman had to leave on emergency leave."

"Yeah. That is real coincidental, ain't it?"

Gidget nodded. "What's happened these last three days is beyond belief. No wonder the Coast Guard is sending in a team to investigate. Oh, I don't think I've had time to tell you. I saw the Schwarzenegger guy standing on the main deck when Harry's towline snapped."

"I been wondering when he'd pop up again."

"Seems he pops up every time we lose a Marx Brother. He was outside Azul when Larry croaked. We saw him in the passageway not long after Jerry took the plunge. And now, he's watching Harry go floating off into the wild blue yonder. I think there's some sort of connection."

"I agree. What should we do?" asked Daffy.

"Don't know. Maybe nothing. What can we do?"

"Good point. We go to the Chief of Security and say, 'Y'all got an Arnold Schwarzenegger guy running loose on this boat that's making people die and disappear, yet he's not on the ship's passenger photo wall. He'd probably send us to Mokulus for a psychological evaluation."

Gidget nodded. "But we don't want to forget about him or E-gor."

"How could you forget someone that looks like Marty Feldman?"

"Despite their weird looks and personalities, I've really grown fond of the Marx Brothers. And now, three of them are dead."

Daffy wiped a tear. "Harry, Larry, and Jerry. What nice guys. Real gentlemen."

"We don't know jack poop."

"You were right that we didn't get much out of trying to interrogate Tyler."

Gidget nodded. "Yeah. He clammed up. Captain's orders."

"I probably could've gotten more out of Mr. Tyler in my bedroom with handcuffs and a whip."

"I think he would have gotten more out of you."

"Very willingly, I might add. Just the thought of handcuffs, a whip, and Tyler working me over gives me the vapors." Daffy fanned her face. "What now?"

"We amp up our investigation. I'm even more determined now to find out what's going on."

Chapter 33

12° 29' 53.7288" North, 69° 52' 56.5464" West
November 17th

The Bahama Princess remained anchored in the same location off the Aruban coastline awaiting the U.S. Coast Guard inquiry team. Gidget and Daffy saw little of Barry and Gary after their meeting on the bridge the previous day. Both brothers were upset and remained in their stateroom that evening despite entreaties by the two women to dine with them.

The next morning, Daffy and Gidget knocked on the brothers' door before going to breakfast. Barry invited them inside and closely looked at Gidget as she entered. "Toots, how ya doing? Any throwing up this morning?"

"None so far. Maybe I'm getting my sea legs back," Gidget said for the others' benefit.

"How are y'all doing?" asked Daffy.

Barry said, "Eh, so-so. Maybe a little better this morning. Captain Omen stopped by late last night to update us."

"And he called this morning. Still no sign of Harry," said Gary.

"We finally accepted the reality that he's probably done for. I don't see how anyone could survive that long in those waters. They would've found him by now if he hadn't drowned."

"Daff and I feel so bad for y'all," Gidget said.

"Yeah. But Harry was seventy-five, after all. He lived a long life, a good life."

Gary shook his head as he looked down. "Anyway, we're kind of bummed out right now. I'm gonna skip breakfast."

"Me too. Youse go on to breakfast without us," said Barry.

They talked a while longer, then Gidget and Daffy went to Azul by themselves. At nine o'clock, they powerwalked on the promenade deck.

"I'm very confused at this point," said Daffy. "There is too much information for my seventy-year-old brain to process."

Gidget nodded. “We’ve got three deaths. One choking or poisoning. One, an accidental or on-purpose slip and fall over the side of the boat. One, a probable drowning from possible tampering with a towline. Agreed?”

“Yeah, and I’m not even gonna chastise you for calling the Bahama Princess a boat.”

“Your generosity is appreciated.”

“What next?”

“We cool our jets until we see what comes out of the Coast Guard’s preliminary inquiry.”

Ten minutes into their powerwalk, they spotted an orange and white helicopter approaching the ship.

“It’s a Coast Guard helicopter,” said Daffy. “It must be the inquiry team.”

“Let’s hustle so we can watch them land,” said Gidget.

They walked at a spot on the stern of the ship overlooking the helicopter deck. By then, the helicopter had completed its required three passes around the ship and was slowly descending. It gradually touched down on the surface of the helipad.

The aircraft’s rotor kept turning as four Coast Guard officers got out. All wore Coast Guard Tropical Blue uniforms, consisting of dark blue trousers and a light blue short-sleeve shirt with shoulder boards. Daffy said, “Looks like some high-ranking people are getting involved.”

Gidget said, “Yeah. Those things they got on their shoulders tell what their ranks are. Let’s see… one guy has four gold stripes, one has three, one has two, and the last guy has one and a half stripes. Let’s get a picture.”

Daffy and Gidget both pulled out their phones. All four officers ducked down to avoid the spinning rotor blades as they fast-walked off the helipad. They also kept a hand on their caps to keep them from being blown away. The large circular crowns and stiff plastic visors of the officers’ combination caps made them extremely susceptible to wind gusts. Looking down, Daffy and Gidget were unable to see their faces, only the tops of their caps. After the four cleared the helipad, the aircraft’s rotors spun faster, and it lifted off.

“Wonder where it’s going?” asked Daffy.

"Probably the airport in Oranjestad to gas up," said Gidget referring to the capital of Aruba. "After that flight from San Juan, it's probably low on gas."

"Let's finish up our walk and see what the boys are up to."

Minutes later, Gidget knocked on the Marx Brothers' door. Barry opened it and invited them inside. Louella, Naomi and Veronica were already there.

"Louella, Naomi. Veronica. Didn't expect to see y'all here."

"We thought we'd check on the boys to see how they're holding up after the latest tragedy," Naomi said.

Gidget looked at the two brothers. "How are y'all holding up?"

Barry said, "Same as we were before."

"We just saw the Coast Guard helicopter land on the ship. Four officers got out."

Gary nodded. "Yeah. We know. Captain Omen just called and told us they'll probably want to talk to us sometime today."

"Have y'all ate breakfast yet?" asked Daffy.

"Yeah. Stokes made something for us a little while ago. The ship's chaplain stopped before that, and we prayed together."

"What are y'all going to do today?" asked Gidget.

"We told the captain that we're probably gonna go play some canasta, so he'll know where to get us for the inquiry. Take our minds off of Harry," said Barry.

"Yeah," Gary said. "Nothing but canasta and booze until tonight."

"Tonight? What's going on tonight?" asked Daffy.

"Don't youse remember? Tonight's the night we all got reservations to see Moriarty the Magician in Neptune's Spectacle."

"Y'all are still gonna go?!" Gidget asked.

Naomi said, "I been debating with 'em. They seemed reluctant, but I told 'em seeing a good magic act will take their minds off of this tragedy. Ronnie and Lou agree."

Veronica and Louella nodded.

"Yeah. Why not?" asked Barry.

Gidget sensed reluctance in his tone. "But your brothers…"

"Not going to see Moriarty ain't gonna bring 'em back."

Gary said, "We've been debating it and finally decided it's not doing us any good to mope around here. We've been holed up in this room since yesterday evening. It's getting to us. The girls is right."

"Besides, tonight is one of Moriarty the Magician's last performances on board. Gary saw his act when he was in Arizona and loved it."

Daffy agreed. "It's probably better for both of you to get out. We'll go too. It'll get all our minds off Harry for a while."

"Naomi's right," said Gidget. "Moping in this room isn't going to make Harry return any faster. Moriarty sounds entertaining."

"Thanks," Barry said. "We could use some company tonight."

Gary said, "The only downside is that we'll have to miss both *MASH* and *Andy Griffith*."

Gidget and Daffy met up with Veronica, Naomi, and Louella early afternoon for rummy. Everyone was gloomy, despite three rounds of Mojitos. Louella's gloom was personal.

"The pickins is getting even slimmer now."

"Poor Harry. Whatcha gonna do now, Daffy? He was such a stud," said Veronica.

"How in the hell would you know?" asked Daffy and roughly discarded a card.

Veronica hiccupped, picked up the card, smiled, and lay down a three-card run. She said, "Pung."

"We're playing rummy, not Mahjong," said Naomi.

"Sorry."

Louella said, "I miss Jerry. He was pretty funny for a short guy."

"You mean short guys aren't funny?" asked Gidget.

"Not in Nebraska."

Naomi hiccupped. "No one' s funny in Nebraska. There is no such thing as fun in Nebraska. Larry could've had me any time."

"Any of 'em could've had you any time," said Veronica.

"And I'd be proud of it."

Daffy said, "I love all their cute little bald heads."

Gidget shook her head. "That's not what you said when you first saw them in the IHOP."

"That was the IHOP, and this is now… It is now, isn't it?"

"Now or never."

"What about that outfit Harry wore parasailing? Perfect camouflage uniform for a food fight in Disneyland," Naomi said.

Louella disagreed. "Not in Disneyland… in Jamaica."

Veronica shook her head. "Nope. Food fight in a Las Vegas chorus line."

"Food fight in a Crayola factory," said Daffy, laying a card face down on the discard pile.

"You're supposed to lay your card face up on the discard pile."

Daffy turned the card over. "Sorry. Three of them dying in three days is kind of suspicious. I wonder if they got some sort of volume discount."

Louella picked up Daffy's discarded card and laid down three cards of three different suits. "Crown me!"

"We're not playing checkers. And your cards are not even in the same suit," said Gidget. She bent over and carefully scrutinized the cards. "Are they?"

After Gidget and Daffy finished rummy, they took the long way back to their stateroom via the main deck to clear their heads. As they approached the stern of the ship, the sound of an aircraft caught their attention.

"Hey, it's a Coast Guard helicopter," said Daffy.

Gidget said, "Must be coming back to pick up the inquiry team."

They stopped and watched the helicopter circle the Bahama Princess three times before landing on the helipad. After its rotor blades stopped, five Coast Guard personnel fast walked toward the aircraft, each bent down and holding a hand on their combination caps.

Gidget said, "Look. Four stripes, three stripes, two strips, one and a half stripes, and one stripe." She pulled out her phone and began recording a video of them climbing into the aircraft.

"I think you're still a little tipsy," Daffy said.

"Why?"

"Your phone is upside down."

Gidget reversed her phone and recorded the aircraft slowly rising into the air. It circled the ship once, then turned eastward and flew off.

As they turned to go to their stateroom, Daffy pointed to a spot above them. “Look up there.”

Gidget looked. “It’s the Arnold Schwarzenegger guy.”

He stood above them. When he saw them looking, he turned and walked away.

“The man that does not exist,” said Daffy.

Both Ladies’ phones sounded the arrival of texts. Gidget looked at her text messages and said, “It’s a shipboard-wide text announcement. Captain Omen says we’ll be weighing anchor shortly and resuming our cruise. Next stop is the Cayman Islands.”

Chapter 34

13° 0' 59.76" North, 70° 32' 22.3404" West
November 17th

Tables in Neptune's Spectacle were arranged so all the room's chairs had good views of the stage. A small combo played bluesy John Coltrane music which eerily befitted the mood of everyone at Gidget and Daffy's table. All five women still felt their afternoon of Mojitos.

Halfway through the meal, Gary sat his empty glass of beer on the table.

"If youse will excuse me, I gotta go appease the prostate god."

Gidget chuckled. "And I thought all y'all were Catholic."

"The prostate god is a lesser divinity, but nevertheless he is a powerful divinity. Saint peter guards the entrance to his kingdom."

"I've paid my respects to saint peter many times," said Daffy.

Veronica and Naomi nodded.

Gary was on a roll. "The prostate god demands frequent offerings, and so, I best make my offering now so's I don't have to during Moriarty. I bid youse, *adieu*."

Gidget's eyes followed Gary as he weaved through the tables. She noticed a familiar person standing in the back of the room whose eyes also followed Gary. She nudged Daffy and nodded in the direction of the man.

Daffy leaned in and whispered, "It's him. The Arnold Schwarzenegger guy."

"The man that does not exist."

"He's leaving the room. Must've seen us spot him. Whatcha gonna do?"

"If Gary's not back in ten minutes, you and I are going to look for him."

Gary returned safe and sound within Gidget's timeframe, and at seven thirty, the jazz combo packed up and exited. A booming voice replaced the room's soulful music.

"Ladies and Gentlemen, as well as anyone not conforming to either definition, you are about to experience the greatest feats of prestidigitation ever performed. Revered by royalty and lauded in capitals around the world, please give a hearty round of applause for Moriarty the Magician!"

Moriarty swept into the room amid enthusiastic applause. Very pale skin, menacing dark eyebrows, and a high forehead with hair long enough to touch the wingtip collar of his white formal shirt. Black bowtie, cape, and pants completed the classic magician's outfit.

Gidget was taken by his eyes. "Look at those round, dark eyes. I'd hate to meet him alone in a Victorian mansion."

"Almost no lips, no chin. He needs a smaller mouth," said Daffy. "Reminds me of a possum."

Moriarty ascended the stage and whirled around, producing a large bouquet of red roses from thin air at the completion of his twirl. He handed them to a beautiful assistant whom he introduced as Alisha. Her low-cut, sequined costume showed plenty of leg and cleavage, intended to keep males in the audience from paying too much attention to Moriarty's sleight of hand. She handed individual roses to women sitting close to the stage.

"Thank you, ladies and gentlemen for your warm welcome," Moriarty said. "You will see real magic tonight. Not tricks. Not sleight of hand. Not the kind of fakery that charlatans pull over simple minds. Real magic. Magic invoked by supernatural forces unseen by humans."

Moriarty spread his arms wide as he spoke. He suddenly brought his hands together and when he opened them, they held a rabbit. He held the creature up for everyone to see before handing it to the lovely Alisha.

"Audiences of magic performances always expect to see the magician make a rabbit appear. I perform this simple trick to get it out of the way so I can show them the real magic."

Gary leaned in. "Get ready. It gets real good real soon."

Gary was not wrong. Moriarty proceeded to perform a number of card tricks, followed by the bullet trick. For this, he asked for a volunteer from the audience.

"I need someone who is a competent marksman," Moriarty said, then pointed to a man in the audience who had raised his hand. "You, my friend."

The man ascended steps up the stage, and Moriarty handed him a revolver. He said, "Sir, please verify that this is a real pistol."

The man opened it, spun the gun's cylinder, and nodded his agreement.

Moriarty had more instructions. "Now, please write your initials with this Sharpie on this bullet and load it into the revolver."

After the man complied, the magician showed him where to stand and further instructed him to fire the bullet at Moriarty's face on command. Moriarty walked to a spot on the stage fifteen feet away and said, "Ready, aim, fire!"

The volunteer pulled the trigger, the revolver roared, and a cloud of smoke exploded from the barrel. Moriarty's head rocked backward, then returned to its original position. He turned to face the audience showing something shiny in his mouth which he extracted and handed to the volunteer.

"Would you attest that this is the bullet with your initials on it?" asked Moriarty.

"Yessir, it is," said the volunteer.

The audience roared with shouts and applause. Alisha took the bullet from the volunteer and walked to each table, allowing them to see the initials 'JR' on it.

Gary clapped frantically. "Unbelievable! I told you this guy was the greatest!"

Moriarty next had an audience volunteer handcuff his hands behind his back. After the woman verified that the cuffs were indeed locked and secure, Moriarty stepped away, then turned his back to the audience so they could see the cuffs were locked. He turned back to face the audience, but as he finished turning, he moved his hands back in front of him. He held the cuffs in his right hand. The audience's applause was deafening.

Gary applauded loudest of all. "It only gets better."

Moriarty performed a number of other tricks with ropes and metal hoops, each trick becoming more amazing. When asked for a volunteer for his disappearing act, Gary's hand shot up.

"The gentleman at that table." Moriarty pointed to Gary.

Gary rose and hobbled onto the stage. After he stood next to the magician, Moriarty said, "Please tell the audience your name."

"Gary Fra… Gary Vanderhoff."

"Mr. Vanderhoff, have you ever disappeared?"

"No, never, but sometimes I wish I could disappear."

Gary's reply elicited raucous laughter from the audience.

"Well, your wish is going to come true tonight," Moriarty said.

Alisha rolled out a large black box out from behind the stage curtain. The box was six feet high and four feet square. Once it was front and center, Moriarty stood on the right side while Alisha stood on the left. They proceeded to rotate the box three-hundred-sixty degrees, showing the audience that it was indeed a square box. Moriarty instructed Alisha to open the front panel, step inside, and push on its three interior walls to verify that it was solid. This she did.

With a flourish of his arms, Moriarty said, "Ladies and Gentlemen, I will now ask Mr. Vanderhoff to step inside the box."

Moriarty helped Gary step into the box and closed the door. "I will now ask my assistant to lock the door panel."

Alisha proceeded to insert a padlock into a latch on the door and lock it. She tugged on the lock to verify it was secure. Moriarty and his assistant then rotated the box to show the audience once again that it was solid.

He asked, "Mr. Vanderhoff, are you okay?"

"Yeah." Came the reply from within the box.

Moriarty stepped back, then walked around the box several times. He said, "I will wave my magic wand, and when Alisha opens the door to the box, you will no longer see Mr. Vanderhoff. He will have disappeared."

He moved to a point next to the box and waved his wand. Alisha walked to the door and unlocked it. With a flourish, she swung the door open. A collective gasp arose from the audience. Gidget and Daffy looked at each other, worry on each's face.

"As you can see, Mr. Vanderhoff is not inside the box. He has indeed disappeared," said Moriarty. With that, he and Alisha rotated the box in a complete circle. When they finished, he said, "I will now ask the lovely Alisha to close the front panel and lock the box again.

Alisha did as instructed, and Moriarty said, "I will now wave my magic wand and cause Mr. Vanderhoff to reappear."

Moriarty made a flourish with his wand. "Alisha, please unlock the box and open the front panel."

Alisha unlocked the box, opened the front panel, then stood aside. The audience remained silent. Standing on each side of the box expecting applause, Moriarty and Alisha's expressions turned from smiles to surprise. Both looked inside the box. Gary was nowhere to be seen.

Moriarty closed the door and waited. "The forces beyond this realm sometimes work at their own pace."

He opened the door, and again, the box was empty.

Barry almost pushed their table over trying to get out of his chair. "Where is my brother!? Where is Gary?!"

He rushed onto the stage and frantically searched inside and behind the box for Gary. Finding no one, he ran to the back of the stage and began violently sweeping the curtain back and forth in a futile attempt to find his brother hiding somewhere.

Mayhem ensued. The audience began booing. Several audience members stood and threw food at the stage. A tomato smashed into Moriarty on the chest. He and Alisha retreated to the rear of the stage in fear. The audience shouted profanities.

Gidget and Daffy sat motionless, horror on their faces.

Naomi said, "Those boys are a magnet for disaster."

"Magic gone bad," said Daffy.

Things deteriorated for the next ten minutes until Captain Omen, the Chief Security Officer, and several other crew members arrived.

Chapter 35

13° 0' 59.97" North, 70° 32' 22.3464" West
November 17th

Captain Omen stepped up to the microphone on the stage and said, "Please calm down. I apologize, but I have to ask the audience to leave. We need to find out what happened here."

As they were companions of Gary's, Barry and the five women were allowed to remain. Daffy leaned into Gidget and whispered, "Four down, one to go… Oh, I'm sorry." She'd forgotten Barry was Gidget's lover.

Looking at Moriarty, Captain Omen asked, "What happened here?"

"I… I don't know. It was my standard bit. I've done it hundreds of times. I get a quote," Moriarty made air quotes with his hands, "volunteer from the audience that I've talked to beforehand. I had talked to Mr. Vanderhoff right before the show started. Caught him when he was peeing in the bathroom before the show. I took him behind the stage through the performers' entrance and showed him the inside of the box and how it worked. He was very enthusiastic. Said he'd seen my act before when he was in Phoenix and would love to do it—"

"Show me how it is supposed to work."

"Sure. Step up onto the stage."

Moriarty led Captain Omen to the box and opened the front. He stepped inside and said, "You can see, Captain, although the box is four by four feet square, inside it is only four feet by two feet. This back wall inside the box can be opened. There's a hidden latch. The subject opens it and simply walks into the back half of the box which is also four by two feet. Because all the inside walls are solid black, the audience can't tell that the inside of the box that they see is only four by two. They're sitting too far away to be able to tell how deep the box is."

Moriarty opened the back wall of the box and showed them the box's other half.

The captain said, "Okay. I see how your trick's supposed to work, but that doesn't explain where Mr. Vanderhoff went. Could he have slipped out through the back of the box?"

"No, as you can see the back is a solid wall connected to the two sides of the box. The outside back wall is not hinged to one of the side walls. It can't swing outward." Moriarty turned and pushed on the back wall, but it remained unmoved. "I don't know how he could have gotten out or where he went. He was supposed to wait in the back half of the box, then move into the front half when we closed the front door. There's no room to slip out. Opening the front door would have been seen by the audience."

"Move the box for us."

Moriarty and Alisha moved the box to one side. Captain Omen walked over and thumped the stage floor with his foot where the box had stood. A hollow sound rang out. The stage floor was about three feet higher than the floor of Neptune's Spectacle. He said, "I don't see a trap door or any other opening he could have slipped through."

Barry was furious. "My brother's missing! What are you gonna do?! We gotta find him! He can't just have disappeared into thin air."

"I'm going to have the crew conduct a thorough search of this ship. Stem to stern, top to bottom. Starting right here. We're going to leave no stone unturned. We will find your brother."

Captain Omen issued instructions to the crew members for conducting the search. They combed every inch of Neptune's Spectacle. Then he and the rest of the crew left, leaving one crew member in the club. Moriarty and Alisha left with the Chief of Security. Gidget turned to Barry.

"What do you want to do now?"

He looked down. "I searched and Gary wasn't behind the curtain on the stage. I looked at the stage floor. There's no trap door. I'm sure of it. Besides, there's not enough room underneath the stage floor for anyone to slip away. I… I just don't know. I guess I'll go back to the room. Nothing I can do here."

Veronica said, "I'm going back to my room."

Louella and Naomi concurred.

Gidget and Daffy stood still as the others walked out of the room. Daffy said, "I bet he's gonna go watch the rest of *Andy Griffith*."

Gidget shouted, “Daffy! The man just lost his fourth brother… Besides, it’s too late for *Andy Griffith*.”

“Is it too late to see a rerun episode of *MASH*?”

Gidget walked to and up the steps of the stage. The sole remaining crew member asked, “Can I help you, ma’am?”

“I just want to look around,” Gidget said as she began walking in a pattern that led her to and around the black box.

“What are you doing?” asked Daffy.

“Just checking to see if there’s a trap door anywhere.”

Daffy joined her, and after they had paced the entire stage floor, she said, “I don’t see any trap doors that he could’ve slipped through. Maybe Gary shifted into a parallel dimension. You and I could be in the midst of a sci-fi story.”

“Now, you sound like Babs.” Gidget looked up. “I don’t see any connector between the box and the ceiling. No way he could have climbed up and out of that box and into a room in the ceiling without being seen.”

“Yeah. There’s too much space between the top of the box and the stage ceiling.”

Gidget walked up to the box, opened the front door, and stepped inside. She pushed against both side walls, then the back panel. “If you look closely, you can see the seam around it. Here’s the hinges on this side. Here’s the latch.”

She pulled on the latch, and the back panel opened, revealing a hidden compartment behind it. “Yeah, there’s enough space for a small person to fit into it.”

Daffy said, “Bet that’s why Moriarty picked Gary.”

Gidget closed the back panel and latched it. “I’m tired.”

“What now? Go to bed?”

“Nope.”

“What?”

“We interrogate suspects.”

At midnight, Gidget and Daffy rapped on the door to Alisha’s cabin.

A sleepy but sultry female voice sounded from inside. “Who is it?”

“Misses Smurfitt and Belvedere. We sat with the Vanderhoffs at your show,” Gidget said.

The door cracked open, and Alisha's head poked out, rubbing her eyes. "Please go away. I just spent two hours being grilled by the Chief Security Officer. I gotta get some sleep."

"No, we need to talk. We're going to find out what happened to our traveling companion."

"There's nothing to talk about. I don't know what happened to Mr. Vanderhoff. And you have no authority to question me anyway."

Daffy stepped into the doorway and dominated the scene with her imposing height. "Step us through it again. We're not leaving until you do."

Alisha remained in place but relented. "Okay. One more time. I open the front door to the box. He steps inside. I close the door. As far as I know, he unlatches the inside panel, steps behind it, and closes it."

"How do you know he stepped behind and closed it?" asked Gidget.

"Well, I can't say for sure. I didn't actually see inside. There's no peepholes where you can see what the subject is doing inside."

"Did you hear anything?"

"Yeah. I could hear the inside panel being unlatched and opened."

"And you heard him moving around inside?"

"Oh yeah. You could hear his steps… shuffling inside."

"And then you heard him close the inside panel?"

"Yeah."

"What about after Moriarty waved his magic wand? What did you hear?"

"Now that you ask, I don't remember hearing anything."

"And you didn't see him open the back side of the box and slip out?"

"No. The back panel is attached to the two side panels. They're fixed and immovable. Only way out of that box is through its front door. If he'd a slipped out of that box, I'd have seen it."

"Who's paying y'all to get rid of Mr. Vanderhoff?"

"The ship's paying us to perform our magic bit. Nothing else. No one's paying us to make Mr. Vanderhoff disappear!"

With that, Alisha pushed Daffy back outside and slammed the cabin door. Daffy looked at Gidget. "You were pretty rough on her. She's lucky you didn't have a rubber hose."

Gidget nodded. "It is late and I am tired."

"You may have been tired, but you made me proud nonetheless. Why you ever fretted about being your own independent woman is beyond me. You would make Gloria Steinem proud. What's next?"

"We interrogate Moriarty."

Fifteen minutes later, they knocked on the door to Moriarty's cabin. A voice from within said, "Who's there?"

Gidget said, "Misses Smurfitt and Belvedere."

"Please go away. I'm bushed and need to go to sleep."

"No. We're not going away. We're going to keep knocking on your door until you talk to us."

The door opened, and Moriarty invited them in. "Nothing compels me, but I'll talk to you out of respect for your missing companion. You know I just spent two hours with the Chief Security Officer. We got nowhere in coming up with any ideas on what happened."

"Well, we know he didn't just disappear. You were next to that box the whole time. You must've seen him slip out."

Moriarty shook his head in despair. "Nothing. I saw nothing. And Alisha told the Security Officer that she saw nothing. It's as if he *did* actually disappear. As amazing as it seems, my magic may have worked. I've often suspected that magic really does exist."

Daffy said, "You sound like our friend Babs."

Gidget rolled her eyes and looked at Moriarty. "We checked the stage floor, and we couldn't find any sort of trap door. Could he have somehow climbed up and slipped through a door in the ceiling above the box?"

"Nope. The box's ceiling is attached to its sides. Besides, the old boy looked like he'd have trouble even climbing a stepstool."

"Did you pick Gary because of his small size?"

"Yep. I met him when I had to pee and figured he would be a good fit."

"Was there a real big guy in the bathroom when y'all were there?"

"No. I wouldn't have asked your friend if there'd been anyone else in the bathroom."

Daffy and Gidget left the room and dragged butt to their stateroom, both feeling punchy from a long day filled with too much alcohol and excitement. Daffy was frustrated.

"Questioning those two was about as useful as a doorknob on a toilet seat."

Gidget nodded. "As useful as a mirror on a refrigerator door."

"Now that might not be a bad idea. What better way to discourage someone from opening the refrigerator door? How about as useful as a speedometer on a blow dryer?"

"Nah. How about as useful as a speedometer on a broom?"

"You could probably get that guy that does those Made for TV commercials to do a commercial for that one. What would they call it?"

"Speed-O-Broom?"

"Broomometer?"

"It's been too long a day. Say goodnight, Daffy."

"Goodnight, Daffy."

Chapter 36

14° 8' 50.0244" North, 72° 37' 31.5804" West
November 18th

Daffy and Gidget again debated powerwalking the morning after another Gary's disappearance but did not know what else to do. Fifteen minutes into their walk, Daffy complained, "Slow up. I'm having trouble keeping up with you. Give an old woman a break."

"Sorry. Too much on my mind." Gidget slowed.

"I don't understand the Marx Brothers."

"Does anyone?"

"Trying to understand them defies rational thinking. I can understand Jerry committing suicide, if that's the case, after Larry chokes to death. But they lose Jerry, and Harry *still* goes parasailing. Then they lose Harry, and they go to see a magic act. I'll be curious to see how Barry handles Gary's disappearance this morning."

Gidget put on her pharmacist thinking cap. "Maybe they've handled these tragedies so well because they're on something."

"You mean like tranquilizers?"

Gidget nodded. "Xanax, Valium. Something along those lines. Something not too addictive. Something that keeps them on an even keel. That might explain why they don't seem to get too depressed when tragedy strikes."

"You've spent a couple of nights with Barry, and I've spent a couple with Harry. I never saw any of those kinds of meds laying around."

"Me neither, but that doesn't mean that they don't take something."

Daffy was impressed. "Once again, you make Hercule Poirot look like Barney Fife. I'm amazed at your powers of deduction."

"I didn't watch *Murder, She Wrote* for twelve years for no good reason, my dear Daffy."

They walked in silence until they rounded the ship's stern and Daffy asked, "I take it you haven't come up with anything since we left Moriarty last night?"

Gidget spoke deliberately. "After we got back to our room, I lay in bed for an hour, looking up at the ceiling, and reviewing everything."

"And?"

"Three things. First. Moriarty met Gary in the john and recruited him for his magic act because of his *small size*—"

"Gary or his weenie?"

Gidget ignored the lame humor. "Second. As Moriarty explained it, his box is rigged to *conceal* the subject during the disappearing part of the bit and *not to escape from it*. The subject never has to come back into the box because he never leaves it. Movement out of and back into the box is unnecessary."

"Good point. But where was Gary when we examined the box?"

"I don't know."

"Moriarty opened the door to the concealed compartment inside the box, and we didn't see Gary in it. You examined the concealed compartment yourself."

"True."

Daffy tried to lighten things up a bit. "Maybe, it's like I said. Maybe, Gary shifted into a parallel dimension or a parallel universe after he entered the hidden compartment."

"Thank you, Mr. Spock." Gidget smirked as her iPhone signaled an incoming text.

Gidget extracted her iPhone and read the text. "Oh no. Sammy woke up screaming and crying this morning."

"Poor thing. What happened?" asked Daffy.

"He lost his Godzilla."

"Godzilla?"

"Yeah. One of those hard rubber Godzilla toys. He sleeps with it every night."

"Did he find Godzilla?"

"Yeah, thank God! It got lost under the covers, and when he woke up this morning, he couldn't find it. He started screaming and crying. He loves Godzilla, takes it everywhere—to church, the playground. Godzilla *must* sit beside him in the van."

"Sounds like my granddaughter's stuffed penguin."

"Anyway, my daughter felt I should know about Sammy's dramatic loss and recovery of Godzilla. Sammy probably cajoled her into texting me. He knows I know how much he loves Godzilla."

"I feel your pain."

"They found Godzilla under the covers at the foot of the bed. I bet the poor creature was probably trying to get away from Sammy. That boy sleeps like a shark."

"Always moving?"

"You got it. Anyway, Sammy's probably got a case of PTSD over losing Godzilla, even though they are reunited. I'll text Sammy and tell him I'm bringing him a special toy to be Godzilla's friend. Maybe that will ease the temporary separation pain. Can I borrow one of your taxidermized reptiles?"

Daffy rolled her eyes. "Over my dead body. Back to our murders. What else did you conclude during the late-night exploration of your consciousness?"

"Nothing."

"Nothing else?"

"Well, I think that the Arnold Schwarzenegger guy is somehow tied into these Marx Brothers' deaths and disappearances. He was once again in the area when tragedy befell one of our boyfriends. Let's go wake Barry up and have breakfast."

Gidget and Daffy knocked on Barry's door only to find him inside with Louella.

Gidget looked at Louella. "Y'all are up early this morning."

Louella said, "I wanted to check on Barry to see how he's holding up."

The sole remaining Marx Brother looked dejected.

Daffy asked, "How are you doing this morning?"

"Not too good," Barry said. "Didn't sleep much last night."

Gidget asked, "Heard anything this morning about the results of yesterday's inquiry?"

He nodded. "Captain Omen came by just before Louella showed up. The Inquiry Board questioned the crew that was in any way involved with my brothers' deaths and said no one caused their deaths. They were doing just a preliminary investigation. Someone back in the States will do a more thorough job. That's why they ordered the boat to head back home."

"What about Gary?" asked Daffy.

"They still haven't found him. They searched high and low."

"We interrogated Moriarty and Alisha after you left last night," said Gidget.

Barry looked worried. "What did youse find out?"

"Nothing. They both clammed up tighter than Dick's hat band."

A look of relief crossed Barry's face. "Too bad. What youse doing today?"

"Breakfast. Want to join us?"

Barry shook his head and looked down.

Gidget said, "I don't know what we'll do after that. What about you?"

"Nothing much. I'm gonna do the MegaSlide one more time this afternoon. Get one more ride in before we dock."

Daffy and Gidget both shrieked, "What?!"

Louella shrugged. "It might be good for his spirit. He's enjoyed the slide a lot."

Barry said nothing.

Daffy couldn't believe what she'd heard. "Yeah. A four-hundred-foot drop will take your mind off anything."

Barry remained silent, prompting Louella to put her arm around his shoulders.

"Besides, it's very safe," she said. "It's an enclosed plexiglass tube. One way in, one way out. He's done it five or six times so far. What could go wrong?"

Daffy was going to object, but Gidget interrupted. "Louella's right. It's a closed system. It should be safe and probably good therapy. Let us know when you do it. We'd like to watch."

On the way to Azul, Daffy said, "I'm surprised you didn't try to talk Barry out of doing the MegaSlide. Why?"

"What risk could it be? It is a closed system. He's done it several times already with no problems. It might be therapeutic somehow for him—these guys are different. Besides, maybe we'll see the Arnold Schwarzenegger guy again. I'd love to get a picture of him."

Raspberry Bellini was the drink of choice later that morning at Mexican Train. The bartender's recipe upped vodka from ¾ to one ounce and two ounces of prosecco. The ladies' conversation reflected the bartender's change in the recipe.

"Your boyfriend seems to be holding up," Louella said.

Gidget managed a ho-hum shrug. "He seems to be hanging in there."

"Any chance of you two transitioning from friendship into something more permanent?" Veronica asked. She flagged their waiter for a refill, having miscounted the number of Bellinis she had already consumed.

Naomi was upset at her best friend's lack of tact. "Veronica! That's rather rude."

"It is a catty question that deserves an answer," Louella said.

Gidget knew all three would love to snare the remaining Marx Brother and decided to be catty herself.

"Barry and I have nothing planned right now, but y'all will all be invited. Have y'all ever been to Santorini?"

"Santorini? Is that an alternative to a bellini?" asked Louella.

"It's a beautiful Greek island. The latest thing for destination weddings."

Naomi was surprised. "You two have talked about wedding locations?"

Daffy grinned. "Gidget and Barry don't smoke cigarettes. What else they got to do after they finish?"

Gidget and Daffy waited for Barry on the weather deck. He wanted to do the MegaSlide at three o'clock—in fifteen minutes.

"I know I didn't discourage him, but I do worry about Barry going down the slide," said Gidget.

Daffy nodded. "You two have gotten pretty close. You were kidding this morning about Santorini, weren't you?"

"The subject has come up."

"And..."

"He's... he hesitates."

"A little something on the side is fine, but marriage is a whole different animal. What man doesn't hesitate when it comes to marriage? You got to give him a little push to get him to take the plunge."

Gidget shook her head. "I don't know. I get the feeling he wants to get married, but something's holding him back. Something he doesn't want to discuss with me."

"Probably his prostate, but I'm optimistic. He'll come around in time. We have to make sure this is his last MegaSlide."

"I keep telling myself that it's a closed system—one way in, one way out, so he can't get lost. And he's done it... What, maybe ten times?"

Daffy nodded. "At least."

"They should rename it Barry's EgoSlide in his honor. Rachel said the slide is four hundred and thirty feet long—"

"That's a long way for Barry to go without peeing."

"Maybe you should suggest they put a rest stop halfway through it."

"Or better yet, a Buc-ee's. They have the cleanest bathrooms."

"As I was going to say, it's four hundred and thirty feet from there..." Gidget pointed at the slide entrance on the weather deck, then in the direction of the stern. "...to there, but there's no way for him to get lost in route. Just the same, one of us will watch him enter it up here, and the other will be at the pool on the stern watching him come out."

Chapter 37

14° 33' 8.6148" North, 76° 37' 24.6864" West
November 18th

Barry acted nervously, even shuffling more than normal toward the pool. Eyes darting back and forth, wringing his hands, beads of sweat sparkling on top his bald head. Daffy was worried.

"Barry looks so nervous than he makes me nervous."

"Second thoughts, maybe?" mused Gidget. "It's not as if this is his first time. His brothers must make him nervous."

Daffy looked at her friend. Barry wasn't the only one worried. "You have grown attached to him."

Gidget nodded, then smiled as they approached Barry. "Buck up, Sweetie Pie. You're an expert sliding four hundred feet down a plexiglass tube."

Barry forced a smile. "Yeah. The expert. It takes a lot of expertise to lie flat on your back and let hundreds of gallons of water propel your body down twelve stories. I debated whether or not to do this, but I told myself, 'Gary would want me to do this.' That was the kind of brother he was."

"Dat's the spirit," said Daffy.

"Let's get on with it."

"Wait ten minutes before you begin," Gidget said. "I'm gonna go to the stern and wait for you to come out and splash into the pool down there. I want to get some pictures. Be sure to smile when you come out. I'll be waiting for you with one of Elyse's special cocktails."

"Have her put *lots* of alcohol in it. Doesn't matter which."

As Gidget walked off, Barry and Daffy walked to the MegaSlide. Freddy stood at the entrance and was sending another passenger, a teenage boy, off into it. After the boy disappeared in the tube, Freddy turned.

"*Hola*, Mr. Vanderhoff. Goin' again?"

"Yeah. This'll be my last trip," Barry said.

"We'll make it a good one."

Freddy checked Barry over to make sure he was okay and put a wristband on his wrist. All slide riders wore one, indicating they had been checked by the attendant and certified okay to make the ride through the curvy, twisting slide. If anyone was found dead at the other end and they weren't wearing a wristband, the cruise line could claim they entered the slide without permission. Freddy repeated his standard instructions by rote.

"Lie down on your back. Cross your arms. You'll feel a rush of water flow under you. Let your body float on the water. Do not fight it. Flow with it. You can slow your rate of descent by spreading your legs. You can speed it up by bringing your legs closer together."

"Bye-bye," Daffy said.

Water gushed through the slide, and Freddy gave Barry a gentle push. Daffy bent down and peered into the tube opening as Barry's little head became ever smaller until it vanished, heading down to the next lower floor.

Gidget sat at a table by one of the pools on the stern of the ship. This one occupied an outcropping just below the main deck, giving the MegaSlide rider an unbelievable view of emerald-green Caribbean Ocean after exiting the tube. She sipped a Caribbean Mule, and another sat on the table beside her, that one containing double the amount of rum. The glass's condensation dripping onto her chest was refreshing in the afternoon sun. Her phone buzzed; it was a text from Daffy.

He just left.

Gidget texted back: His Mule is ready with lots of ice.

He'll probably need a good kick in the head after it's over.

Based on Barry's past rides, it took him anywhere from eight to twelve minutes to complete the MegaSlide. Gidget looked at her watch—three-fifteen. She figured Barry's little bald head would be sailing through the air above the pool sometime between three-twenty-three and three-twenty-seven.

A teenage boy splashed into the pool from the MegaSlide at three-twenty. She looked at her watch and again at three-twenty-one and three-twenty-two. At three-twenty-three, she checked her watch again but was not surprised that Barry had not emerged. A funny thought popped into her head. He was very floatable since his large tummy probably acted like a personal flotation device. She smiled, remembering how she enjoyed rubbing his hairy tummy after they had sex. The thought, 'rubbing his tummy for good luck' subconsciously entered her brain.

Three-twenty-four and three-twenty-five passed and raised no concern on Gidget's part. As three-twenty-seven, three-twenty-eight, and three-twenty-nine passed with no Barry, she began to worry.

She texted Daffy.

3:30 and no Barry. You sure he left when you texted me?

Absolutely.

At three-thirty-five, Gidget again texted Daffy.

"Still no Barry. Something's wrong.

I'm on my way down.

"So, where is he?" Daffy asked after she arrived at the stern pool ten minutes later. She stood next to the exhaust end of the MegaSlide and looked up into it.

"You tell me, and we'll both know," said Gidget. "And you *saw* him slide down?"

"Absolutely. I looked until I couldn't see his little bald head anymore, then I went over to the bar, got a drink to go, and cooled my jets. And you haven't *left* the pool since you got here?"

"Nope."

"No way he could have slipped by when you went to pee or something?"

"No. I did not have to go pee… I don't have a prostate. Did anyone go down after Barry?" Gidget asked.

"No. No one after Barry until I left to come down here. I don't know about after that. I didn't see anyone queuing up to ride. What do we do now?"

"Put on our bathing suits."

At four-thirty, Gidget and Daffy stood in front of Freddy. Gidget asked, "Has anyone gone down the slide since Barry went down?"

Freddy shook his head. "No'm. No one. One of the sewage treatment techs called me right after Mr. Vanderhoff left and told me they wanted to flush the water in the slide. They started flushing the water shortly after he left. No one goes down while they're flushing."

"That sounds terrible. Can't they come up with a less disgusting term for exchanging the water flowing down the slide?" asked Daffy.

"It sounds nasty, but it's accurate. And it keeps the water clean. You'd be surprised what a lot of people do while they're sliding down."

"I don't want to know."

"Oh look. Here comes the water again. Looks like they're finished flushing."

Gidget said, "Do me a favor. Don't let anyone go down after Mizz Belvedere goes. Mr. Vanderhoff never came out of the end of the slide." Freddy's face froze in horror as Gidget continued. "We think he's stuck somewhere in the slide. If he is, we'll get him unstuck."

Freddy nodded. "For sure. I'll hold everyone up till I hear from you."

"I got my phone. It's waterproof. Give me your phone number, and I'll call you and let you know when it's okay to send people down."

Freddy told her the number, which she entered into her Contacts. He looked at both women, misgiving written all over his face. "I don't know if I should let y'all do this—Him being missing and all. Y'all sure y'all wanna do this?"

"I don't," said Daffy. "I'm claustrophobic."

Gidget said, "Come on. Barry did it a bunch of times, and—"

"And where is he now?"

"Look. It only lasts about ten minutes. You're a grown woman… just like me," Gidget said in an attempt at false bravado. She never dreamed of doing something as scary as the MegaSlide. The zipline in Antigua had cured her of scary rides.

Daffy was adamant. "I'm grown, and I'd like to stay grown for a while longer. Transitioning to a dead woman has no appeal for me."

Gidget shamed Daffy by setting the example. Freddy helped her lie flat on her back in the tube, feet first. She heard none of the instructions he regurgitated after he put a wristband on her. She felt water gushing beneath her, then a push before sliding down a moderate fifteen-degree slope for twenty feet. Then the bottom dropped out.

The angle of descent had increased to forty-five degrees while sharply curving left at the same time. She passed from the weather deck to the next floor below it. She never noticed when several passengers in one of the ship's lounges waved at her. One of them gave her the finger, thinking her rude for not waving back. She kept her arms crossed over her chest as Freddy had instructed. That part was fairly easy; the hard part was keeping her eyes open as she had told Daffy.

"Keep your eyes open so you don't run into me. Be on the lookout for Barry."

The angle leveled out to about thirty degrees, and the tube curved once again as she slid past another two floors. So far, no Barry. The tube itself was clear acrylic plexiglass affording excellent views of the ship's interior as well as the ocean when its path took it next to the ship's exterior. Although her sixty-two-year-old stomach turned, Gidget began to feel less fearful. She started observing things like joints in the plexiglass where sections connected to each other. They appeared secure; no water leaked from the connections. The thought occurred that Barry could not have slipped through one of these connections, even as short as he was.

The tube passed through more floors, frequently varying in its angle of descent and its repeated left-right-left-right direction. All the while, Daffy's screaming echoed many yards behind her. Gidget came close to smiling.

A silent prayer of gratitude passed her lips when she saw 'Level Six' on a wall outside the tube. Only five more levels until she would splash into the pool. She breathed a sigh of relief, then noticed the Arnold Schwarzenegger guy. He stood close by the tube in an open area of the floor where passengers normally played pickleball, but now strangely deserted. He appeared to be looking through the plexiglass down into the tube at a point further ahead of her. When he saw her, he turned and walked away.

Gidget looked in the direction of his focus and saw it—a large hole in the plexiglass thirty feet below her. It was in a section of the MegaSlide running along the exterior of the ship and affording riders an excellent view of the ocean below as they passed from Level Four to Level Three. She screamed as she plunged toward it.

The hole was large enough for a person to pass through and had jagged edges. If the edges did not kill you, the fall into the ocean below would. Gidget instinctively spread her legs as wide as possible but realized little traction from it. The tube's steep angle fought against her straining legs, and her speed only decreased marginally. She uncrossed her arms and added them to the opposing force her legs exerted. Her speed slowed… until a screaming Daffy slammed into her.

Chapter 38

14° 41' 9.1121" North, 76° 50' 15.6154" West
November 18th

Gidget had neither time nor presence of mind to experience any of Kübler-Ross' stages of grief. The famous psychiatrist said one passes through five stages when facing death: denial, anger, bargaining, depression, and acceptance. Gidget went straight to an undocumented sixth stage as she screamed, "OH, SHIT," which Daffy now heard. She followed that expletive with more screaming.

"DAFFY! Quick! Spread your legs wide."

By the time Gidget finished her sentence, both women were ten feet closer to the jagged hole in the plexiglass, and water continued to flow under and around them.

Daffy opened her eyes, saw their predicament, and passed on into the sixth stage herself. "OH SHIT!"

Gidget shouted, "Spread your arms and legs wide! We've got to stop somehow!"

Four arms and four legs strained with all their might against the plexiglass walls. Their rate of descent slowed, but not enough. The hole kept closing in on them.

"Turn sideways," Gidget said, and quickly turned her body such that her shoulders pressed against one side of the tube, while her feet pressed against the opposite side. Daffy followed suit, and their rate of descent decreased. They were twelve feet away.

"Press harder! Harder!" Gidget pressed her shoulders and feet against the plexiglass as hard as she could. Daffy did also. Daffy's height mattered, and three feet from the hole, their progress halted.

Daffy said, "When I heard your first 'spread your legs wide,' I wondered if you had found us two more boyfriends or a new gynecologist. What now?"

"Keep pressing against the walls of the tube. Thank God for your tall body. I've got to call Freddy."

Gidget extracted her iPhone from her bathing suit and speed dialed. "Freddy, this is Mrs. Smurfitt! Stop the water flow now!"

Pause.

"Because there's a hole in the MegaSlide plexiglass on Level Three. It's on the side and part of the bottom of the tube that runs next to the exterior of that level."

Pause.

"Because Daffy and I almost went through it."

Pause.

"Call the sewage treatment people and the bridge. We're hanging on… for now. We're gonna very carefully edge our way around it and slide on down to the pool."

Pause.

"Don't worry about that. With Daffy's height, we should be able to make it around the hole. We're gonna do it one at a time, holding hands. Tell Captain Omen what's happened and what we're gonna do."

Pause.

"Let him know that this must be where Mr. Vanderhoff fell through. He's probably in the ocean right now."

Pause.

"Exactly. They need to start a man overboard drill ASAP. Has anyone else gone down the slide after Missus Belvedere? Good. Don't let anyone else come down. Look, I gotta go now. I don't wanna stay here any longer. I'll call you after we land in the pool."

Gidget hung up. "Now, we got to navigate our way down."

"Be careful on your way down," said Daffy. "I think I contributed some of the reason why Freddy said they have to flush the MegaSlide."

After exiting the MegaSlide and pool, Daffy and Gidget made their way back to their stateroom and quickly changed before heading up to the weather deck. They saw Captain Omen and several staff who were walking away at a rapid pace. The women made a beeline for Freddy.

"Freddy! What did the captain say?" Gidget asked.

"They've already started the man overboard drill. The Chief Security Officer grilled me about Mr. Vanderhoff's ride and about yours."

"What'd you tell him about Mr. Vanderhoff's ride?"

"That it was a typical ride, no different than any of his other rides, except that you said he didn't come out of the slide into the stern pool. And that y'all went down the slide to see if y'all could find him, but that y'all found a big hole in the tube on Level Three. That's where he and the others are headed for now."

"Freddy, tell me all you can remember about Mr. Vanderhoff's ride."

"Well, it's like I told Captain Omen. He got here about three o'clock. I helped him get positioned in the tube. It was no different than with any other rider—"

"Tell me exactly what you did."

"Y'all watched. I put the wristband on—"

"The standard wristband?"

"Yes'm. It was standard. Then I positioned him, gave him the standard instructions, and when he seemed ready, I gave him a push, and he was off."

"And that was it?"

"Yes'm. I watched him go down the tube. He seemed okay as far as I could see. Didn't notice anything different until you called me."

"What about the flushing?"

"Oh yeah. I got a call from Sewage Processing a minute or two after he left. I believe you had left to go to the stern pool, and Mizz Belvedere had walked over to the bar for a drink. One of the sewage treatment techs called me and told me to send no more riders for a while. He wanted to flush the tube."

Gidget noticed a slightly puzzled look on Freddy's face. She asked, "What is it?"

"Umm… just that I thought it was an odd request."

"Why?"

"They don't normally flush the MegaSlide at three o'clock."

"When do they normally flush it?"

"Early in the morning… before it opens for rides."

"Which tech called you?"

"Uh… Let me think. I think he said his name was Karl. Yeah. Karl."

"Karl? One of the sewage treatment techs?"

"Yes'm, I suppose so."

"You suppose so. Why you say that?"

"Well, now that I think about it, I've never talked with anyone named Karl in that department."

"Didn't you find that strange?"

"No'm. All I got in my Contacts is one number for Sewage Treatment… see." Freddy opened his phone and pulled up his Contacts. He scrolled to the S's and showed them the entry for Sewage Treatment. He continued. "It don't say which tech it is, just that it's a call from that department. I just listened to what he said and did what he told me."

"What did he sound like?"

"Now that I think about it," Freddy said. "He sounded just like the Terminator."

"The Terminator?"

"Yeah. You know. Arnold Schwarzenegger."

"How so?"

"Sort of a foreign accent like Schwarzenegger had in the movie. You know, 'I'll be Bach.' Freddy performed a pretty good imitation of the star's Austrian accent.

Gidget proceeded carefully, not wanting to antagonize Freddy. "But yet, you did what he told you to. You didn't let anyone else go until he got back to you?"

"Yes'm."

"Even though you didn't recognize his name or voice?"

"Yes'm."

"Why?"

"Why not. There's several sewage processing techs, and I don't talk to them all that often. There's a lot of crew on the Bahama Princess—over two thousand. And a lot of turnover. I don't know all of the crew on the ship, especially the ones that work below deck."

"Did you tell Captain Omen or the Security Officer this?"

"No'm."

"Why not?"

"They didn't ask."

Gidget and Daffy discussed Gidget's interrogation of Freddy back to their stateroom. Daffy enthusiastically praised her friend.

"Wow! You were great again! I couldn't believe how well you handled him. And found out stuff even the captain didn't find out about."

Gidget waved the praise aside. "It was nothing. Just common sense."

"But you heard what he said about the tech's accent."

"I know. But just because he sounded like Arnold Schwarzenegger doesn't mean the guy that Freddy talked to was the same guy we've been seeing."

Daffy sighed. "No, it doesn't. What does it mean?"

"All it means is that whoever called Freddy to stop the flushing was someone he didn't know that had an Austrian accent."

"Anything else?"

"Starting the flushing process at that particular time may or may not be connected to the hole in the plexiglass that we think Barry went through."

Daffy nodded.

Gidget said, "We'll have to see what happens with the man overboard drill. Hopefully, they'll find Barry and find him alive."

"What do we do while we're waiting?"

"I think we need to see if we can find this mysterious sewage treatment technician."

"The Arnold Schwarzenegger tech?"

Gidget nodded. "I haven't had time to tell you that I saw that guy on Level Six. Near the pickleball courts. Looking like the Hulk, standing there, looking down the tube at the hole below me."

"My God! You think he has some connection to the hole?"

"He must. He sure wasn't just there to look at me in my two-piece bathing suit, wrinkles and eczema on full display. I realized on the way down why Freddy tells you to keep your arms crossed."

"Why?"

"So, your bathing suit's top doesn't get swept off by all that water flowing around you. If that had happened, the Schwarzenegger guy would've seen more than just my wrinkles and eczema."

Chapter 39

14° 41' 9.1121" North, 76° 50' 15.6154" West
November 18th

The man overboard drill worked in Gidget and Daffy's favor. Much of the ship's deck crew was too busy with those tasks to be distracted by two women prowling below deck. The few crew hands they ran into largely ignored them.

The two women prowled below deck as a result of a question Gidget asked Daffy in their stateroom.

"Why did the sewage processing staff decide to flush the MegaSlide while Barry was riding in it? Freddy said they normally flush it early in the morning before most people wake up."

Gidget led the way through the dimly lit, narrow passageways. She looked over her shoulder at her tall friend and said, "How's your claustrophobia holding up?"

Daffy said, "This place doesn't do it any good. I don't see how people could actually work down here without a psychologist coaching them all the time. Isn't there a pill for claustrophobia?"

"Xanax might help."

"Is there anything Xanax doesn't help? I don't know why I let myself get talked into coming back down here. I swore I'd never come back down here with you after our visit to the morgue."

"Wah, wah. Daffy Downer," Gidget teased in a reference to a Rachel Dratch character on *Saturday Night Live*.

"Do you remember where the sewage processing facility is?"

"Yeah. I remember passing by it on the way to the morgue."

"Ahh, our visit to the morgue! The experience of a lifetime. And now, we top it with a visit to the sewage processing facility."

"Aren't you the queen of sarcasm? Look. Here it is." Gidget pointed to signage on a door ahead of them.

The Sewage Processing Facility door was unlocked, allowing them to walk inside. Gidget said, "This must be like the morgue. So little traffic this far below deck that they don't worry about locking doors."

"I wonder why?" Daffy teased. "It's such a lovely place."

They stood inside a room whose dirty beige walls were covered with pipes running horizontally and vertically. Blue-grey rolled steel floors were textured with a raised diamond pattern intended to prevent falls. Several large green machines occupied much of the floorspace.

"That has to be one of the ugliest shades of green I've ever seen," said Daffy.

"Lilly would have a seizure, given her obsessive compulsive decorating disorder," said Gidget.

"What shade is this? Pea soup green?"

"Either that or vomit green."

"You ain't supposed to be in here." The speaker stepped around from behind one of the nearby sewage processors. *Intimidating* popped into Gidget's mind. Short and burly, wide chest and large shoulders, grease spots on his t-shirt, hairy arms, worn-out blue jeans with holes revealing hairy legs.

Gidget was speechless. "Uh…"

"You ain't supposed to be here."

She found her voice. "We're passengers and we got lost. We saw the sign on the door and got curious about how they treat the sewage on these big cruise ships. It's fascinating to think that y'all can provide drinking water from salt water and from reprocessed sewage."

Burly Man flashed his biggest grin. These two women were obviously a couple of passengers who got lost in the massive ship. All Bahama Princess employees, including below deck crew, received instruction on customer relationship as part of their employee orientation. Passengers were to be treated as if they were owners of the ship. This might be an opportunity to accumulate some brownie points. Burly Man said, "What ya wanna know? I can give ya a quick tour of Sewage Processing if ya want."

"Would you mind? We'd love a tour."

Daffy was amazed at her friend's quick thinking.

Burly Man said, "Yeah. No problem. We don't often get passengers down here in Sewage Processing. In fact, you're the first. Right over here is one of the ship's six Sewage Treatment Processors. We call them STPs for short. You see that pipe coming down from the ceiling? That pipe feeds this STP's primary chamber with raw sewage. It's got a macerator pump inside it that breaks up the raw sewage's solid components so they can be separated from wastewater……"

Daffy and Gidget listened as Burly Man explained both his equipment and steps for processing sewage. Despite the gross nature of the subject, they listened politely—Southern ladies are polite if nothing else. When an opportunity arose, Gidget asked, "Does the MegaSlide wastewater come into one of these processors when they flush it?"

"Yep. It does," said Burly Man. "You asking 'cause of the man overboard today? We heard they had a man overboard drill after someone rode the MegaSlide."

Gidget nodded. "Flushing the MegaSlide. Y'all do that on a regular basis?"

"Yeah. We do it on a regular schedule."

"Is that why y'all flushed the MegaSlide at three o'clock this afternoon?"

"We didn't flush it at that time. We flushed it early this morning. Like we always do."

"Are you sure?"

"Yeah. Positive."

"So, you were here at three o'clock this afternoon, and you know no one flushed the MegaSlide at that time."

"No, I wasn't here. No one was."

"No one was here at three o'clock. That you know of—"

Gidget's phone suddenly rang. She looked at it and said, "Hold on a second. I gotta take this call. Whatcha want?"

Pause.

"Look. I'm kinda busy right now. Can't this wait?"

Long pause.

"I understand, but he's your husband. You talk to him."

Long pause.

"It'll only start a pissing contest between me and his mother."

Long pause.

"Look. I'm kinda busy right now. I'll give you a call back in a few minutes. Okay? Great. Toodeloo." Gidget hung up, looked back at Burly Man and said, “Sorry for that. Crisis back home. Back to the topic at hand. You said that no one was here at three o’clock?”

“Correct. No one is ever here that time of day. The first shift locks the facility at two o’clock and leaves. The Sewage Processing Facility is always closed from two to five o’clock, every day. Second shift don’t come on board until five o’clock.”

Gidget said, “You’ve been very helpful. One more question.”

“Make it quick. I gotta go pee,” Burly Man said.

“You have a tech down here named Karl?”

“Nope.”

“You have any foreigners that work down here?” Gidget asked.

“That’s a second question, but yes, most of the Bahama Princess’ crew are from foreign countries. It’s a way out of the third world for them.”

“Anyone from Austria or one of the Eastern European countries?”

“Not in Sewage Processing. And that’s question number three. Let me show you out. I gotta go pee.”

“Thanks for your time…” Gidget stopped speaking as Burly Man escorted them out and headed off.

“What was the phone call about?” asked Daffy.

“My middle daughter is in a huff about her husband playing online video games on his phone. She says that’s all he does all day. They’ve only been married four years. She ain’t had time to housebreak him yet. Wants *me* to talk to him. No way.”

“Young men and their smartphones. They don’t know how to interact in person with other people anymore.”

“You got that right. I nicknamed him the Couchman because he’s always sitting on the couch, phone in hand, playing games. I tell my daughter, ‘Give him a phone and leave him alone.’ That’s all you can do.”

Gidget and Daffy ate a late dinner in Azul. Daffy stuffed her face while Gidget picked at her food.

“This thing gets more interesting day by day.”

“How so?” Daffy asked.

“We got someone initiating a flush of the MegaSlide—”

“Please don’t use that term.”

"Whose name is Karl, sounds like Arnold Schwarzenegger, and who does not work in Sewage Processing, the department that is supposed to initiate the process."

"You forgot the most important thing."

"What?" asked Gidget.

"Remember what he said about how the water that's treated by an STP can be reused for bathing and cooking. Yuck!"

"Where do you think astronauts on the International Space Station get their fresh water from?"

Daffy frowned. "No wonder you've been picking at your food."

"The other things he said that were interesting is that they flush the MegaSlide early in the mornings, and they are closed from two to five in the afternoons."

"Yeah."

Gidget said, "That means whoever flushed the MegaSlide this afternoon wasn't supposed to."

"I can tell you're upset over losing Barry," Daffy said after they had returned to their stateroom. "You barely ate anything."

Gidget said, "You know, I been thinking. It's as if the Marx Brothers had a death wish… doing all those risky things like parasailing and ziplining. Weird people… but I do miss them already."

"Me too. I feel bad about losing Harry. I admit I didn't love him, but I really liked him. He was a good companion. You really miss Barry, don't you?"

"Yeah. He was very special to me."

"I know. I remember the first time I had sex the week after Royce died. I remember it felt real special. But any sex after Royce would feel real special."

"Are you trying to cheer me up?"

"I know, I know. It's Daffy's perverted sense of humor. Anyway, Barry was your first sex since Sam passed. I know it's hard losing him since he was special. It was hard losing Harry."

Daffy noticed tears running down Gidget's cheeks and realized this was her friend's first opportunity to grieve since losing Barry. She embraced her and cried with her.

Chapter 40

17° 14' 44.6784" North, 74° 33' 37.0944" West
November 19th

Daffy heard Gidget throwing up before breakfast, the first time in two days. She walked into Gidget's bedroom and saw the light on in the bathroom.

"Seasick again, Hon? Captain Omen needs to slow this boat down."

Gidget walked out of her bathroom. "I heard he received a directive from corporate to return to Jacksonville without delay. The Feds will have an investigative team meet us at the dock."

"Five mysterious deaths and disappearances. No wonder the Feds are gonna do a formal investigation."

The team's composition was unknown, as it was still being assembled. The Bahama Princess navigator had charted a shorter course back to port that took it through the Windward Passage, a strait of water between Cuba and Haiti.

"Getting underway this fast must've got your tummy churning again," said Daffy, "Maybe you need to go see Doctor Mokulus."

Pale as a ghost, Gidget said nothing and shook her head.

"I heard you crying off and on all night. That probably didn't do your tummy any good either. You're taking Barry's death pretty bad, ain't you?"

Gidget started crying.

Daffy struggled to console her friend. "It's understandable. I know you feel bad about not finding whoever's killing our travel companions. And I know you have a special place in your heart for Barry. Same for me with Harry. Women always do with the men they have sex with. But today's a new day. You gotta get a grip. You can't go around depressed all the time. Understand?"

Gidget said nothing.

"You really should go see the doctor. I'm sure he can give you something for your seasickness."

"It ain't seasickness."

"If it ain't seasickness, what is it?"

"Morning sickness."

Gidget gently wiped Daffy's face with a cold wet washcloth. Her friend lay prone on the floor. She barely caught Daffy after the woman fainted but was able to ease her down without injuries.

Daffy regained consciousness. "Did I hear you right? You mean you're pregnant?"

Gidget nodded. "Yep. I've suspected it for over a week."

"How do you know?"

"I've had five babies. I know. I checked all the retail stores on board the ship. None of them stock pregnancy tests, which is weird on a boat where everyone's having sex." Gidget wrung her hands. "I can't verify it, but I can tell I'm pregnant. I know it's been a long time since I birthed my youngest, but… you know you're pregnant when you've been pregnant as many times as I have."

"I thought you started menopause about a year ago. Didn't you finish it?"

"I thought I had. It did start about a year ago, but it was kind of a weird menopause. My periods got shorter and smaller, but nothing major like in the old days. It went like that on and off for months and months until last August. I thought it was a sign that I was beginning to go through menopause. My momma had periods up into her late fifties, and I told myself, 'Well, I guess I'm finally gonna go through menopause just like old Ethell did.' Yeah, I figured I was gonna take after her—weird periods for a while, followed by a late menopause."

"I've heard of late menopause."

"Sam's been dead for three years, and I haven't had sex since he died… until I had it with Barry. I didn't think I needed any contraception because I hadn't had a real period for a while. And I am sixty-two—"

"I didn't think women could get pregnant in their sixties, unless it was with some sort of in… in something fertilizer."

"In vitro fertilization. But some women in their sixties do get pregnant without IVF. After I started throwing up and worrying, I looked it up on the Internet, and there are examples of women getting pregnant in their sixties without IVF. And there are examples of women not starting menopause until they're in their mid-sixties. Heck, my momma had me when she was fifty-eight."

"When *did* you and Barry first have sex?"

"October 23rd. I remember it well. First time in almost four years. God, was it wonderful. And he's in his seventies. Sheesh! I would have thought he would be shooting blanks."

"Blanks! If he could get a sixty-two-year-old like you pregnant, he must've been shooting .357 magnums."

Gidget managed a limp smile.

"So, your morning sickness has been going on for how long now?" asked Daffy.

"Two weeks."

"If you got pregnant the first time you had sex… Let's see, from October 23rd to November 19th… How many days is that anyway?"

"Twenty-seven days. Three weeks and six days. I've been calculating it for a week now. I know it's real soon. Most morning sickness doesn't start until about the sixth week, but I *am* an oddball. I always got morning sickness early on with my babies."

They sat silently for several minutes before Daffy said, "That explains why you've been so upset with Barry's disappearance. He's the father of your baby."

"Yeah. I felt like something was happening even before I started getting the morning sickness. It just confirmed my feelings. But I didn't tell Barry I thought I was pregnant until Larry died. Barry was so happy when I told him…"

"But?"

"He was happy at first, but then he got kind of melancholy. I asked him why, but he only beat around the bush… never really gave me a good answer. I took it that maybe he was concerned about being in his seventies… fathering a child when he probably wouldn't be around to see it grow up. He grew moodier, and I figured because he was alive and had fathered a child while his brothers were dead. I figured it was bound to have affected him."

"And now he's gone," said Daffy.

"Yeah, that's right. Now, I'm wondering if the reason he seemed melancholy about the baby was because he worried about his own life. Was he worried that he himself might be murdered and wouldn't be around to see his baby born and grow up? I could tell that he was excited at the thought of having a son or daughter. He never got married, you know… though I guess that doesn't necessarily mean he may not already have children."

"He apparently knew what he was doing in that regard."

Gidget nodded. She agreed with Daffy's assessment but did not like the thought that the father of her child might possibly have other offspring, unknown to her. "And it must've gotten worse for him after Harry died parasailing, and then Gary goes missing. I bet he thought somebody or something was out to get him and brothers."

"Why the heck did he even consider going down that slide with all that going on?"

"Who knows? It seems like those brothers had a death wish."

"This is super scary," said Daffy. "I wanna go home."

"I do too, but not right now. I was determined to find out who killed his brothers until Barry died. Now, I'm not determined. I'm *obsessed*. I've got to find the killer of my child's father."

"We don't know that Barry is dead. We just know he's not here."

"He's dead. I know it. I feel it in my body. He will never walk the earth as the father of my baby. What I don't know is who, what, and why made this so. This is a coordinated attempt… No, it's not an attempt. It's a coordinated killing of all the Marx Brothers for some reason."

"I agree. All five of them dying… getting murdered. It's not just a coincidence."

"Absolutely."

"What are we going to do?" asked Daffy.

"We agree that all five of them disappearing or dying ain't coincidental. That tells me we need to revisit all the evidence we have, beginning with Larry's poisoning. We start with that and work our way through Barry's disappearance out of the MegaSlide. We need to investigate the circumstances surrounding each of their deaths. See if we can find more clues."

"How do we do that?"

"I want to question everyone involved in the deaths, like Chef Dreyfus, Doctor Mokulus, Tyler, Freddy."

"Yeah. Makes sense. What about Jerry's plunge overboard? Who do we interrogate about that?"

"We start with Stokes and Yvette."

"Good thinking."

Gidget was determined. "We've got to move quickly. I want to get all this done before we reach Jacksonville. Once the Feds get on board, I suspect we won't be allowed to question anyone."

Chapter 41

Thomasville, Georgia
November 19th

Babs had called and texted Daffy and Gidget repeatedly since six o'clock in the morning to no avail. No responses. Nada. Lilly and Lizzie had tried to contact them too, but also had no luck. Daffy's text congratulating their *Real Widows* success was the last communication they had received. That was last Thursday. Until today, no one worried. Daffy and Gidget were probably preoccupied with sightseeing on Caribbean islands and with the Marx Brothers.

Babs could take it no longer. She was sixty-three years old and did not trust her memory, but as best she could remember, her friends were supposed to be back by now. They were supposed to have docked in Jacksonville yesterday and stayed overnight to celebrate returning to the States with the Marx Brothers. The drive back to Thomasville should not have taken this long.

She jumped in her Escalade and headed for Daffy's house to see if maybe she was inside. After all, Daffy was closing in on seventy and could have fallen. Her friend might be lying in her house and unable to get to the phone, or worse. Babs vowed to make Daffy buy one of those Life Alert necklaces so she could notify 911 in case she ever fell again.

No one answered the door, and Daffy's Lincoln was in her driveway, furthering Bab's fears. Her brain's gears suddenly began turning faster. Daffy and Gidget had been chauffeured to the ship; her Lincoln was supposed to be in the driveway. What if something happened to their limousine somewhere along I-10 on the way back?

Babs stood on the porch. Something was definitely wrong. She texted Lilly and Lizzie.

Babs: Y'all heard anything yet?
Lilly: Nothing.
Lizzie: Same here.
Babs: I'm getting worried. What if something happened to them on the road from Jax?

Lizzie: That may be, but there's nothing we can do about it. We just have to wait and see.
Babs: I'm going to call the cruise line and check on their boat.
Lilly: Good idea.

Babs called the cruise line and panicked when she heard the news. There had been a series of mysterious deaths onboard the ship beginning last Friday. There was unrest in Haiti, and authorities there had ordered the Bahama Princess to be detained in Port-au-Prince. The ship's communications network, which provided international cell phone service, had been disabled. That was the extent of the information available. The cruise line was obviously keeping a lid on news about the situation for public relations purposes.

Babs called Lilly and Lizzie, and they agreed to discuss the cruise situation over late breakfast at the Plaza Restaurant. A waitress approached their table and asked, "What can I get y'all to drink?"

Lizzie said, "A martini. Tell the bartender that if he only thinks about putting vermouth in the cocktail shaker, that's plenty."

The waitress took their drink orders and asked, "Y'all mind if I ask y'all something?"

"You just did," said Lizzie.

"Your reality show. The episode where y'all went to Area 53 and met that Monroe guy. He wasn't really from outer space, was he? He was just someone wearing one of them Halloween monster costumes, wasn't he? He was my favorite person on that episode."

"He wasn't a person."

"He wasn't? What was he?"

"An extraterrestrial alien."

The waitress shook her head as she walked away.

Babs got down to business. "I called the cruise line and got the scoop. The cruise people told me the ship is heading for Port-au-Prince—"

"Why? Some voodoo queen put a spell on the boat?" asked Lizzie.

"There's been a series of mysterious deaths on the ship—"

"Oh my God! Are Daffy and Gidget okay?" asked Lilly.

"I don't know. The cruise line won't release any names. I guess they have to notify the next of kin. We don't know that Daffy and Gidget *aren't* okay. All communications services with the ship have been cut off for security reasons. That's probably why Daffy and Gidget haven't been texting us lately. There'll be an investigation so they have to keep a lid on things."

"I knew there had to be a good reason why Daffy and Gidget weren't texting us. Texting is in our female DNA," Lizzie said.

After their drinks arrived, Lilly asked, "You're saying the cruise line wouldn't give you any information on who mysteriously disappeared?"

"Nope," said Babs. "We gotta do something. Daff and Gidg may be in trouble."

"Port-au-Prince. Too bad you ain't there, Babsie. You are the Voodoo Queen," Lizzie said.

Lilly displayed a rare boldness. "I think we should go there."

"No way. Go to Haiti. Uh-uh. That country's a disaster."

Babs said, "We can't go there. Cordell's flying in this afternoon with his production crew. They start filming on another episode tomorrow."

Lilly was adamant. "But we have to go! Daffy and Gidget are our best friends. We can't leave them stranded and helpless… or who knows what, in Haiti."

Lizzie said, "Let me repeat. Haiti is a disaster of a country. They have problems with their government all the time. It's very unstable. They have military coups and revolutions and such. The Times-Enterprise had an article last week about country-wide protests in Haiti. People are upset with the way the government is run. They have bad inflation. Their healthcare system sucks. Problems with government services and so on."

Babs seemed to have drifted off into her own world, then suddenly snapped out of it. "Now that I remember it, the Marche de Fer did have some great voodoo supplies. Everyone who stops in Port-au-Prince goes there to shop."

Lilly said, "This is about our friends. To hell with shopping in Haiti—"

A look of horror crossed Lizzie's face. "Not care about shopping? That sounds like blasphemy."

"You sound like Amazon Anonymous isn't working," Babs said referring to the support group Lizzie regularly attended to help with her spending addiction.

Lilly was adamant. "We HAVE to go to Haiti to see if Daffy and Gidget need our help."

"It would be a good opportunity to pick up on some more voodoo supplies."

"Uh-oh." Lizzie shook her head. "I think I'm about to be outvoted."

Babs said, "Hear me out. Cordell gets here this afternoon. I bet he'd go for filming the next episode of *Real Widows* in Haiti. It could be as exciting as the episode with the UFOs in Area 53, if Haiti's in some sort of a military coup. The voodoo stuff in Haiti might make the UFO stuff we filmed in Area 53 look tame."

Lizzie looked at Lilly. "I think Babsie has finally gone Hollywood."

Chapter 42

19° 10' 16.0068" North, 74° 3' 30.24" West
November 19th

Daffy had late breakfast in Azul with Gidget. Her friend seemed energized, quite a change from last night's depressed mood and this morning's sickness. She took note of Gidget's appetite.

"Never seen you eat like this before."

"Not since my last pregnancy," said Gidget. "I haven't had lox and bagels in ages. These taste so good."

"Lox and bagels; you *must* be pregnant. What're we gonna do about investigating Larry's death? I'm getting to where I'm kind of getting into this sleuthing stuff."

"Let's review what we know so far. First, Doctor Mokulus said Larry choked to death as a result of having a seizure brought on by acute alcohol poisoning. Correct?"

"Correct."

"Yet, he was throwing up all day the day before he had acute alcohol poisoning. I would have thought he'd gotten rid of a lot of the alcohol in his system from all that throwing up. Correct?"

"Maybe, but he was having a Bloody Mary at breakfast."

"True." Gidget's eyes looked upward as if looking into her own brain for more information. When they rolled back down, she said, "But Larry's heart stopped, didn't it? Remember, I checked his pulse and could not feel one."

"That's true."

"Okay then, if his heart had stopped beating while he was choking here in Azul, why didn't his phone go off like it did when he had that heart arrhythmia climbing those stairs in Saint Thomas? Remember, his pacemaker transmitted an alert to his cardiologist in Arizona when the arrhythmia was detected, and the cardiology clinic called him to check on it."

Daffy nodded vigorously. "That's right! It did! I remember his phone playing the theme to *The Godfather* when it did."

"Yeah. Larry's phone always played *The Godfather* theme when it received an incoming text or call. If his heart had stopped beating in Azul, why didn't we hear *The Godfather*? We would have heard it when the cardiology clinic called to check on him. Since we didn't hear it, did his pacemaker not send an alert to Arizona then? Why not? Was it malfunctioning? Did he have the ringer turned off? Or was something else going on?"

Daffy shrugged. "But Doctor Mokulus told us his heart stopped."

"Yes, he did, but I don't think that is the final word on Larry's death."

"What do we do next?"

"We need to see if we can find out why his phone didn't play *The Godfather* theme. He did have his phone with him when he choked. I remember feeling it in his shirt pocket right before I was about to start CPR."

"*The Godfather* theme playing while Larry choked would have been appropriate. They had several people get choked to death in that movie."

Gidget frowned. "I don't know which is worse—your logic or your taste."

"Sorry. You're right. What else?"

"Where is Larry's phone?"

Daffy shrugged. "In his room, I guess. Surely, it wouldn't have been on him when they offloaded his body in Saint Georges, would it? I want to have my iPhone buried with me along with Sophie's ashes, but I'm a woman."

"I can relate to that."

"Should we check in his room to see if we can find it after breakfast?"

"Yes, but first I want to talk to Chef Dreyfus before we leave Azul."

Azul's staff was too busy to notice the two women at a two-top rise and slowly walk toward the kitchen door.

En route, Daffy asked, "What do you hope to find out from Chef Dreyfus? I thought Louie's analysis revealed no traces of poison."

Gidget said, "That's correct; nevertheless, Larry exhibited some signs of poisoning. He could have eaten something not normally identified as a poison that might have acted in a toxic manner when eaten by a human. Dreyfus cooked his empanadas that morning, and I want to know what he put in them."

"He's not the only person who cooks in the kitchen."

"That's true, but he's in charge of what goes on in the kitchen. Nobody does anything in there without the head chef's knowledge. If Larry was poisoned, someone in the kitchen must have put the poison in his empanadas. We need to check out the kitchen—how things operate there and how they made Larry's empanadas."

"Uh-oh. Recipe espionage. A culinary capital crime," said Daffy. "What do we look for? They won't have bottles of rat poison sitting on the counter."

"We look for evidence of anything suggesting the presence of poison substances. Certain kinds of food ingredients—mushrooms or cassava fruit, for example—have poisonous variants. It might be something that looks innocent but really is poisonous. Look around to see what kinds of ingredients they have lying around at their cooking stations."

"What do we tell them when they ask what we're doing in the kitchen?"

"We tell them we're interested in finding out more about how they prepare their delicious dishes. Just follow my lead and act natural."

"You mean act like a senile old woman? No problem."

Daffy followed Gidget through the kitchen door. Six kitchen staff, including Chef Dreyfus, worked at different cooking stations. Gidget headed toward Dreyfus. He looked up as she approached.

"*Mesdames* Gidget and Daffy. What are you doing here? Diners are not allowed in the kitchen."

Gidget said, "We have enjoyed your cuisine so much that we wanted to see how you prepare your excellent dishes before the cruise ends. Can we watch for a while?"

"I would be honored."

"If it's okay with you, we'll just stand around and watch."

"Please."

Gidget and Daffy stood quietly next to the salad preparation table, pretending to observe. After a few minutes, Gidget said, "It was so terrible about Mister Vanderhoff's death the other morning. Choking on your empanadas. Tsk, tsk."

Dreyfus nodded. "*Oui*, the Chief Security Officer talked to me shortly after his death. He wanted to know what Mister Vanderhoff ordered for breakfast. What the ingredients were."

"Surely you didn't tell him what they were! I know how secretive you chefs are about your recipes."

"No, not in this case."

"Why?"

"It was a common recipe I got off the Internet, although I did put my unique touch to it—a pinch of Vadouvan."

"Vadouvan?"

"French curry powder."

"Surely, you must feel some guilt about Mister Vanderhoff's death as he choked on your empanadas?"

"Absolutely not! Not at all! In fact, I did not even prepare his empanadas. I oversaw their preparation."

"Who did prepare them?"

"Colette, our Pâtissier, prepared the shells used in Mister Vanderhoff's empanadas. Lucien, our Chef de Partie, prepared their ingredients. Gigi, our Sous Chef, assembled them, and Francois, our Friturier, fried them."

"Only the French would make the preparation of empanadas more complex than assembling a Cadillac," said Daffy.

"*Madame!* I do not appreciate your sense of humor. Preparing fine food is an art, not a manufacturing process."

Back at their table, Daffy asked, "Did you see anything?"

"Oysters. They contain algal toxins. Cassava, bamboo roots, and almonds all contain cyanogenic glycosides, and I saw all of those. I could go on, but I did see a variety of foods containing natural toxins that could potentially poison someone under the right circumstances."

"Wow! Anything else?"

"Yeah. Four people prepared Larry's empanadas. That's four opportunities to slip something that could have poisoned him into the recipe."

"I was surprised Dreyfus didn't get his hackles up at your questioning."

"It's all in the technique. Coming on strong as I did when I implied Dreyfus shared some of the blame for Larry's death sometimes shakes a person up. If he's complicit in something illegal or nefarious, he may stumble on his answers or give off some sort of tell that he's lying."

"What now?"

"We need to question Stokes."

"Why?"

"I met with him after he came out of Larry's room early the morning of his choking. He said he'd been helping Larry prepare something for his stomach. I want to see if there's something more to that story."

Chapter 43

19° 10' 16.0068" North, 74° 3' 30.24" West
November 19th

Back in their stateroom, Gidget rang for Stokes. He arrived shortly. "Yes, mum."

"Stokes," Gidget asked, "Do you remember the morning Mister Vanderhoff choked in Azul?"

"Yes, mum."

"Remember earlier that morning, I was up early throwing up and I rang for you?"

"Yes, mum. I do."

"And you were here in a flash, and I said, 'That was quick.' Remember?"

"Yes, mum. I had been next door. Mister Vanderhoff was also throwing up. I remember thinking you both must have eaten the same thing the night before."

"Excellent thinking. What did you do for Mister Vanderhoff?"

"I made him the same thing I made for you. Peppermint tea."

"Tell us about the morning when Mister Vanderhoff fell off his balcony. Where were you when he fell, and what were you doing?"

"Not much to tell, mum. I was busy in another passenger's stateroom at the time. I found out about the fall during the man overboard drill. I was horrified to find out it was Mister Vanderhoff."

"Usually, you and Yvette are up and busy in our staterooms around the time Mister Vanderhoff fell off. But not that morning. Why?"

"One of the other passengers had a request for some special cleaning. She spilled a bottle of lotion on the carpet while dressing and needed it cleaned up. I was attending to that."

"When *did* you go into Mister Vanderhoff's suite?"

"I never did that morning, mum. The Chief Security Officer informed all Premier Suite staff to stay out of his suite as there would be an investigation. Mum, if I may be excused, I have to serve a bottle of Veuve Clicquot in another passenger's stateroom."

"One more question. We went into Mister Vanderhoff's stateroom right after he fell. There were empty vodka and gin bottles strewn over the floor and liquid—probably vodka and gin—spilled on the floor. Did you bring Mister Vanderhoff the vodka and gin before he fell?"

"No, mum."

"Not even earlier in the morning or late the night before?"

"No, mum. May I be dismissed now?"

"Sure. We may want to talk to you later."

"That was quick," Daffy said after Stokes left their stateroom.

"But productive."

"How so?"

"Stokes said he made Larry some peppermint tea. What was one of the first items on Louie's list from the analysis of Larry's vomit?"

Daffy shrugged.

"$C_{10}H_{20}O$, the chemical formula for menthol, and primary component of peppermint oil."

"So, Stokes's story holds water?"

"That part does."

"What doesn't?"

"The part where he said he never brought gin or vodka to Jerry's suite the night before he fell. It conflicts with what Yvette told us that Stokes did bring them the booze."

"You're right. I'd forgotten that. What next?"

"Yvette. We need to get Larry's iPhone and find out why we didn't hear the theme from *The Godfather*. Remember?"

They rang for Yvette and met her in front of Larry's stateroom. Gidget asked, "Yvette, would you be a dear and please unlock the Vanderhoffs' three-bedroom suite for us? We need to get some of our belongings out."

"Oh, *madame*. I cannot do that now without permission. Ze captain has ordered both Vanderhoff rooms to remain sealed until ze inquiry is finished."

Gidget summoned her scary voice. "But we have things in here that we need now. We can't wait until after the inquiry."

Yvette was perplexed. Should she do as a passenger requested or follow the captain's orders? She pointed to a room two doors down and said, "But… but… I have to go into this other room right now. I have been summoned."

Gidget detected the maid's nervousness and remembered similar nervous behavior outside their staterooms after Jerry fell from his balcony.

"You seem uneasy, Yvette. Tell me why."

"Oh, uh… uh I am uh… not nervous."

"What's going on?"

"Nothing *madame*. I have been summoned by ze guest in ze room… I do not want to get into trouble." Yvette fidgeted, and her eyes darted back and forth as she spoke.

Gidget thought the maid's agitation offered an opportunity and pretended to know more than she did. "Yvette, we know what you were doing the day Mister Vanderhoff fell off his balcony. We saw you coming out of that stateroom three doors down." Gidget pointed to the room Yvette had indicated as her intended destination.

"Oh *madame*! Please say you will not tell anybody! Senator Ma—" Yvette caught herself and abruptly stopped, then resumed speaking haltingly. "He… he will be very… uh upset. This could be a… a *très gros scandale* for him. His wife! If she finds out, it will be catastrophic. His political career would be over. Please do not say anything. I will lose my job."

"I won't tell anybody anything if you open the door to the Vanderhoff stateroom. If you open it and go on about your business, no one else but the three of us will know."

Yvette looked up and down the hallway, then opened Larry's door.

"One more question before you go. You did previously tell us that Stokes had brought some gin and vodka to Mister Vanderhoff's suite the night before he fell off his balcony, didn't you?"

"*Oui, madame*."

"Thank you. You may go now," said Gidget.

Yvette left and Daffy and Gidget entered Larry, Jerry, and Harry's suite. Daffy looked at Gidget. "You truly are amazing. You've really taken control of finding how who killed the Marx Brothers. Getting Yvette to open their suite like you did was truly cool. And now we know we got a senator fooling around with her."

"A senator fooling around on his wife is not exactly news. No big surprise there," said Gidget.

"True. And Yvette repeated her assertion that Stokes brought the booze to the boys. What do you think?"

"I don't think Yvette has a motive to lie. That's probably not the case with Stokes. If he brought the alcohol that had a role in causing Jerry's death, he would probably not want that fact known. He could have lied because he is worried about getting blamed for contributing to Jerry's death by supplying him with too much alcohol."

Chapter 44

19° 10' 16.0068" North, 74° 3' 30.24" West
November 19th

Gidget and Daffy entered the three-bedroom suite Larry had shared with Harry and Jerry and closed the door.

Daffy said, "I didn't know a United States senator was staying just three doors down from us."

"I guess he's traveling incognito for a reason, and it sounds like an amorous reason," said Gidget.

"And that explains what Yvette was doing coming out of his stateroom the day Jerry fell off the balcony and why she doesn't want anyone to find out."

"Yes, indeed it does."

"Remember how she was pulling down her short skirt that day?"

"Yep. Yvette had probably just finished her business," said Gidget. "Let's get on with our business. You take a bedroom, and I'll take a bedroom, and we'll see what we find. We'll go through all three bedrooms, bathrooms, and kitchen. Look in drawers, closets, under the bed, medicine cabinets, and so forth."

Fifteen minutes later, Daffy screamed, "I found a phone! I found a phone!"

"Which bedroom?"

"Jerry's!"

"Keep looking. Let's get the other phones if they're here and anything else suspicious."

Ten minutes later, Gidget hollered, "I found Larry's phone! Check inside Harry's room! See if you can find his phone. We're probably gonna want it as well. I'm gonna keep looking in here."

Thirty minutes later, they had all three phones and the jackpot—a printed list of logins and passwords to various accounts, including all five Marx Brothers' iPhones. They also found several other interesting items.

"Let's get this stuff back to our room. We'll get Yvette to open Barry and Gary's room for us later," said Gidget.

Back in their stateroom, the Ladies started with Larry's iPhone. The device appeared relatively new.

"This list of login IDs and passwords is a goldmine," said Daffy. "There are so many things online nowadays, and no way a seventy-year-old can keep track of them without having them written on a list. I pack my list every time I travel."

Gidget said, "It's our luck that the boys put all of theirs on a consolidated list. Probably easier to maintain one list. What's the password for Larry's phone?"

Daffy scrolled down the paper. "Hmmm, should have known it... same as his nickname—T-I-T-T-Y."

Gidget keyed in Larry's passcode, and the device opened, displaying a screen full of app icons. She carefully perused them, then swiped to the next screen. "Ah ha! Here it is—an app called MyHeartCareLink. Let's see what's in here."

She tapped the app icon, and a menu screen appeared. "Let's see. There are several things to choose from—My Device, Vital Sign Tracking, Activity Journal... ah, here's one we want to look at. My Clinic. We need to find out if they ever received an alert from his pacemaker."

Gidget tapped My Clinic, and the screen displayed the name and address of a clinic.

> Banner Cardiovascular Clinic
> 104 Thunderbird Drive
> Sun City, AZ 85351

It also listed a phone number. Gidget pulled out her phone and dialed it. She turned on her speakerphone.

"Hello, Mister Fratelli?" said a voice on the other end.

Gidget lowered the pitch of her voice. "This is Larry."

"Mister Fratelli? You sound funny. You okay?"

"Bit of a cold."

"Did everything go as planned? We didn't expect to hear from you so soon."

"Yeah. Everything went well." Gidget's voice cracked, emitting a high-pitched 'yes.'

An audible 'click' sounded.

"They hung up. What do you make of that?" asked Daffy.

"The person on the other end expected someone named Fratelli would be calling from this number. When the person on the other end realized it wasn't Larry, they hung up really quick."

"This is real strange."

"Very suspicious. Larry's cardiologist and pacemaker. Both are connected to a clinic way far away in Sun City, Arizona instead of someplace closer to home in Florida. I know he said they had a great cardiology clinic, but there are great cardiologists at a lot of places in Florida near or in The Villages. Or back in New York where they came from."

Daffy nodded. "Yeah. I hate having to go see a specialist in Tallahassee instead of Thomasville... although it is a good excuse to have lunch in Tallahassee. I wonder if Larry acquired a taste for Sonoran empanadas in Sun City when he went to see his cardiologist. Wonder why Banner Clinic cut you off like they did?"

"My most generous thought is because of HIPAA concerns. Not wanting to talk clinical stuff and find out it wasn't with the patient."

"Yeah, that sounds plausible. What's your least generous thought?"

"Something sneaky going on that we stumbled into. Let's go find Stokes. I want to talk to him more about Jerry's death."

Stokes did not respond when they rang for him. Gidget said, "Let's take a walk and see if we can find him."

"Aye, aye," Daffy said, and she opened the door for her friend.

They walked down the passageway and spotted a familiar figure.

"Look," Daffy said. "It's the Arnold Schwarzenegger guy. He just left one of the rooms up ahead. He's walking away from us, and I think he didn't see us."

"Let's see where he goes," said Gidget.

They acted casually, hoping to go unnoticed but were unsuccessful as the guy picked up his pace. Daffy said, "He must have seen us."

The ladies likewise walked faster, but Gidget began huffing. "That guy is too fast."

"They should provide courtesy Hoverounds for older sleuths like us."

The guy disappeared down a side passageway and was nowhere to be seen when Gidget and Daffy got there.

"Damn. He's a slippery little devil," said Daffy.

As they started back for their stateroom, the Bahama Princess's public address system suddenly blared a series of short staticky tones.

"What the hell is that?" Daffy asked. "Never heard it do that before."

Gidget stopped walking, looked up at the nearest overhead speaker, and counted, "Three, four, five, six, seven. Seven short tones. That means it's a general alarm. Remember. Rachel mentioned that during our tour of the ship—"

A familiar voice blared over the public address system. "This is Captain Omen. I have important information for you. I am directing all passengers to return to their cabins immediately. I repeat. This is Captain Omen, and I am directing all passengers to return immediately to their cabins."

"All crew members will immediately proceed to their assigned emergency duty stations. I repeat. All crew members will immediately proceed to their assigned duty stations. Crew members will be given instructions by their managers once they report."

"Passengers are advised to tune in to Channel Two, the ship's information channel, on the televisions in their rooms. We will provide updated information on Channel Two as soon as we are able to provide it. Also, we will be texting updated information to all passengers' smart phones."

"That is all."

Chapter 45

19° 10' 16.0108" North, 74° 3' 30.01" West
November 19th

Back in their stateroom, Daffy asked, "I wonder what's going on? Omen's announcement was a little short on information."

Gidget said, "Rachel said a ship's general alarm is sounded for some sort of emergency like a collision, a fire, or when it's time to abandon ship."

"Abandon ship! You think we're sinking?"

"I don't think so. Rachel said the captain would specifically give the order to abandon ship over the PA system after the general alarm was sounded, and he didn't do that."

"What do we do now?"

"Nothing we can do except sit tight and wait for Omen's information updates. Let's turn on Channel Two."

"You left out the most important thing we need to do."

"What's that?"

"Make some cocktails."

"Excellent idea, my dear Daffy."

After twenty minutes and a tall, strong gin and tonic each, Gidget and Daffy had exhausted all possible reasons they could think of for the general alarm, except one.

"I thought I heard some explosions when we were looking for Stokes," said Gidget. "They sounded far off."

Daffy nodded. "Yeah, I heard 'em too, but I thought it was just my tinnitus. Too bad I don't have a hearing aid to blame it on."

Gidget hiccupped. "It was probably a minor accident somewhere on the ship, and they're trying to fix it. What were we talking about before the alarm?"

"Stokes. You wanted to talk to him about him leaving Larry's stateroom the morning he choked in Azul. He denied having been in Larry's suite that morning he died. He was obviously lying. I bet he had something to do with Larry's choking."

"You're confusing Larry's choking with Jerry's plunge the next day. I wanted to talk to Stokes some more about the spilled liquor and bottles lying on the floor after Jerry fell."

Daffy slapped her head. "There's been so many Marx Brothers deaths, I can't keep them straight. It could be its own category on the *Jeopardy* board."

"These deaths *have* gotten pretty convoluted. Stokes said he *was* in Larry's suite the morning he choked to make him some peppermint tea. He also made some peppermint tea for me that morning because I was throwing up."

"Correct. Larry was sick because he drank too much, and you were sick because you screwed too much." Daffy laughed and hiccupped. Her brain fogged for a few seconds. "Because you got pregnant."

"Keep it up, and next thing, they'll be hiring you to entertain at funerals. Stokes isn't a suspect in Larry's death. Doctor Mokulus is. He said Larry choked while having a seizure brought on by acute alcohol poisoning. I remember reading an article a year ago in *U.S. Pharmacist* about choking deaths—"

"*U.S Pharmacist*? Talk about racy reading. Ooh-la-la. Do you sell that mag from behind the counter at the pharmacy along with the *Playboys* and *Penthouses*?"

"Once again, my dear Daffy, your sense of humor underwhelms me. Anyway, I believe the article said choking deaths are rare—less than five thousand a year in the U.S. Usually, someone administers the Heimlich Maneuver, or the person coughs it up on his own. Why didn't Mokulus attempt the Heimlich Maneuver? Why did he take Larry to his clinic before administering CPR? Why wasn't his body in one of the dispensary morgues?"

"You think he was in on Larry's death?"

A painful look came over Gidget's face. "It's a possibility."

"Ooooh."

"I thought about all his symptoms while I was awake last night. Vomiting, low blood pressure, loss of consciousness, cardiac arrest. These kinds of symptoms are typically associated with those poisons such as cyanide—"

"I thought Louie's analysis of Larry's vomit didn't reveal any cyanide."

"Correct, then what *did* cause those symptoms? That's part of the conundrum about Larry's death. Also, other symptoms like his flushed skin point to arsenic which Louie's analysis also failed to turn up. The alkaloids in his vomit are puzzling. They could have been present from some sort of narcotic like morphine."

"You think Larry OD'd on dope?"

Gidget shrugged. "He displayed some of the signs of OD'ing such as vomiting and loss of consciousness, but not some of the other OD'ing symptoms such as pinpoint eye pupils, pale clammy skin, and blue fingernails. Remember how he foamed at the mouth?"

Daffy said, "A lot of foam. I could've cleaned a toilet with it."

"Foaming of the mouth is not a symptom of either arsenic or cyanide poisoning. All this is why it's been so hard to say if Larry was poisoned or OD'd, or maybe there's something else at work."

"Something else? What?"

"I can't figure that out. I wish the Saint George's med school would have done an autopsy. Why didn't they? That's why Larry's death is so perplexing. I don't think he choked, but I have no idea who murdered him or how."

"Well, we know he died of something. We saw them roll his body off the boat in a body bag."

Gidget nodded, then hiccupped. "I wish I could solve this thing."

Fueled by gin, Daffy's warped sense of humor tried to inject a little humor into the situation. "Maybe it wasn't Larry in the body bag. Maybe it was Dobby, the elf in the *Harry Potter* movie."

"Daffy, all these decades I've known you, and I never realized what a morbid sense of humor you have."

"I get my sense of humor from my Uncle Hannibal, on the Lecter side of my family. Also, from this gin and tonic."

Daffy mixed another round of G&Ts. "We're getting nowhere on solving Larry's murder. Let's talk about Jerry. What's your thinking on his death?"

Gidget said, "I don't think Yvette is a prime suspect. I did at first because she and Stokes were two that had easy access to Jerry's room. Remember right after Jerry fell, we ran back upstairs—"

"Ran? I'm seventy. I quit running anywhere forty years ago."

"When we saw Yvette leaving the stateroom three doors down from the Marx Brothers' suites, she admitted that she had been screwing a United States senator when Jerry fell. That rules her out."

"Did Jerry fall, or was he pushed?"

"At this point, it's a toss-up. If Jerry was pushed, it raises the question of the identity of the person I saw in his room."

"I say it was Arnold Schwarzenegger guy."

"Yeah, but the spilled liquids and empty bottles indicate Jerry may have accidentally slipped and fallen, which clears that guy."

"Yes, it does."

"Unless he put them there to make his death look like an accident. And that's part of the problem."

"Why?"

"It all seems too convenient. That's why Jerry's death puzzles me."

"What does your gut tell you?"

"My gut tells me that I don't know whether Jerry committed suicide or was murdered, and if he was murdered, who did it. I feel more like Jacques Clouseau than Hercule Poirot."

Daffy one-upped her friend. "I feel like Scooby-Doo."

Daffy sipped on her drink as she thought. "I'm confused. Let's switch subjects. What about Harry's death?"

"What about it?" Gidget hiccupped.

"He was probably buried at sea."

"You really need to work on your humor. Besides that?"

"His towline broke?"

"Or was it intentionally snapped?"

"Someone was out to get him? But who?" asked Daffy.

"E-gor acted suspiciously. Tyler clammed up. One of them is a likely suspect in the towline mishap."

"Which one?"

Gidget shrugged. "Maybe both. Also, why did Captain Omen allow Tyler to take Harry parasailing in questionable weather and sea conditions?"

"Oooh."

"Harry's death is as puzzling to me as Larry and Jerry's."

Daffy asked, "Can I make you another drink?"

"Please. Maybe the more I drink, the less confusing these murders may get," said Gidget.

"What about Gary?"

"What do we know so far about Gary's disappearance?"

"Moriarty knows how to do real magic?"

"I won't dignify that with a response. It's all about Moriarty's Magic Box. He explained that the trick depends on the box's false wall that the subject, which in this case was Gary, hides behind."

Daffy nodded. "Yeppers."

"And we inspected the box and the stage. We know there was no way Gary could have climbed up and slipped out through the ceiling, or down and out under the stage."

"Correct."

"Yet, he wasn't in the hidden compartment behind the false wall."

Daffy nodded. "Moriarty opened it and showed it to us and Omen. So, where did he go to? I say again, he transitioned to a parallel dimension."

"Either that or he died."

"You think he might be dead? Not just magically disappeared?"

"Looks to me like someone wants all the Marx Brothers to meet fatal ends, which would probably include Gary. The problem again is who and why and how?"

"I hate to even ask about Barry's death."

"It must be related to the unscheduled flushing of the sewage processing system and the Arnold Schwarzenegger guy I saw near the hole in the plexiglass. Looks like he was in on Barry's murder."

"What a mean looking dude. What else?"

"Was he the Karl with the Austrian accent that Freddy says called him about flushing the MegaSlide at three o'clock today? The guy in the Sewage Treatment Facility said no one is ever in there at that time of day. And he said it was flushed early this morning. Why would they flush it twice in one day?"

"After talking with Freddy, they can never flush the MegaSlide enough for my taste. Wait. That didn't come out right."

"I'm so confused over all these deaths, Daff. I don't think I'll ever be able to figure out who the murderer is, or if it's more than one murderer."

"Give me your glass," said Daffy.

As Daffy mixed their drinks, the elevator music on the TV suddenly stopped, and Captain Omen's image suddenly appeared on the screen.

"I want to provide you with an update. As you know, the Bahama Princess was ordered to return to Jacksonville as soon as possible. Accordingly, I directed our navigator to chart the shortest possible course back. This required us to pass through the Windward Passage, a narrow straight of water between the islands of Cuba and Hispaniola. Haiti occupies the western half of Hispaniola and borders the Windward Passage."

"During our transit through the Windward Passage, the Bahama Princess came under attack by several ships of the Haitian Coast Guard earlier this morning. The Haitian National Police had overthrown the former Haitian government and ordered the attack. The new Haitian government has charged us with violating their territorial waters and ordered us to follow their ships to Port-au-Prince."

"I have vigorously objected and contacted our corporate office for instructions. They ordered me to do as Haiti directs while they undertake measures under international maritime law to get us released. We expect to dock in Port-au-Prince today. I will endeavor to keep you informed as events unfold. Please remain in your cabins until directed otherwise. That is all."

Chapter 46

Port-au-Prince, Haiti
November 19th

Daffy and Gidget kept sipping gin and tonics off-and-on until six large black men burst into their stateroom that evening. As all passengers were confined to their rooms, the two women had snacked from things in the mini kitchen. They had heard nothing from Captain Omen since his announcement that they were being commandeered by the Haitian Coast Guard.

The intruders appeared to be some sort of military personnel. All wore khaki uniforms, differing only in symbols of rank on their collars or sleeves. Their jabber, as Haitian Creole sounded to Gidget and Daffy, contained no English they could understand.

"They must be speaking some sort of Haitian Creole. I wish I spoke it," said Gidget.

Daffy asked, "Where is Babs when you need her? She *thinks* she speaks the language, but it might be better than nothing."

Gidget grimaced. "I don't know about that. Her mangled Creole has screwed up more than one of her voodoo rituals."

Another man wearing the same khaki uniform entered. This one possessed a more authoritative manner than the others.

Gidget surveyed him. "Looks like we're in deep doo-doo."

"Except here in Haiti, it's probably called very deep voodoo doo-doo," Daffy said.

The authoritative man laughed. "Madam. Perhaps you will not mind if I adopt your 'very deep voodoo doo-doo' as my own. Permit me to introduce myself. I am Inspector Principal Guerrier of the *Le Groupe d'Intervention.*" He pronounced his surname as 'gare-re-er.'

"*Le Groupe d'Intervention*?"

"Intervention Group. Like your police force SWAT teams. We are a unit of the Haitian National Police."

"Well then maybe you can tell us what in the hell is going on," said Daffy.

"There is not much to tell, Madam. You are in the middle of another Haitian coup… in a long history of Haitian *coups d'état*."

"The captain of our ship said the Haitian National Police had overthrown the existing government," Gidget said.

"He was correct. This is not the first, nor will it probably the last coup."

"Inspector, you make it sound as if coups in Haiti are more regular than a woman's menstrual cycle," Daffy quipped.

He chuckled. "The best comedy has an underlying element of truth. *Coup d'états* occur in Haiti on a regular basis. We've had thirty-two coups since we won our independence from France in 1804. In my lifetime, we had one in 1986, two in 1988, one in 1991, and one in 2004."

Guerrier's short history lesson provided no measure of comfort to Daffy or Gidget. Gidget said, "We understood from the captain's last update that the Bahama Princess would be boarded. I take it, that's why you're here."

"*Oui*. You are correct. The Revolutionary Government of Haiti has impounded the Bahama Princess," said Guerrier.

"Impounded?"

"*Oui*. Our government considers the Bahama Princess to have entered Haitian territorial waters, and therefore, is being impounded until a resolution to the violation can be negotiated. The ship is now anchored in the harbor at Port-au-Prince."

"We could see that out our window. What are you going to do with us?"

The smile on Guerrier's face reminded Gidget of Cruella De Vil's smile—wide, full of white teeth, and malicious.

"We understand there are over four thousand people on this ship, which is too many to house and feed in Port-au-Prince. For that reason, most passengers and crew will remain on board until a resolution of our grievances is negotiated. The Revolutionary Government of Haiti has decreed that your *Capitáne* and key members of his senior staff such as the Navigator, Chief Engineer, and Senior Communications Officer will accompany us and be retained in the city. The rest of the ship's crew will remain on board. Likewise, most passengers will remain on board."

Gidget knew what was coming next. "But some will go ashore."

Guerrier smiled again. "You are exceptionally bright. A few of those privileged to occupy Premier staterooms will go ashore with us."

"And Daffy and I are two of the privileged Premier passengers."

Guerrier's smile became even more Cruella-ish. "Ah, Madam, you are very clever. You two have been selected to be two of our guests. We will be honored to have you spend some time with us."

Gidget and Daffy accompanied Inspector Guerrier and his men down the gangplank toward three black-and-white police vehicles. Daffy and Gidget piled into the one in the middle, a rusted 1995 Toyota Land Cruiser. Guerrier sat next to them.

As they pulled away from the dock, Gidget asked, "Where are you taking us?"

"We have accommodations set up especially for you. Not far from here," Guerrier said.

Daffy asked, "Would it be considered rude to ask if it has hot and cold running water?"

He chuckled. "Another example of your humor."

"Yeah, but I hope it doesn't have an underlying element of truth."

"I'm sure you will find your accommodations not quite as lavish as a Premier stateroom on the Bahama Princess, but they should be more than adequate for your needs."

They rode northeast along the main shoreline road, *Boulevard la Saline*, to a building whose signage indicated it was a Haitian National Police station. It appeared to be a remnant of the Cubism movement in art that had infected Haitian architecture. Two smaller cubes attached themselves to a larger central cube upon which another smaller cube rested. All cubes were painted white with a wide horizontal baby blue stripe separating each of its five floors.

"I love the blue and white horizontal stripes," Daffy said.

Gidget asked, "What about black and white horizontal stripes? You may be wearing them shortly."

"Right this way," said Inspector Guerrier as he led them out of the car toward the main door of the building.

Inside the police station, a desk officer completed paperwork on Gidget and Daffy and gave directions to two guards. Accompanied by the two guards—one leading, one following—they passed through an open entranceway into one of the smaller side cubes attached to the main one. A sixty-foot corridor lined with jail cells afforded an unpleasant introduction to their prospective accommodations. Before entering, one of the guards said, "Avoid contact. These prisoners can be dangerous."

Black and brown arms squeezed through iron bars lining both sides of the corridor. Many hands flailed at the two new prisoners and their guards who proceeded in single file down the middle. The two guards swatted back with batons, but with limited success.

"Guerrier overstated it when he said our accommodations wouldn't be as lavish as our stateroom," said Daffy.

Gidget nodded. "The guy's a real comedian. At least they're putting us in the women's section."

"*Silans*!" said one of the guards.

Daffy looked behind at Gidget who raised her forefinger to her lips and shhh'ed.

Near the end of the corridor, the guard in front stopped before a cell and opened its door with his key. He motioned for Daffy and Gidget to enter. Daffy stepped forward, then hesitated at the filthy sight inside the cell. Dirty walls, floors, and ceiling, as well as disgusting smells, assaulted her senses and proved Guerrier to be a bald-faced liar. The guard shoved her inside. Gidget followed.

A female lay on the bottom mattress in the cell's solitary bunk bed. She bolted upright and began frantically cursing in Haitian Creole at the guards. One of the guards spat in her direction, then both stepped outside, slammed and locked the door. After both guards had disappeared, the female prisoner sneered at Gidget and Daffy and said in broken English, "You white *beechess* can fight over who gets the top bed."

Chapter 47

21° 20' 25.9728" North, 74° 29' 49.0344" West
November 20th

Cordell's Gulfstream G650 cruised at 20,000 feet over the Atlantic Ocean. Six-hundred-fifty miles per hour was considered cruising speed for the quintessential corporate jet. Passengers occupied less than half of its eighteen seats.

The pilot spoke over the plane's intercom. "Folks, this is Captain Stevenson. You might engage in a little sightseeing if you look out of the starboard side of the aircraft. You can see Cuba in the distance. On the port side, you can see the Turks and Caicos Islands. We'll be landing shortly at Toussaint Louverture International Airport in Por-au-Prince. Temperature in Port-au-Prince is a balmy eighty-three degrees Fahrenheit. No rain. Time there is 12:40 PM Eastern Time. Hope you enjoyed your flight."

Cordell, Lilly, Lizzie, and Babs accompanied the *Real Widows of Thomasville* film crew—two video cameramen, the show's director, and a writer. The *Real Widows* stars had little difficulty convincing Cordell that a couple of episodes filmed during a Haitian *coup d'état* would be a ratings bonanza.

"Can't you make the pilot make this thing go any faster?" Babs asked Cordell. She fretted over a news report they watched on a TV monitor mounted behind the flightdeck. A CNN reporter stood in front of a wrought iron fence, speaking into a microphone.

"Behind this fence is the residence of the President of Haiti." She turned and pointed to a white two-story building. Six columns fronted a veranda flanked by two wings. "As you can see, members of the Haitian National Police stand guard outside the fence. They are here both to protect and detain the President who has been removed from office in the two-day old *coup d'état*. National Police have also surrounded the Haitian Legislative Palace and expelled all members of the Haitian National Assembly."

"We also have word that most of the passengers and crew of the Bahama Princess cruise ship are confined to the ship until all grievances of the Haitian Revolutionary *Gendarmerie* are resolved—"

Cordell abruptly turned the TV off. “Cool your jets. We’ll be landing there soon."

“I can’t help it. That reporter is saying The Bahama Princess is being detained in port by those Haitian revolutionaries. And all those deaths onboard the ship. No telling what’s happened to Daffy and Gidget,” said Babs.

“What do y’all think they’ll do to us after we land?” asked Lilly.

“Whatever it is, these guys will get it on camera.” Lizzie flicked her thumb at the two cameramen, Tim and Allen, sitting beside her. She looked at them. “Make sure y’all get my better side.”

Lilly asked, “Which side is that?”

“It’s been so long since I had a good side, much less a better side, it’s hard to tell. Probably my backside. That butt lift I had done two years ago still seems to be holding up. Cordell, when are we going to get enough time off from filming so I can get my vampire breast lift?”

Cordell said, “We go into hiatus in February.”

“Shouldn’t we be talking about our safety instead of breast lifts?” asked Lilly.

Lizzie smirked. “You will realize the foolishness of that remark after you see my revitalized puppies after surgery.”

“Our safety is inside that case right over there on the seat beside Tim.” Cordell pointed to a black, hardshell rollable video camera case sitting on the floor next to the cameraman. “That is our security. Those Haitian revolutionaries will play to the camera, and that’s to our advantage.”

Cordell left his seat, walked down the aisle, and sat close to his writer and director. He leaned in to speak privately.

“I want the script to focus on one or two of the revolutionaries and how they react with the Widows. Don’t just show only crazy Haitian soldiers firing guns into the air. Some of that’s great, but pick one guy and get into his head, his past, his motives. Make sure you get some good video of the Widows interacting with him.”

“How do we do that?” asked the Director.

“You’re the director. Figure it out. Listen, if we do this right, *Real Widows* ratings will go through the roof and on up to the moon.

We're looking at full employment for all of us for the next decade if we do this right."

"That could be kind of dangerous, couldn't it? Some of these revolutionaries might get violent. Shouldn't we keep the Widows away from them?"

Cordell's solution addressed the Director's concern by relying on the personality characteristics each of the ladies naturally displayed on the *Real Widows* show.

"We'll let Lilly dazzle them with her Cate Blanchett looks. Lizzie can entertain them with her Joan Rivers humor. And Babs' non-stop Gracie Allen chatter will put them to sleep."

While the Gulfstream cruised toward Port-au-Prince, Gidget and Daffy paced their cell's dirty floor, tired. They slept little last night and looked haggard. They took stock of the jail cell they now occupied. Their cellmate lay on the bed, looking at them and mischievously grinning. Fearful of what might happen to them if they both fell asleep at the same time, Gidget and Daffy had alternated staying awake through the night.

Daffy said, "These walls and ceiling are chipping the same pea-green paint we've seen before. Must be the standard color for all jails worldwide."

"It would be nice if they'd use a little Rust-Oleum paint on the iron bars..." Gidget pointed to the window and cell door. "That's a lot of rust."

"It wouldn't be a jail without a nasty concrete floor. At least we got a sink in the room." Daffy pointed to a small rust-stained, stainless-steel sink mounted on a wall.

Gidget looked at a ten-gallon orange plastic bucket sitting next to the sink. The diagonal Home Depot logo adorned its side. "At least we got a toilet."

Their cellmate's mischievous smile broadened. "You beechess don't like the accommodations?"

Daffy nodded. "I never thought I'd miss the Duval County Jail."

"You miss jail?" Their cellmate laughed. "No way! You rich American beech. Doan boolsheet me. You never see inside of a jail before now."

Gidget smirked. "That's what you think! Daffy and I spent a night in the Duval County Jail in Jacksonville, Florida just last month, *AND* one of our cellmates was from Port-au-Prince."

"Boolsheet. You lie like a dog. A Haitian in you jailcell. Hmph!"

"I beg your pardon. Our cellmate was from right here in Port-au-Prince, and her name was Delphine Lafleur."

The cellmate bolted upright. "Delphine?! No way! Describe her."

Daffy said, "She's a lovely young woman. About five feet, six inches tall. Slim. Very dark, smooth skin. Black, straight hair. High forehead—"

"She has a small scar on the right side of her neck. She told us it was from some sort of a voodoo ceremony she participated in about five years ago. Some sort of voodoo ritual. The scar was from a snake bite—" Gidget said.

"We figured she was bullshitting us about the snake bite. She told us her mom was a..." Daffy looked at Gidget. "What'd she call it?"

"A Manbo."

Their cellmate enthusiastically nodded. "*Oui*, a Manbo! A voodoo preestess! I knew Delphine and her *manman* well. Delphine and me used to go to different schools together."

Puzzled expressions on Daffy and Gidget's faces prompted their cellmate. "I make a funny. Going to different schools together is old Haitian joke."

Gidget frowned. "Sounds like a very old joke. You might want to retire it. Anyway, Delphine told us she practiced voodoo herself. Apparently, she had to leave Port-au-Prince after the Haitian National Police caught her scamming tourists. She immigrated to Jacksonville."

Their cellmate laughed. "I remember it well. Last spring. A cruise ship docked. She and Miss Monique—"

"Yeah," said Daffy. "Delphine mentioned Miss Monique was one of her competitors."

"Delphine and Monique always try to out-voodoo each other for tourist business. They did not realize one of the tourists they tried to swindle was actually a constable." Their cellmate let out a good belly laugh.

Gidget and Daffy both joined in the laughter. Gidget said, "Our friend Babs told us about Miss Monique after she visited Port-au-Prince a couple of months ago. She bought some voodoo stuff from her shop. Anyway, all of us—me, Daffy here, Babs, and two of our girlfriends—spent the night in the jail with Delphine and twelve other ladies who had also been arrested."

"Did you say, Babs?"

Daffy nodded. "Yeah. Babs Neauxgeaux."

Their cellmate's eyes widened. "Babs Neaugeaux?! Is your girlfriend Babs, the same Babs in *The Reel Widows of To-ma-vee*?"

"The same one. You know about The Real Widows of Thomasville?" asked Gidget.

"*Real Widows* is most popular TV show in Port-au-Prince, in all Haiti. I love Babs' *vodou* ceremonies. They are hilarious."

"Well, it was Babs and our other two girlfriends, Lilly and Lizzie, that spent the night with us in the Duval County Jail."

Their cellmate laughed. "Lilly and Lizzie. I loved the episode about Lilly's shoe closet. And she was in jail with you? When was that? What were you arrested for? How did you get out?"

Daffy said, "It was about a month ago. It was the night after the five of us streaked the Georgia-Florida college football game during the halftime—"

"Streaked?"

"We ran naked across the football field. It was a televised game. Streaking was real popular in the 70s when I was in college."

"Why you do that now at you age? You no that young anymore."

"Another grandmother insulted my granddaughter. She said Tara's plié—"

"Ple-ay? What is that?" asked their cellmate.

"It's when you put your heels together and turn your feet outward, then bend your knees halfway so you lower yourself. Then you straighten back up." Daffy demonstrated as she spoke. "The other grandmother said Tara's plié looked like she was trying to pick up marbles with her butt—"

Their cellmate laughed as Daffy plowed on. "Anyway, I got mad and let my ego get the best of me. The bitch proposed a bet based on which of our two six-year-old granddaughters would win the dance recital. The loser's grandmother had to streak the football game. I lost, and my friends streaked the halftime ceremonies with me."

"Insulting grandchildren is vile." Their cellmate stood up and spit on the concrete floor. "My *gran mama* would kill to protect my honor. Next time you see this beech who insult you grandchild, tell her Fabienne will rip her tongue out."

Fabienne put her fist to her chest in a sign of solidarity with Daffy.

Chapter 48

Port-au-Prince, Haiti
November 20th

Aéroport International Toussaint Louverture takes its name from the leader of the revolution that led to its independence from France in 1804. Among the first of the Latin American countries to achieve independence from a colonial ruler, revolution has been part of its culture ever since, just like voodoo. Cordell planned to combine the current revolution in Haiti with its voodoo in tonight's *Real Widows* episode, aired live in real time. He spoke with Captain Stevenson as they approached the airport.

Stevenson said, "We received clearance from the control tower to land, Mister Isler. We'll be the first non-military aircraft to land in Port-au-Prince since the *coup* began."

Cordell smiled. "I want you to make a couple of loops around the airport before landing. At an altitude low enough for Tim and Allen to get some good video of the Widows looking out the windows at people and planes on the airport tarmac."

"Sir, I need to get control tower approval to make those kinds of passes."

"No way. It's like they say in the military. It's easier to ask for forgiveness than to seek permission."

Five minutes later, Tim and Allen filmed as Babs looked out a window. "Look at all those soldiers in front of the terminal."

Lilly had a change of heart. "Look at all the guns they got. I knew this was a mistake. I know they're gonna start shooting when we get off the plane. We need to turn this thing around and go back to Thomasville."

Lizzie said, "Babsie, do some sort of voodoo hex and turn their guns into water pistols."

Tim exited the plane first so he could film the women as they descended the plane's foldout airstairs. Allen stayed on the plane to get video from behind the women. Cordell wanted a high-angle, over-the-shoulder camera shot from above showing each widow as she descended into the cluster of military uniforms. There were twenty soldiers. They wore camouflage uniforms and formed a semi-circle around the bottom of the plane's airstairs. Each soldier held an assault rifle at port arms position, but as Tim began walking down the airstairs, a sergeant barked a command. Every soldier immediately pointed his rifle at Tim. He paused, then kept descending, although at a slower pace. Once on the tarmac, Tim carefully positioned himself to record the widows' descent.

Lilly began her exit, saw what she faced below, and halted. "I… I don't know if this is such a good idea, Cordell."

Cordell placed his hands on her shoulder. "Go on. Don't back out on me now. Those guys down there are just playing to the camera. You'll be fine."

Lilly hesitantly continued. Lizzie followed with trepidation. "Cordell, if this thing backfires on us, my ghost is gonna hunt you down."

"Don't worry, Liz. Babs is gonna charm these guys with her chatter." Cordell looked at Babs. "Ain't you?"

Babs stepped onto the first step. "If I can make it down in these Bruno Magli's."

"Only you would wear four-inch heels into Haiti."

Lizzie looked back up over her shoulder. "She needs the extra height."

All the soldiers had been quiet when the Gulfstream's hatch opened, and Tim descended. As Lilly began walking down the steps, they looked at each other quizzically and began talking in Haitian Creole amongst themselves. This intensified after Lizzie exited. When Babs stepped out, their chattering reached fever-pitch levels although their assault rifles remained pointed at the women.

Lizzie asked, "Lil, what do you think is the latest style of POW clothing in Haiti?"

"My pale skin doesn't coordinate well with black and white horizontal stripes," said Lilly as she stepped onto the tarmac.

"I wonder if there's anything in the Geneva Convention about fashion requirements for POW uniforms?"

Babs stood on the third step when the unit's sergeant raised a walkie-talkie to his mouth and began excitedly speaking into it in Haitian Creole. She looked back at Cordell.

"I'm getting bad vibes."

Lizzie stepped onto the tarmac. "Something's up. I don't know what they're saying, but I don't like it either. Let's turn around and go back up into the airplane."

"I can't. I can't turn around in these heels and go back up without falling."

"I wonder who he's talking to?" asked Lilly.

"I wonder what they're talking about?" asked Lizzie.

"Whatever it is, they're sure excited about it," said Babs.

"Must be about who gets sloppy seconds."

"Lizzie!" Babs and Lilly shouted in unison. Tim lowered his camera and doubled over laughing.

Meanwhile, Daffy and Gidget had made a new friend in their cellmate, Fabienne. Daffy asked, "What are you in for?"

"This time, it's for picking tourists' pockets. What you in for?" Fabienne asked. Her fairly good English surprised Daffy and Gidget, but as she had explained, Port-au-Prince catered to a lot of American tourists.

"We were on a cruise ship—" said Gidget.

"Investigating the murders of the gentlemen friends we were traveling with," said Daffy.

"Gentlemen friends, eh?" Fabienne smiled deliciously. "I hope they paid you before they were murdered."

Gidget frowned. "It's not like you may think. They saw our calendar—"

"Calendar?" Fabienne's smile broadened.

"Not a nudie calendar, although you wouldn't want to pin it up in your Sunday school's classroom," said Daffy.

Gidget said, "All five of our boyfriends—"

Fabienne was impressed. "Five boyfriends? I never managed five boyfriends even on my busiest day on the Rue du Centre."

Gidget gave up. "Anyway, your government impounded the ship we were on before we could solve who murdered our boyfriends. Figuring it out is still on my to do list. They left most people on the ship but took some of us as hostages, I guess—"

Daffy said, "You'd know they'd leave Veronica and Naomi on board—"

"Do we know that?"

Daffy shrugged. “I bet they are.”

“Why did the government impound you ship?” asked Fabienne.

“The Haitian police officer said they impounded the ship because it supposedly strayed into a part of the Windward Passage that Haiti considers part of its territorial waters,” Gidget explained.

“That sounds like something the Bouchard government would do.”

“Bouchard is no longer the president of Haiti.”

“No? Who is?”

“We don’t know. The Haitian National Police overthrew your government two days ago.”

Fabienne shook her head slowly. “That is not good.”

“Why?”

“That means Director General Francois is in charge in Haiti. He is in charge of the National Police and a most evil man.”

As she asked her question, two prison guards began rolling a cart down the corridor, opening cell doors, and depositing trays with food on them.

Fabienne nodded her head in the direction of the guards. “They began feeding us regularly again yesterday.”

“Huh?”

“It is the law in Haiti that prisons must provide prisoners with water and two meals a day.”

As Fabienne spoke, one of the guards opened the door to their cell and placed three trays on the floor. Each contained a bowl of porridge and a bowl of rice with fish. He smiled maliciously at the women.

When he was out of earshot, Fabienne said, “Be careful of that one. He has his way with the women prisoners.”

Daffy and Gidget began eating ravenously. Gidget quickly said, “This stuff sucks. No wonder you’re so skinny.”

“I’ve lost nine pounds in as many days, but not for much longer.”

“What do you mean?” asked Gidget.

“Tonight, I’m breaking out of this hellhole. Eight o’clock.”

The soldiers guarding the *Real Widows* crew talked excitedly until an officer exited the airport terminal and briskly walked toward them. They lowered their rifles a bit and nervously looked back and forth between the women and the approaching officer. Their sergeant stepped away and met him out of earshot. By this time, Cordell had joined the ladies on the tarmac.

The officer kept looking over at the *Real Widows* stars as he talked with the sergeant. When they finished, the sergeant saluted. The officer returned his salute, took one last look at the assemblage of people standing next to the jet, then turned and strutted back to the terminal. The sergeant shook his head and returned to the stars.

Cordell took charge. "I'm the executive producer of *The Real Widows of Thomasville*, a nationally televised show in America. We are here to film a couple of episodes in Haiti, which could be very good for Haiti and for yourself if you—"

The sergeant nodded toward a corrugated metal building at the far end of the airport. A half-ton military truck painted camouflage green had pulled out of the building and drove toward them.

"You will please climb aboard that vehicle when it stops."

"Why? Where are you taking us?" asked Lilly.

"You will find out."

Cordell looked up into the Gulfstream's hatch at the cameraman. "Allen, grab your and Tim's gear and get on down here with us. Tell the director and writer to stay with Captain Stevenson in the Gulfstream. Tell them to stay put until we return."

Cordell, his two cameramen, Babs, Lilly, and Lizzie had climbed into the bed of the half-ton truck, and it rumbled toward the corrugated metal building next to the airport. The truck was a standard military green color including the canvas cover over the truck bed and the metal bench on which they sat. The only light came from a small opening at the rear of the truck.

The sergeant and two other soldiers also sat in the back of the half-ton. Smiles on their faces unnerved everyone.

Lilly looked at Cordell. "I thought you said we'd be safe? You said the Haitians would want the publicity that our show could give them. Now, we're being hauled to who knows where for who knows what's gonna be done to us."

Cordell stiffened. "We got a top-rated nationally televised show that's viewed by millions of people. I just need to educate these guys on the value of the cargo they got in the back of this truck."

Lizzie looked around. "Valuable cargo, my ass! If we're valuable cargo, then this truck must be Haiti's version of a Rolls-Royce limousine."

A commotion down the hallway outside their cell roused Daffy, Gidget, and Fabienne from their bunks. They pressed their faces against the iron bars in order to see what was happening.

"What is it?" asked Daffy.

"Eet looks like they are bringing in more prisoners," said Fabienne.

Three guards prodded three females. Daffy recognized them. "Lou, Ronnie, Naomi! Over here! It's Daffy and Gidget!"

Chapter 49

Port-au-Prince, Haiti
November 20th

The sergeant sat across from Lizzie and Cordell in the back of the half-ton truck. A thin smile creased his lips as the words "Rolls-Royce limousine" rolled off her tongue.

"None of my men would ever call this a limousine. I am sure you would agree after riding in it for thirty seconds."

Lizzie rubbed her backside. "Anyone climbing in this truck for a ride should be issued a tube of Preparation H. Have you thought about selling this godawful machine to Six Flags Over Georgia as a replacement for one of their roller coaster rides?"

Noise from the truck's knobby tires almost drowned out the sergeant's laughter. When he spoke, he had to shout. "Permit me to introduce myself. I am *Sergent* Brière Labonté of the Haitian Aviation Corps. We are Haiti's counterpart to your Air Force, although not quite of the same magnitude."

Cordell leaned forward so he could be heard over the noise. "Where are you taking us?"

"The colonel directed us to transport you to Aviation Corps headquarters. It is in one of the corrugated steel buildings you may have seen on the other side of Toussaint International Airport."

"Are all of you in the Aviation Corps?"

"*Oui*. The Corps' Military Aviation Base is located next to the airport. We have facilities there to house your group."

"I need to communicate to your colonel exactly who we are so that we can be treated appropriately."

"I communicated who you are on the radio to the colonel. That is why he came over to us. When I told him who had landed, he insisted on verifying that himself."

"Who do you think we are?"

"These three ladies are the stars of *The Real Widows of Thomasville*." Labonté pointed to Lilly, Lizzie, and Babs and pronounced Thomasville as To-ma-vee.

"How do you know about our show?" asked Lilly.

"Our island is not as backward as you may think. We get cable television just like you do in America. *Real Widows* is very popular in Haiti. Every TV in Port-au-Prince tunes into *Real Widows* on Thursday nights."

Cordell looked at the *Real Widows* stars and beamed. They beamed back.

Labonté said, "Haitians especially enjoy Babs' *vodou* rituals. They are very entertaining."

Babs looked at Lilly and Lizzie. "Well, well, well. What do y'all doubting Thomases think about my voodoo now?"

Before the other women could respond, Labonté smiled. "Haitians especially enjoyed your *vodou* ritual under the Big Oak in the first episode of Real Widows."

"I'm so glad you enjoyed it. I try my best when I perform my voodoo rituals. I'm kind of proud of them."

"I have one thing to offer."

"What's that?"

"Your Creole was incorrect, *Madame* Babs. In the ritual, I believe you meant to say, 'Let our boyfriends tell them mammas to kiss their asses and think only about the Casserole Ladies,' did you not?"

"Yes, of course."

"What you actually said in Haitian Creole was, 'Oh great spirit, let me find an alien nearby here, so I can make a new friend!'"

Fabienne's explanation of the escape plan gave Gidget and Daffy little comfort.

"One of the city's largest gangs, the New Macoutes, will gather in front of the jail at eight o'clock. They will burn tires in front of the building, then rush inside and overwhelm the guards. They want to free as many prisoners as possible before the police and the Haitian National Guard can react."

Gidget was skeptical. "I don't know if it's a good idea to go along with this escape plan. We could get hurt. We might want to stay put in this here jail."

"But armed gangs storming jails is pretty much how jailbreaks are done in Port-au-Prince. It's an accepted way of protesting."

"You mean this is not the first time a jail break has been attempted?"

"Of course not. Prison conditions in Haiti are deplorable. Jailbreaks happen all the time."

Daffy said, "I don't know… I think I agree with Gidg about staying here and waiting for the American embassy to free us."

A more serious look replaced the sober expression on Fabienne's face. "Something you should consider. The guard that served our dinner… the one that smiled wickedly at both of you this evening. We call him *Vyolèt Malad*, the Sick Rapist. He typically makes his nighttime rounds at nine o'clock. I am sure he would love to add you to the notches on his belt."

Labonté agreed to let Tim and Allen start videotaping inside the half-ton during the short trip to the Aviation Corps' Base on the other side of the airport. Cordell wanted video of the women inside the truck interacting with the three Aviation Corps personnel who all spoke passable English.

Babs said, "The main reason we came here was to find our friends, Daffy and Gidget. They're on the Bahama Princess, and we understand that the ship is being detained here against its will. We're very worried about our friends."

A serious look came over Labonté. "The Haitian National Police has impounded the Bahama Princess. I am told that most of the crew and passengers are still on the ship."

"I hope they won't be detained onboard too long."

Lizzie said, "They may go into withdrawal if they can't buy souvenirs very soon."

"Don't listen to her. She's the one with the overspending compulsion. You say most of the passengers are detained onboard?"

Labonté nodded. "A few have been taken in custody and are being held in Port-au-Prince."

"How can we find out who they are?" asked Lilly.

"I do not know. The Aviation Corps and the National Police do not have close relations. There is competition. The Police are the ones who initiated the coup and are now in control of the government."

"We need to go to the ship and see if we can find out about them," Babs said.

"Certainly. The colonel gave me no instructions as to what to do with you, so I will use my own authority. When we get to our facility, we will transfer to one of our other vehicles and ride over to the ship."

The other vehicle turned out to be a 1996 Buick Roadmaster Estate Station Wagon. Labonté and an enlisted driver sat up front; Babs, Lilly, and Lizzie were in the second row; and Cordell, Tim, and Allen crowded into the third. The vehicle's olive-green paint job failed to hide much of its rust and dents.

The trip to the Bahama Princess was short. Haitian National Police personnel surrounded all entrances to the dock. After the Roadmaster stopped, one of the guards walked toward it. Labonté turned around.

"Let me do the talking. What are the names of your friends?"

Lilly said, "Daphne Belvedere and Gloria Smurfitt."

Labonté exited the Roadmaster and engaged in conversation with the policeman. Afterward, he walked back to the station wagon and explained, "The policeman told me they have no list of who is on and who was taken off the ship. You will have to wait to find out."

"Did he say how long that will be?" asked Babs.

"Till hell freezes over."

"Cordell, what should we do?" asked Lilly.

"Let's make good use of the down time and keep filming," Cordell said.

"Is that all that's on your mind? We came here to find Daffy and Gidget."

"Any suggestions as to how to go about that?"

Silence ensued until Babs said, "Let's go to the Marche de Fer."

"What's that?" asked Cordell.

Labonté said, "A place visited by all Port-au-Prince tourists."

Babs had visited the Marche three months prior on a short Caribbean cruise she had taken. For those shopping for voodoo supplies, Marche de Fer is a must. It was located close to the harbor, and vendors crowded its open-air marketplace, selling a variety of goods to gullible tourists. Babs had been one, the prey of a vendor known as Miss Monique. Babs eagerly led the others to a small rundown shop inside the Marche.

"Miss Monique! Miss Monique! It's me. Miss Babs!"

A small, dark woman wearing a loose linen dress decorated with mysterious symbols looked up from the voodoo materials she was arranging on a table. A greedy smile spread across her face.

"Well, I will be cursed," Monique said. "Madam Neauxgeaux, one of my very best customers. You could not stay away, could you? Back for more *vodou*? I hope you did not accidentally create too much chaos with your *vodou* rituals."

"Me and my friends are here filming for a television show we're doing—"

"Yes! *The Real Widows of Thomasville*. It is a big hit here in Port-au-Prince. I love it! The city closes down every Thursday so everyone can watch your show. I have told everyone that I sold you all of the *voudou* supplies you use on your show. I love your *vodou* ceremonies. They are very funny."

"They work real well."

Lizzie whispered under her breath, "When they work… which is never."

"Why are you here in Port-au-Prince? Did you run out of *vodou* supplies for your television show?" asked Monique.

Cordell stepped up. "Permit me to introduce myself, Miss Monique. I have heard so much about you from Babs. I'm the executive producer of *Real Widows*. We're here filming a couple of upcoming episodes of the show and thought it would be good for ratings to film them in Haiti. We especially want to get some voodoo scenes on film. We will be airing tonight's show live in real time."

"That might be hard given the *coup d'etat* the National Police have pulled off. The police are all over the streets. Some of them are not very encouraging of the role *vodou* plays in Haitian society and culture."

Labonté said, "There are a lot of police on the streets."

"Surely, something could be arranged for us," said Cordell.

"Ah! Now that I think about it, there is something. It will be perfect for your show tonight. I was just putting things away to close up, and all of you are welcome to accompany me."

"What exactly are you talking about?"

"Come with me tonight and find out."

Chapter 50

Port-au-Prince, Haiti
November 20th

Daffy hovered over the orange Home Depot toilet, her shorts and underwear lowered to her ankles. When she finished, she pulled them up, washed her hands, and looked disgusted at the results.

"I don't get a warm fuzzy feeling from washing my hands in brown water."

"I would not recommend it," said Fabienne.

Gidget said, "Urine is sterile, you know. Brown water usually is not. Keep that in mind next time you pee."

"Water treatment in Port-au-Prince is rare."

"Let's talk about something else... please," said Daffy. "My watch says it's getting close to eight o'clock."

"How did you manage to keep your watch when you were jailed? That does not happen in a Haitian jail."

"I hid it in my underwear when I peed in the bathroom on the ship before they hauled us off. I ain't losing my Rolex without a fight."

"How close is eight o'clock?" Fabienne asked.

"About five minutes."

"What should we do when the riot starts?" asked Gidget.

Fabienne said, "We stay put. They will come through the corridors with the keys and open as many cell doors as they can before police reinforcements arrive. So, you have decided to escape with us?"

"Yes." Gidget looked at Daffy, who nodded in agreement. "After we get out of here, we'll try to make it to the ship or the American embassy. And we want to take three other women they brought in this afternoon with us."

"I think they are only a couple of cells from us."

Five minutes later, they heard explosions outside the jail—front, sides, and back. Fabienne said, "This is it. Stay put, but get ready. It should not be too long."

Chaotic sounds quickly followed, soon spreading into the jail itself. They heard gunshots. Gidget grew worried.

"You didn't say anything about guns."

Fabienne smiled. "They're mostly for show. They fire them into the air like fireworks. The police do it as well. Everyone has to put on a show. Nobody would dare aim their gun at someone else. They might accidentally hit them."

Soon Haitian rioters ran down the women's corridor cursing and opening cell doors. A large black man opened Fabienne, Daffy, and Gidget's door and immediately looked surprised when he spotted the two Caucasian women. He quickly moved on as he had other cell doors to open.

"Let's go. Follow me," said Fabienne.

"The three other women," said Gidget.

They quickly walked down the hallway, peeking into each cell along the way. Five cells down they struck paydirt.

"Gidget! Daffy!" shouted Naomi. She was crowded into a small cell with Louella and Veronica and two Haitian women. One of the rioters had just opened the door to their cell.

Fabienne said, "Come with us! Queek!"

Gidget and Daffy vigorously nodded, and their three traveling companions rushed out of the cell. Fabienne led everyone down the corridor to an open side door. Outside, clumps of rioters cursed and threw empty bottles against the jail walls.

Fabienne pointed as she walked briskly. "This way. This street empties onto the N1 Highway. We can catch a ride there."

"Is that safe?" asked Daffy as she and the other four women struggled to keep up. "My momma always told me hitchhiking was very dangerous."

"Hitchhiking?"

"Thumbing a ride. Catching a ride with strangers."

"It's less risky to hitchhike than to get caught by the Haitian police. They do nasty things to prison escapees."

"You didn't tell us that before," said Gidget.

Daffy went Debbie Downer. "Oh great. The Haitian police don't shoot you. They just do nasty things to you."

Fabienne did not respond and kept walking at a fast pace. Gidget and Daffy figured that they had no choice but to rely on her street savviness. Louella, Naomi, and Veronica followed suit. Everyone soon reached the N1 to find it crowded with cars, trucks, and buses. Fabienne noticed her companions' looks of surprise.

"Port-au-Prince streets are always crowded during a city-wide prison escape. We should have no trouble 'hitchhiking.' Let me do the talking."

She soon caught a ride for all of them in the bed of a 2003 Toyota Tacoma.

"Where are we going?" asked Gidget.

Fabienne said, "We lucked out. They are headed to a *Dans* not far from here. We can go to that and be safe from the police. They will never disrupt a *Yanvalou Dans*."

"Dance?"

"It is a very old part of Haitian culture. It is a nighttime ceremony that involves a formal dance by a *vodou* congregation."

"Congregation?"

"It's like one of your Methodist or Catholic churches."

"What happens at this dance?" asked Daffy. "I ain't line danced in decades."

Fabienne turned out to be a goldmine of information. "It is a *vodou* ceremony in which the congregation wears white clothes and performs a special dance. They invite an *Iwa* into their midst."

"*Iwa*? What's that?" asked Gidget.

"It is a spirit."

"A spirit? You mean someone who's dead?"

"Yes. They invite the *Iwa* for a specific purpose."

"What's that?"

"They want the spirit of the dead person to leave the spirit world, come into the world of the living, and possess the body of one of the dancers. The person being possessed is called the *Chwal* or horse. The *Chwal* can be either a man or woman. While the *Chwal* is possessed, or mounted as it is known in Haitian, he or she actually becomes the possessing spirit."

Daffy's eyes widened. "Mounted? This just keeps getting better and better."

"Daffy! Don't interrupt," said Gidget. "Please continue, Fabienne."

"While the person is possessed, the spirit communicates with the other congregants via that person. It is a two-way conversation between the spirit from the otherworld and the living. All this is done while the congregation is singing and dancing."

"This kind of sounds like that voodoo sacrifice scene in the James Bond film, *Live and Let Die*."

"Exactly. And that is why we want to go to the *Dans*. The Haitian National Police would not dare interrupt a sacred *vodou* ceremony like a *Dans*. We will go there… It's in the forest not far from here. We will stay there through the night. The police and military would never invade a *Dans* ceremony. Things will have calmed down by morning, and you will be able to safely return to your ship. You should easily be able to hitchhike a ride."

The truck followed the N1 for several miles then turned onto a side road leading into a heavily forested area. It was not long until it again turned onto another unpaved road. The forest consisted of subtropical trees and colorful plants. They soon encountered bumper-to-bumper traffic, barely moving on the narrow road.

"Looks like this is a popular dance," said Daffy.

"Very popular. Hundreds of congregants will be here. It will be very easy for you to get lost among them if, by chance, some of the authorities should arrive," said Fabienne.

"You think Daffy and I can get lost among a bunch of native Haitians?" asked Gidget. They were tanned, but not that tanned.

"Oh, there will be a lot of whites there as well."

"No kidding?"

"*Dans* are very popular among tourists. They get invited all the time, usually for the tithes they are expected to donate. There will probably be lots of white tourists."

By the time they arrived at the location of the *Dans* and parked the Toyota, it was close to midnight. They parked in an open space surrounded by palms, giant tree ferns, and mesquite-like trees. A variety of brightly colored native orchids and small green ferns were interspersed among the trees. A full moon illuminated the area, allowing them to see hundreds of Haitians in a clearing in the forest beyond the parking lot.

Daffy, Gidget, and the three other women followed Fabienne through the parking lot and into the crowd. Many were dressed in white as Fabienne had foretold.

"Those in white are members of the congregation. Those colorfully dressed, like yourselves, are visitors—either tourists or local Port-au-Prince residents. If you can look over the heads of those in front of us, the two Haitians in the center of the congregants are the *Manbo* and *Ougan* of this congregation."

"*Manbo*. Babs told us that's a female *Vodou* priestess," said Gidget. "What's an *Ougan*?"

"He is a male *Vodou* priest. The *Manbo* and *Ougan* run the *Dans* ceremony. We are a little late. As you can see, the *Dans* has already begun. It usually begins before midnight. The exciting part happens after midnight."

All five women followed Fabienne as she pushed deeper into the crowd. Something going on in the epicenter of the dancing congregants attracted a lot of attention. They could see and hear several black men on the periphery of the crowd rhythmically pounding on what looked to be large, crudely built conga drums. Others played bamboo flutes, and a few had simple horns made of cheap metal.

The dancers themselves swayed back and forth in unison. Each woman enhanced her sway by clasping both sides of her white skirt with her hands and waving the loose skirt back and forth. Likewise, all the dancing men wore loose white shirts and baggy pants that swayed back and forth as they moved rhythmically. No one wore shoes, and they all moved their bare feet to and fro on the hard-packed dirt.

Gidget and Daffy forged ahead with Fabienne, trying to get closer to the center of the congregants. That was where the most exciting part of the *Dans* appeared to be happening. As they closed in, both were shocked beyond belief at what they saw.

Chapter 51

Port-au-Prince, Haiti
November 20th

Gidget and Daffy remained frozen at the spectacle before them. Dressed in a billowing, ankle-length white dress, Babs swayed in the epicenter of the hundreds of *Dans* congregants. Other dancers, of whom there were many, moved in unison with her. She clutched the sides of her dress below her waistline and twirled them seductively back and forth in time with the music. Her bare feet, *sans* the Bruno Maglis, rhythmically slid back and forth on the dirt. As her head and shoulders swayed right and left, so did her large, pendulous breasts. Her movements seemed to captivate several of the male congregants close by. The steady beat of the drums was overpowering, and Babs appeared to be entranced.

Gidget's eyes were as wide as saucers. She turned to Daffy. "Babs was always an awful dancer, but look at her now."

"She's the only woman I ever knew that dances with a white man's overbite." Daffy referred to Billy Crystal's line in *When Harry Met Sally*. She motioned for Fabienne to come closer, then pointed at Babs. "That's our friend, Babs. What is going on?"

Fabienne said, "The rhythm of the drums creates an avenue… a pathway between the spiritual world and our world. The rhythm invites an *Iwa* into the ceremony. The *Manbo* and *Ougan* have chosen your friend Babs to be the *Chwal* of the *Dans*. Probably because of her famous role in the *Real Widows* TV program."

"The one who gets mounted?" asked Gidget.

"Yes. She will be possessed by a spirit."

"Possessed by someone dead?"

"Yes."

"What happens when she becomes possessed by a dead person's spirit?"

"She will have spasms—her body will shake uncontrollably, like she is walking over hot coals."

Daffy asked, "Whose dead spirit will possess her?"

"Anyone. It could be a dead relative, a dead lover, a long-lost friend. Many come here praying for a specific dead person to possess the *Chwal* so they can communicate with the dead person's spirit."

"It sounds like something a lot of fake spiritual advisors in America stage when they're trying to fool their victims," Gidget said.

"Except this works. *Vodou* is real. The *Dans* is real, not fake."

Gidget wanted to make certain she understood the *Dans*. "You are saying that the congregants and visitors at this *Dans* can pray that an *Iwa*, a dead person, will possess Babs' body and communicate with them through her right here and now while the *Dans* is in process?"

"Exactly."

"Interesting. Will everyone who prays get their prayers answered?"

Fabienne shook her head. "No. Only one or two at most."

"Who decides whose prayers are answered?"

"My Manbo always told me that the spirits themselves decide. Among those at this *Dans*, the person whose prayers are the most powerful, the most earnest, those prayers will be perceived by all the spirits as being the most powerful of all the prayers. That person will be blessed to have his or her dead spirit possess the *Chwal*."

Daffy asked, "You're saying the person among all these people here in this dance who most wants to hear from someone who's dead, that dead person will possess Babs?"

"Yes."

Daffy looked at Gidget in disbelief and noticed something. "You got a look on your face, Gidg. What's going on in that brain of yours?"

"Nothing, except that Babs seems to really be into her voodoo. I wonder who at this *Dans* will get lucky and have their prayers answered?" Gidget looked upward and closed her eyes.

Babs continued dancing with such enthusiasm that it was evident she was really into it, no faking for the crowd. A look of recognition flashed across her face when her head eventually turned in Gidget and Daffy's direction. She waved at them, then continued her movements, which gradually increased in their intensity. She seemed transformed. Her efforts oozed with an increasing eroticism her friends had never witnessed.

Fabienne explained, "Your friend Babs looks as if she is ready to be possessed. It is getting close to midnight—the witching hour. That is when the *Iwa* will possess the *Chwal*."

Five minutes passed, then spasms started in Babs' arms. Next, the spasms spread into her upper torso. Soon, her whole body shook so violently that Daffy and Gidget panicked and started to rush to Babs' side. Fabienne grabbed their arms.

"No. Do not go to her. Do not do anything."

"But she needs us," said Daffy. "She's having convulsions."

"No. Those are not real convulsions. She is being possessed. It looks bad, but trust me, it really is not. I have seen these possessions many times. The *Iwa* is entering her body at this moment. After it is all over, she will be fine."

"What happens next?" asked Gidget.

"The spirit will speak through her."

"Like in Bullwinkle?" asked Daffy.

Fabienne looked perplexed. "I do not understand."

"The cartoon. Bullwinkle would say, 'The spirits are about to speak,' and Rocky would say, 'Are they friendly spirits?' But the spirits that spoke were always just cereal commercials."

What Babs did next surprised and shocked everyone who watched. Her spasmodic movements suddenly ceased. The thin cotton fabric of her dress clearly revealed the erotic gyrations of her pelvis. Left, right, left, right. As her pelvis went left, her bent knees twisted right. As her hips swayed right, both knees shifted to the left. Her knees repeated this left-right movement slowly and rhythmically several times. The sheer cotton fabric clung to her legs, revealing their shape.

Next, she introduced another movement by occasionally bending her knees inward toward each other, then outward. Her feet sometimes turned outward and moved out away from her body, then reversed inward. All this as the speed of her pelvic gyrations steadily increased. The sheer, gauzy fabric clung to her body, its sensual movements unmistakable.

Babs' arms were not idle. They moved up, and her hands clapped together slowly above her head several times. When she lowered her arms, she moved them back and forth in front of her body and started snapping her fingers. Her erotic—some in Thomasville would have called it pornographic—movements left many wide-eyed bystanders immobile with mouths agape. Her movements seemed to be choreographed by someone not visible, some hyper-sexed entity.

The musicians—those on drums, flutes, and horns—lowered their volume in awe.

Gidget asked, "What's happening?"

"The musicians realize the *Iwa* is about to communicate with the congregation. They have lowered the music volume so everyone can hear what the *Iwa* is going to say," said Fabienne. "Be quiet and listen."

Babs opened her mouth and began singing, but it was not Babs' voice that came out of it. It was a totally different voice, but one not unfamiliar. It was a voice very familiar to both Daffy and Gidget as well as others in the crowd. Low at first, its volume increased until Daffy and Gidget recognized why it was familiar.

The voice possessed a rich, smooth tone. Some would describe it as a velvet baritone, yet others might say it blurred the lines between baritone and tenor. A beautiful timbre. The voice possessed a familiar Southern accent. Both Gidget and Daffy were absolutely certain the words coming out of Babs' mouth in no way sounded like her normal, high-pitched voice.

The *Iwa* in Babs began to sing. "You ain't nothin' but a hound dog, cryin' all the time. You ain't nothin' but a hound dog, cryin' all the time. Well, you ain't never caught a rabbit, and you ain't no friend of mine….."

Gidget and Daffy listened to the words of *Hound Dog* in rapt silence. After the *Iwa* in Babs completed the song, Daffy said, "If that wasn't Elvis Presley coming out of her mouth, I'm Buddy Holly. I saw Elvis live in Macon in 1972 and heard him sing *Hound Dog* in that concert. I'd swear that was him singing just now."

Gidget nodded. “I’ve got *Hound Dog* on a couple of Elvis albums. That was definitely Elvis the Pelvis, singing *and moving* through Babs. I mean, those were Elvis’s movements exactly.”

“Babs moved exactly like Elvis moved. It brings new meaning to the old phrase Elvis has left the building. Don’t it?”

“Oh?” Gidget made a face. “I’m afraid to ask.”

“Elvis has left the metaphysical world.”

Gidget rolled her eyes. “Fabienne, what happens next?”

“The *Iwa* will continue communicating through your friend Babs until it has said all it feels compelled to or wants to communicate. Usually, it is not for too long.”

Daffy smiled. “I got a new nickname for Elvis.”

What?” asked Gidget. “No. I retract that. Please don’t tell me.”

“Instead of Elvis the Pelvis, how about Elvis *Iwa*?”

Elvis *Iwa* finished his set with *Rock-A-Hula* from the movie *Blue Hawaii* and *It’s Now or Never*. Gidget, Daffy, and the entire congregation raptly listened, awed by the beauty of Elvis Presley’s voice. After Elvis *Iwa* finished singing *It’s Now or Never*, Gidget asked, “Fabienne, what happens to Babs after Elvis *Iwa* goes away?”

“Usually, the *Chwal* returns to their normal self. No after effects or personality changes at all.”

Daffy said, “Some personality changes might be good in Babs’ case.”

“Will anymore *Iwas* try to communicate through Babs?” asked Gidget.

Fabienne said, “No. Usually only one. More than that is too much of a strain on the *Chwal’s* body. If another *Iwa* communicates, it would be through someone else.”

“If someone has prayed really hard for a particular spirit and it does not possess and communicate through the *Chwal*, what does it mean?”

Fabienne thought for a moment. “It means that the spirit did not feel compelled to communicate with that person.”

“And you said that’s because the prayers of that person were not more intense or more powerful than the prayers of the person whose spirit did communicate through the *Chwal*?”

“Correct.”

"But what if a person's prayers to communicate with a particular *Iwa* were more powerful, more intense? What if they were the most powerful and most intense of all the congregants in the *Dans*? If an *Iwa* did not possess the *Chwal* in that case, what does it mean?"

"I would have to say that something was wrong during the *Dans*. Something was amiss in the connection between the spiritual world and our world. There must have been an overpowering reason why that dead spirit was unable to communicate with the living."

A look of triumph mysteriously appeared on Gidget's face. Daffy noticed. "What? What are you thinking?"

Gidget said, "I just solved the Marx Brothers murders."

Chapter 52

Port-au-Prince, Haiti
November 21st

Before Daffy could ask Gidget who had murdered the Marx Brothers, Babs collapsed. Daffy, Gidget, and Fabienne rushed toward Babs' prone body as it lay unmoving on the dirt. Louella, Naomi, and Veronica were prevented from following by the crush of dancers crowding in on Babs. She appeared to be unconscious. Gidget and Daffy worried that the possession of her body by a dead spirit had extracted a toll too horrible to contemplate.

As they pushed through the crowd, Daffy said, "I had a gut feeling all along that Babs shouldn't be letting Elvis *Iwa* into her body like that. She's no spring chicken."

"You might be right," said Gidget, physically shoving congregants aside to get to her friend. Doing something as rude as shoving others was something she had never done before in her life. As she neared Babs, a taller woman elbowed her way in front. Gidget was furious and grabbed the aggressive woman by the arm. The woman wore clothes only a tourist would wear and seemed frantic to get to Babs. As the woman's face turned to scold Gidget, there was mutual recognition.

"Gidget!"

"Lilly! What are you doing here?" asked Gidget.

"Lizzie!" said Daffy recognizing the woman next to Lilly. "What are y'all doing here?"

"We're here looking for you two," said Lizzie.

"And they're here filming an episode of *Real Widows*," said a strange man nearby. "Let me introduce myself. I'm Cordell Isler, executive producer of the show. You must be Gidget and Daffy."

"Yes, we are, but we have to get to Babs now! She may be in bad shape," said Gidget. She continued to push through the crowd. Lilly, Lizzie, Daffy, Cordell, Fabienne, Miss Monique, and Sergeant Labonté and his driver followed. Tim and Allen captured everything on video.

Babs was sitting up by the time Gidget reached her, shaking the wooziness from her head. Gidget knelt down.

"Babsie, don't try to get up just yet. Wait till your head clears."

"Gidg? We came to Port-au-Prince looking all over for you." Babs slurred her words.

Lizzie said, "We heard about the Bahama Princess being detained in Port-au-Prince."

"The three of them talked me into flying them here to find you," Cordell said.

"What are y'all doing here at a *Dans*?" asked Daffy.

Lilly said, "Miss Monique brought us here. In Sergeant Labonté's station wagon."

Miss Monique stepped forward and smiled. "Welcome to Haiti."

"We went to the Bahama Princess to find you, but the Haitian Police wouldn't let us onboard to see y'all," Lizzie said. "We figured they didn't want us to see the disgusting spectacle of five old men puttin' the make on a bunch of old women."

Gidget looked down. "I have terrible news. The Marx Brothers are dead."

"Which ones?"

"All five."

Lilly gasped. "How horrible! Those must have been the mysterious deaths we heard about from the cruise line. They never told us who it was. We were so worried that it might have been y'all. That's the main reason we got Cordell to fly us to Port-au-Prince… to see if it was y'all."

"How did they die?" asked Lizzie.

Gidget said, "Each one died—"

Daffy interrupted. "We think they were all murdered. Gidg thinks she's solved the murders."

Gidget nodded. "It's very suspicious. One died each day over a five-day period. One death every day, beginning with Larry who supposedly choked while having a seizure brought on by acute alcohol poisoning. The next day it was Jerry who was pushed or jumped overboard. Next day, it was Harry, who disappeared after his parasail towline snapped over the open sea. The next day, it was Gary, who mysteriously disappeared in Moriarty's Magic Box. The last day, Barry slid down the four-hundred-foot MegaSlide and fell into the ocean through a huge hole in the plexiglass."

Lizzie, who was unaware of Gidget's pregnancy vis-à-vis Barry, blurted, "Sounds like y'all got the makins' of a juicy Marx Brothers murder mystery going."

In a few minutes, Babs had recovered sufficiently to talk more clearly. With Elvis *Iwa* no longer commanding her voice, she said, "I hate hearing that about the Marx Brothers. I was really looking forward to seeing them again. And Cordell wanted to film some voodoo stuff here for a couple of episodes. That's why I thought a good place to start would be the Marché de Fer. We went straight to Miss Monique's shop after we left the boat—"

"Babsie, your shaggy dog story is beginning to show again," said Lizzie.

"Y'all know I got to tell it just like it is in my brain, or it don't come out right. Anyway, before I was interrupted, this nice man—" Babs pointed to Sergeant Labonté. "What am I saying, he ain't just a nice man, he's a full sergeant in the Haitian Air Force, although it ain't quite as big as our Air Force, anyway he's got this nice big Buick station wagon and took us in it to Miss Monique's shop after we couldn't see y'all at the boat. There wasn't much else we could do." Babs paused to catch her breath before continuing.

"We hooked up with Miss Monique in her shop in the Marché de Fer. And I introduced Miss Monique to Lilly and Lizzie and Cordell and his two cameramen, Tim and Allen here." Babs pointed to the two cameramen who were recording the entire Casserole Ladies reunion, then to his driver. "And Private Guillaume—I hope I'm saying that right—has been nice enough to drive us around Port-au-Prince all night….."

As Babs chattered, Daffy whispered into Gidget's ear, "Private Ghe-yahm may have been driving Babs around, but she's been driving him crazy."

"Anyway, Cordell told Miss Monique he wanted to film some voodoo stuff for a couple of episodes, and she said she had just the ticket." Babs looked at Monique for affirmation, and Monique nodded. "So, we toured Port-au-Prince a little bit so Tim and Allen could film us interacting with the people behind this *coup d'etat*—"

"The Haitian National Police," said Miss Monique.

"Yeah, the Haitian National Police. Those are some tough guys by the way—"

"We got some great live video," said Cordell. "I can't wait to see the ratings for tonight's episode."

Babs became incensed. "I certainly hope you will edit some of that video out of the film. I don't want any of my grandchildren seeing me handcuffed again. Anyway, Miss Monique said she knew just the ticket for us to film some voodoo stuff, and so here we are. Apparently, all of Haiti watches *Real Widows*, and they love the voodoo stuff I do in it, so when we got here, the people in charge of this thing were eager for me to be the Charles thing—"

"*Chwal*," said Miss Monique.

"Yeah. That's it. These folks have been the politest folks I've ever met. They made me feel like I'm one of the family. Just like folks do in Thomasville, although now that I think about it, those Haitian police weren't very nice. Cordell, you have just got to edit out that scene of them handcuffing me. My grandchildren—"

Cordell said, "Babsie, we were filming that scene live, in real time. Remember?"

"You mean you can't delete the scene of them handcuffing me?"

"No, it was shown live. The whole world has already seen it."

While Babs absorbed what Cordell told her, Gidget asked, "What did y'all film live?"

Cordell said, "It was great stuff. We weren't supposed to go live until 8:00 PM, so we filmed some scenes at the Bahama Princess, then the girls interacting with Miss Monique in the Marche de Fer, then some scenes at a couple of locations around Port-au-Prince. While we were filming in the city, Haitians kept telling us about a prison riot and jailbreak that was supposed to start at 8:00 PM, the exact time we were due to go live."

"I figured a prison riot and jailbreak would be a gold mine. So, we got set up at seven-forty-five and were ready when it started. I called my writer—he's back on the plane—and told him to work up some good stuff and get back to me with it. He did, and he called back to Hollywood and prepped the narrator with it as well. She narrated while the girls interacted with the rioters outside the prison. It was dy-no-mite."

Babs said, "Those rioters were the nicest people. They loved being on camera."

Cordell smiled. "They all knew about the *Real Widows* and were fans. The dialogue was priceless."

Daffy said, "Y'all must have been filming in front of the jail when we were breaking out of the side of the jail."

"I wish we would have known. But we got some great footage anyway. The best part was when Babs, Lilly, and Lizzie showed the rioters how to use their pistols."

Lilly said, "All they were doing when we got there was waving their pistols in the air. No one really knew how to aim at someone and shoot."

Gidget looked horrified. "Oh, my God! Y'all didn't show them how to shoot?"

Babs nodded. "Oh yeah. They was nothing but a bunch of amateurs."

"Where's the NRA when you need 'em?" asked Lizzie.

"And their gun safety procedures was non-existent."

"What did you do?" asked Daffy.

Lilly said, "We pulled out our pistols—"

"You brought your pistols with you?"

"Of course," said Babs. "I never go anywhere without a pistol in my pocketbook, unless I forget my pocketbook."

"What kind of pistol?" asked Louella.

"A Sig."

Naomi asked, "You carry a Sig Sauer?"

"Yeah. A P238."

"And you brought it into Port-au-Prince?"

"Right in here." Babs patted her Alfie Leather handbag.

Veronica looked at Lilly and Lizzie. "What about y'all?"

Lizzie patted her handbag. "Mine's a Defender. I like the option of hitting the bastard with either a shotgun shell or a .45 caliber."

Lilly said, "I just carry a small automatic. A .38 caliber."

Babs explained, "Those rioters had automatics but didn't know how to use them. They were real impressed when Lilly and I pulled out ours. We showed 'em how to rack the slide, set and release the safety. They didn't even know how to do simple stuff like that."

Lizzie joked, "They were pretty harmless rioters when we got there, but when we left, they were dangerous hoodlums."

Chapter 53

Port-au-Prince, Haiti
November 21st

Gidget and Daffy gave a much shorter version of their escapade in Port-au-Prince. Afterward, Gidget looked at Cordell.

"I hope you're gonna be able to give Daff and me and our three Bahama Princess friends here a ride."

"Plenty of space on the Gulfstream, but it's gonna be pretty tight in the Roadmaster. We had to squeeze Miss Monique in. Luckily, she's on the small side," said Cordell, who then turned to Sergeant Labonté. "You think you can rustle us up another Roadmaster?"

"No, but I can get a 1990 Ford Country Squire Station Wagon here," he said.

"Is it the same barf-green as the Roadmaster? Does it still run?" asked Lizzie. "It seemed like your Roadmaster was on life support."

Miss Monique said, "No need for additional room on account of me. I want to stay here for some after-*Dans* activities."

"Same for me. I will not be going back into Port-au-Prince anytime soon," said Fabienne.

"Why's that?" asked Babs.

Daffy gave Babs a look. "Didn't you hear what we just explained? We just escaped from jail with Fabienne. It wouldn't be smart for her to go back into town right away. She might get picked up by the police if she goes back into town."

Cordell looked around at the hundreds of adoring Haitian congregants, all eager to meet Babs, the Vodou Queen of the *Real Widows*. "It looks like it's gonna take us a while to get out of here anyway."

The congregants kept Babs occupied well past two o'clock in the morning. Everyone wanted to be near and touch her. A non-Haitian *Chwal* was a once-in-a-lifetime event. And an Elvis *Iwa* to top it off. Haitians are big Elvis fans. Eventually, Babs and her coterie were able to extricate themselves from the adoring Haitians and walk back to the parking lot.

All five Casserole Ladies, Cordell, Tim, and Labonté rode in the upchuck-green Roadmaster. Everyone else piled into a Country Squire coated with rust and spray paint. On the way back to the Gulfstream, Cordell asked, "Sergeant, how can all of us get off this island?"

Labonté said, "That could be a problem, *Monsieur*. The Direction Générale of the Haitian National Police has taken control of the government. They are exercising very tight control over arrivals and departures to and from Port-au-Prince whether by ship or by airplane. In the four days since the *coup d'etat*, no one coming into Haiti has been allowed to leave. You will need Director General Francois' permission to fly out of Haiti." Labonté pronounced the Director's name as Frahn-swa. "You picked a bad time to come to Haiti."

"True, but the video we've gotten so far makes it worth it."

"That may be the case, *Monsieur*, but Director General Francois is not likely to let your aircraft use the airport's runway to leave Haiti anytime soon."

"How long do you think we'll be here?"

"It wouldn't surprise me if Francois kept you here for several weeks. You are celebrities, you know. The longer the revolution keeps you in Port-au-Prince, the more publicity it gets."

Gidget's anger exploded. "Damnit! I can't wait weeks until I'm able to resolve Barry's disappearance. I need to get back to the States immediately."

Cordell panicked. "Today's Thursday. We need to get back to Thomasville on Monday to start filming on the *Real Widows* episode that airs on December fifth—"

An incoming call interrupted Cordell. He put his iPhone to his ear. "Yeah. It's me. I'm kind of busy right now. What's up?"

Long pause.

"No kiddin'! An eighteen share! That's unbelievable."

Pause.

"You do? Will the network go for it? Hell yes, I do. This will blow *RuPaul's Drag Race* out of the water. Tell them the writer and I will work up something when I get back to the Gulfstream in a few minutes, and he'll call them back with the script for the narrator. Yeah. Gotta go. Bye."

Cordell looked like he had just finished an electroshock therapy treatment as he put his phone back in this pocket.

Lilly asked, “What was that about?”

“That was corporate. Last night’s show garnered an eighteen share!”

“Eighteen share? What’s that?” asked Gidget.

“That is unbelievable. It is fantastic. *Real Widows* was watched by eighteen percent of all adults under age fifty who had their TVs on from eight to nine o’clock last night. That percentage is unheard of. Last night’s episode blew the roof off of television ratings.”

Blank stares greeted his announcement.

Cordell swept his arm in Babs, Lilly, and Lizzie’s direction, “Ladies, you are megastars. The network wants another *live* episode, and they want it tonight. They’re going to bump the regular 8:00 PM show off and replace it with tonight’s *Real Widows* live episode. I’ve got to put our writer to work on another script ASAP. The network wants to put us up against *RuPaul's Drag Race*. They’ve wanted to sandbag that show for years, but nobody’s been able to do it… so far. They’re going to flood the airwaves with a commercial blitz announcing tonight’s live *Real Widows* episode."

As the vehicles pulled into the airport, Cordell continued to rave about the possibilities for tonight’s show. After everyone exited the vehicles, Tim lowered his camera and walked up to Cordell.

“Boss, I’ve got an idea.”

“What?”

“I think I may very well have come up with a way to get us out of Port-au-Prince.”

“How?”

“It’s iffy, but it might just work.”

“Tell me.”

Tim and Cordell huddled together for ten minutes before they headed directly for the Gulfstream, saying nothing to the others in the process.

Lilly asked, “Wonder what they’ve got in mind?”

“Hopefully, they’re figuring out something that’ll get us off this island,” said Babs.

Lizzie said, "Or more likely into a Haitian jail. How does a Haitian jail compare to the Duval County Jail, Daff?"

Daffy missed Lizzie's question as she was in the process of getting Gidget's attention. She asked her friend, "When are you gonna tell us who murdered the Marx Brothers, Gidg?"

Gidget nervously looked around and whispered, "Not now. Later. Too many people around here."

Chapter 54

Port-au-Prince, Haiti
November 21st

Tim provided the general concept, but Cordell filled in the details on how to get out of Haiti. Most of the Casserole Ladies loved his plan, especially Lizzie, as it involved two of her favorites—sex and booze. Lilly's off-and-on puritanical nature led her to object.

"It's extortion plain and simple. Ain't that illegal?"

"Get real. We're in Haiti," Daffy said.

Cordell made several calls to his network via the airplane's Wi-Fi satellite Internet connection. He relayed their proposed script. Of course, the network execs did not want to go along at first. It was too risky. Never been done before. Blah, blah, blah. But *Real Widows* was a megahit, and in the end, they had to agree to Cordell's demands.

They planned to execute the plan at eight o'clock in the evening. That left several hours to kill, so Labonté first took them to a shopper's paradise—Papillon Enterprises. Lizzie was in heaven.

"I'm off the wagon this afternoon," she said. "I promise I'll shred one credit card as penance when I get back to Thomasville."

"I'll believe it when I see it," said Daffy.

Lilly smiled. "She'll just open up a new credit card right after she shreds one. Which one are you gonna shred?"

Lizzie said, "My Hello Kitty Card."

"Hello Kitty? Does such a credit card exist?" asked Tim who kept filming despite his surprise.

Gidget said, "Don't let her BS you, Tim. Hello Kitty was a Visa card that gave you points on purchases you could use to purchase Hello Kitty stuff from Sanrio. That's the company that markets Hello Kitty merchandise. My granddaughters badgered me into getting one years ago. The only reason Lizzie is willing to tear her Hello Kitty card up is because they killed the card years ago."

Daffy said, "Killing the Kitty card reminds me. When are you gonna reveal who killed the Marx Brothers? I really would like to know who the bastard is."

"Not now. I want to make sure I got my facts straight."

Next stop was the Barbancourt Rum Distillery. Labonté took special interest in this part of the tour.

"Barbancourt Rum is distilled and bottled right here in this distillery. They began in 1862 as a family business. Barbancourt rum is Haiti's largest export."

"You seem to know a lot about Barbancourt," said Lizzie.

"They have a tasting room, which I have taken advantage of many times. They give military personnel generous samples in their tasting room. Follow me."

After several samples of the various rums in the distillery's collection, Gidget had an idea. "We gotta include Barbancourt in our extortion plan."

A resounding chorus of "YES!!!" followed, which Tim and Allen dutifully recorded.

By seven o'clock in the evening, *Real Widows* stars and crew milled around in front of the Haitian National Police Headquarters. The wide two-story building boasted official Haitian Police colors, on which Daffy commented.

"The police in Haiti sure do like their white and baby blue color scheme."

Gidget said, "Except that the police station uses a horizontal striped pattern, while the headquarters uses a vertical striped pattern."

"It makes a great background for our wide shots," said Cordell. He had cobbled together a script with his writer and director earlier in the day inside the Gulfstream. He began pointing. "Tim, I want you to set up over there. Allen, you over there. Babs, Lilly, Lizzie… you guys stand near the front gate, but not too close. Gidget and Daffy, you guys hang close by. I'm gonna have the narrator introduce you two as the last but not least of the *Real Widows* about five minutes into filming."

Veronica, Loella, and Naomi stood behind Tim. All three declined the opportunity to appear in the *Real Widows* live episode.

Veronica had explained, "My ex would use me becoming famous on TV as an excuse to cut my alimony."

Louella said, "If the IRS gets wind of me vacationing in the Caribbean, they'll for sure audit the tax returns for my farm."

Naomi's excuse was simple. "I ain't appearing on live TV with no makeup. No way."

Tim's solution to their problem was iffy, just as he had said. A major part of Cordell's plan involved the Haitian National Police. It depended on getting Director General Francois on camera while shooting live and extorting him into letting the *Real Widows* cast and crew fly out of Haiti. Extortion would be the fun part.

Two things were key to success. Cordell wanted the show to be televised live when the majority of Haitians would be watching. *Real Widows* was not only a megahit in the United States; it was a hit worldwide, including in Haiti. Babs, Lilly, and Lizzie were stars. Especially Babs—voodoo was still practiced in places such as Brazil, Togo, Nigeria, Ghana as well as Haiti.

Televising the show in real time would put Director General Francois in the limelight worldwide, particularly in Port-au-Prince, where its residents would watch it live. The script was critical. It had to put Francois on the spot. Could he be maneuvered into a compromising situation? Lizzie volunteered to take the lead on this part of the plan.

Things seemed to go according to plan. As Cordell figured, Port-au-Prince was no different than any other city; its rumor mill was very efficient. By seven forty-five, over two-thousand Haitians had gathered on the streets in front of and around the Police Headquarters to be part of filming a live episode of the *Real Widows*. Cordell looked at them and turned to his crew.

"This crowd of Haitians is our security."

Just as he spoke, two dozen Haitian National Police ran out of the headquarters building and surrounded the *Real Widows* cast and crew. They immediately began gesturing and shouting orders in Haitian Creole. Labonté translated.

"The captain of the police detail orders you to disperse. You are attracting a crowd that will become unruly and create a protest. This is on the direct orders of Director General Francois."

Cordell said, "Good. That means the Director Francois is inside. Tell the captain that we will be filming tonight's episode of *Real Widows of Thomasville* live right here in Port-au-Prince, beginning in fifteen minutes, and we want to include some video of the Haitian Police interacting with the stars of the show."

Labonté translated Cordell's instructions to the captain in charge of the police detail. His eyes lit up.

Cordell said, "Look at him. He's excited about the possibility of being on TV. Tell him that we need a handsome face like his in the video. It will appeal to the show's younger female viewers."

Labonté translated, listened to the captain, then said, "He likes your idea and is very enthusiastic. All of his girlfriends love *Real Widows*.

"Perfect. Tell him that we also want to get Director General Francois on camera. It will be good public relations for him."

Labonté translated again, listened again, then watched as the captain spoke into his walkie-talkie. "The captain relayed your desires to Francois, and he eagerly accepts your offer. He will be right out."

"Tell him to wait about twenty minutes. We need to get the show's credits and intro out of the way first." Cordell's smile stretched ear-to-ear.

Chapter 55

Port-au-Prince, Haiti
November 21st

EXTERIOR SCENE: HAITIAN NATIONAL POLICE HEADQUARTERS, THURSDAY NIGHT 8:00 PM

Lilly, Lizzie, and Babs stand in front of a wrought iron fence in front of Haitian National Police Headquarters. They are surrounded by a large Haitian crowd repeatedly yelling "Manbo Babs!" "Manbo Babs!" "Manbo Babs!" in unison.

NARRATOR: [Speaks off camera.] We are televising this special episode of *Real Widows* live in real time in Port-au-Prince, the capital city of Haiti. [Camera slowly pans Babs, Lilly, and Lizzie.] Babs, Lilly, and Lizzie have been reunited with the other two Real Widows, Daffy and Gidget. [Camera slowly pans to Daffy and Gidget, standing several feet away.] After their cruise ship, the Bahama Princess, experienced a series of mysterious deaths, it was ordered to return to Jacksonville, Florida. En route through the narrow straight of water between Cuba and Haiti, the Bahama Princess was impounded by the Haitian Coast Guard on the orders of that country's National Police. [Wide shot of Headquarters building.] That organization had just overthrown the previous Haitian government two days before. [Second camera pans Headquarters with Real Widows in front of gate.] All five Real Widows now stand in front of the Haitian National Police Headquarters [Camera pans crowds surrounding Widows.] alongside thousands of Port-au-Prince residents who are *Real Widows* fanatics.
DAFFY: [Shouting to be heard over the noise.] They're all yelling for you, Babsie! Thousands of Haitians! They love you here in Port-au-Prince!
BABS: [Shouting.] It's sure nice to be loved!

[Several Haitian demonstrators push through the crowd with pen and paper.]
DEMONSTRATOR: [Shouting.] *Manbo* Babs! *Manbo* Babs! Your autograph please!
[Babs signs several autographs.]
BABS: I just can't believe they want my autograph!
DEMONSTRATOR: [Runs up to Babs.] *Manbo* Babs! Haiti loves your *vodou* rituals! They are fantastic!
BABS: Thank you very much!
DEMONSTRATOR: *Manbo* Babs! I do have information for you!
BABS: What is that?!
DEMONSTRATOR: *Manbo* Babs! Your *vodou* ritual under the Big Oak in the first episode of *Real Widows*, your Haitian Creole was so funny, but your Creole was incorrect! You meant to say, 'Let our boyfriends tell them mammas to kiss their asses and think only about the Casserole Ladies,' did you not?"
[Babs nods.]
DEMONSTRATOR: *Manbo* Babs! What you actually said was, 'Oh great spirit, let me find an alien nearby here, so I can make a new friend!'
[Babs smiles but says nothing.]
LIZZIE: [Camera zooms in as she speaks to Daffy.] I wonder how many more people are gonna tell her that?
DAFFY: Did you put that demonstrator up to saying that?

Close camera shot follows Director General Francois as he pridefully strides out of the building and sees the size of the crowd. His face shows surprise. The Widows watch him anxiously engage in conversation with his armed retinue en route to the Real Widows. The Director, a small black Haitian, looks comical in a formal National Police uniform—white barracks cap, white shirt, black tie, white coat, and black pants with gold stripe down the sides. He begins speaking passable English when he reaches the Real Widows.

FRANCOIS: I am Director General Francois of the Haitian National Police. Which of you is *Monsieur* Isler, the Director of *The Real Widows of Thomasville*?

CORDELL: [Steps into camera shot.] That's me. Happy to meet you, Director General.
FRANCOIS: Likewise. I understand you will film tonight's episode of *The Real Widows of Thomasville* live in our great city?
CORDELL: That is correct. In fact, we are filming live right now. [Points to Tim and Allen.] I would greatly appreciate incorporating some dialogue between you and the show's stars if you have the time.
FRANCOIS: But of course. I would be delighted. Your show is a hit in our country. Most Haitians will be watching tonight.
DAFFY: [Wide shot she steps into camera view. She pulls other Real Widows into shot.] Director Francois, let me introduce you to the Real Widows. [Francois shakes each woman's hand as introduced.] This is Babs, this is Lilly, this is Lizzie, this is Gidget, and I'm Daffy. We are so happy to meet you. Your city is lovely, and folks here have treated us so nicely.
LIZZIE: [Moves next to Francois so they are touching.] I love your uniform. You look so sexy in it. I bet the women can't keep their hands off you. I know I'm having trouble myself.
FRANCOIS: [Beams] *Merci*, *Madanm* Lizzie. May I say you look lovely tonight.
BABS: Mister Francois… is that your first name or last name? What should I call you?"
FRANCOIS: Francois is my last name. My first name is Henri. You may call me Henri."
BABS: On-ree? I don't believe I've ever heard that one before. Is that some sort of football player name?
FRANCOIS: No *Madanm*. Henri is spelled h-e-n-r-i and is the French version of the English name Henry.
BABS: But you pronounce it On-ree? That's different—
GIDGET: Babsie, we are in Haiti you know, and Haiti was a French colony.
FRANCOIS: Let me say to all of you, the stars of *The Real Widows of Thomasville*, how happy I am to welcome you to Haiti. I am honored to have you here as our guests. I hope you

find the city of Port-au-Prince to be an exciting and colorful backdrop to your very popular TV show.
GIDGET: Henri. Where should we film this live episode in your lovely city? What are the nighttime attractions in Port-au-Prince that you want showcased in *Real Widows* for the rest of the world to see?
FRANCOIS: Ah, my dear… is it Ghee-jay or Ghee-ghet? Gee-ghet. You must first start out at Yanvalou. It is not far from here on Rue Pacot in downtown Port-au-Prince. A restaurant in the daytime, a nightclub at nighttime. Everyone goes there to dance. And, tonight is Live Groove Thursday, which is especially entertaining.
LIZZIE: [Rubs up against Francois.] You will go with us, won't you? I can't wait to get you on the dance floor. I bet you got more moves in those hips of yours than John Travolta.
FRANCOIS: [Beams] Of course. I would love to escort you to Yanvalou. [Turns to his aides, issues commands in Haitian Creole. One of them leaves.]

[Wide camera shots of thousands of Port-au-Prince residents dancing and repeatedly cheering Manbo Babs! A chauffeured black Cadillac Escalade, the eight-passenger version of the SUV, pulls into view and is followed by a Dodge Ram and Toyota HiLux. Both trucks have National Police decals on their sides. Close shots of all five Real Widows climbing into the Escalade with Francois and Cordell. Tim and Allen enter off camera.]
NARRATOR: Looks like a night of excitement and fun for the Real Widows. Port-au-Prince loves them. What kind of voodoo magic will they pull off tonight?

Chapter 56

Port-au-Prince, Haiti
November 21st

INTERIOR SCENE: HAITIAN NATIONAL POLICE CADILLAC ESCALADE, THURSDAY NIGHT 8:20 PM

LILLY: [En route to Yanvalou.] Mister Francois, how does it feel to be in charge of a country like Haiti?
FRANCOIS: [Puffs up.] Wonderful. Sobering.
LIZZIE: [Slides closer to Francois.] And, now you've been in charge for how many days… two or three?
FRANCOIS: *Oui*. Two days this time.
BABS: This time?
FRANCOIS: Yes. Last time, I was Prime Minister for nine and a half months.
GIDGET: How long ago was that?
FRANCOIS: That is a good question. Let me see. Hmm… about four years ago.
DAFFY: What happened at that time?
FRANCOIS: The usual—the Haitian Coast Guard overthrew the government, and I was replaced by a filthy animal, Joubert Dorvil. The Coast Guard made him President.
BABS: I just have trouble imagining someone with a pretty name like Zho-bey Dor-vee being a filthy animal. Sounds more like an interior decorator, and they're always such nice people.
FRANCOIS: Trust me *Madanm* Babs, Dorvil was a filthy animal. *Coup d'etats* happen quite regularly in Haiti.
LIZZIE: [Places her hand on his thigh and slowly rubs.] Henri, tell us about yourself? Are you married?
FRANCOIS: [Nods] Many times. How about you?
LIZZIE: Four so far. [Eyes Francois seductively.] Currently looking for number five. [Tim can be heard off camera snickering.]
FRANCOIS: Oh, here we are at Yanvalou, *Mesdames*. [Looks at Lizzie.] Please stay close to me. It is quite crowded in

Yanvalou on Live Groove Thursday, and I don't want to lose you. Things tend to get wild on the dance floor… if you know what I mean. [Lizzie gives Francois a seductive look. Francois smiles, then exits vehicle.]
DAFFY: [Leans into Lizzie and whispers.] Too bad you ain't had that vampire breast lift yet. Henri would be putty in your hands right now instead of just eating out of 'em.

EXTERIOR SCENE: PARKING LOT AND WALKWAY TO YANVALOU, THURSDAY NIGHT 8:30 PM
Long Tracking Shoulder Level Shot as camera follows the Partygoers exiting the Escalade and walking along the pathway into a sand-colored, three-story brick building. Lizzie is wrapped around Francois.

NARRATOR: [Speaking off camera.] Let's go inside to Yanvalou's dance floor and watch the action. I'm sure it will be worthwhile.

INTERIOR SCENE: YANVALOU DANCE FLOOR, THURSDAY NIGHT 8:38 PM

Real Widows and Henri Francois are dancing together as a group, surrounded by dozens of Haitians and tourists. A Cocktail waitress approaches them with drinks—Barbancourt rum and lime juice over ice. As onlookers cheer them on, Lizzie and Francois intertwine arms and drink from each other's glass nonstop until both glasses are drained. Noise on the dance floor is deafening.

LIZZIE: [Throws her glass on the floor.] That was the best rum drink I ever had!
FRANCOIS: [Hiccups] It is one of Haiti's most popular drinks!
DAFFY: Let's have another!
BABS: Yes!
FRANCOIS: This time, let us drink a Port-au-Prince Cocktail! It is one of my favorites!
LIZZIE: [Hiccups] I bet you have a lot of favorites! [Rubs up against Francois.]

BABS: [Hiccups] What's in it?!
FRANCOIS: Demerara rum and clairin, a rum-like alcohol made in Haiti from sugarcane! [Rubs up against Babs until Lizzie pulls him back.]

Wide camera shot of Yanvalou dancefloor with dozens of Haitians crowded around Real Widows and Francois as they dance together and with other Haitians *en masse*. A cocktail waitress brings another round of drinks for the Real Widows group. Francois and Lizzie repeat their non-stop, arms-intertwined drinking routine to bystanders' loud cheers. Camera shots have become increasingly unsteady as Tim and Allen have also been drinking cocktails. As planned, Lizzie and Gidget excuse themselves for a bathroom break. Three minutes pass before they return to execute a key part of Cordell's plan. Noise level has increased.

GIDGET: [Hiccups] Henri, when Lizzie and I went to the bathroom, one of the ladies there told us about one of the most famous cocktails in Haiti! She called it the Haitian Jacmel Cocktail!
FRANCOIS: *Oui*! It is wonderful! Very potent! One of my favorites! [Hiccups]
LIZZIE: The lady [Lizzie hiccups.] said it has Barbancourt rum, mango rum, and Grand Marnier in it!
FRANCOIS: [Hiccups] *Oui*! Very potent! [Hiccups] One of my favorites!
GIDGET: She said the best ones are made at [Hiccups] Le Belvedère in the port of Jacmel, not far from here!
FRANCOIS: Eh… Jacmel is about twenty-five, thirty miles from Port-au-Prince! [Hiccups] Le Belvedère is where *the party* is always happening! And I mean *the party*! Fast music! Wild women! You name it!
LIZZIE: I got an idea! [Hiccups then smiles at Francois.] Why don't we go to Toussaint International and hop in Cordell's Gulfstream?! The lady in the bathroom… [Hiccups, then bats her eyelashes at Francois.] She was real nice! She said Jacmel

has an airport! We could fly in the Gulfstream down there, party at Le Belvedère! [Hiccups while rubbing against Francois.] And see what happens, if you know what I mean!

FRANCOIS: [Turns to an aid.] Go get the Escalade and call the airport. Tell them to get the *Real Widows* Gulfstream ready for takeoff!

NARRATOR: I'm sorry to say that it is nine o'clock, dear viewers. That means it is time to close this episode of *The Real Widows of Thomasville*. But, do not worry. We will continue filming our group of Real Widows partygoers as long as their party continues. And maybe, just maybe, we will show you what happens after they leave Yanvalou in the next episode. Bye bye.

The Real Widows stars, their crew, and Francois landed at the Jacmel airport at twelve fifty-one, having consumed several to-go rounds of Goslings 151 Proof Rum and Coke during the ride to Toussaint International as well as in flight. Francois nodded off as they approached the Jacmel airport and was allowed to sleep while the Gulfstream was refueled. After Captain Stevenson had powered up the jet's engines for takeoff, Gidget shook Francois. "Time to wake up."

Francois was still drunk. "Are we in Jacmel yet?"

Lizzie said, "Yes, we are, sweetie. It's after one AM in the morning. Time for you to deplane."

He managed to sit up and weakly smile. "Let's go."

"Sorry sweetie, but we gotta head back to Thomasville."

"But you cannot leave now. We have to go to Le Belvedère."

Babs said, "Oh, Francois, we'd love to go with you, but I gotta get back for one of my grandkids' birthdays. You know how it is."

Francois nodded but became irritable. "No! You must stay in Haiti until I allow you to leave. We go to Le Belvedère now."

"Francois, I think you should allow us to leave when we want to," Gidget said.

"No. You leave when I allow you to leave… At least Lizzie must remain in Haiti."

"You may want to change your mind when you see some of the video we got on the flight from Port-au-Prince to Jacmel. Tim, can you show Henri what you videoed?"

Tim smiled then pointed at the monitor on the wall outside the flight deck. A scene appeared. The Real Widows crew and stars lined the Gulfstream's aisle, clapping and whistling as Francois danced up and down the aisle, performing a clumsy striptease. Lizzie kept shouting, "Take it all off, you great bid stud!"

Francois periodically looked at the camera, smiled, then turned a bottle of Goslings 151 Proof Rum he held upside down over his mouth, and chug-a-lugged. At the end of his striptease, he turned his back on the camera, bent over, and passed gas to the delight of the other passengers.

After the video ended, Daffy asked, "Are you sure you don't want to let us leave Haiti?"

Francois hung his head. "Go! Go!"

"What about the rest of the Bahama Princess passengers and crew?" asked Gidget.

Francois said, "For the Real Widows, I will immediately authorize the ship to weigh anchor at their discretion. Let me off this plane, and I will make the necessary calls."

Chapter 57

24° 1' 57.6048" North, 77° 16' 35.2992" West
November 22nd

Cordell's Gulfstream cruised at twenty thousand feet above the area of the Atlantic Ocean in which the Bahamas Islands are located. They headed north toward Nassau, one hour and thirty minutes flying time from Port-au-Prince. Most were too wired to sleep, except Tim, the writer, and the director. The latter two had been confined to the jet for over twenty-four hours. Allen kept his video camera ready to film any Widows' interactions Cordell wanted recorded.

Five of the eight women passengers produced material worthy of recording, but Naomi, Veronica, and Louella were subdued. They stayed to themselves on the flight to Jacmel. Shaken up after their Port-au-Prince experience, they entreated Cordell to give them a lift to Nassau, where they could catch a flight back to the safety of the United States. Now, they sat at the front of the plane, napping. The Casserole Ladies debated over where to go after dropping their female traveling companions off.

Lizzie grumbled and looked around. "Are we there yet? I'm channeling the grandson who sat next to me on the drive to Disney last summer. Ask me how many McDonald's there are along I-75 between Lake City and Wildwood in Florida."

"Please. We'll be landing pretty soon, and we need to decide where to go after we drop these three off." Daffy pointed to the front of the plane where the others napped.

"Thomasville," said Babs. "I gotta get back for Little Bobby's birthday party."

Lilly said, "Thomasville. I got a contractor waiting on me."

"Let's go back to that nude beach in Martinique y'all were telling us about," said Lizzie.

Daffy looked at Gidget. "Gidg? What do you say?"

Before Gidget could respond, Captain Stevenson's voice squawked over the plane's intercom. "Folks, please buckle up in your seats. We'll be landing at Lynden Pindling International Airport in Nassau in ten minutes."

Naomi, Veronica, and Louella were anxious to go their separate ways, but appeared sad as the plane taxied to a stop. They had been through a lot with the Casserole Ladies. Veronica voiced it. "I know Lou and Naomi hate leaving y'all as much as I do. Once things get settled, y'all are all invited to my place in Dallas to play rummy until our hearts' content."

"Even though our time together ended in such a tragic way, we did have some great times with y'all." Daffy's tenure as Chairman of Sawgrass Bank had taught her to lie with the best of them.

"I wish we could've gotten to know y'all better in different circumstances," said Lilly. "A voodoo ceremony ain't exactly my idea of the best way to get acquainted."

Louella looked as if she would cry. "Me too. I'm sure we will get together with you in the near future."

Naomi simply said, "Folks, we gotta get off this bird. I know Gidget and Daffy are anxious to get back home and catch up on their sleep."

Hugs and kisses abounded, and the three women descended the Gulfsteam's steps.

After the others had debarked, Captain Stevenson taxied to one of the airport's Jet-A storage tanks for refueling. While the plane was being serviced, Cordell asked, "Where to? I agree with Babs and Lilly. We should go back to Thomasville. We can film another episode or two."

Three heads nodded, Daffy's and Gidget's remained still. Daffy said, "Before we decide where to go, I want an answer to who murdered the Marx Brothers. Gidg, right before Babs collapsed at the *Dans*, you told me you had solved their murders. Now that we're out of Haiti, tell us who did it. I been dying to find out."

Gidget shook her head. "I don't want to say who murdered the Marx Brothers until I get some more info."

"So, get your information," said Lizzie.

"I need to get on the Internet."

Cordell said, "Why didn't you say so? We have Internet connectivity on the plane and several laptops. Solving a multiple murder would be great for ratings."

He opened a laptop, logged onto the jet's Wi-Fi network, passed it to Gidget, then nodded at Tim and Allen.

Daffy pointed at Gidget. "Sherlock Holmes goes Hitech."

Everyone crowded close to Gidget in silent anticipation. As they waited for her to speak, Captain Stevenson informed them that refueling had been completed, and they were ready for takeoff. Cordell went forward, leaned into the cockpit, then came back into the main cabin.

"Where'd you tell him to take us?" asked Daffy.

Cordell said, "I told him to head west for now."

After five more minutes of silence, Lizzie nudged Gidget. "Don't keep us in suspense. Talk, Sherlock."

"Right now, I'm looking into things I didn't pay enough attention to at first, but probably should have."

"Such as?"

"First off, the Marx Brothers' names—Barry Vanderhoff, Harry Vanderhoff… and the other three Vanderhoffs. I thought those were strange names for five short, olive-skinned men who say things like 'youse goils' and 'duh' instead of 'the,' and pronounce words that normally end in er with 'ah' like 'bruddah' instead of brother. But when we first met them, I thought, 'They have Brooklyn accents because they grew up in New York.' But I kept thinking that something was screwy. Things just didn't fit quite right. Their appearances didn't match their names. Vanderhoff just seemed out-of-place for those guys."

"So, what are you looking for on the Internet?" asked Babs.

"I'm on a couple of people locator search sites looking up Vanderhoffs. I found our five Vanderhoff boys in The Villages. They do… or did own property there. Now, I'm looking at online birth and property records in New York City."

"Whatcha see?" asked Lilly.

"There are some Vanderhoffs in the New York area."

"Maybe you should also search on the name Marx Brothers," said Lizzie.

Gidget rolled her eyes. "Yeah, but unless our Marx Brothers first names were Harpo, Chico, Groucho, Zeppo, and Gummo, it wouldn't match."

"That's what I get for trying to be funny—a real answer."

"Here's several Vanderhoffs in the Bronx and in Queens, but none with first names that match Barry, Larry, Gary, Harry, or Jerry. Here's one in Brooklyn. First name is Johanna. Here's a couple in Manhattan, but none that have our boys' first names. Ah ha. Here's our five Marx Brothers in Brooklyn."

"So, Vanderhoff is their real name," said Daffy.

Gidget typed furiously. "Not necessarily. Hold on a second… Yeah. Yeah. Look here. When I try to go deeper into their history, I'm getting almost nothing. It's not like the other names in these databases. You can click on other names and go deeper into the records for more detailed info. Not with Barry Vanderhoff. And not with Harry Vanderhoff. All you get with these guys is just some very superficial birth record info and scant property record info. Guys that old, I'd expect much more info on them."

Daffy said, "Okay. Keep it simple for me. What does not finding detailed birth and property records on them in New York City mean?"

Gidget said, "It's as if Barry, Jerry, Larry, Harry, and Gary Vanderhoff didn't exist before The Villages—at least not for real in New York City."

Chapter 58

24° 49' 53.796" North, 78° 28' 18.3972" West
November 22nd

Gidget resumed typing as the others looked on in stunned silence until Lilly asked, "What's happening? I can't stand the suspense."

"Try sitting down," said Lizzie.

"Ho, ho, ho. Excuse me if I don't laugh. I lost my sense of humor about eight or nine of your lame jokes back."

"Ladies," said Cordell, "let's remain friendly. It's been a long night."

Gidget ignored the other ladies' snarky conversation and continued typing with her head down. "I'm using several speech analytics sites to analyze the Marx Brothers' speech patterns. Their accents still bother me. I want to see if these programs can reveal anything about their accents beyond that they sound like they're from Brooklyn."

"Find anything?" asked Lilly.

"I'm using several free analytics packages, and they all point to our boys' speech as displaying speech patterns characteristic of Italian-Americans living in the Northeastern part of the country."

"How so?"

"Like how they said 'duh' instead of the, 'goil' instead of girl, 'caw-fee' instead of coffee."

Daffy asked, "So what if they're from the Northeast? We already figured they weren't from the South. I could tell that the minute they opened their mouths in the IHOP."

"And I don't hold not being from the South against 'em," said Lizzie. "Doctor Beauvisage is from North Carolina, and I don't hold that against him."

Babs said, "I thought North Carolina was a Southern state. At least it is on the globe I got in my den."

"Anything above Macon is in the North as far as I'm concerned."

"Why Macon?" asked Daffy.

"You can't get ladyfinger peas above Macon," said Lizzie referring to the small green pea grown only in the deep South.

Gidget continued typing on the laptop during the others' distracting exchange. Finally, she looked up.

"We knew the Marx Brothers were from New York. Now it opens up the possibility of them being Italian-American instead of Dutch-American."

Daffy said, "We should have been suspicious about those guys when Gary said their ancestors came over on the Mayflower with the other Dutch settlers."

"Even I knew the Pilgrims came over on the Mayflower," said Lilly.

Lizzie said, "I probably would've known that if I'd paid attention in the fourth grade."

"Did you ever pay attention in school?"

"I paid attention in the eleventh grade."

Babs asked, "What was so special about eleventh grade?"

A dreamy look came over Lizzie's face. "Mister Bohannon, my geography teacher. He was twenty-eight, single, and looked just like Paul Newman. I couldn't take my eyes off him."

Gidget looked up again. "And the fact that, other than canasta, they played bocce ball all the time on the ship was itself telling."

"Huh?" asked Lilly.

"Bocce ball is the favorite sport of Italians and Italian-Americans. And remember how they'd say 'ciao' instead of goodbye. They always said 'ciao' right before they'd hobble off for their afternoon naps."

Lizzie sighed. "Isn't it sad how afternoon naps replace nooners after age sixty?"

"There are other things in life besides sex," said Lilly.

"Other than shopping, I haven't found anything."

Daffy said, "I haven't heard the term 'nooner' in years."

"It was one of the words in a crossword puzzle in the Times-Enterprise the other day. I had to ask Siri what word describes 'a sexual liaison during lunchtime.' It took her three tries to find the right answer."

"Gidg, what's your conclusion?" asked Babs after her friend had been head down for several minutes.

Gidget looked up. “The Marx Brothers ancestors more than likely came over from Italy in the late nineteenth or early twentieth century during the mass migration of Italians at that time. Not Holland in the 1600s with the Dutch. Like the Dutch, a lot of Italian emigrants settled in and around New York, probably including the Marx Brothers’ ancestors. And remember how the brothers said ‘mamma’ with an ‘a’ instead of ‘momma’ with an ‘o’? Italians and Italian-Americans say momma that way.”

“Why did the Marx Brothers tell us their ancestors were from Holland?” asked Lilly.

“It seems obvious to me that a lot of the clues Daffy and I uncovered while we were on the Bahama Princess about the Marx Brothers’ deaths were nothing but red herrings.”

“What do you mean? Are we talking about seafood or murder?” asked Babs.

“Red herrings in the murder mystery genre are misleading clues. Clues that don’t point to the real culprit and instead, make you go off on the wrong pathway, looking for the wrong person. In the Marx Brothers’ case, I think someone has put out some red herring clues to throw us off the scent.”

“Who?” asked Daffy.

“Good question but hard to say. We know the Marx Brothers themselves put out one red herring, the Vanderhoff fake names, to keep their Italian-American heritage secret.”

“Why didn’t they want us to know they were Italian-Americans?”

Before Gidget could answer, Babs asked, “Any other red herrings?”

Gidget nodded. “The spilled liquor and bottles lying on the floor in Jerry’s room were probably put there to make it look like he slipped and fell off the balcony.”

Daffy said, “We know that the maid didn’t put it there.”

“The maid?” asked Lilly.

“Yeah. Yvette—”

“They had a maid named Yvette? Was she French?”

“Does the Pope poop in the woods?” asked Babs.

“Babsie, you got your jokes mixed up,” said Gidget.

“You know what I mean.”

Cordell chastised them. "Ladies, I'm gonna have to send a couple of you to your corners for a timeout if this continues."

"Yvette must have done it. Wasn't there a French maid named Yvette in the movie *Clue*? French maids are always the murderers," said Lilly.

Gidget frowned. "That's a stretch. Anyway, we saw Yvette acting suspicious around our staterooms the morning Jerry jumped. At first, we thought she might be a suspect in Jerry's death, but after we talked to her, we ruled that out."

"Wait, didn't we get distracted? I thought we were talking about spilled liquor and bottles on the floor in Jerry's room, and you said it was to make it look like he slipped and fell off the balcony."

Babs nodded enthusiastically. "Correct. But why would someone want to do that?"

Gidget pointed out the obvious. "To make it look like his death was an accident."

"Sounds like you don't think his fall *was* an accident," said Daffy.

"Correct. I don't think Jerry accidentally fell off his balcony. All that spilled liquor and bottles on the floor were red herrings."

"What makes you say that?"

Gidget said, "I don't want to say right now."

Chapter 59

24° 48' 59.9544" North, 79° 19' 42.4344" West
November 22nd

Gidget resumed typing, head down. Minutes later, she paused and looked up.

"The Marx Brothers' told us they were in a number of different businesses. Restaurants, convenience stores, Vegas entertainment, Hollywood, waste management, and a Chicago credit business. There's something in common there… a common theme to their business…"

Lizzie said, "When I think of Vegas and Hollywood, I think of glitz and celebrities. When I think of Chicago, I think of *The Sting* and crime. Like it was a crime Paul Newman and Robert Redford weren't in the movie's sequel."

"Who was in the sequel?" asked Babs.

"Jackie Gleason is the only one I can remember."

"*That* was a crime," said Daffy. "Gidg, why don't you just tell us now who murdered the Marx Brothers?"

"Not now. Right now, I'm thinking about glitz in Vegas." Gidget resumed typing. "When I think of glitz, I think of bling. Notice how the Marx Brothers all wore a lot of bling?"

Lizzie asked, "How could I miss? I'd like to have all the diamonds they wore on just those five pinky rings."

Lilly added a touch of sarcasm to her voice. "I'd like to have a couple of their Hawaiian flower shirts. Nice fashion statements."

Gidget kept typing and said, "Yeah, they wore a lot of that kind of stuff, didn't they? Let me check something."

As Gidget focused on her Internet research, Allen moved to the front of the cabin to film a long shot of the other women bunched around her. He sat on the edge of an aisle seat and rested his camera on the top of the seatback to steady it. Something wedged deep between the seats caught his attention, and he extracted it.

"I found an iPhone. Isn't this where Lou and Veronica were sitting? Must've fallen out of one of their pockets."

"Yeah. That is where they were sitting," said Daffy.

"I'm surprised they let y'all keep your phones with you in jail," said Lilly.

"Anyone trying to take mine away would have done so at their peril."

"It looks like Veronica's. I noticed her phone was in a pink camo case. At least it gives us an excuse to get together again with them. We can fly it to Dallas."

Babs said, "Ronnie must be gettin' senile."

"She's not the only one. Talk about flaky. The whole time we were with them on the cruise, I kept thinking that all three of them were possible candidates for some sort of dementia care." Daffy shook her head. "They must've been tired from our Haiti adventure. Forgetting her iPhone. What woman in her right mind would do that?"

"A woman would forget her grandkid's birthday before she'd forget her iPhone."

Lilly said, "A woman would forget her makeup before she'd forget her iPhone."

Lizzie said, "A woman would forget her credit card before she'd forget her iPhone."

Gidget kept typing through the one-upmanship. "I've been researching the Internet about some of the Marx Brothers' notable characteristics."

"Such as?"

"They all sported a lot of bling, they all had diamond pinky rings, all of 'em wore those Hawaiian flower shirts. I'm googling to see who is most known for wearing that kind of stuff. And if what I'm seeing on the Internet is true, I'm starting to worry."

Lizzie said, "Truth and the Internet. Aren't those two things incompatible?"

Gidget kept typing. "The phrases the Marx Brothers liked to use—like 'sleeps with the fishes' and 'make him an offer he can't refuse' and—"

"Those are lines from *The Godfather*," said Daffy.

"What about goombah?"

Daffy shrugged.

"And you think it's likely the Marx Brothers were Italian-American?" Lilly asked.

"Bingo. Don't Italian-Americans like cannoli? The Marx Brothers did." Gidget quit typing and looked up. "All these clues point to something else."

"What?"

"Italian-Americans. The kind of businesses they're in. Their bling and their Hawaiian flower shirts. Those point to something… scary. And the ringtone on Larry's phone."

"What about his ringtone?" asked Babs.

"He had the theme from *The Godfather* as his ringtone. Not one you often hear on a phone. Oh! I almost forgot another clue. I must be getting old."

"Getting old ain't a clue," said Lizzie. "It's a tragedy."

"Getting old is not the clue I was thinking of. They use Bitcoin. Isn't Bitcoin one way of hiding illegal transactions from the government?"

"What do all these clues point to?" asked Lilly.

Gidget said, "I'm thinking the Marx Brothers must be Mafia."

Tim woke up from his sleep about the time Gidget finished speaking. "Mafia? What's this about the Mafia?"

Daffy said, "Gidget's been reviewing a bunch of clues about the Marx Brothers' deaths, and she thinks they may have been Mafia."

Gidget nodded. "Daffy can back me on this. Two different people at two different times and locations walked up to the Marx Brothers. One guy came up to Larry and said, 'Hey, Little Titty—'"

Tim interrupted, his eyes wide open. "Little Titty?"

"Yeah why?"

"Eh... Go on."

"And the guy kisses Larry. Then, another time a woman comes up to Jerry and says, 'Hey, Tushie,' and kisses him."

"Tushie?"

"Yeah, Tushie. I think I know where you're going, Tim. Gary's nickname was Big Burrito."

"Big Burrito?"

"Yep."

A look of fear came over Tim. He seemed to freeze and said nothing.

Babs jumped into the conversation lull. “Remember how they used to make you kiss your grandmother while she’s lying in the casket? It just popped into my head. Don’t know why. Maybe because the Marx Brothers got kissed and died?”

Gidget rolled her eyes. “As I was saying, two Marx Brothers got kissed before they died. Isn’t that some sort of Mafia custom?”

Tim unfroze. “Yes, it is. I grew up in Brooklyn. Brooklyn has a lot of Mafia in it. I can tell you that Little Titty, Tushie, and Big Burrito were nicknames for three powerful Mafia bosses in Brooklyn. They were part of a powerful Mafia family—one of several Mafia families in New York City.”

Gidget asked, “Do Mafia use terms like ‘goombah,’ ‘sleeps with the fishes,’ and do they wear a lot of bling and Hawaiian flower shirts?”

Tim nodded. “I used to hear Mafia guys using those terms and wearing bling all the time. They love Hawaiian shirts. And those kisses on the cheeks—the Mafia calls it the kiss of death. It’s a sign that the Mafia has designated the kissed person to be killed.”

“We found out that Harry’s nickname was Big Banana, and Barry’s nickname was Medallions.”

“Little Titty, Medallions, Big Banana, Tushie, and Big Burrito were five of the most notorious Mafia mobsters in Brooklyn. They disappeared about five years ago after testifying against the Mafia. I was still working in New York at the time, and I remember the headlines. There was a lot of speculation about how they died because the bodies were never found.”

Chapter 60

24° 54' 40.8564" North, 79° 35' 35.2104" West
November 22nd

Cordell had remained silent through most of Gidget's investigative work. At Gidget and Tim's revelations about the Mafia, a worried look appeared on his face. He had not met the Marx Brothers and had not paid much attention when Babs, Lilly, or Lizzie mentioned them. This changed when Gidget offered the possibility that the Marx Brothers might be Mafia.

"Ladies, I think we're heading into dangerous territory here."

Daffy nodded. "Yeah. Smart people don't mess with the Mafia."

"So, what do we do? Just drop everything?" asked Lilly.

"Sounds like a good idea to me," said Lizzie. "Anyone wanna play some Bunko? How about going back to the nude beach in Martinque?"

Cordell said, "I think y'all should act like you believe the Marx Brothers are dead and stay in Thomasville for a while."

Four heads nodded. Gidget's did not. "Even if I wanted to do that, which I don't, I don't think we can act like we think they're dead and just go on about our business."

"Why is that?" asked Daffy.

"Because of the Arnold Schwarzenegger guy."

"I'd forgotten about him."

"Who's the Arnold Schwarzenegger guy?" asked Lilly.

"Trust me. You don't wanna know."

Gidget said, "He was a huge intimidating-looking guy on board the Bahama Princess."

Daffy nodded her concurrence. "He looked just like Arnold Schwarzenegger did in his movies… except for *Kindergarten Cop*."

"I loved it in *Terminator* when Arnie time-traveled to LA in the buff, showing them cute little buns of his," Lizzie said.

Babs enthusiastically nodded. "Me too."

Cordell said, "Ladies, I think we've gotten Gidget off track. What is it about the Arnold Schwarzenegger guy that makes you think we can't act like the Marx Brothers are dead?"

"I don't know," Gidget said.

A frustrated silence followed Gidget's answer. She used it to go head down on the laptop. The others stared, anxious for something from her, anything. Finally, Babs could stand it no longer.

"Okay. That's enough. 'You don't know' ain't good enough. You had something in your mind when you first brought up Schwarzenegger. What's on your mind?"

"Tell us what's on your mind even if it's stream of consciousness," said Lizzie. She noticed the others staring at her. "It was the answer to last Friday's Times-Enterprise trivia question: What is a narrative mode in modern literature that depicts thoughts passing through the mind? I don't know what I'd do without Siri."

"I do," said Daffy. "Use an encyclopedia."

"Encyclopedia? What's that?"

"Someone remind me when we get back to Thomasville to cancel Lizzie's newspaper subscription."

Gidget had barely glanced up from the laptop during all this. "The Arnold Schwarzenegger guy was a huge, intimidating man that mysteriously popped up every time a Marx Brother was murdered."

"You think he killed them?" asked Lilly.

"No. He didn't kill them, but we did see him around every time a Marx Brother met a mysterious fate, which is awfully coincidental."

"And that's why you think we can't act like we think they're dead and just go on about our business?" asked Daffy. "I'm not following you."

"You forget a couple of things. He knows we traveled with them and saw us snooping around, so he might not want us alive. Also, he wasn't included on the passenger manifest, according to the cruise director. His picture wasn't on the bulkhead. That says he's working undercover, which is troubling."

"Yeah, but in what way?"

"What are the implications of a person you see that doesn't exist?"

A light bulb went on for Babs, and a look of horror appeared on her face. "You think he's a Mafia hitman! Wait, you said he did not kill the Marx Brothers. Maybe it was one of those guys that gave them the kiss of death."

The possibility of running afoul of Mafia hitmen sent shivers up everyone's spine.

Gidget said, "The Schwarzenegger guy might be a Mafia hitman, or not. I don't know at this point. What I do know is that neither he nor any of the 'kiss of death' folks killed the Marx Brothers."

"If it wasn't any of them, who did murder the Marx Brothers?" asked Daffy.

"No one."

Skeptical silence followed. Gidget's assertion seemed too absurd. Daffy broke the silence.

"You must mean they accidentally died. But that doesn't make sense because you said at the *Dans* you'd solved the Marx Brothers murders. How could it be an accident if they were murdered?"

Gidget said, "I did say that, and it syncs with what Tim just said about those mobsters that testified against the mob. They never found their bodies. I solved the Marx Brothers murders—which unintentionally solves the Mafia mobster murders in New York—when I realized at the *Dans* the Marx Brothers weren't dead."

"Not dead? How do you know that?"

"When Elvis *Iwa* possessed Babs, I realized that meant the Marx Brothers weren't dead. I was wishing with all my heart that one of their spirits would possess her and talk to me. When that didn't happen, I realized it was because he, and the others, weren't dead."

"Explain."

"Remember Fabienne said that the person whose desire to speak with the dead was greatest would be rewarded by that person's spirit possessing the *Chwal*?"

All heads nodded.

"No one at the *Dans* wished for a spirit to cross into our world and communicate with us any more than I wanted Barry to. I wanted it with all my heart. When he didn't possess Babs, that told me he wasn't dead."

"Somebody must've really, really, really wanted to communicate with Elvis Presley," said Lilly.

Lizzie lowered her head and kept quiet.

Gidget said, "Anyway, I figure if Barry isn't dead, it's likely the other brothers aren't dead as well."

"Iiiii dunno," said Daffy.

"The thing is, if the Marx Brothers are *not* dead, things begin to make sense. Why else didn't the other brothers seem more depressed when one of them died unless he didn't really die?"

"I don't know."

"Why couldn't we find Larry's body in the morgue?"

"Good point, but we did see his body when they rolled it off the boat in Grenada."

"We saw them roll something off. Maybe another body or maybe a live Larry inside. And why didn't they do an autopsy on Larry in Grenada?"

"What about Jerry? We *saw* him fall overboard. How could anyone survive that kind of a fall? I mean, he was turning over and over very fast. And hitting the water from that far up would have to have been fatal. No one could have survived that."

"Yes, *if* it was a human that hit the water. It must have been a dummy dressed up to look like Jerry. Remember, the body was spinning so fast that we couldn't see his face. If it was a dummy dressed in a Hawaiian flower shirt, Bermuda shorts, and huaraches and not Jerry, that might explain why we saw more Coast Guard personnel leaving the Bahama Princess than came on board. Maybe the extra one was Jerry dressed in a Coast Guard uniform. We were looking down at them, so we couldn't tell how tall they were. One of them could have been short, like Jerry. Here are the pictures of the Coast Guard people I took that day."

Gidget extracted her iPhone and showed them the two pictures.

"You're starting to convince me they may not be dead," said Lilly. "Anything else?"

"Why were Jerry's, Harry's, and Barry's bodies never found in the ocean?" asked Gidget. "I would have thought they'd recover at least one or two."

Daffy asked, "How could Gary disappear in Moriarty's Magic Box and never be found on the Bahama Princess while it was still at sea unless he died and the body was disposed of? And we saw the empty hidden compartment in the Magic Box."

"We did, but remember you said that Gary might have shifted into a parallel dimension or a parallel universe after he entered the hidden compartment?"

"I was joking."

"That's what I thought at the time. But now that I think about it, you were onto something."

"How so?"

"What if Gary shifted from one hidden compartment into another hidden compartment? What if there was a second hidden compartment that we did not know about? What if it was parallel to the first hidden compartment that we examined? What if it was the same size as the first hidden compartment and behind it?"

Gidget was making sense. She continued.

"The inside of the Magic Box is black and dark for a reason. It's black and dark, so the audience looking at it can't determine the depth of the main compartment. Likewise, you and I could not determine the depth of the hidden compartment. There must have been enough room behind the first hidden compartment for a second hidden compartment. Gary could have hidden in it until everyone was out of Neptune's Spectacle."

Blank stares followed.

Gidget said, "And Jerry, Harry, and Barry's bodies were never found at sea because they never died."

Chapter 61

24° 53' 29.1084" North, 80° 12' 31.5" West
November 22nd

Lilly had a follow up question. “If they aren’t dead, what happened to them?”

“Good question,” said Gidget. “I suspect the Arnold Schwarzenegger guy is involved in this thing somehow.”

Daffy nodded. “Yeah. He acted too suspiciously not to be involved.”

“He was a hulk of a man. Short blond hair, fair complexion, muscles on his muscles. He didn’t fit the picture of a Mafia hitman you always see in the movies. Tim, you ever run across Mafia hitmen when you were growing up?”

“All the time. I grew up in a rough neighborhood where you always kept an eye out for them so you could avoid ‘em,” Tim said.

“What did they look like?”

“You could spot a Mafia type a mile away. Mean-looking. Tough. Wide. Dark clothes. Lots of bling.”

“That didn’t look like the Schwarzenegger guy. He looked more like Arnie in one of his special ops movies.”

“He had a couple of scars on his face that probably came from fighting a platoon of Russian soldiers,” said Daffy.

Cordell asked, “And you couldn’t find him on the ship’s manifest?”

Gidget nodded. “Correct. We couldn’t find out anything about him. We even went cross-eyed looking at a thousand photos. They were passenger photos that they take of *every* passenger who boards. They hang them on the bulkheads. He wasn’t in any of them. It’s as if he didn’t exist.”

“That’s probably for a reason.”

“Such as.”

“Sometimes, people who work in the clandestine services purposefully want it to look like they don’t exist.”

“How do you know?” asked Babs.

“I’ve produced enough spy movies.”

Gidget agreed, "Cordell's right. Maybe some secret government agency is behind the Marx Brothers' disappearances, and the Arnold Schwarzenegger guy is part of that agency."

"What about the FBI?" asked Daffy. "They're always catching and prosecuting the Mafia."

"Daff, remember what Barry said when we watched the *Real Widows* episode where the girls go into the UFO and meet the aliens?"

"No, what?"

"He said don't believe everything you see. I think he was trying to send me a message."

"What message?"

"That the Marx Brothers weren't what they seemed to be. Remember how they all loved the Captain Tuttle episode on *MASH*?"

"What's the Captain Tuttle episode?" asked Lilly.

"It's the episode where Trapper and Hawkeye make up an imaginary soldier, Captain Tuttle. Someone who doesn't exist. The Marx Brothers seemed keen on people who weren't real, who didn't exist. Maybe they were looking for pointers on how to make others think you no longer exist."

Daffy asked, "But who exactly is behind this grand deception? Some organization must be helping hide the Marx Brothers."

"Not the Mafia. Those kisses of death say the Marx Brothers must have been running *from* the Mafia, which answers why they disguised their real identities."

"But 'not the Mafia' doesn't answer where they are now, assuming your realization at the *Dans* about Barry is correct."

"Why did you want to have Barry speak to you so badly?" asked Babs.

Gidget said, "Because he's going to be the father of my baby."

After Cordell and Tim revived Lilly and Babs, Lizzie turned to Gidget.

"Aren't you a little too old to be having a baby?"

"Apparently not," Gidget said, "As I told Daffy, my momma had me when she was in her late fifties. I'm only sixty-two-years-old, and women have been known to have periods in their sixties."

"But I thought you went through menopause this past summer?"

"I did, too. That's why I wasn't taking any precautions with Barry. I guess it was a false menopause."

"How do you know you're pregnant?" asked Lilly.

"I know. After five babies, I know. Besides, I've been having morning sickness for several weeks. Haven't I, Daff?"

Daffy nodded. "Oh yeah. And I thought it was seasickness."

"Did… does Barry know?" asked Lilly.

Gidget said, "Yeah. I told him a few days before he disappeared."

"How'd he take it?"

"He was happy but melancholic. I guess he must've known they would have to disappear, and it made him sad."

Babs began jumping up and down in her seat.

"Oooh, I can't wait to host the baby shower."

The Casserole Ladies immediately began planning Gidget's baby shower. They debated doing a shower, a reveal, or both but each separately, or combining them into a big shower-reveal. Lizzie declared her ambivalence as long as there was enough wine. They discussed baby names for twenty minutes.

Cordell reeled them back in.

"Ladies, you've been arguing about types of baby showers and whether to buy baby clothes one or two sizes too big and which stuffies babies like best for so long now that you've forgotten what the real problem is—"

"I beg your pardon," said Lilly, "but breast feeding versus bottle feeding is pretty important."

Cordell recognized he was defeated. "Conceded. Next to breast feeding, we need to talk about what happened to the Marx Brothers, if they're not dead."

Gidget's jaw tightened. "They're *not* dead. They're most likely hiding from the Mafia. They received the kiss of death. The questions we have to answer now are who's hiding them and where?"

"It sounds like the Arnold Schwarzenegger guy is probably behind all this," said Daffy.

"That's what I think. Don't forget, someone who looked big enough to be Arnold Schwarzenegger was on the balcony right after Jerry, or something, fell off."

"What about all of those scuba- and skindiving reading materials in Jerry's room?"

"Good question. Maybe Jerry, or even Harry, was reading about skindiving because they knew they'd be in the ocean at some point. Maybe even Barry. Skindiving tells me that someone like the Arnold Schwarzenegger guy, someone who's an expert in that kind of stuff, was involved. However, I think the most reasonable explanation is that someone pushed a dummy dressed up like Jerry off his balcony."

Lilly said, "I think you're onto something."

"Too many things about their supposed 'deaths' says they were planned beforehand."

"Such as?"

"Take Harry's death. Parasailing at 1:00 PM, exactly when you shouldn't because the water is usually too choppy. Parasailing way above the approved safe height. Why? Someone wanted him to get lost on purpose so he could be recovered and taken elsewhere. Why did the towline looked like some sort of charge was set off to snap it, unless it was preplanned? I think Harry planned to parasail out to sea, where he would be picked up."

"What about Barry?"

Gidget said, "Someone ordered the MegaSlide to be flushed in the afternoon instead of the usual early morning time for a reason."

Lizzie said, "Flushed? Remind me never to go on one of those waterslides."

"Flushing the slide probably somehow allowed Barry to control his rate of descent. Someone blew a hole in the plexiglass right before he got to a pre-arranged place where Barry could be extracted. He never fell into the ocean. I think the Schwarzenegger character somehow snared him through that hole."

"There's a bunch of unanswered stuff about Larry's death, ain't there?" asked Daffy.

"Yes. Why did Larry's iPhone not ring with a notice that his pacemaker had alerted his cardiologist when his heart stopped in the restaurant? Something just occurred to me. Maybe his pacemaker was preprogrammed to slow his heartbeat enough to make anyone checking his pulse think he was dead. That is possible. And why, after Larry showed symptoms of arsenic and cyanide poisoning, was there no poison in his vomit?"

"It was icky. All that foam all over everything," said Daffy.

Gidget's head nodded vigorously. "That's important! Foaming at the mouth. High levels of anhydrous citric acid, sodium bicarbonate, and aspirin in Larry's vomit. That's the answer to his death!"

"How so?" asked Babs.

"Those are the main ingredients in Alka-Seltzer. I bet he popped an Alka-Seltzer in his mouth while he was eating so he could fake his seizure. It was all preplanned."

Cordell asked, "You know who else did that?"

"Who?" asked Lilly.

"Johnny C, the ex-mobster in the Arnold Schwarzenegger movie *Eraser,* swallowed Alka-Seltzer. I was at Warner Bros. at the time and had a hand in producing it."

"I remember *Eraser*. Great picture," said Lizzie. "Arnold still had a yummy body in that one."

"The storyline had Arnold working for the DoJ WITSEC—"

"WITSEC? What's that?" asked Lilly.

"It's a term for the Federal Witness Security Program. Arnie would erase his witnesses' identities and hide them from bad guys who wanted them killed. Johnny C was an ex-member of the Italian mob who became one of Arnie's WITSEC protectees. He chewed on an Alka-Seltzer tablet to make it look like he was foaming at the mouth and having a seizure in order to help get Arnie into the Cyrez building."

Babs said, "The Marx Brothers are hiding out in the Cyrez building?"

"No, silly," said Lilly. "All Cordell is saying is that the Marx Brothers were members of the Mafia and are being protected under some sort of WITSEC program."

Cordell nodded. "It makes sense."

Gidget said, "I think Larry faked choking, but was really rolled off the boat in a body bag. And I think at this point we can say the Arnold Schwarzenegger guy might have been part of the Mafia, but more likely was some sort of WITSEC operative. Whichever, Doctor Mokulus must have been in on it. Y'all know what that means, don't you?"

"What?" asked Daffy.

"The Marx Brothers didn't come to meet us in Thomasville because they liked our calendar. We were patsies. We were set up to be witnesses to their fake deaths."

Lizzie said, "What a bunch of liars. They said they wanted to meet some 'good-looking fillies.' To think that I fell for that line. But I always fall for a good line… especially when it's wearing a lot of gold."

Chapter 62

25° 5' 43.9764" North, 83° 35' 38.1552" West
November 22nd

Cordell's worst fears were coming true. "If they *are* in a WITSEC program, what Tim said about the Marx Brothers testifying for the Feds against the Mafia makes sense. And if the Mafia is out to get them, anyone associated with them is at risk. Like I said before, y'all should return to Thomasville, tell everyone they died on the cruise, and hope the Mafia believes that's what you really think."

"We can't do that," said Gidget. "And you know why. I've got to find Barry."

"So where is he?" asked Daffy. "Definitely not in The Villages. They probably moved there in order to escape from the New York Mafia—"

Lizzie said, "I thought old people only moved to The Villages to get in on the pickleball action there."

"Lizzie! Be serious for once," said Lilly. "We're talking Mafia."

"The Villages is serious about pickleball. It has twenty-two pickleball courts."

"How do you know?"

"Remember when you and I hit the road headed there in September? When we were going prospecting for gold in the 'Fort Knox of Old Widowers?'"

"How could I forget? You insulted my Mercedes' GPS, and she got peeved at you and shut down, so we got lost and instead of The Villages, we wound up at that gay nudist colony in Florida. Twenty-two pickleball courts? You sure about that?"

"Before we hit the road, I looked up things old guys would probably do there and read they have fifty-six golf courses and twenty-two pickleball courts. I figured we'd be more likely to find our quarry by hanging out around those places—"

Gidget said, "As I was about to say before I was interrupted, the reason the Marx Brothers went on the cruise was because the Mafia was closing in on them in The Villages, and they wanted to fake their deaths on a boat on the ocean. It'd be tough to deny they died in a closed environment like a ship."

"I'm not liking where this is going," said Daffy.

"You're reading my mind. They hooked up with the five women in the *Widows of Thomasville* calendar, then purposefully left a trail from The Villages to the Bahama Princess. That's why those kiss of death people were able to track them down. The Marx Brothers must've figured having us and two thousand other passengers on the Bahama Princess as witnesses to their deaths would give the Mafia proof they had died."

This revelation enraged Lilly. "You mean we were just a bunch of pawns?"

"Exactly. We were witnesses that could attest to their deaths, which were staged for the Mafia's benefit. That's why they wanted to meet 'doze good looking fillies.'"

"It must've disappointed them when Babs, Lizzie, and I didn't go on their cruise."

Gidget nodded. "That's probably why they were so eager to accept Lou, Ronnie, and Naomi as additional traveling companions, filling in for you three. They probably thought two thousand passengers would be pretty good witnesses to their deaths, but five traveling companions giving personal interviews to TV reporters would be icing on the cake."

Lizzie said, "And that damn Barry gets you pregnant and runs out on you."

"Where are those bastards? I wanna get my hands on someone's gonads," said Daffy.

Gidget said, "Cordell, tell Captain Stevenson to head for Arizona."

Cordell's megastars overrode his objections to flying them to Arizona; all supported Gidget in her quest for the father of her baby. However, the women and Cordell wanted an explanation as to why she thought the Marx Brothers were hiding out in Arizona.

"Several clues point to Arizona," Gidget said. "First, Larry choked on a Sonoran breakfast empanada because he loved Sonoran food, and that type of cuisine is rarely found outside of Arizona. He probably ran across it while he was in the state."

"How'd you know it's rarely found outside of Arizona?" asked Babs.

"Found this article on the Internet while Cordell was whining about going after the Mafia earlier." Gidget turned the laptop around so they could see the title 'What is Sonoran-Style Mexican Food?' on its screen.

"It says 'Sonoran-style…' blah, blah-blah, blah… 'is rarely found outside of Arizona.' Yeppers. That's what it says," said Daffy as she read the first paragraph of the article.

"I figure Larry developed a taste for Sonoran cuisine while he and his brothers traveled there for his cardiology appointment and to scope out an area as a possible place to relocate under WITSEC."

"Hmmm. Sonoran empanadas. Good dietary choice for a guy with heart disease," said Lizzie.

"Another clue pointing to Arizona is when they said Larry always loved a warm climate. Harry said the main reason they moved to The Villages was Florida's warm climate."

"May he find his warm climate when he goes to hell," said Daffy.

Gidget said, "And it was in Arizona that Gary saw Moriarty's magic act which he wanted to see again on the Bahama Princess. He said he loved it when he watched Moriarty saw a woman in half in Phoenix."

Lilly's antagonism toward the Marx Brothers continued to grow. "I'd love to watch Moriarty sawing every Marx Brother in half."

"That's pretty cruel," said Lizzie. "Those guys are already short enough."

The Casserole Ladies engaged in five minutes of one-upmanship as to appropriate punishments for the Marx Brothers until Gidget interrupted to finish her sleuthing.

"The biggest clue pointing to Arizona is Larry's cardiologist is in Arizona, not in The Villages. He said Banner Health had one of the best cardiology programs in the country. At his age, he probably does have some sort of heart issue, so going to a good cardiologist makes sense."

"With men his age, it's either heart problems, prostate problems, or both," said Lilly.

"And diabetes," added Babs.

Daffy winced. "Or hemorrhoids."

Lizzie said, "Speaking of which, did anyone remember to pack any Preparation H?"

"I did, but it's back on the boat."

Cordell groaned, "Ladies, please—TMI. Allen, Tim—did either of you get all that on film?"

Both Tim and Allen nodded.

Gidget said, "As I was about to explain before we got off track, his cardiologist practices at the Banner Health Clinic in Sun City."

Babs asked, "How'd you know that?"

"While we were in Saint Croix, Larry's pacemaker sent an alarm to his cardiologist's office. They called his iPhone to check on him. We asked him about his cardiologist's doctor, and he said he was with Banner Health in Arizona because it has one of the best heart programs in the States."

"I always thought the best thing in Arizona was no Daylight Savings Time," said Lizzie.

"Don't get me started on Daylight Savings Time," said Daffy.

Gidget continued, "The clincher was when Daff and I found the name of his cardiologist and his Sun City address on Larry's iPhone. I called the clinic, and they confirmed he's a patient."

Cordell steered the conversation back to the Mafia.

"Let's think this through. We're possibly dealing with five ex-Mafia members who might be under WITSEC protection on the run from the Mafia. They're in the program for a reason. They're in danger. And this Arnold Schwarzenegger-type guy? He could be a good WITSEC agent or a bad Mafia guy. We don't know. There's another possible danger for you. If you ladies go charging into Sun City and actually find the Marx Brothers, your lives will be in danger just like theirs. You can't do it. Drop it and move on."

Cordell looked at Tim and Allen. "Did you guys get that?"

Tim and Allen nodded.

"You just don't want to lose the stars of your megahit TV show," said Lilly.

"Neither do I," said Lizzie.

Gidget said, "I have to find the father of my baby. Y'all can drop me off in Sun City and go on back to Thomasville."

"If you go, I'm going," said Daffy.

Babs nodded. "Me too."

"I don't wanna go, but if y'all go, count me in," said Lilly.

Lizzie never let Lilly go on a Casserole Ladies misadventure without her. "If Lilly goes, I'm in."

Cordell sighed. "Sounds like y'all have your minds made up. I've learned not to go against that. But listen—dealing with a coup in Haiti is one thing, but the Mafia..."

Daffy said, "Think of the ratings, Cordell. Everyone loves TV shows about the Mafia. You're passing up another blockbuster episode if you don't go."

Tim lowered his camera. "She's got a point, Boss."

Cordell was silent for a moment, wheels turning. Finally, he said, "How could we work this into the show without putting you, me, my crew, and the Marx Brothers at risk? Let me work on that."

"So, you'll fly us to Sun City and stick around?" asked Gidget.

"We'll see."

"If I know Cordell," said Lizzie, "he'll figure out something."

Cordell looked at the *Real Widows* writer. "I have faith in this guy. I'll go tell Captain Stevenson to head for Arizona."

Chapter 63

Sun City, Arizona
November 23rd

Development of the first retirement community in the United States began in 1959. Del Webb Development purchased 20,000 acres in Maricopa County and expanded over the years. Over forty-thousand people called Sun City home by the time the Casserole Ladies drove into it from the airport in Phoenix. Cordell's Gulfstream landed in Arizona's capital after an overnight stop in Thomasville for meals, baths, and sleep.

All of the *Real Widows* production crew—except for Cordell, Tim, and Allen—headed back to Los Angeles. They had enough footage for several episodes, all of which needed editing. The decision was also motivated by concern for the safety of as many crew members as possible.

Meanwhile, the Casserole Ladies, Cordell, and his two cameramen cruised down West Grand Avenue in a rented GMC Yukon Denali. Lilly confirmed that Sun City had been built as a magnet for senior citizens.

"I haven't seen this many Lincoln Town Cars since my last visit to Clearwater, Florida. I thought they quit making Town Cars over a decade ago."

"And the little bald heads and gray heads peeking through the steering wheels," added Lizzie. "I haven't seen this many blue-haired old ladies since I was last in Clearwater with you."

"What is it about Town Cars and little old ladies?"

"Little old ladies need a lot of metal around them when they run redlights and get sideswiped."

Babs said, "I haven't seen this many palm trees since I watched that Tom Hanks movie *Castaway*. What is it about 55+ communities and palm trees?"

"I'm not sure, but it probably has something to do with all the palm trees on old men's Hawaiian flower shirts. Camouflage, maybe?"

Not to be left out, Daffy said, "I think Sun City must be competing with The Villages for the most golf courses. We passed Quail Run golf course, now here's Sun City North golf course.

There's a sign for Sun City Lakes up Del Web Boulevard. My God! Golf must be the national sport of retired old men. Gidg, are we here to play golf or find the Marx Brothers?"

"Once we check-in at the hotel," said Gidget, "I plan on doing just that. And I'm not talking about playing golf.

Once they were settled in a local motel, Gidget connected her laptop to the Wi-Fi.

Daffy leaned over her shoulder. "Whatcha gonna do?"

"See if I can locate where the Marx Brothers are living," Gidget said.

"How 'ya gonna do that?"

"If they're living here, they've got to live somewhere. I don't think they'd rent. They didn't rent in The Villages. They—or someone on their behalf—probably bought property here. If I can't find something they purchased, I'll have to figure out a way to check for recent rentals. But first, I'm going to look up recent real estate sales to see if they bought something."

"How?" asked Lilly.

"By going to the Sun City government website that records real estate sales. They'll have all the documents associated with the property transfers."

"Ahhh. Excellent. You're going to search the records to see if the Marx Brothers bought a house here."

"Yes, but it's not going to be that simple."

"How so?"

"I'm sure they didn't use the name 'Vanderhoff' to buy anything, so I can't search by their last name."

"I bet they didn't even buy property using the name 'Marx Brothers,'" said Lizzie.

Gidget chuckled. She googled 'Sun City Arizona government' and looked at the list of recommended websites. She selected a link to Sun City Government Offices, which led to a page for Sun City Property Records. That, in turn, linked to the Maricopa County Recorder's Office. The site was titled 'Recorded Document Search' and displayed a form for accessing a wide range of records.

Daffy looked over her shoulder. "Whatcha got there?'

"Y'all know as much as I do about navigating this site," Gidget said, moving her cursor to a dropdown menu labeled 'All TYPES.'

She began scrolling through a long list of document types—Abandonment of a Mine, Abandonment of Any Type, and so on. She tried a few, including Deed of Trust and Certification of Purchase, but those weren't what she needed. She struck gold with Certificate of Sale of Property.

"Bingo! This looks like what we're looking for. A Certificate of Purchase records the purchase of a real estate sale between the buyer and the seller."

"Okay, but so what?" asked Babs.

"I'm gonna run a search on all real estate sales to see if anything looks like it might be them."

"That could be a lot of purchase records to look through," said Lilly.

"We'll see. I'm going to start with sales in the last six months and see what comes up."

After Gidget entered the date range, a long list of records appeared on the computer screen. She opened the first one and scammed it for any clue that might point to the Marx Brothers. It quickly became clear this would be a time-consuming process.

"This is gonna take some time," she muttered.

Two hours later, Gidget lit up. "Eureka! I bet this is it."

"What? What?" asked Daffy.

"Look at this." Gidget read select lines aloud as the other Ladies looked on. "Certificate of Purchase… Da, da, da… Property Address 121 Camelback Road, Sun City, Arizona 85351… Da, da, da… for the sum of THREE MILLION ONE HUNDRED THOUSAND DOLLARS."

"Whose name is listed as the buyer?" asked Babs.

"Get this—buyers are Cary Jankowski, Perry Jankowski, Terry Jankowski, Guerry Jankowski, and Ari Jankowski."

"My God! They used *no* imagination on those first names," said Daffy.

"Or the last names," said Lizzie. "I wonder if their Jankowski ancestors sailed over on the Mayflower."

Gidget said, "They bought it less than three months ago—right before they showed up at the IHOP in Thomasville."

"That's proof they were setting us up," said Lilly. "We were part of their scheme."

"Hey, look at this," Gidget added. "The certificate lists their previous address as one in Brooklyn."

Chapter 64

Sun City, Arizona
November 24th

A massive, two-story structure filled the view in Gidget's binoculars. She let out a low whistle and then handed them to Daffy in the passenger seat. The rest of the crew—Lilly, Lizzie, Babs, Cordell, Tim, and Allen—sat in the second and third rows of the Denali. Daffy raised the binoculars to her eyes and echoed the whistle.

"What a spread. I'm jealous."

Lilly said, "That place isn't even listed in the National Register of Historic Places like your house in Thomasville."

"I'd love to toilet paper their lawn," Lizzie muttered, "but I couldn't afford that much toilet paper."

They were parked a block away from the house. A six-foot wrought iron fence enclosed the entire property, with a spear-tip finial on every picket to discourage intruders. The house sat on three acres of meticulously groomed Bermudagrass. A U-shaped cobblestone driveway prompted Lilly to estimate, "That's at least twenty grand right there." Sunlight sparkled off the house's pristine white limestone block.

"Easy to see why this place sold for over three mil," Daffy said.

"Must've flown in Egyptian slaves straight from the Pyramids to lay those blocks," Lizzie added.

They'd begun their stakeout at 7:30 AM. It was now 9:30 AM. Lizzie, as expected, complained. "This is above and beyond. I should've slept-in like normal."

Lilly groaned too. "Why didn't someone stop me from having that second cup of coffee? How do real detectives deal with needing to pee?"

"You think you've got it bad. Thank your lucky stars you're not pregnant. I got a baby pressing up against my bladder," said Gidget.

"Have you decided what you're gonna do if Barry is actually living in that house?" asked Daffy.

"Hit him up for fifty thou a month in child support," said Lizzie without missing a beat.

"Gidge's got plenty of money without child support," Lilly pointed out.

"Mo money never hurt anyone," Lizzie said. "Make him suffer."

Babs said gently, "I don't think you should meet with him."

"Then why did we even come here?" Lizzie countered.

"To satisfy our curiosity. If we see them, then we can go home satisfied."

"Out of the mouth of Babs," Lizzie said, half amused.

Cordell said, "If they are here, they're under WITSEC protection. Don't forget that. I'd love to get your reunion on camera, but not if it puts y'all at risk."

Tim and Allen exchanged bewildered looks. That was remarkably uncharacteristic of Cordell, the guy who'd do just about anything for ratings.

Ten minutes passed in chatter.

Daffy finally said, "A sawbuck for your thoughts, Gidge. You've been quiet while the rest of us have been running our mouths."

"I'm just stewing. I'm mad—not just at Barry but at all the Marx Brothers. We were pawns," Gidget said.

"Lord knows you've got every right to be miffed," Lilly said.

"Barry's a little stinker," Lizzie added, "but he must have a healthy sperm count for seventy-year-old."

"I hate the thought of my baby growing up without a father," Gidget said. "I can't imagine done that without Sam around—for the births, for raising the kids."

"Trust me. Sometimes things work better without a husband," Lizzie said.

"I keep swinging between hating Barry and wanting him here. I thought we had something real—something I never thought I'd find again after Sam."

"I think you should give up and move on," Lilly offered.

Daffy shook her head. "Not me. I vote for tracking the bastard down and cutting off his nuts."

"I'm with Lizzie. At least get child support," Babs said.

"Why? She's loaded," Lilly said.

Lizzie frowned in disbelief. "Money is money. Get all you can, girl."

Gidget tapped at the Denali's infotainment screen. "This thing has a nice GPS system. Look at this map."

"Be careful. Those things have a mind of their own," said Lilly, thinking of the GPS in her own Mercedes.

"If that thing acts up, just bitch slap her," Lizzie said. "Show her who's boss."

Gidget said, "Look. This thing also has Alexa. Daff, reach in the glove box and hand me the owner's manual."

"Careful," Daffy said. "Alexa's worse than a GPS."

Babs nodded enthusiastically. "Don't I know it. I got this thing in the mail last winter called a Better Marriage Blanket—"

"A what?" Lilly asked.

"Sounds like something I could've used in a couple of my marriages," Lizzie said. "Especially husband number three. What a dud in the sack he was!"

Babs frowned. "It's not that kind of blanket. It has nothing to do with sex. It eliminates fart smells. Don't laugh. You lay it over the bed, and it absorbs the odor."

Daffy burst out laughing. "Wish I'd had one when Royce ate Mexican."

"It turned out Alexa had ordered it behind my back," Babs said, indignant. "Y'all know she's on my smart TV—"

Lizzie cut in. "Somebody make note of this. Babs is telling a shaggy dog story that actually relates to the conversation."

Unbothered, Babs went on. "Alexa saw one of those 'As Seen On TV' commercials for the blanket and thought I needed it. Talk about insulting!"

"How'd you find out she ordered it?" Lilly asked.

"After the Blanket, I got a 'Fanny Bank' in the mail."

"What's that?"

"It's a piggy bank shaped like a bare butt. You drop a coin in the butt-crack and it farts. I kid you not." Babs puckered her lips and made a 'pfffffft' sound. "Alexa laughed when I asked her about it and said 'If the shoe fits, wear it.' Y'all ever heard of Alexas that can smell?"

"They can hear and talk," Lizzie shrugged. "Why not smell?"

Tim and Allen could not contain their laughter, their bodies shaking so hard they had to lower their cameras.

Daffy asked, "And Alexa was ordering these things online?"

Babs nodded vigorously. "She kept seeing those 'As Seen On TV' commercials and ordered them as a joke."

"How'd you figure out that it was Alexa ordering them?" Lizzie asked.

"When she ordered a 'Talking TP' that came in the mail—"

"Talking TP?" Lizzie echoed.

"It replaces the plastic cylinder that goes inside the toilet paper holder—the thing that actually holds the roll of toilet paper. This one has a recorder in it, so you can record a funny or insulting message. When somebody takes care of business and pulls on the toilet paper, it plays the message."

Babs paused to glare at Tim and Allen who were doubled over with laughter. "As I was trying to say, when Alexa ordered it, the online order form had a space to leave a message for the recipient. She filled it in, thinking she was being cute."

"What did she say?" asked Cordell, grinning.

"I hope everything comes out all right. Love, Alexa."

The group erupted. Tim and Allen howled with laughter again.

Babs huffed. "Go ahead and laugh, but let me just say—whatever y'all do, don't ever say your credit card number where Alexa can hear it."

As the laughter finally died down, Gidget looked up from the infotainment screen. "Got it working."

"What?" asked Lilly.

"The Denali's Alexa."

"I'm amazed," said Lizzie. "You must've promised to have sex with it."

Babs perked up. "That reminds me of something funny that happened at Harvey's while y'all were off on that cruise. Something Mary Ellen at Harvey's said to me when I was checking out… Jimmy and Ethan have been begging me to make a pumpkin pie for them for Thanksgiving dinner—"

"Oh no," Daffy said. "Babsie, your shaggy dog story is showing again."

"There's a point in their somewhere," Lizzie added. "The trick is getting out of Babsie's brain."

Babs nodded earnestly. "You're darn right there is."

"There is what? A point to your story or a trick to getting it out?" Daffy teased.

"Uh… I forgot. Darn it. Oh yeah, it's coming back now. I was unloading my cart at Harvey's and put this fat ole pumpkin on the conveyor belt for Mary Ellen to ring up. She scans it and says, 'This pumpkin reminds me. Sonny Biskit told me he's running for City Council next year.'"

Lizzie smirked. "Sounds like he was trying to impress Mary Ellen. Must have the hots for her."

Babs continued. "Remember at the IHOP when we all had breakfast that day the Marx Brothers stopped by to woo us—"

"Woo us?" Lilly interrupted. "I ain't heard that word in thirty years."

"Wooing us must be the connection to having sex with Alexa," Lizzie muttered.

"Lizzie, Lilly. Please. Don't interrupt her shaggy dog story, or she'll never finish it," said Daffy, turning to Babs. "Please continue."

"Thank you," said Babs with a prim nod. "Anyway, Mary Ellen looked at that pumpkin and said it reminded her of Sonny Biskit. And I tell you I couldn't stop laughing. Just the thought that the pumpkin reminded her of Sonny Biskit was more than I could handle."

Lilly chuckled. "Sonny *is* fat."

"I laughed so hard I leaked a little in my Depends."

Tim, Allen, and Cordell grinned at each other. Cordell felt vindicated in his decision to produce *The Real Widows of Thomasville*.

Just then, Gidget sat upright. "Look! Someone's pulling out of the garage."

Chapter 65

Sun City, Arizona
November 24th

A black Ford Expedition SUV eased down the cobblestone driveway and out through the wrought iron gate, which swung open automatically. Gidget raised the binoculars.

"It's Barry," she said. "It looks like he's alone." She started the Denali's engine.

"That's a lot of SUV for such a little guy," Lizzie said. "You can barely see his bald head over the steering wheel."

"It's one of those Expedition MAX models," Daffy chimed in. "Probably seats eight."

"Enough room to haul the whole Marx Brothers crew together at once. That's a lot of little bald heads packed in like sardines," Lizzie added.

"Don't get too close, Gidge." Cordell warned. "Stay at least a block behind. He's Mafia—might know how to spot a tail."

Gidget narrowed her eyes. "He's driving a Platinum model. Not cheap. Looks like the Marx Brothers are living large after all. Maybe Daff is right about the satisfaction I'd get from cutting off his nuts."

Lizzie shook her head. "There are less drastic ways to get revenge. I remember my second… or maybe my third husband? I caught him with my neighbor when I was supposed to be at a Junior League meeting one afternoon. That night, I smeared Vick's VapoRub inside the crotch of his Fruit of the Looms and left him a note in his medicine cabinet: '*Remember this next time you screw around with Rhonda Jernigan. Love, Lizzie*.' His balls were on fire all day."

Gidget didn't laugh. "Stinging his nuts doesn't seem satisfying enough."

Barry's Expedition crawled along several residential blocks before turning onto a slightly busier road near a golf course. He turned onto Del Web Boulevard. Traffic picked up a little, but not much. A few blocks later, he veered east onto Highway 60.

Gidget kept half a block behind, unaware of the drone hovering six hundred feet above and one hundred feet behind her Denali. Traffic remained light, and she had no problem keeping Barry's SUV in sight while maintaining a safe distance. After a couple miles, he turned north onto State Road 101—a four-lane loop around Phoenix. The road snaked north, then bent sharply eastward.

"Where's he going?" Daffy wondered.

Gidget gestured at the Denali's infotainment screen. A GPS map of the Sun City-Phoenix area filled the display. "Highway 101 loops around Phoenix. He must be heading east around the city."

"Go East, old man," Lizzie quipped, parodying Horace Greeley.

Barry's SUV continued through residential neighborhoods and eventually crossed I-17. Instead of staying on 101, Barry veered onto an entrance ramp and headed north on the interstate. Gidget followed.

The homes thinned out. Development gave way to raw desert, and the colors shifted—coarse sand with red-tinged clay stretched out in all directions. Sparse vegetation dotted the landscape—creosote bushes and yucca plants like lonely sculptures.

"This is more like the Arizona I imagined," Lilly said. "Kind of… deser-ty."

"Deser-ty," Lizzie repeated. "Add that one to the dictionary."

A few miles farther, brownish-grey hills from the parched terrain.

"Where the heck is he going?" Daffy asked.

"Somewhere away from the city," said Gidget.

"And people," said Cordell.

After seven miles, the Expedition exited the highway and took a four-lane road due east. The area was mostly deserted.

"Drop back more," Cordell advised. "He'll spot you if you're too close."

Gidget eased up, keeping the SUV in sight. The road passed scattered brush and the occasional tiny subdivision. After two miles, it forked. One branch curved sharply north, while the other continued east. Barry stayed east—until he turned onto a dirt road heading south.

Gidget pulled over and studied the GPS. "He's heading into the Sonoran Preserve."

"What's that?" Daffy asked.

"Let's find out." Gidget tapped a button on the touchscreen. "Alexa. What is the Sonoran Preserve?"

The screen displayed a spinning circle. Then Alexa's voice filled the Denali's sound system:

"The Sonoran Preserve is a nature park maintained by the City of Phoenix. It spans over 9,600 acres of arid desert. Three trailheads—Desert Vista, Desert Hills and Apache Wash—offer access to thirty-six miles of trails. Visitors are advised to be aware of hazards such as limited water, dangerous wildlife, rough unpaved roads, and infrequent ranger patrols."

"I don't like this," Lilly murmured. "I don't see many cars coming and going this way."

"Let's be cautious," Cordell said.

Barry inched deeper into the Preserve, even slower now than on paved roads. Gidget shifted into drive and from a distance, followed the cloud of dust kicked up by his Expedition.

The dirt trail twisted between rocky hills, winding through narrow valleys. Scattered patches of cactus and scrub struggled to survive the unforgiving terrain.

"Not much plant life," Gidget observed.

"How do animals survive out here?" Daffy asked. "And where are the other cars?"

"I wonder if that's why he is driving out here?" Cordell asked.

Gidget trailed the Expedition at a safe distance for thirty minutes, winding along a series of curvy desert roads between hills. Though both vehicles stayed under thirty-five miles per hour, the constant motion began to wear on the group.

"I feel like we're on a roller coaster," Lilly groaned. "My tummy is woozy."

"Can we swing back to that last hill and pick up my tummy?" Lizzie asked. "Alexa warned us about the limited water, but she forgot to mention packing Pepto-Bismol."

Suddenly, Gidget eased off the gas. "Look up ahead. Barry's dust trail just vanished behind that hill."

"What?" Daffy asked, leaning forward.

“It was kicking up a cloud like always—right up to that bend. Then… nothing.”

“He must’ve stopped. Sight-seeing? By himself?” Daffy wondered aloud.

“I bet he stopped to take a leak,” Lizzie said.

Babs wrinkled her nose. “I hope that’s all it is. I hope there’s a Porta Potty back there.”

Cordell glanced toward Gidget. “You sure you want to keep going?”

She nodded. “Absolutely.”

“Just remember, our Denali’s been kicking up its own a dust cloud. He’ll be able to see us coming up on him just like you could see him ahead of you. And we have no clue what’s waiting behind that hill.”

Chapter 66

Sonoran Preserve, Arizona
November 24th

Tracking the Expedition by its dust tornado had worked well so far. Gidget was able to follow the SUV at a safe distance without being seen. But now, Cordell's comment about the Denali's kicking up its own dust trail left her uneasy. The Expedition had vanished behind a hill, but he'd surely see them approaching.

Gidget grew apprehensive. Still, she pressed the gas pedal. The SUV surged forward, its dust plume climbing higher as they sped toward the hill.

The road narrowed into a shallow valley, funneling them toward a small, pyramid-shaped hill, about fifty feet high and three hundred feet wide. As the road neared the base, it began to curve around the right side of the hill in a long 180-degree arc.

As they rounded the far side, Barry's Expedition came into view.

"There he is," said Daffy. "He's outside the vehicle."

Cordell narrowed his eyes. "Looks like he's waiting for us. He must've known you were tailing him."

Gidget nodded. "Yeah. Doesn't feel like a good sign."

Barry had parked the Expedition squarely in the middle of the narrow dirt road—there wasn't room for two cars parked side-by side.

One thing was odd, on which Daffy commented. "It's facing us. Wonder why he turned it around?"

Gidget didn't hesitate. "So he could make a quick getaway if he had to. Didn't want us blocking him in."

Gidget eased off the accelerator. As the Denali slowed, its dust cloud caught up and engulfed them. When the dust finally settled, the two SUVs faced each other, ten yards apart.

No one exited the Denali immediately.

Gidget studied the scene. Barry leaned casually against the Expedition's grill, the driver's door hanging open. He looked calm—too calm.

"Looks like his Expedition is empty. He must've known it was us," Gidget said.

"Why you say that?" Daffy asked.

"He's not nervous. He wouldn't act so relaxed if he thought he was being followed by someone dangerous."

"What now?" Daffy asked.

Gidget didn't answer. She put the Denali in park and opened her door. Cordell nodded at Tim, who opened the door on his side and exited the vehicle, camera in hand.

Gidget left her door open and walked toward Barry.

"Hey, baby!" Barry called with a grin. "I knew it was you. I've missed you."

"You have a funny way of showing it," Gidget said. "You look awfully alive for a dead man."

Barry's smile faltered. "I—"

Gidget's right hand slapped his face, the crack of it audible inside the Denali.

"You and your brothers played me and Daffy like fools," she said, voice tight. "Used us as pawns to fool the Mafia. We figured it out. Invited us to go on a cruise with you just to be witnesses to your fake deaths—"

"I, I—"

"Shut up! I'm not done." Her voice broke slightly. "You didn't just use us. You got me pregnant—"

"How was I supposed to have known a woman your age could still get pregnant?"

Gidget slapped his face again, this time with her left hand. "My age! You son-of-a—"

Barry winced. "Baby, are you sure you're pregnant? You might've just been seasick, you know."

"Do you think I'm somehow trying to trap you? You bastard! You think I want to marry you? If I did, it wouldn't be with an ugly shrimp like you!"

Barry looked down, stunned into silence.

Gidget's anger softened, regret flickering across her face. "I… I shouldn't have said that. I was really beginning to love you. And then you guys start dying on me. What am I supposed to think?"

They stared at each other for a moment.

Behind them, the rest of the Denali's occupants had exited and were gathering near their vehicle. Tim had captured the whole confrontation from ten feet away, low afternoon sun casting perfect light across the scene. Its reflection off the Expedition's windshield and chrome grill forced the group to squint.

No one noticed the small dust tornado on the horizon behind them steadily growing.

Barry's voice broke the silence. "Gidge, trust me. If I'd a known you could get pregnant, I never would've… you know."

"I know," Gidget said. "I know you're a crook, or whatever you and your brothers are. Probably in a WITSEC protection program and need to hide from the Mafia."

Barry nodded, saying nothing.

Gidget's gestured toward her group. "You used us. You needed witnesses to make it look real."

He said, "You've guessed everything right so far. We did want youse as witnesses."

"Y'all made up the whole story about seeing us in the calendar."

"We did see the calendar and knew you'd be perfect. But we never meant for anyone to get hurt. Everything was going exactly according to plan before that damn Haiti mess happened."

Gidget wanted to get more answers, but Barry kept glancing over her shoulder. Uneasy, she turned. A dust tornado was growing behind her.

"What is that? You've got the rest of your brothers and who knows who coming for us, I bet."

Fear washed over Barry's face. Everyone turned to look. The dust tornado rapidly grew larger as it sped toward them.

Cordell squinted. "That looks like another SUV. Black Chevy Equinox. And it's flying."

The Equinox skidded to a stop about twenty yards behind the Denali. Its own massive dust cloud surged forward, swallowing both SUVs and everyone nearby.

They heard car doors open—followed by the sound of footsteps. As the dust began to settle, three women emerged from the haze, standing in front of them with assault rifles raised and aimed directly at them.

"Naomi!" Daffy called out. "What are y'all doing here?"

"I doubt it's for a game of Mexican Train," Lizzie muttered.

Gidget kept her voice calm and steady. "Veronica. Louella. I'm surprised—but not that surprised—to see y'all here. I always thought y'all acted a little strange, but I never imagined this."

The three women approached slowly, rifles held loose but pointed toward the group. Louella waved her rifle toward a sandy patch about fifteen feet off the dirt road. "Everyone. Over there."

Veronica pointed her rifle at Barry. "You too, Fratelli. And take her with you."

Barry touched Gidget's arm lightly, guiding her toward the others as they trudged into the desert. He leaned in and murmured, "Don't say a word. The Chicago mob must've sent these dames. We heard the families were bringing in some outside help but never figured they would be women."

"What are they gonna do with us?" Cordell asked.

"Just do what she says. She's Mafia. A hitwomen. All three of 'em are."

Tim and Allen slowly lowered their cameras, and Daffy asked, "Hitwomen? What does that mean?"

"It means it ain't your day," Naomi said coldly. "Now move. And don't waste my time."

Louella, Veronica, and Naomi trailed behind them as the cast and crew of *Real Widows* slowly coalesced in the designated spot. Louella chuckled. "Smile for the camera. Everyone get nice and close."

"You're not…" Lilly could not finish her sentence.

"I knew I should've slept-in this morning," Lizzie muttered.

Naomi swept her assault rifle across the group. "We can make this quick and painless if you don't try to run away. If you do try to run away, then it's gonna be slow and painful for everyone."

Chapter 67

Sonoran Preserve, Arizona
November 24th

The *Real Widows* crew and cast stood in the desert sand, twenty feet from the three SUVs, their backs to their would-be executioners, who stood between them and the vehicles. Fittingly, the group faced a setting sun.

They heard the clink of an assault weapon's slide as it racked a bullet.

Each Casserole Lady nervously looked left and right. Fear etched every face. They awaited death—hoping it would be quick.

Then came a voice.

"Pull those triggers and make my day."

Gidget stiffened. The voice was male, unfamiliar, and carried an odd accent. It came from behind—from the direction of Barry's Expedition. She feared turning around might prompt the three hitwomen to pull their triggers. She continued looking at the sunset. Along with her condemned teammates, she waited in silence, nervous about the scurrying sounds behind them.

"If you point those rifles at us, you're dead."

From his accent, Gidget guessed the speaker to be European.

"At least one of us is bound to get at least one of you." Gidget recognized this voice as Louella's.

"You three might want to look up in the sky." The European accent again.

Gidget looked up as did her condemned teammates. She saw sunlight glint off an object hovering far above them.

The unknown voice narrated.

"That's a TIKAD drone, hovering two hundred-fifty meters above you. It's armed with an M4 that's loaded with thirty rounds of 5.56-mm ammunition. It can fire either single shot or seven hundred rounds per minute on full auto. It can hit a fifteen-centimeter target from a distance of five hundred fifty meters. It is remotely controlled by a pilot with whom I am in real-time communication with via satellite phone. Stan, you copy?"

The voice paused while listening to Stan's reply and then said, "Roger that. Let's give these three a little demo."

Gidget heard three loud thuds strike the ground in the vicinity near the hitwomen. Less than two seconds later, she heard sounds from the muzzle blasts of the weapon itself.

"Drop your weapons," the voice said, "or the next three rounds will be through your skulls."

Clatters followed as assault rifles hit the dirt.

"Barry," the voice said, "you and the others can turn around."

Gidget and the others slowly turned and saw the Arnold Schwarzenegger guy and three other men in desert camo aiming rifles at Louella, Naomi, and Veronica. The Arnold Schwarzenegger guy walked up to the hitwomen followed by his companions.

"Cuff 'em. Load 'em in the Expedition and get 'em the hell out of here."

Lizzie muttered, "Well, I guess that rules out a game of Mexican Train."

The Schwarzenegger guy drove the Equinox out of the Preserve with Cordell, Barry, Gidget, and Daffy inside. The rest of the crew and cast piled into the Denali. His three associates had departed fifteen minutes earlier in the Expedition with Louella, Naomi, Veronica, Tim, Allen, and all the video equipment.

"Where were y'all hiding?" Gidget asked. "Barry's Expedition?"

The Schwarzenegger guy nodded. "Correct. We folded the second and third-row seats down and laid down flat for the ride from the safehouse to the hill where Barry parked. It was so smooth, one of my guys fell asleep. We got out and hid before you arrived."

"You must've gotten an earful while Barry and I argued."

He smiled. "You and Bart were… entertaining."

"Bart?"

Barry shrugged. "Short for Bartolomeo. My real name."

"Bartolomeo Fratelli?"

"That's me."

"The four Fratelli brothers?"

"That's us."

"What are your brothers' real first names?" Daffy asked.

"Harry is Enrico. Larry's Lorenzo. Jerry's Girolamo. And Gary's Gerado."

"The Fratelli brothers."

"Exactly," Barry said. "Appropriate, right?"

"Why you say that?" Gidget asked.

"'Fratelli' means 'brothers' in Italian."

As the two vehicles exited the Preserve, the conversation turned to the operation.

"You must have known we were following you," Gidget said.

The Schwarzenegger guy nodded. "Of course. Bart identified you the minute you began surveilling the safehouse this morning. We called in the drone shortly before he left."

"And you purposefully sent Barry to draw us into following him so you could trap Louella, Naomi, and Veronica?"

"Correct. We knew Lola—"

"Lola?"

"Her real name. Dolly and Rita are the others. We knew they had tracked you to Sun City—"

"How'd you know that?"

"We searched your Gulfstream after you landed in Thomasville. Found an iPhone. You forgot to take it with you when you landed. Rita had left it on purpose with Location Services turned on. Our tech hacked into it and traced it back to another phone we figured belonged to them. We tracked that phone via the cell towers it used while they followed you."

"Nice to have a geek at your disposal," Daffy said.

"We *are* the Federal government."

"And you've been tracking… Rita while she was in Sun City."

"We began tracking her phone shortly after we found the phone she had 'forgotten' on the Gulfstream. Tracked her from a location in Dallas all the way into Sun City."

Gidget said, "I take it you didn't go ahead and pick her up when she arrived in Sun City because you weren't sure how many or who she was working with."

"Correct. We could have nabbed her any time. And we would have eventually broken her into telling us who she was working with and where they were, but that would have probably taken several days. Mafia hitwomen are tough to crack. Better to lure them into a remote location and grab them all at once."

"Why didn't the Marx Brothers recognize them?" asked Daffy.

"They weren't from New York. The families imported them from Chicago so they wouldn't be recognized."

"Ronnie *did* mention her power kept going out in her Chicago condo."

"You put all of us at risk," Gidget said.

The Schwarzenegger guy shrugged. "I judged the risk to be acceptable. We had drone coverage the whole time outside the safehouse. Stan matched the location of Rita's cell phone with the Equinox on Highway 60."

Gidget crossed her arms. "I don't care. You and… the Fratelli brothers used us as pawns. Twice. Daffy and I were at risk the whole time we were on that cruise."

"Why do you think you kept seeing me? I was watching out for you, just like I was watching out for the Fratelli's."

"Why didn't you arrest the hitmen that gave them the kisses of death?" Gidget asked.

"The kiss of death just marks someone for death—it doesn't mean the person giving it will kill them at that moment. Sometimes it's just to frighten the victim. We wanted to catch the hitman in the act. We didn't know who the hitman would be. We wanted whoever it was to witness the Fratelli's die on the cruise and report back that they were dead."

Barry added, "None of us guessed it was Naomi, Louella, and Veronica."

Gidget and Daffy sat in silence, reeling from the realization that they had been used. Daffy finally asked, "Are the rest of the Marx… Fratelli brothers safe at the house in Sun City?"

"Everything in Sun City—the safehouse, the property records, the fake names—all those are dummy things set up in case the Mafia didn't fall for the fake deaths. That trail ends in Sun City. The others went straight from the Bahama Princess to a permanent secure location. They are waiting there for Bart."

"Where is it?" Daffy asked.

The Schwarzenegger guy smiled. "If I told you, I'd have to kill you."

Gidget's curiosity compelled her to ask Barry, "What happened back in Brooklyn? Why'd you have to leave?"

Barry sighed. "After we testified, the guys we put away had family and friends who came after us. Wolfgang's been moving us around ever since. When things got hot in the Villages, he comes up with the cruise plan—fake our deaths and have witnesses the mob will believe."

Wolfgang chimed in, "I figured five deaths on a major cruise ship would generate a lot of media coverage, which it has. Haiti detaining the Bahama Princess was an unintended gift in that respect. Now every New York family is pointing fingers at each other. You got dragged into it because we needed people close to the dead Fratelli's who could provide personal testimony to the media."

Barry smirked. "It's like we told youse back at the IHOP. We saw your calendar during a game of canasta and said, 'Bingo. Those is the ones we want as witnesses.' Five gorgeous women—ideal witnesses."

Gidget's glare silenced Barry. She directed her questions at Wolfgang. "Lorenzo chewed an Alka-Seltzer tablet, faked a seizure, and his cardiologist temporarily stopped his heart remotely, right?"

"Correct."

"He was in the body bag we saw being rolled off at Grenada, but he was alive?"

"Correct."

"You pushed a dummy off Girolamo's balcony, and made sure it tumbled to hide the truth?"

"Correct. I waited until I saw you walking up the promenade deck."

"And Girolamo was one of the extra Coast Guard officers who boarded the helicopter two days later?"

"Correct."

"And Enrico's parasail line was rigged to explode, and he guided himself out to sea to be picked up by a boat?"

"A United States submarine to be exact."

"Gerado just hid in the second secret compartment in Moriarty's Magic Box until the coast was clear?"

"I measured him and made sure the second secret compartment was big enough for him to sit down in it."

"Bartolomeo's death must have been the hardest. He slid down the MegaSlide and at a designated point, triggered a small explosion?"

Wolfgang nodded. "It was tough, and you're close. Bart didn't trigger the explosion. His bracelet was a two-way radio. He gave me a description of the last person who entered before him. I had a harness rigged up and lowered myself to a point outside the plexiglass where I waited to retrieve Bart. When I saw the person who entered before him go past, I stuck a plastic explosive charge on the plexiglass, detonated it, then kicked out enough glass to retrieve Bart. I caught him when he arrived and helped him into another harness I had, then winched both of us up and disappeared with him. The news media attributed Bart's death to a freak accidental break in the MegaSlide's plexiglas."

"Unbelievable."

Wolfgang nodded. "Yes, it was. The Haitians did do us a favor though when they impounded the Bahama Princess. I used that event to sneak Bart and Gerado off the boat."

Daffy asked, "Why didn't the hitwomen try to kill the Fratelli's during the cruise?"

"They did, although I didn't realize it was them at the time. The first time was at Gibbs Cay," Wolfgang said.

"The chicken liver pâté," Gidget said.

"Yes. Since Lola had Chef Dreyfus prepare it, she must have done it on purpose to attract dangerous fish. And Dolly must have told Stokes to pick out green bathing suits for them, knowing they would attract fish. She told him the boys looked cute in green."

"I bet the second time was on the zipline in Antigua," Gidget guessed. "I was suspicious of Jerry's nylon strap breaking, but I blamed you, not Rita."

"It was Rita," Wolfgang confirmed. "The last attempt was on Saint Lucia when Gary was almost run off a cliff by the bike."

"Did the hitwomen hire a guy for that job?"

"Nope," Wolfgang said. "It was Dolly. She wore cyclist gear, and with her smaller chest and the helmet covering her head and much of her face, she easily passed for a man."

Lizzie muttered, "Transgender gone wild."

They rode in silence for several miles. Finally, Gidget asked, "You've told us a lot, but what happens next?"

Wolfgang spoke slowly. "We will take you back to your Gulfstream and ultimately fly you to Thomasville. All of you will forget everything that has happened since you left Port-au-Prince."

She looked at Barry. "What about us?"

Barry looked down and said nothing. Wolfgang answered instead. "You and Bart are finished. You two will never see or contact each other ever again. It's for your sake as well as Bart's."

"And the baby's," Barry said.

Gidget held back tears yet managed to say, "Our baby will grow up never knowing its father."

Wolfgang's words came hard and fast. "You need to understand. You and your friends are lucky to be alive. So are the Fratelli's. If anyone fails to do exactly what we tell you to do, you greatly increase the risk of losing all your lives. Bart has no say in this whatsoever."

Chapter 68

Thomasville, Georgia
December 2nd

> **You are invited to a**
>
> **Faux Baby Shower**
>
> **honoring Gidget Smurfitt**
>
> **Tuesday, December 2nd at 3 o'clock**
>
> **110 Tockwotton Place**
>
> **RSVP to: Daffy@SawgrassBank.com**

Gidget had been in the doldrums ever since Wolfgang escorted her and her coterie—minus Barry—into an empty private aircraft hangar at Phoenix Sky Harbor International Airport. The WITSEC team used the hangar as a temporary debriefing location. For three days, the detainees answered questions and were briefed on permissible conduct moving forward. The agents were stern, no-nonsense professionals who repeatedly stressed the severe penalties for disclosing any information about the Marx Brothers, other than being witnesses to their deaths. Each person was required to sign a Non-Disclosure Agreement, agreeing to federal criminal penalties if breached. The whole experience left Babs plagued with WITSEC nightmares for weeks afterward.

Five days after Cordell's jet lifted off from Phoenix, thirty-eight people crowded into Daffy's spacious dining room in Tockwotton. Babs peeked out from behind the sheer curtains for the fifth time in less than five minutes. Daffy finally ran out of patience. "If you don't calm down, I'm getting the Xanax for you… and for me."

Babs scurried from the window. “I can’t help it. I *love* surprise parties, especially a surprise baby shower! That is the ultimate. Gidge is going to be so surprised. I can’t wait to see her face.”

Most of the women in attendance were there out of curiosity. As one of Thomasville’s prominent citizens, Daffy’s home—her decor, her art, her antiques, even her knick-knacks—were all subjects of constant interest. Daffy had hired Amy at The Hare & The Hart to decorate her house for the shower. Some of the catty snippets being offered by guests included:

“I wish I could afford to hire Amy for my parties.”

“This must have cost a small fortune—though I’m sure it was pocket change for Miss Daffy.”

“Silver dollar eucalyptus garlands around those columns. Only Amy would’ve thought of that. I heard they were over three hundred bucks alone.”

“That sofa’s either Bernhardt or Hooker. I can always tell.”

“You are wrong on both counts. It’s Theodore Alexander.”

On Babs’ eighth peek through the curtains, she gasped. “Quiet everybody! Gidge’s car just pulled in.”

“I’m surprised she could find a place to park,” someone whispered.

Babs narrated, “She’s getting out of her Cadillac now—looking around at all the other SUVs. It looks like she’s surprised that many women showed up.”

“I told her I was having a wine tasting,” Daffy said.

“She’s probably surprised that there are this many wine drinkers in Thomasville,” Lilly quipped.

Lizzie added, “Yeah. Most women in Thomasville drink vodka. Talk about hardcore.”

“Wait,” asked one guest. “She doesn’t know it’s a baby shower for her, right?”

Daffy nodded. “Not a clue.”

The guests erupted with a big “Surprise!” as Gidget stepped into the living room, which was awash in pastel pink and baby blue bows, steamers, flowers, and balloons. A banner hung over the fireplace: 'Welcome Baby Smurfitt!!!!!' One corner of the room was stacked high with beautifully wrapped children's gifts.

"What in the hell is all this!?" Gidget exclaimed as she walked into the dining room. "I thought this was supposed to be a wine tasting."

Daffy smirked. "I'm surprised a sleuth like you catch on. When has anyone in Thomasville ever hosted a wine tasting?"

"There's always a first for everything."

Lizzie chimed in, "The only time anyone drinks wine in Thomasville is in the backseat of a car in the drive-in on Saturday night. And the wine is always Boone's Farm, and we all know what that tastes like."

Gidget's cheeks flushed—not from being duped, but from the acknowledgement of her presumed indiscretion. A baby shower meant a baby, and in her case, no marriage. She had been a bad girl, a loose woman. And now all Thomasville knew it.

Rumors had started after it became known that she and Daffy had traveled with five older gentlemen from The Villages. Photos of the Casserole Ladies and the Marx Brothers, laughing it up at the IHOP, had even been posted on several Facebook pages as they dined. Women's clubs buzzed with speculation over what the men might've expected in exchange for joining them on the cruise.

Gidget dreaded the firestorm her pregnancy would ignite. That's why, on her first day back from Phoenix, she tried to sneak a home pregnancy test kit out of Smurfitt Phamily Pharmacy.

Keeping something secret in Thomasville is impossible, especially when it involves pregnancy. A customer saw Gidget slip the test kit into a bag and not ring it up for one of her customers. An hour later, another customer walked in and asked Gidget who it was for. Gidget claimed it was for her youngest daughter, but after the girl was bombarded with numerous phone calls, the truth unraveled. By nightfall, Facebook was ablaze with speculation.

When Daffy called and Gidget told her the test results, Daffy said, "The best offense is sometimes another good offense, and we're going to go on offense. I got this. Leave it to me."

After the guests had gushed over the shower and departed, the five Casserole Ladies relaxed in her living room, finishing off the remainder of the Peach Sangria punch.

"See Gidge?" said Daffy, "That wasn't so bad. You're sixty-two and widowed. No sane adult expects you to remain celibate forever."

Gidget grimaced. "I know, but there are some old biddies in town—I see 'em every day at the pharmacy—who still tut-tut about sex outside of marriage. I just wish I could have taken the test before anyone found out about that damn kit."

Lilly asked gently, "Do you wish the test results *had* been positive instead of negative? That your seasickness was really morning sickness instead?"

A wistful look crossed Gidget's face. "Yeah, I do. It was just wishful thinking on my part. I've been missing having kids running around the house so much. I was glad when I thought I was pregnant. I truly believed I was pregnant. Given my mother's history, I just assumed it was happening again. I guess it wasn't meant to be. I talked with Doctor Fischel about it, and he thinks I had a very mild case of antepartum delusional psychosis—"

"What the hell is that?" asked Daffy.

"It's a type of psychosis where you experience delusion—believing something is real when it's not. In my case, I was convinced I was pregnant. Some women go through postpartum psychosis after giving birth. I experienced the delusion that I was pregnant antepartum, before the baby's birth, only I *never was* pregnant. Fischel said it was one for the books."

Lizzie said, "I got the solution. You should identify as pregnant. That way, it wouldn't be a delusion."

Gidget chuckled, shook her head, and looked at Daffy. "You went to a lot of expense and effort for a *faux* baby shower."

"It's like I told you. The best offense is a good offense. I knew the best way to counter all the sniping the old biddies in Thomasville would be taking at you was to acknowledge that you had sex but didn't get pregnant, and do it up front and directly. Sex is something to celebrate, not to hide or ignore. The way to attack it head on would be to have a *faux* baby shower. Besides, a lot of Thomasville children will get great presents for Christmas this year as a result of this shower." Daffy had privately informed all the guests that their gifts would be donated to the Marine Corps Toys for Tots.

Once again, the Casserole Ladies made lemonade out of lemons.

Epilogue

Thomasville, Georgia
December 2nd

The Casserole Ladies continued consuming Daffy's Peach Sangria punch and gabbing. As Babs stood to refresh everyone's punch glass, she noticed someone walking onto Daffy's porch. "You got a late guest, Daff."

"Damn! I assumed anyone would know that a shower that starts at three would end around five o'clock. Who is it?" asked Daffy.

"Looks like Sonny Biskit."

Daffy opened the door. As he walked inside, she said, "Sonny, how nice to see you. We just finished having a baby shower."

Sonny's face looked as if he was going to a funeral. "I know. I heard about it at Harvey's."

"But it's a shower just for ladies. What brings you here?"

"I need to speak to Gidget."

Gidget got up and walked over. She asked, "How can I help you?"

"I heard about your pregnancy and your baby shower. You know how much I've always admired and respected you. You're the best of the Casserole Ladies in my opinion."

Gidget started to speak. She wanted to tell Sonny how much she appreciated his opinion of her, but that she was no better than any of her friends in the room. She also wanted to say that she certainly was not pregnant. Instead, he kept talking.

"I feel so bad for you… I mean, having your baby with no father. And everyone here in Thomasville knows about it. They've all been talking about you, and what they've been saying ain't very nice. When Mary Ellen at Harvey's told me Daffy was giving you this *fo* shower… What is a *fo* shower, anyway?"

All the Casserole Ladies were biting their tongues so hard, none could respond to his question. Sonny gave up waiting for an answer and continued. "Anyway, I said to myself, 'Sonny, you got to make an honest woman out of Gidget. You can't let her baby be born without a last name.' So here I am. I'm offering my hand in marriage, if you'll have me."

Authors' Notes

Although we make use of dramatic license at times to enhance the reading experience, much of the plot incorporates facts, places, and things gleaned from our research. Here are some of our sources, all of which can be found on the Internet.

Fish and Scuba Diving:
1. "What Attracts Fish The Most?"
https://fishfinderstips.com/what-attracts-fish-the-most
2. "13 Scuba Diving Rules You Need to Know (OWSI Explained)" by Adeline Ee February 29, 2024
https://oceantrust.org/scuba-diving/rules/
3. "Private Gibbs Cay and Snorkel Charter"
https://www.shoreexcursionsgroup.com/tour/private-snorkel-gibbs-cay/cagtgtdprisnk
4. "Triggerfish Teeth and Other Interesting Facts about These Animals"
https://www.dresseldivers.com/blog/triggerfish-teeth-facts/#a2

Voodoo and Folklore:
1. "Folklore of Italy" Wikipedia
https://en.wikipedia.org/wiki/Folklore_of_Italy#Traditional_characters
2. "Haitian Vodou" Wikipedia
https://en.wikipedia.org/wiki/Haitian_Vodou#Practices

Picking Locks:
1. "how to pick a lock with a bobby pin" on youtube
https://duckduckgo.com/?t=h_&q=how+to+pick+a+lock+with+a+bobby+pin&iax=videos&ia=videos&iai=https%3A%2F%2Fwww.youtube.com%2Fwatch%3Fv%3D3HcV_2CB7jc

Weird Stuff Sold on TV:
1. "The Weirdest "As Seen on TV" Products by Nathan Davidson
https://www.ranker.com/list/weird-as-seen-on-tv-products/nathandavidson
2. "The Blanket That Absorbs Farts" By Rico Mossesgeld

https://www.tomsguide.com/us/this-blanket-absorbs-farts,news-6678.html
3. "The Original Fanny Bank" sold by BigMouth Inc. https://bigmouthinc.com/products/the-original-fanny-bank-1
4. "Talking TP- Talking Toilet Paper Roll Holder" sold on Amazon
https://www.amazon.com/Talking-TP-Toilet-Paper-Spindle/dp/B01M9JVBUX

Languages and Accents:
1. "How to Say Mom in Italian: A Simple Guide for Beginners" by Ellison Clapton
https://promova.com/blog/mom-in-italian

Mafia and Military:
1. "How can you tell if someone's in the mafia?" Quora Blog https://www.quora.com/How-can-you-tell-if-someones-in-the-mafia?share=1
2. "Which Hand Do Mafia Members Wear Pinky Rings On?" By Staff Writer
https://www.reference.com/world-view/hand-mafia-members-wear-pinky-rings-6deb7d4559fc3347
3. "Joe Barbaro Costume Guide" by Quetzalcoatl https://www.costumerealm.com/joe-barbaro-costume/
4. "US firm reveals gun-toting drone that can fire in mid-air" by Mary-Ann Russon, Technology Reporter, BBC News https://www.bbc.com/news/technology-40901393
5. "Meet TIKAD: the gun-toting drone that can aim, fire, and compensate for recoil" By Luke Dormehl
https://www.digitaltrends.com/cool-tech/duke-gun-robot-tikad/
6. "U.S. Navy Diving Manual, SS521-AG-PRO-010, Revision 7," 01 DECEMBER 2016.

Food and Poisons:
1. "What is Sonoran-Style Mexican Food?" By: Someburros Familia
https://www.someburros.com/news/what-is-sonoran-style-mexican-food

Sun City, Arizona:

1. Maricopa County Property Records (Arizona) https://www.countyoffice.org/az-maricopa-county-property-records/

About the Authors

Billy and Linda Johnson live in Florence, Alabama. MURDER ON THE BAHAMA PRINCESS is the third Casserole Ladies zany misadventure. Previous Casserole Ladies books include:

- THE CASSEROLE LADIES, Zany Misadventures in the Quest for Postmortem Romance. ISBN: 978-1-7374282-0-6
- AREA 53, The Casserole Ladies Go Where No Woman Has Gone Before, ISBN: 978-1-7374282-3-7.

Billy has published a collection of eight short stories in ATTACK OF THE iFONES and Other Vertically Challenged Stories, ISBN: 978-1-7374282-1-3.

Billy wrote and illustrated a children's picture book titled LION IN MY BACKYARD, ISBN: 978-1-7374282-2-0.

All Billy and Linda's books are available on Amazon. You can visit Billy's Author Page on Amazon at: https://www.amazon.com/stores/author/B091FY4CSM/allbooks

You can visit Billy's Facebook page at: https://www.facebook.com/Billy4GoodBooks.

www.ingramcontent.com/pod-product-compliance
Lightning Source LLC
Chambersburg PA
CBHW030527190726
48283CB00006B/1799

* 9 7 8 1 7 3 7 4 2 8 2 4 4 *